Visible Amazement

GALE ZOË GARNETT

SIMON & SCHUSTER
NEW YORK
LONDON
TORONTO
SYDNEY
SINGAPORE

SIMON & SCHUSTER
Rockefeller Center
1230 Avenue of the Americas
New York, New York 10020

First published in Canada in 1999 by Stoddart Publishing Co. Limited

Book Design by Ellen R. Sasahara

Manufactured in the United States of America

1 3 5 7 9 10 8 6 4 2

Library of Congress Cataloging-in-Publication Data

Garnett, Gale Zoë.
Visible amazement / Gale Zoë Garnett.
p. cm.
1. Teenage girls—Fiction. I. Title.
PS3557.A71678 V5 2001
813'.6—dc21
00-055611

ISBN 0-684-87306-0

Acknowledgments

To the "House People"—who freed Roanne from my household clutter of ghosts, and let me see the sea (or, looking at lakes and rivers, believe I could). Most particularly: Patricia (Patsy Louise) Neal of Packard, Kentucky, and Martha's Vineyard, Massachusetts (where this book was begun); Bill Glassco of Tadoussac and Quebec City, Quebec; Randy and Sue Hague of Niagara-on-the-Lake, Ontario; and Harriet (Sis) Bunting Weld, also of Niagara-on-the-Lake (where this book was completed).

To the "Music People," whose CDs and cassettes were background companions and moodbringers during long days and nights running after Roanne and those people and things she was chasing: Daniel Lavoie, Christy Moore, Kostas Hadzis, Björk, Daniel Seff, Alanis Morrisette, Stavros Xarhakos, Gabriel Yared, Ferron, Paolo Conte, Marianne Faithfull, Petru Guelfucci, Lhasa De Sela and Cesaria Evora.

To Susan Musgrave, for her clear, muscular editor's eye and vibrant, Pacific-coastal poet's heart. To all those at Stoddart, my Canadian publishers, especially Nelson Doucet, Don Bastian and Simone Lee, for the enthusiasm and belief they have given and continue to give to this book.

To the "relay-team" who lovingly passed *Visible Amazement* along—from Martin Sherman to Leila Livingston to Margaret Korda to Chuck Adams—until it reached my American editor, the uniquely remarkable Michael Korda (whose father and uncle made my favourite film; *The Third Man*), who happily said, "Yes, Simon & Schuster will publish this book."

To Philip Metcalf, for soulful copyediting of an English that is both Anglo-Canadian and the personal language of Roanne Chappell.

To the "Three Graces" of S & S, Carol Bowie, Rebecca Head and Cheryl Weinstein, who have been warmly helpful to this first-novelist.

To my "Internet Friends," particularly David Chadderton, Lynne Perednia, Janet McConnaughey and Kit Snedaker, for cheering me on as I worked. To Tony Marra, who taught me to use the computer, starting with painting and solitaire (a good game for writers). To Malcolm Woodland, for putting this book onto floppy disks before I knew how, and to Nicole Winstanley, for her endless and gracious help navigating me through my subsequent "newbietude."

To Neil Bissoondath, for saying, "You must finish this," and to my agent, Jan Whitford, who always believed I would. To all these, deep gratitude and thanks.

GALE ZOË GARNETT
Abingdon Guest House,
Greenwich Village, New York
April 14, 2000

For Jerry Purcell,
Who has always been there—
And for Jay Scott,
Who should've been here.

The film director turned to those assembled in his Roman hotel suite:

"I think we should take the kid to Venice,
For the Biennale," he said.
"Paintings, palazzos, houses rising out to the sea.
She'll be visibly amazed . . . she's at that age."

This is the story of another kid . . . at that age.

Visible Amazement

GIVE THE LITTLE GIRL A GREAT BIG HAND

1

July-August stuff, 1981 (For my sister, if I ever turn out to have one.)

Until the thing happened with Marcus, I was glad, sometimes very glad, that Del was my mother. Sure, she was a little Out There in some ways, but she was fun. And I always knew she loved me. I know it now. I mean, I had classmates with Regular Mothers and I could see I was having a better time with Del. Which is why I'm sorry about the terrible thing I did. Which is why I'm in bed with this dwarf.

I think part of what makes Del and me close is the Body Thing. Even though she's 39 and I'm 14, we have the same body. Big tits. Big asses. Little waists. Del says it gets to be fun when you're older, but for a young person it's mostly a drag. Teenage guys are jerks anyway, and they say really dumb things to girls who have majorly conspicuous fronts and backs. I did want guys to like me, but I didn't want it to be about pretending to bump into me in the hall at school just so they could feel my stuff.

So I decided I'd only consider older guys. Not Del's age or anything. Mid- to late-twenties guys. I decided this last year, when I was 13. I was too shy to do anything about it, though, and didn't know what to do about it anyway. Until Del taught me the Bend Over Thing.

It happened a few months ago, at this grown-up party. There was this cute guy there. So I did what I always do. Wedged myself into a corner and watched him across the room, thinking as hard as I could, "See me! See me and think 'I must know this person.'" Del caught me doing this. "What's wrong, Rosie?" she asked. I said nothing was wrong. Del knew better. She pressed it. So I told her I wanted to meet "that guy over there" and didn't know how. She said the guy was a twit and too old for me anyway, but that getting his attention in a positive way would be "easy as kiss your hand." Then she took a pencil out of her pocket and handed it to me. "Now, you take this and walk over to where he is. Then, you turn your back on the fella, drop the pencil and bend over to pick it up." I said I didn't see what good picking up a stupid pencil would do. Del smiled. "Just do it. I promise you it'll work a treat. I'll explain it to you later." So I did. Walked across the room, keeping my eyes down because I felt like a jerk. I could feel Del watching me and I hoped to hell my ankle wouldn't turn in, which sometimes happens when I'm nervous. I got to the coffee table in front of where the guy was talking to his friends. "Boy, is this ever dumb!" I thought, but I did it the way Del said. Turned around. Dropped the pencil. Bent over to pick it up. Amazing! When I straightened up, the guy was standing right next to me, chatting away! So were two other guys!

Later, at our place, when we were having hot milk and cinnamon, Del said the Bend Over Thing was "primal," that the original cavepeople courted that way. That four-legged animals still do. That it would always work.

I haven't used it again yet. But I know it's there for me. A special secret power. Del knows lots of stuff like that. Stuff that Regular Mothers don't know. Or don't share.

I don't know who my father was. That's not a tacky thing about Del. Del knows, but she won't talk about it because she thinks he was a shit. A "thoroughgoing" shit, she says (Del is English). He's never shown any interest in meeting me (Del says he knew where we were for the first four years of my life), so I guess that's true. I mean, do I need to know a guy who isn't even curious about his own kid? Why break your heart, right?

Only thing is, if I have a father, even the most hopeless father ever, that means I could have a sister. Or a brother. And that person could be really super and great to know. So I keep my eyes open for a girl who looks like me (staring at boys is too much hassle. They always think you want some sex thing. If it's a brother I've got, he'll have to do the looking, because girls are more used to ignoring being stared at). My sister might not even look all that much like me. She might just have a "me-ish feeling," which I would, of course, recognize immediately. So far, no luck. But I thought I'd start this journal so that, if we do find each other, I can give it to her and we won't have to take forever catching up, and can go out and do stuff together. If she doesn't have a journal, I will listen to her stuff for absolutely as long as she wants. Being an artist's model, I can sit still for long periods of time.

My name is Roanne. It was ROSE Anne, but I took the "s" and the "e" out when I was 10 and have no intention of putting them back in! I look older than 14 because of the Body Thing. I'm not a virgin. When I told Del about the first time (rock-band roadie. Great face, great hair, great hands. A drunk. A disaster!), she said, based on my description, that I haven't come yet, so I'm still half a virgin. Del says coming is one of the absolutely BEST things that can happen to a person, so, naturally, I'm looking forward to it.

Del also said that I now needed "some form of birth control," and that we could see her doctor, together, when we got back to Kitsilano, before school started.

I still feel mad at Del sometimes, but I miss her. Fucking Del. Fucking Marcus. Fucking gay dwarf. No, that's not fair. He's being really nice, and has this wonderful smell. It's just that when things are scary it feels good to say fuck a lot. Don't know why. Just does.

We'd been in Oregon for two months. On the coast, in a neat little house in the woods. The town's called Yachats, an Indian word. Pronounced "YaHOTS." I was born in England, but have lived in Canada since age four. We came down from Vancouver when Del had a sculpture show in a Yachats gallery. The show sold well and Del was offered a job teaching summertime Adult Extension sculpture classes at a college not far away, in Eugene. I got to make some money too, being her model, which I've done, on and off, since I was little.

It was there, in Eugene, where I met Marcus. I had finished modelling for Del's 2-to-4-o'clock class. She still had her 6-to-8 once-a-week night class to do (with a male model), so I decided to go into town and pick up the white sweater I was paying off. I love white things, even though they get dirty fast. The best colour of all, I think, is like the skin in Renoir paintings. It's real hard to find. "Deco peach," Del says it is. Art stuff, instant-home stuff, bend-over stuff and 60s English music and clothes are Del's strongest areas of knowledge.

So, I was on my way to the Fashion Plate (which Del spells p-l-a-i-t. It's a Del joke; in London slang "plait" is going down on a guy, and Del thinks Fashion Plate clothes suck) when I saw this guy. Truly, the best-looking guy I had ever seen. I mean personally seen, as opposed to film, telly, poster or album cover. For a start, he was HUGE! Not fat huge. Tall huge. Six-something. And he had this great hair. It's hard to describe Marcus's hair colour. It was red, brown, gold—and the whole thing went crazy with beautifulness when the sunlight hit it. And he had this really sexy lower lip. And hands. Big hands.

As far back as I can remember I've had this thing about guys with big hands. When I was little, 6 or 7, I'd see a big-handed guy and suddenly all at once I'd love that person so much! Then, when I was about 9, I would look and think, "Please pick me up! Lift me up!" I like leaving the ground. Del does too. It's inherited. Sometimes, I'd dream I was being held in the palm of his open hand and he'd take me around town. Not any town I've actually ever lived in. A fantasy beach town with this incredible carousel right on the beach. Beautiful carved lacquer-shiny painted horses going round and round. Me watching, sitting in the palm of this huge, beautiful hand. And the hand never closes on me or drops me. I think it's going to, but it doesn't.

At about that time, when the dreams first started happening, I won this drawing contest at school (to make the illustration for a poster about how reading was good). When the man from the library gave me the prize, he said, "Let's give the little girl a great big hand." That made me think of my dream and I got these stupid giggles. People looked at me like they thought I was weird, which I know some of them thought anyway. There was no way I could explain, so I just giggled until the giggle died.

Anyway, this guy in Eugene had hands that were so big and so amazingly beautiful that I loved them all at once and completely and could hardly breathe. He was looking at me. (It's possible I looked weird. If I looked on the outside like I felt on the inside, I'm SURE I looked weird!) He laughed. It wasn't a mean making-fun-of-a-person laugh, but I was embarrassed and took off running for the Fashion Plate.

The night, no surprise, I had the Hand Dream again. Only this time, ditto no surprise, the big hand belonged to the guy from Eugene.

Usually, when I would see somebody I thought was hot, I'd tell Del about it, and she'd tease me and say semi-gross things, and we'd both laugh. This time, though, I didn't say anything. I didn't feel like being teased about it. I think because the hands were in it so much. The hands thing was just so MAJOR for me that I'd never told ANYONE about it. Not even Del. I think people need to keep some stuff. Not tell it.

The following Tuesday I was modelling. I modelled nude but it was OK. Most of the people in Del's classes were really trying to make some kind of art. There was one guy with a sort of pervo way of looking at people. Del told me he was just a little walleyed. Besides, they all knew I was Del's daughter. While I was holding the pose, I kept thinking about the Eugene guy's hands. "Stop fidgeting, Rosie," Del said.

After modelling, while I was waiting for Del to finish her night class and drive us home, I looked around town for Mr. Big Hands, but he wasn't anywhere.

He was somewhere the following week. I wasn't even looking. Things like that are like that. If you want to find someone, it's better if you don't look. I think there's a sort of mystical phantom committee whose whole job is to keep people from getting what they want, and if you don't let on, they get bored with watching you and go off to deny other people stuff and your Wanted Thing slips past them.

Anyway, I was in this croissant place having an apple juice (apple is my favourite juice. Orange churns my guts up. Del's too. Inherited) and drawing. I'm not an artist-artist professionally. I'm a cartoonist. Like Searle and R. Crumb and D.D.A. I've had cartoons printed in school papers, and once in a real newspaper. In Salmon Arm when I was 11. When Del was with Stavro.

So there I was, in the croissant place, drawing this cartoon of a starfish regenerating, when in came the big hands guy. He sat down at the table next to mine, smiled this terrific smile and said, "Hi." I was so glad, this great huge gladness, that I said, actually said, "Yay." It was so right out there in the road we both laughed.

That was Marcus. He said he was 29 so I said I was 16. I knew that 14 sometimes made older guys nervous but 16 was usually OK. We were both lying. Him down, me up, but I didn't know that then.

It was really easy talking with him. He was working at the college too. Teaching Adult Extension short-story writing. Same as the thing Del was doing with drawing. He came from Seattle and had written a book of short stories. He walked me over to the BookNook so I could see it. Bought me a copy. I didn't tell him not to (I think people who say "You shouldn't have!" when they're really happy about being given something are dishonest jerks). He signed, "To Roanne, who has just begun to regenerate—from Marcus Willoughby, who is still doing so as best he can." He wrote that because of my starfish cartoon, which he said he really liked. So I gave it to him. He asked me to sign it. I'm usually good with words, because of having an English mum, and reading a lot, but all I could think of to write was, "Glad you like this, from Roanne Chappell." Pathetic, eh? Then he had to go teach his night class. I said "Bye" and that it was nice to meet him. Then I stuck his book inside my denim jacket and went back to the croissant place to wait for Del. She was already there, parked at the curb. I could see that the two young guys at the table by the window were impressed. It wasn't about Del. It was about the Morgan.

Being an artist means sometimes being majorly broke. Del and I both know how to make do with whatever. When I was little and there was nothing to eat but bologna (which I hated), Del would point at the slimy pink slices pooching up in the pan and say, "Look, Rosie! Chinese hats!" It didn't make the pink slime taste any better but at least she was trying to make it interesting. Last year, she told me she hated bologna too. It had just been at a good stealing location in Mac's Milk.

The Morgan was Del's extravagance. Even when we were broke, she took really good care of it, telling people it was "a classic," that it had a "wooden frame" and ran "like a thoroughbred." It's dark green and shaped like a Labrador retriever's head. Being a sportscar, it only has two proper seats. With all the paintings and sculptures Del has to haul around, she really needs something like a station wagon, but she loves the Morgan like family, so she just goes back and forth with stuff a lot.

Del was in this really terrific mood. I could tell because she was singing old Brit rock stuff, and when we got to the coast road she did some four-wheel drifts. That's a crazy steering thing you can do in sportscars on winding roads. It feels like the car's going to lose it, but there's a technique to it. Del learned it from this racing car driver she went out with for a while when I was five. He was Italian, with a really low voice and a pretty name. Corrado. When I was little I was scared of four-wheel drifts. I'm used to them now.

So there was Del, singing "Guhn, guhn, gilly guhn guh-uhn, walk on gilded splin . . . TAHS" and driving all over the road while I felt the sea wind in my face and Marcus's book inside my jacket against my body. It was a happy car.

• •

That night, in my bed, I read one of Marcus's stories. I've always loved to read. Since I was three. Del taught me because I pestered her all the time. I wanted to be on the inside of the secret of the black squiggles. I think when you move around a lot and don't relate really well with kids your own age, books can be an important alternative to suicide. I'm usually more optimistic about my life now. Books helped with that by showing me possible ways out when my wherever and whatever weren't as terrific as they could be. I still read a lot, but now it's mostly just because I like to.

I started one Marcus-story, about a divorcing couple who were fighting over books and records. I couldn't get into it. Then I found "Ursa Major." The woman in the story is on a camping trip with her boring husband. She sees a large, beautiful bear. She leaves food out for him. The next day, she finds a bright blue bead where the food had been. She knows it's crazy, but she's certain that the bear left the bead. She strings it on a shoelace and wears it around her neck, telling her husband she found it in the woods. After a week, she has seven bright blue beads on her necklace. At night, while her husband is sleeping, she leaves their tent and walks to the food and beads place. The bear is there. The woman, Alice, feels there's a sense, "an echo" of a man's face within the bear face, "an echo of a man's body within the bear body." The bear kneels in front of her. She drops to her knees facing him/it, smiling. "Alice saw the arrow glinting in the night sky, lit by the moon. It described a wide arc. As she cried out, the arrow found its mark. The bear's mouth opened in surprise, making no sound. His great Kodiak body pitched sideways and fell with a thud to the ground. Once again, as he had deliberately and by accident for ten years, her husband had stepped between Alice and something interesting." I really liked that one. I understood it PERSONALLY. For a while I'd been feeling that something interesting was trying to happen to me, and that someone, or something, was in the road between me and it.

I loved the words "described a wide arc." I wanted to make a cartoon of that, but was too sleepy. I dreamt I was held in the bear's paw. Inside the paw was a man's hand. It was, of course, Marcus's.

The next day, in the teachers' room, while Del was changing into her smock, I looked up Marcus's schedule on the bulletin board. He had a 2:30 to 4:30. I decided that after I finished modelling in Del's 2-to-4 class, I would casually walk by in front of his room. Say hello and see what he said back.

At four, I toreassed out of Del's class and ran upstairs to the women's loo on Marcus's floor. Hair up or hair down? Down was sexier but Del was always saying I had "a gorgeous neck and clavicles" that I "obscured with too much hair." Marcus was closer to Del's age than mine, so I decided to go for a high ponytail. Did lips, did eyes, and hauled my heartbreaker clavicles down the hall. Timing, perfecto! Marcus's class was breaking up and people were coming through the door. Then Marcus came out. He was talking to a woman. She looked low end of older. About 25, 26. Blondish. Fattish. He didn't see me. "Hi," I said brilliantly. They both looked at me. "Oh, hello, Roanne," he said, sounding like what a beige wall would sound like if a beige wall could talk. The woman was looking at me with that "Oh, really?" face female persons sometimes use to make other female persons feel stupid and wrong. It worked great. I said something truly babbloid about having to model for my mother's class, then ran off down the hall. Behind me, I heard them laugh. I was sure it was something about me. Probably about my body. "You're in no position to do body jokes, Miss Lard-ass Bleacho Bloato!" I wanted to say, but I got a grip on it. Back on the second floor, all flushed, I turned on the water fountain, stuck my hand in it and wet my face. Damn, I thought, I don't know how to do this stuff! What was I supposed to do, turn around and bend over?

• •

"Hello, you." It was Marcus. I was still mad at him for laughing at me the day before, with the fat blonde. It had been my plan to cut him dead the next time I saw him.

"Hi!!" I said. Then I remembered my plan and went back to my cartoon of a fat blonde being penetrated rectally by a schoolbus.

"May I sit down?"

"If you like."

I was pleased with that. Cool, but not rude.

Marcus, however, didn't seem to notice. He sat down, smiling his terrific smile. "I want to use some lapidary, different colored stones, as part of a writing exercise for tomorrow's class. There's a shop, Clyde's Rock House, out on the coast road. Would you like to take a ride out there with me?"

1) I'm too busy. 2) Sorry, I'm meeting somebody. 3) Fuck you. I couldn't decide which one to use. "OK," I said.

I knew Clyde's. Knew Clyde. Nice old guy. Skinny. Missing his two bottom front teeth. He'd owned the Shell station next to the rock shop. Sold the station to his nephew Buzz and opened the Rock House because he loved rocks. Clyde had a big black dog, mostly Lab, named Geronimo. Geronimo really liked me, and Clyde let me take him for runs on the beach. I had bought some stones from Clyde too. His prices were lots better than in Vancouver. Even with the money difference between American and Canadian.

I told Marcus all this as we drove along the coast road. It was a gray day and a little cold, so Marcus gave me his jacket to wear. It was green corduroy and smelled like him. It felt like I was wearing Marcus. Like I was the man echo inside the bear.

Marcus drove a Jeep. I liked it. Funky-elegant. Like Marcus. He was wearing a green-and-gray checked flannel shirt and old black jeans. Button fly. He looked incredibly hot. I felt like screaming "Yippieshit!" I told him I'd read "Ursa Major," and that I thought it was "quite good."

He smiled, but kept his eyes on the road. "Did you? I'm glad." He squeezed my knee for a quick minute. I thought I was going to explode.

Clyde was happy to see me (which made me look important in front of Marcus), but nowhere near as happy as Geronimo, who jumped all over me and licked my face. Marcus looked through the boxes of stones. He bought amethysts, carnelian, lapis, malachite and, I think, topaz. Geronimo was galumphing back and forth. He wanted a beach run. I asked Marcus if he'd mind.

"Not at all," he said. "I'd enjoy a beach run myself."

There was about a minute of drizzle, then *bam!*, it was pissing with rain. Geronimo didn't mind. He was already soaking wet from running in and out of the sea. Marcus and I ran for cover under the pier.

I'd love to say it was this incredibly perfect experience. Two Bodies Moving as One and all that. But it wasn't. Not even a little bit. What it was was:

1. A boulderette in the sand grinding into the left cheek of my bum.
2. Rain coming through the boards of the pier into my eyes (which I closed). And my nose (which I could not close).
3. Sand in pretty much everything I had that could get sand in it.

As for two bodies moving as one, forget it! My fault. I kept trying to go up when Marcus went down. But, what with the rock and the sand and the rain in my nose, I would lose the rhythm. When I moved down as Marcus moved up, he'd fall out and one of us, sometimes both of us, would have to put him back in. I was very wet inside and it made his thing slippery and sticky and it took forever to put it back. Marcus asked me to say his name over and over, and to say "fuck me," so I said "Marcus, Marcus, fuck me, fuck me." Or, "Marcus, fuck me, Marcus, fuck me." Then he came, saying, "Yes, baby, *yes!*" I didn't come. While he was coming and yessing, I said, "I love you." I said it very softly so he wouldn't feel obligated to love me back.

When Marcus pulled out I found out why I was so wet. His thing was covered with blood! Perfect, Roanne! Absolutely fucking brilliant! I felt like the scummiest, grossest person anybody could possibly be with. I started to cry and couldn't stop. I kept sobbing these huge gulpy sobs and saying, "I'm sorry, I'm sorry." Marcus was very sweet, sweeter than I would've been if somebody bled all over ME! He sat up and held me. He rocked me in his arms and petted my hair. He kept saying, "It's OK, baby, it's OK." Geronimo was trying to lick between my legs.

It had gotten dark while we were under the pier, so we put just our shirts on and sat in the shallow water to wash ourselves off. Then we finished dressing and walked Geronimo back to Clyde's.

Driving me home, Marcus asked, "How do you feel?" I said I was OK. He held my hand and played with my fingers. I asked if he wanted to go for a pizza. He said he couldn't. That he had a meeting with a writing student. That he'd see me at the college.

After you're with someone for the first time, it's really, really important that they ask you out again. With someone sexually, I mean. Not that I would've blamed Marcus if he didn't want more actual sex with me. I wasn't very good at it. And I bled on him. But after a first time, a woman or girl or whatever feels really open. It's like you give yourself over, give up a lot of the control you have over who you are, over how it is with you. With the roadie, I knew when we were doing it that he was only in town for the one night. And he was a rock 'n' roll person. Marcus was going to be in Eugene all summer. And he wrote books, which isn't occupationally as flaky. So I needed to have him at least ask if I wanted to have lunch or something. He didn't.

When I got inside the house, I called the college and asked the woman who answered to please tell Delores Chappell, the art teacher in 232, that her daughter got a ride home and would see her there. Then I put on a Bob Marley tape, washed out my panties and the crotch of my jeans, took a hot bath and put in a plug. Then I made a grilled cheese sandwich but had this awful, majorly large crying gulpo after I ate it which made me throw the sandwich back up. Then I started crying again. Felt like a real jerk. Went out and sat on the porch. It had stopped raining. There was a breeze. Everything smelled green and good. I had to stop thinking of Marcus's beautiful hands on my body or I'd start crying again. So I got the Interesting and/or Pretty Words book that I had been making, turned to the Foreign Words section and said the words out loud.

Chiaroscuro
Vertige
Pipistrello
Farfalla
Sizwe
Pamplemousse
Jacaranda
Iliovasilema
Mousseline
Auto-da-Fé

"Pipistrello" felt best in my mouth, so I rocked back and forth in the swing chair and said it over and over until the crying burned off.

I woke when I heard the Morgan pull up.

"Hullo, Rosie mine! Give us a hand, would you, love?" She was trying to wrestle an enormous wood sculpture out of the passenger seat. It was supergood! A cluster of naked people all tangled together. We hauled it onto the porch.

"This is great, Del. I love it."

"It's not finished. I decided to bring it home and refine it on the porch so I can work naked. Have you eaten?" I gave the short answer, "No." Del set about to make us a salade Niçoise. I've always loved watching Del do stuff with her hands. It fills her with energy and makes her glow. That night, she was looking particularly beautiful. She was wearing her floaty dress, the one made out of old chiffon scarves. White, pale blue and pale green. The odd flower print here and there. Her amazing Irish setter-colored hair was all curly and shiny. My hair, which is almost black, is the same type, only Del's looks Art Nouveau whereas mine mostly looks messy. Big hair is like big tits and bums. You have to grow into it.

We had eaten our salads and Del was smoking a joint when she asked, "Who drove you home?"

Oh well, what the hell. "One of the teachers from the college. He had to go to Clyde's. Name's Marcus."

"Marcus Willoughby?"

"Uh-huh. Do you know him?"

"Yes, I do. He's a lovely guy."

As far back as I could remember, whenever Del was fucking somebody, she'd describe him as "a lovely guy."

• •

I couldn't get it out of my mind. No matter what else I was doing or thinking about, "lovely guy" would come into my head. Del and Marcus. I tried to remember if there'd ever been a "lovely guy" Del hadn't gone to bed with. Couldn't think of one. I knew I had no real right to be mad at Del. She didn't know I'd done it with Marcus. I thought of telling her. Telling her what? That he wanted me to be his girl? Since Blood on the Beach, he hadn't even phoned me or looked for me. The one time I saw him, in the hall at the college, he was walking with two very tall women, nodding and saying "Mm-hmm" while the one with the largest nose nattered away about a person or place called "Dooney Barns." He saw me, said, "Hi, Roanne" and kept walking.

Del and I had always spent a lot of time hanging out together. Talking. Laughing. Just goofing on stuff. After the Lovely Guy Thing, I couldn't do that. I was all turned around inside, and afraid I'd start to cry or say something dumb. When I wasn't doing Del's classes I was real pulled-in and quiet. Del and I are both sort of moody people, and I knew she wasn't pressing it, was trying to give me room.

I was in the croissant place, drawing.

"I've been looking for you. Would you like to have lunch at my place on Saturday?" It had been five days since we drove out to Clyde's. Maybe he had just been waiting for me to stop bleeding.

I decided to tell Del. There was no point expecting her to respect a situation she didn't know about. She was lying on the chesterfield in a long white shirt, listening to Dr. John the Night Tripper on the stereo. I didn't want to be too intense.

"Hi," I said and went into the kitchen. "Want a spiced milk?" She didn't, but asked me to have mine out on the porch with her.

She was in the swing chair. I still felt shy, which I wasn't used to feeling with Del. I sat on the top step, facing her. We talked for a while about a woman in her class who was doing a really good sculpture of me. Then I said, "I like Marcus Willoughby."

She laughed. "Of course you do. He's bloody gorgeous!"

I looked down. I didn't know why, but it was all a little scary. "He's asked me to lunch on Saturday."

"I see . . . isn't he a bit old for you, Rosie?"

"I've sort of given myself a 30 ceiling. Marcus is 29."

"He's 34."

"He told me 29."

Del lit a cigarette. Her eyes, in the Zippo light, looked . . . I don't know what. Something. Worried?

"Look, Rosie . . . I give you lots of room. Always have, right? I do it because I know you're smart. Always were. Even when you were small you did fewer arsehole things than most people. Do . . . what you like. You will anyway, you're my kid. But, please . . . be careful. Don't get yourself into a bad corner. People aren't always as they seem. They rarely are, in fact . . . do you understand?"

"I think so."

Del got up, walked up to me, lifted my face, tapped my nose. "Good. I'm going to crash. It's been a long day. I'm drained." She went inside.

I walked over to the wood sculpture. I ran my hands over the bodies and little round heads of the naked wooden people. What did she mean, "bad corner"? Should I have told her that Marcus already did me? That I wanted, very much, for him to do me again, with me being better at it?

• •

I've reviewed Thursday night over and over in my mind. I know that what I did was violent and wrong. That I did an injury to somebody who loves me because of somebody who did not. When I play it back, though, which I do all the time, I cannot see myself doing anything other than what I did.

I had submitted some cartoons to *The Eugene Weekly Thang,* an alternative newspaper that was working out of the college. Their editor left a note for me in Del's box saying the editorial board liked my stuff and inviting me to a staff meeting at the college on Thursday evening. Del congratulated me when I told her about it and agreed to let me out of her night class a half hour earlier.

Some woman was reading her article on cosmetics and feminism. It wasn't that I wasn't interested. It was just a very long article, so I was sort of looking out the window. I could see Del outside, sitting in the Morgan, talking with a guy in the passenger seat. I couldn't see the guy's face. I could see his size. I could see his hair. The Morgan pulled out of the parking lot. I excused myself and ran downstairs. I had modelling money in my bag. I could afford the taxi home.

I heard them upstairs. Not words, just laughing and mumbles. I went up the steps on all fours, because my knees and hands make less noise than my feet. Del's bedroom door was open. It was a full-moon night, moonlight came through the window and onto the bed. Del was on top. Marcus's hands were moving over her body. From her tits to her sides to her ass and back up her sides to her tits. Del's ass was moving. Up and down, up and down. In the moonlight, it looked HUGE. I didn't snap until Marcus said, "Say my name," and she did.

It happened very fast. I got to the bed as Del's ass was moving up. I remember it as being the size of the world and pale yellow. As it rose, I sank my teeth into it. I knew I went through the skin because I tasted blood. There was screaming and cursing. I heard my name as I ran down the stairs and out the door. Then I was running through the woods to the coast road. I kept on running. Running as fast as I could to nowhere in particular.

Clyde's. Pigsweat and panting, standing in front of the Rock House. There weren't any lights on in Clyde's apartment above the shop. Geronimo, who was guarding the Rock House and Shell station, started to bark, but stopped when he saw it was me. He put his front paws on my shoulders and licked my face. I let him do that for a while because it felt really good and was helping me to slow down inside. Then I walked him behind the building to the toolshed where he slept. Wasted, I flopped down on the shed floor. The shed was dank-smelling, but the cement floor felt cool. Geronimo curled up beside me. I threw an arm over him. He licked my hand. I nuzzled his fur. I think he was glad to have company.

I closed my eyes but couldn't sleep right away because I was thinking about the grenaded kid, like I always do when people do bad surprises. The kid was American. From Iowa or Ohio (I always get those two places confused. Whichever one you say it feels like you're mispronouncing the other one). Anyway, one day this kid, he was eight years old, found a grenade. He didn't know what it was, but he thought it was interesting so he kept it. The newspaper said he told his little sister it was "pretty." Then one day he was in his room playing with all the found stuff he'd collected. He was looking at his pretty grenade, holding it real close to his face. It exploded and blew his face off. Away. Gone. I thought then and I think now that people are like that. They're interesting and they're pretty and because you don't know, or just keep forgetting they can blow up, you take them home and you're all relaxed and looking at them up close when *blammo!* they go off in your face. Always, when people grenaded me, it was Del who helped me put myself back together. Some of my Grenade People were kids. Some were teachers or other grown-ups. Some were even real close friends, like Brian. Sober Brian. But when Drunk Brian turned into a Grenade Person, that one night, Del threw him out. She really liked him, but when he grenaded she packed him off. So OK, Marcus grenaded, but this time Del grenaded with him and I got double-*blammo!* With one of the blammers being my major protector. To be fair, I don't think people always mean to grenade. It's just they've got this grenade-y stuff inside and it goes off whenever. So you need at least one put-you-back-together person. That was Del. Now maybe it wasn't.

Then there's the Starfish Thing. When I was eight we found a starfish on the beach. Del told me that when they lose one of their starpoints, it "regenerates." Grows back. So, maybe if everybody else is a grenade, I had to learn to be a starfish. But how? I'm a person. Could a person learn starfishness, or did I have to learn grenading and go off before the other grenade does?

Lying there with Geronimo, that's what I was thinking about. I didn't want to be a damn grenade. I mean, that boy in Ohiowa lost his whole face. Lost his whole fucking life! I didn't want to do things that did like that. What I wanted was for other people to not do it to me. If I didn't want to learn grenade, I would absolutely have to learn starfish. When I fell asleep I dreamt I could do it, but I almost always do really well with stuff like that in dreams. Awake Life is harder.

When the morning light came through the shed window, I woke up. At first I didn't know where I was, like when I was little and we moved around really a lot. My hands and arms were filthy, my pink tanktop was all black-smudgy from the shed floor and my armpits smelled like rotting roast beef and puppy's breath. Geronimo was in a corner, slurping from his water dish. I crawled over and nudged him out of the way. His water was dusty-tasting but I was thirsty. He didn't seem to mind sharing, but he tilted his head to one side. I laughed. "Looks weird, eh?" It was probably about 6 A.M. We went for a beach run, though I was still pretty tired and mostly walked along the beach while he did his regulation goofy freaking-in-the-sea thing. I knew that I had to go home and deal with the whole shitstorm.

• •

Del was not there. I knew she wouldn't be. She was at the college, using God knows who as a model. It was supposed to be me, but just showing up as usual seemed like a less than brilliant idea. I took a major bath, with bubbles, then baked a couple of potatoes. When I was seven, and Del was seeing Brian, who was Irish, he said, "When all else is out of the question, a person needs to eat a potato," that potatoes would "soothe you, whether you were sick at heart or sick in body." I don't know if it was just the power of suggestion, but ever since he said it, baked potatoes have been one of my major comfort foods.

There had never been any violence thing between Del and me. I knew other kids had violence with their parents, but Del never hit me. It was also true, however, that I'd never before bit her ass while she was fucking. This was all really new stuff and I had no idea what the appropriate behavior was. I decided to write a note:

Dear Del,

I am in the woods. I'd like to come in and work out all our stuff, but I don't want to if it's going to be scary. If you still like me (dumb joke) and want to talk, please come out on the porch and call my name. If you're too pissed off to do that I will understand.

Roanne

Then I grabbed my bag of drawing books and wordbooks and went into the woods to wait.

• •

"RO-SIEEE . . ."

I came out from behind the tree. I was pretty sure it wasn't a trick or anything, but because of the general weirdness of recent events I stopped some distance from the porch and asked, "Honest? It's cool?"

Del smiled. "Honest, it's cool."

I sat in the swing chair. Del stood. I figured I must've broken skin. Not so she needed stitches or anything, but enough so that sitting was not her favorite thing. Del said something about being "savagely bit in the bum by me own kid," and we both laughed. Then she said, "We were a bet, baby."

"What?"

"A bet. We were a bet. Some slag bitch in one of his bloody classes bet him he couldn't pull both of us. The mum and the kid."

"Was she a fat blonde?"

"I've no bloody idea. I only know we were a bet."

I was glad I'd eaten potatoes. Potatoes were the one food I never puked back up no matter what.

"What did they bet?" My eyes must have filled up, because Del came to the swing chair and sat, crossing her legs and putting her assweight on one cheek. She wiped under my eyes with her finger and then petted my face.

"Money."

"Yuck."

"Yuck, indeed. Then, when we were both 'accomplished,' said

slag bitch upped the ante. Said she'd only pay up if he did both of us at once. And took a Polaroid."

"Oh, God, Saturday. Did he invite you to have lunch this Saturday?"

"Yes."

I put my arms around Del and rested my head on her chest, hoping to Christ the potato-puke rule held. Finally, I said, "He seemed, I dunno . . . gentler than that. Sweeter. We were a . . . a bet? That's so ugly."

Del kissed the top of my head. Then she went over to the porch railing and lit a cigarette.

"He is gentle, Rosie. I think we were both something he genuinely wanted to do. Without a bet. The bet wasn't his idea, but when it was suggested, I reckon he saw it as a sort of dare. Men are stupid about dares, Rosie. I reckon he saw it as a way of taking the dare, doing something larky and making a bit of money in the bargain."

I looked down at my bare feet for a while, listening to the night noises in the woods and wishing I were a baby kangaroo.

"Is this what it's gonna be like?"

"What?"

"Fucking."

"Sometimes."

There was another thing, an important thing, that had to be worked out between Del and me. Later, when we were in the kitchen having spiced milk and listening to Ewan MacColl sing about some Scottish guy who danced around a gallows tree, I brought it up. "OK. So we were a bet. But you knew I liked him. How come you fucked him anyway?"

Del put her hand over mine. "Yes. I knew you liked him. I did not know you'd . . . been with him. To be truly honest, Rosie, I do not know . . . what I would have done if I had known."

I pulled my hand away. Not violently or anything. But definitely away. I didn't shout. In fact, I remember my voice as being very quiet, but there was a shouting feeling inside me.

"How can you not know? I mean, I'm your daughter."

I think the stuff Del said next is the major reason I split. Not

Marcus. As amazingly beautiful looking as he was, with his big perfect hands and his multi-coloured hair, after I knew about the betting thing, I thought of him as a gross, gutless jerk. But what Del said next, being as honest as she always had been with me, that was the big thing. The thing I have to work out.

She looked at me for what felt like a year and a half, not saying anything. Her eyes seemed full of love. And something else. A kind of sadness or pain. Then she started to pencil doodle on the back of a magazine on the table. I asked her to stop. She stopped, and looked back up at me.

"Rosie," she said. "I love you. Very much. More than anyone. Have since the day you were born. No. That's not true. When you came, and you were a girl, I was fuckin' terrified! I had wanted a boy. Boys liked me. Girls didn't. I was afraid of having to raise a person, have a person living with me who wouldn't like me. I could get away from the other bitches, with their jealousies, their resentments. But now there was going to be one under my roof. A bitch-in-training. An enemy."

"But, I was just a kid, a little baby."

"Of course you were. And you were nothing like that. Not then, not now." She laughed, a little tiny snort-y laugh. "Except for the pooping and the pissing, which I never came to love the way they all swore mums did, you were a treat from the start. Full of love. Funny. And so bright. You wanted to read, wanted to draw, wanted to know! I was that sort of kid, and was damn near kilt for it. I thought, 'I will not do to her what was done to me. I will endorse her, keep her close and safe, give her room. I will celebrate this kid!' And I've tried to do that, have . . . loved doing it. Oh, yeh, sometimes we'd have problems, but you were rarely the problem. The problem was the problem and we were the team who solved it."

Water was running out of Del's eyes. She wiped her face with the heels of her hands.

"Then you got your Rolling Red River at nine-and-a-fucking-half years of age! Christ! I had been eleven and my family treated me like a damn circus freak! I thought, I'm not going to do that with her. But I saw the way guys would look at you and I was frightened. Frightened as I had been when you were first born. Not for the same reason. Something very different." She slammed her hand on the table. "Damn! I bloody hate this! . . . Rosie, can you name the three most important things in my life?"

"Your work?"

"That's two. YOU are number one. *Then* my work. Do you know what the third most important thing in my life is?"

"The Morgan?"

"No! Not the fucking Morgan! Pulling! Pulling guys is the third most important thing in my life. Pretty fucking silly for a grown woman, I grant you, but there it is. Since I was 11, 12 years old, I've known I could walk into a room and most of the fellas there would want to take me to bed. I haven't gone with most of them, but just knowing I could gave me a sense of power. And that sense of power gave me the guts to leave home, to do my work. To raise a kid on my own.

"Then, one day, that kid starts having her own pull power. The same sort I have. What would happen, I wondered, when we started pulling the same guys? Would I clear off for her? Would she for me? Well, now it's fuckin' happened, and it's a right fuckin' mess, innit?" She leapt up and headed for the stairs.

"Don't go!"

"I'm not going. I'm just . . . catching me breath." She shook her head, like it was full of too much stuff, then came back to the table and pressed her palm alongside my face.

"Rosie, my being your mum, you being my kid has always come first. It still does. I'm just not sure how mum and daughter works when there's a fella. When a fella gets in the mix, it gets tangled. Look, Rosie, this is all as new to me as it is to you. I've no idea how it's all going to shake out, how we're going to handle it. It may not be of much help to know it scares me as much as it does you, but that's the truth and there you bloody well are!"

Now we were both crying! I stood up and we held each other and made dumb snurfly noises. It was like we were balanced together on the flat head of a very long thumbtack and if either of us moved, one or both of us would fall a long way down.

• •

Del was asleep on her back, naked with a sheet pulled up between her legs. I guess she felt me looking at her. She opened her eyes, one at a time. Smiled. "More biting?"

"Uh-uh."

She held out her arms. "Come."

I curled up on my side next to her. She held me from behind, like when I was little and she was alone and couldn't sleep. She smelled like my whole life, the smell I knew best in the world. I closed my eyes and breathed in that smell. Paint and Player's cigarettes. Honeydew melon oil and baby powder. Del.

• •

I had $200 in modelling money. I also had these amazing Victorian see-through chiffon and velvet dresses, plus some other retro clothes Del had given me. Stuff she wore in the 60s. I thought I could get pretty good money for them from Arabella at Le Temps Perdu in Eugene.

People in Eugene had figured Del and Arabella would be natural pals. They were both English, both in their thirties, both from London. There was this Big Hate between them, though. They had known each other slightly from when I was three and we lived in Dickie Siggins's house in Hampstead. Del was doing incredible fairy-tale fantasy album covers for some of the top pop bands then, and the house was always full of these amazing-looking people. Feathers and velvet, sandalwood and kurtas, scarves and music. Del said Arabella was "a groupie and a thief," and that she got her overbite from "oral encounters with the Coarse Animal Members of every rock drummer in the U.K."

Del knew how I loved retro clothes, so she didn't mind my sometimes hanging out at Le Temps Perdu. At first, Arabella would ask me questions about Del, and about whether Dickie Siggins was gay. I didn't know about Dickie and would never tell her anything about Del. Because Del didn't trust her, I didn't either. It was a family loyalty thing. Arabella was nice to me, though, and I did like the way she looked. Really tiny with huge brown eyes and short shaggy blonde hair. She wore dance tights and tunics and could juggle three beanbags. She looked like a small boy who'd run away with a travelling circus. Del said that had always been "Rubella's look," and that when she was 60 she would be a "tiny, titless, wizened, buck-toothed old androgyne." Del didn't say mean things about other women unless they'd done something to her, but she wouldn't tell me what Arabella had done, saying it was "sewage under the bridge" and not worth discussing.

Arabella was in the window, fitting a wine-red puffy-sleeved velvet dress onto a mannequin. "Hullo, Roe, be with you in a tick." I looked through the racks. There was a majorly beautiful satiny-silky belted jacket in the Deco peach colour that I loved. "No, Roanne," I thought, "you're here to sell, not to buy."

Arabella really liked what I brought. Particularly the beige, turquoise and orange geometric-print 1940s suit and the long black velvet and chiffon dress with jet beads. She said, "I remember this dress on yer mum. She wore it to Ronny Scott's club one night. She was with Billy Dane. You remember Billy?"

"Not really. A little bit."

"Overdosed, poor bugger. Best damned white blues singer in England, 'e was."

I said I'd heard his albums, the ones Del did the covers for.

"Oh, right. She did do some of 'is covers, di'n't she?"

"She did all of them except the first two."

I actually remembered Billy Dane very well. He used to play with me. Taught me all these rude pub songs his father had taught him. My favourite went:

> *Please go easy, for I've never been done before,*
> *Please go easy, an' you can 'ave me on the floor,*
> *Oh, I don't care what the neighbours say,*
> *You can put me in a fam'ly way,*
> *But PLEEEZE go easy, for I've never been done before.*

I had no idea, being three, what the words meant. It had a happy little melody, though, and Billy would sing it in this girlish squeaky voice and make all these big gestures. I would try to do exactly what he did and we'd both fall about, larfin'.

When I was six, each kid in my class was asked to sing a song we'd learned at home. I sang that. The teacher sent a note to Del, which is when I found out what it meant.

Billy and Del were really close. "Vertical," Del said. Pals. Not lovers. When he died in that hotel room in Paris, she cried for two days. I wasn't going to tell any of that to Arabella, though, because Del wouldn't want me to. I knew Arabella didn't like talking about Del's accomplishments—when I'd done it other times, her face would sort of prune up. So I mentioned the album covers. It worked. She changed the subject.

"She give you this clobber, then? How come?"

"She didn't think she'd wear them anymore. And she knew I loved them."

"If you love 'em so much, how come yer sellin' 'em?"

"Well, I want the money for something special. A surprise for Del. So I'd prefer you didn't say anything to her, OK?"

"Mum's the word, Roe . . . no pun intended."

I wasn't sure the word would be mum. I had tried to sound casual. I knew if Arabella thought it would hurt Del's feelings she'd tell her. But I had clothes to sell and Arabella had the only retro shop in Eugene.

She bought the lot for $500. Dresses, suits, scarves and beaded bags. Plus two Peking glass rope necklaces, one green, one lavender. Knowing her high prices to the two-parent rich kids at the college, I'd asked for $800, but five was her top offer. Plus the Deco peach jacket. I now had $700 U.S. And a great jacket. And a sort of a plan.

What with the sculptures and the paintings and the Morgan and all, Del is used to major heavy hauling. She actually likes it. Says it's good for the "lats and pecs," and that "lats and pecs" are the muscles that hold your tits up. Well, I may wind up with tits for leg warmers, but I hate carrying stuff. So I packed light. A second pair of jeans, my silky red-and-black wide-leg pants, three black tank-tops, two pairs of panties—one pink, one white—and a genuinely old Victorian ruffle-bottom white petticoat. I'd travel in jeans, peach-and-lavender deck shoes, black tank and denim jacket. I also packed sandals and green suede elf boots for possible buggy-snakey places. Everything fit into my banana-shaped canvas army bag, with some room left over. Toothbrush and paste, ladyplugs, underpants, etc., went into my bookbag, on top of the wordbooks and drawing books, along with a handful of different-colored felt-tip pens. I pulled my new peach jacket real taut over all this, hoping it might stay less wrinkled. If not, there'd probably be an iron. Most people have irons. Even Del has an iron, and we have less "traditional domestic" stuff than just about anybody.

I left a letter on the kitchen table:

Dear Del,

I need a few weeks to try and figure out what happened with M.—what that means to us. I still love you. Very much. I know, I really do, that you love me. I just can't seem to stop feeling like one of those air-sucking dogs people leave in cars with the windows open just a tiny bit. I need to put my whole face, my whole self in the air for a while to try and figure out who I am when I'm not standing next to me amazing mum! I will phone in a few days to let you know I'm OK. I promise. Please please PLEASE don't worry or call the police—I know calling in the Bills isn't your usual way, but I also know that going off alone isn't mine, and I'm sort of not sure what ANYONE is gonna do these days. I just need to try and shake out all the new/weird stuff in my head.

On Friday I sold some of the '60s gear you gave me. At Le Temps Perdu. Please don't be mad. I know you'd want me to be OK for money if I'm on my own. Please don't look for me. I WILL be back in time for our trip home to Vancouver. I know how important the School Thing is to you.

Love always, always, always!

Rosie

P.S. Yesterday (Thursday), I spoke to Jonas. He's that black bodybuilder guy with the barkless African dog who licks toes. The dog licks toes, I mean. He, Jonas, said he'd be happy to model for you in my place. He'll come by the college today, before the 4 o'clock class, and you can see if it works out. He seems like a v. nice person. XOXO. R.

I had this big postcard. D.D.A. sent it after I mailed him some of my cartoons, care of his publisher in New York. The cartoons that won the prize in Salmon Arm. Based on Canadian place names. Salmon Arm, Moose Factory, Medicine Hat, etc. He wrote, "Very good. Original. Full with humor. If one day you are near to here come visit. Follow the stones with 'D.'"

The other side of the card was a cartoon of a forest. It said "The Forest" on one of the tree branches. At the bottom was written "Gasquet, Cal." There was a scribble of a fast-food stand called "Redwood Burgers" to the right of what looked like a large garbage can shaped like a brown bear with its mouth wide open. A word-balloon coming out of this open mouth said "Commence Here." The bear made me think of Mucus's story. I decided this was a good omen. If woods/bear/man was part of the poison, maybe woods/bear/man would be part of the cure. In the upper-right-hand corner, in the forest, he'd drawn a largish house, its windows coloured in with yellow. There was a porch with what looked like hanging Japanese lanterns. They also had yellow bits. Above the house door was a sign. It said INN NAINITY.

There was a 5 P.M. bus that went to a place with a great-sounding name, Eureka, California. The bus passed through Gasquet. The ticket woman said it stopped at Redwood Burgers for people to stretch, get food and "relieve themselves."

• •

It was an eyefood ride. First, we went along the coast road. Tall craggy rocks with amazing shapes grew out of the sea like wizards in mytho stories. For beauty, and amazingness, the trick was to keep looking to the right, where the sea was, not to the left, where the Dairy Queens were. Sometimes I would feel scared. When this happened, I'd say "Eureka," very softly so nobody'd notice, and the scaredness would mostly calm down.

After a while, the bus turned inland. Then we were in a forest with huge trees. I mean REALLY huge! Some of them were so high you couldn't see the tops. The driver announced that these were redwood trees and that some of them were thousands of years old.

• •

"Redwood Burgers! Pit stop!"

We all got off the bus. It was a funky little place. Picnic tables made out of redwood. A hotdog/hamburger stand. To the right was a tiny store whose sign said REDWOOD BOB, TRAVEL NECESSARIES. To the left of the food stand was another tiny building, also redwood, with two doors marked LADIES and GENTS. To the left of the Gents was a garbage can shaped like an open-mouthed brown bear.

My face looked really young in the tin washroom mirror. I put on more lipstick and mascara, which usually adds a few years. Then I queued up with the other bus people and ordered a cheeseburger, pink lemonade and a bag of corn chips. So far, I was doing OK, but I'd done these sorts of things before. Going into the forest and finding D.D.A.'s house would be the new part. The maybe-hard part. I took the postcard out of my jacket pocket. "Follow the stones with 'D.'"

I watched the others get back on the bus, making myself stay where I was. I didn't know any of the bus people, but it still felt like they were leaving me. After they'd gone I noticed how dark it was. And that was by the side of the road. Inside the forest it would be what Del calls Welldigger's Arse. I thought I'd better find out if Redwood Bob considered flashlights a Travel Necessary.

Mr. Bob, or whoever it was behind the counter, looked like God in the Italian Ceiling Thing where the guy is falling out of heaven. And he did have flashlights. Bought one, and some batteries, thinking I'd better start watching my expenses. I hadn't even been on the road one whole day and, including bus fare, I was already down almost $40.

Mr. Bob asked me where I was "headed for." Yanks do that. Ask strangers snoopy questions. Sometimes it makes me feel poked at, but this time I thought it might help to tell.

"To Inn Nainity. Do you know where it is?"

"Inn Nainity? No, can't say as I do."

I showed him the postcard.

"Oh, yeah, that place. These direction's'll get you there. Just follow the Ds on the rock along the path like it says. It'll take a while. . . . Why don'tcha getcha self coupla sandwiches and some pop?"

I passed on the sandwiches because they were all on white bread, which I hate. Bought a bag of M&M's, the American version of Smarties, and a plastic bottle of water. Another $5 spent. Money. Like Del says, "Piss through a goose."

Mr. Bob loaded up my flashlight. He was looking at me funny. Not pervo funny. Sort of like I was some sort of wrong. I put everything in my bookbag and thanked him for his help.

"You're welcome, youngster," he said.

Next to the garbage bear was a path leading into the forest. Just the way it was on D.D.A.'s postcard. I headed into the forest figuring everything was pretty cool. A little spooky but basically OK.

After a few minutes of walking along, watching the ground, I saw three marked rocks. Three in a row, on the left-hand side of the path. D.D.D. "Fine," I said out loud, "everything's going fine."

For a while there was moonlight coming through the humungus trees. Then, as I went deeper in, it got to being a major welldigger-type situation. Seriously dark. I shone my flashlight up into the trees. Something flew. A bird? A bat? There were noises. Crunches and hoots and stuff. I wondered whether using a bear as a garbage can related in any way to the presence of real bears. I thought about going back to Redwood Burgers and starting again in the morning. Then I saw three more D rocks and decided they were an omen, meaning don't be a major sucky baby. I kept going. I did start singing, though, which is something I do when I'm alone and scared.

My old man said, "Follow the van,
And don't dilly-dally on the way . . ."
Off with the van wit' me old man in it . . .
I followed on wit' me old cock linnet . . .
I dillied, I dallied, I dallied and I dillied . . .

The next line was about losing my way so I decided to sing something else.

Gentlemen will please refrain
From passing water whilst the train
Is standing in the station, I love yooouu . . .
We encourage constipation,
Whilst the train is in the station,
Surely, you've got—

There was a fucking great SCREECH! I crouched down, screaming, wishing like crazy that I was in my room in Vancouver or Yachats or Salmon Arm or even boring gross fucking Burnaby where somebody once put dogshit in my locker. I wished I was any place but this great huge welldigger's arse of a great huge dark fucking forest where something superlarge was about to rape and kill and eat me all to death! I was in too deep to turn back. I had no idea what time it was. Was Del home? Did she get my note? Would she ever find out if I was eaten by a bear? Or a cougar? A cougar? I didn't even know what the fuck a cougar was or even if they had them here, but it sounded like one of the many sorts of things that might be what was about to eat me. I sat down on the ground, uselessly hiding myself behind a tree. Del says sitting on damp ground gives you piles. So what, eh? Who cares? Only the bear/cougar/lion would see them. "Eat my piles, cougar!!!" I drank some water and ate the whole damn bag of M&M's, one M at a time.

When I'm scared, I sing. When I'm totally terrified, I pick something out of my wordbook and say it over and over. There was this really neat phrase I found once. On a bottle of Polish vodka the colour of piss. Brian drank this vodka sometimes. It has a blade of grass in it. I stood up. Took some big yoga breaths. In through the nose, out through the mouth. Then I shouted, "ZHOOBROVKAAA! FLAVOURED WITH THE HERB BELOVED OF THE EUROPEAN BISON!!!" I said this over and over, walking faster and faster until I came to a fork in the path. There were three more D rocks on the right side of the fork, so I forked right.

After a bit, I thought I could see lights through the trees. I wanted to leave the path and just run through the trees to where the lights were, but there was another batch of D rocks and the postcard had said specifically to follow D rocks. So I did. I wanted to at least run down the path, but the army bag and the bookbag were feeling lots heavier than when I started into the Forest Without End. Five years ago, seemed like. I drank more water. Shouted, "HELLLOOO! DEE . . . DEE . . . AAAYYY!" No answer except for a weirdassed low fucking rumble. Decided to run. Followed the rock path. Fell down. Skinned holy hell out of my palms on little phantom roadrocks or whatever. Got a killer knot on the right side of my rib cage. Went back to fast walking. "Zhoobrovka . . . flavored with the herb . . . beloved of the Euro . . . pean bisonzhoobrovkaflavouredwiththeherbbelovedoftheEuropeanbisonzhoo—"

It exploded into my eyes like a Magritte floating castle! A huge redwood house. Paper lanterns strung along an enormous porch. I was standing in front of a big boulder. Red-painted words: ET VOILÀ! BIENVENUE! Bienvenue. I knew that word from Del's show in Montréal. Welcome.

The porch went from one end of the house to the other. It was really pretty, with wooden rockers and white wicker chairs like the ones in Le Temps Perdu. An outdoor rocking chesterfield with flower-print pillows. A white wicker table with magazines on it. In different languages. Above my head, all along the length of the porch, were the paper lanterns from the postcard. They had electric bulbs inside, and up close I could see the designs on them. Flowers or Asian writing.

"Bon soir."

I dropped my gear and screamed.

I think what it was was that, after walking for what seemed like ever in a great huge dark forest all by myself for the first time in my whole entire life, I needed to see somebody real. I don't mean real. I mean regular-size. And Didi was. Is. A dwarf. And a dwarf in the middle of a forest is somehow even less regular-size than a dwarf crossing the street in Vancouver. Not that I'd ever actually seen a street-crossing Vancouver dwarf. I may be forgetting somebody, but I think Didi was my first dwarf. So I screamed.

He was very nice about it. "Pardohn," he said in that whispery voice he has. "I did not want to give you fear . . . I am Didi."

"D.D.A.?"

"Yes, the same."

"I'm . . . I'm Roanne Chappell."

"Ah, yes. As I t'ought. Medsenat. Moose Factoree."

He remembered my cartoons! "Yes! Right! That's me!"

"Welcome to Innanneetee. Would you like a laymo nayd or a coca?"

"Lemonade?"

"Oui."

"Yes. Yes, I would, thank you. I'd love a lemonade."

"Bon. Sit. I will return." He went into the house. I flopped down on the chesterfield, wasted. And happy. I was in D.D.A.'s actual house! He knew right away who I was! And he was real. Really little, but absolutely real. And I'd made it through a megaforest without fucking up. Amazing!

That forest was now all around me. Dark, dark, dark. And from where I sat it felt like there was nothing on the earth but this one house and four thousand trees in the darkness.

Didi scootched around the screen door and onto the porch, carrying a tray. On it were two large glasses of lemonade with lots of ice and a glass bowl of strawberries. I took a glass and he put the tray on the wicker table.

"You 'ave t'irst?" he asked, smiling at me gulping down the lemonade.

"Yes. I have lots of thirst, I'm sorry."

"For what? 'Ave the other glass."

"That's yours."

"No. It is for you. The two are for you. I believed you would 'ave t'irst after your long time in the forest. I bring two glasses at the same time because I do not like going two times to the kitchen."

He had a really sweet smile. Little teeth, sort of scalloped like the hang-down part of a white awning. His eyes were bright brown buttons sewn onto a sock doll. He wore tiny blue jeans and a pale yellow shirt. His hair was longish, light brown and gray. It looked soft like baby hair. He had a bristly little beard and moustache, also brown and gray but more gray than his headhair. The hands that made the brilliant cartoons were small and slightly pudgy. The lemonade tasted great and Didi seemed to like me, seemed glad I was there. I felt my shoulders roll down. Yes, I thought, I think I'm safe. I think this is good.

Now that I wasn't worried about being raped by a cougar, I noticed that the forest had a wonderful smell. Tree bark and green things. Didi asked how old I was.

"Sixteen."

"No, I do not believe so . . . Bob, from the little store, watches to be sure everyone 'oo come to vizeet 'ave card from me. 'E telephone to say you are arriving. 'E give a description. I 'ad the sense of Roanne Chappell, so I look for your correspondence. The letter of last year of Roanne Chappell say she 'as thirteen years."

I unrelaxed and was scared again. There was no way I wanted to be sent back into the forest in the dark.

"OK, OK, I'm fourteen. But I'm a very grown-up person. Everybody says so!"

"Yes, yes, Petite, I can see you are. 'Ave you run away from 'ome?"

"No . . . not really. My mother is a painter and sculptor. Her work is really good. She's a terrific person. I'm just taking a sort of holiday before I go back to school . . . I have . . . some new things to figure out and I was hoping I could do that here. Visiting you. And thinking. And drawing, which helps me think. I won't be a bother. I promise. I won't even talk to you unless you talk first." My eyes were filling up but I believe I was successful at keeping major cry or whinge out of my voice.

I reminded Didi that he did invite me to visit him. And I promised to call Del the next day, and he could listen if he wanted. If Del said I had to come back to Yachats at once, I would, of course, do that. He smiled. He nodded. He said, "Bon."

The inside of Inn Nainity was even better than the outside (and the outside was perfect!). Lots of phlumphy chairs to sink into. Funny little objects everywhere, too many to take in all at once, though I immediately connected to a huge green malachite egg, out of which an oversize chicken leg in a red high-heeled shoe was struggling to hatch. And a lit-up neon daisy in a Coca-Cola bottle.

And the Amazing Clock Thing. We'd only been inside a few

minutes when it turned midnight. The glass door of a tall wooden cabinet swung open. Out of it came a carved and painted wooden boy the same size as Didi. The carved boy had a brass mallet in his hand. He hit a brass gong in the cabinet, which went *bonnnggg*. Then the wooden boy went back inside the cabinet and the door closed.

"Wow! Does it do that all day?"

"Ah, no. Only at the twelves."

There were framed D.D.A. cartoons on the walls. I recognized a lot of them. And "serious" oil paintings too. I thought one was really great. Two beautiful naked women with bald heads. They were in dark, jungly-looking water, with lily pads around them.

"You like it?"

"Oh, yes, very much."

"Léonor Fini. She was married wit' Ernst."

"Ernst?"

"You do not know Max Ernst? You would, I believe, like 'im. I believe Ernst would like also 'Moose Factoree.' I will give you a book. Come, I will do it now. And show you your room where you sleep."

I grabbed my gear and followed him up the stairs. He had a little sand-dune-shaped mound sticking out of his back and he walked like a big wind-up toy. Like Charlie Chaplin without the cane.

Three walls of Didi's studio were floor-to-ceiling with books. More books were stacked on the floor. The fourth wall had a brown corduroy-covered daybed in front of it, and was filled with framed cartoons by other people. Many of them were autographed and said nice things about Didi's work. I recognized Searle, Feiffer, Brilliant and Crumb. There were also framed lithos by dead people like Boilly and Daumier. And in the middle of all these great cartoonists was MOOSE FACTORY! My cartoon! Two "completed" moose trying to keep their balance on a conveyor belt while factory workers applied antlers to a third moose.

"You . . . you put me on your wall."

"Oui. I like very much 'Moose Factoree.'"

"I'm glad . . . I really am."

He reached up and patted my arm. Then he climbed a ladder and hauled down a large book.

"Ernst! You can look at it in your bed. Would you like first a bat'?"

"A bat?"

"Oui. A big bat' wiz bool. To wash yourself."

"Oh, a bath!" Stavro told me once that when people were scared, which I had been in the forest, it made them smell bad. I said yes, I'd really like a bath.

He flashed his tiny awning-scallop teeth into a quick smile. "Bon. Follow me." The Ernst book tucked under his arm, he headed down the hall. I followed, hauling my gear. Bool?

Different people have different things that are important to them. For Del and me, one of those important things has always been large old bathtubs with feet. Didi had one. It looked too big for him to bathe in without sliding around a lot. Maybe there was a little tub somewhere in the house.

It was a great-looking loo. In addition to the tub with feet, there was a sink shaped like a large white tulip. Next to the sink stood a wooden washstand with a black marble top. Large pale green towels hung from black marble racks on each side. In the middle of the marble top was a big white bowl with a pitcher in it. The toilet had an unpainted wooden seat. The tiny window next to the toilet had see-through curtains the same pale green as the towels. I could see that D.D.A.—Didi—took time to decorate his house, which most guys I'd met, except maybe Dickie Siggins, didn't.

"This is a wonderful house. I love tubs with feet. And those pitcher-and-bowl things. We lived in a house with a pitcher and bowl like that when I was three. In London. London, England."

"'Lavabo.' The pitcher and bowl are called lavabo. The stand is called also lavabo."

"Lavabo. Nice word. It's nice in the mouth."

"Lavabo? . . . Yes. Yes, it is, Petite. Follow again."

The parade of superterrific rooms continued. "My" room was perfect! Tiny and cozy, two windows with one of those iron grillework beds between them. Painted white. Covered in a green-and-white patchwork quilt with a diamond design. There was a wooden dresser with an oval mirror attached to it by wood things that curved out like snakes' heads. There was a little bookcase with eight or nine books, some upright, some lying on their sides. On each side of the bed was a small square wooden table with a bell-shaped glass lamp on it. The glass was Deco peach. I dropped my gear. Home!

"Bon. Now I go to sleep. I will see you in the late morning. You will find me in the kitchen or on the porch or up the stairs in my studio. Good night, Petite. Bo rev . . . the bool are in the lavabo." A quick smile and he turned, Chaplin-ing out of the room.

"Bool"? What were bool? Bulls, maybe. Rubber bulls. There were lots of weirdassed objects in the house, so rubber bulls instead of rubber duckies made sort of sense. I grabbed my toothbrush/toothpaste and went to look in the lavabo.

"Captain Jim's Morocco Mint Bubblebath." Bubbles! Bool were bubbles. Perfect! I filled the humungotub, tore off my woods-grubby clothes, put my hair up and wove the toothbrush handle in to hold it. The water was steaming and the bubblebath made the room smell like chewing gum and wet leaves. I was pretty sure that D.D.A. wasn't any kind of pervo but I latched the door because people can be sudden grenading disappointments. "Petite." That was French for little. Funny, him calling me that, what with his being barely as tall as just below my tits. I climbed into the hot minty-bubbled water and closed my eyes. When I woke up the bubbles were gone, the water was cool, and the tips of my fingers were pruney.

I was too sleepy to focus on Ernst. Fell asleep as soon as I crawled under the covers, the Ernst book next to me. I woke up in the still-dark, having a full-out anxiety attack. Like when I was nine and Del would leave me alone at night because I insisted I was old enough to stay without a baby-minder. I wasn't then, and it was hideously, embarrassingly possible that I wasn't now either. I turned on one of the bell-shaped lamps. Started to look at the Ernst pictures, which I recognized as being surrealist, like Magritte. Surrealism was one of my favourites, but, in the middle of the night, in a strange house, it was not the best choice for calming down.

In my brilliantly economical packing, I'd forgotten a nightdress, or even a big shirt, so I wrapped the top-sheet around me, found my flashlight and headed downstairs, thinking I'd sit on the porch and wait for morning.

I don't know why I started to cry, but it felt good, so I let it roll, trying not to make too much noise. A light went on up on the top floor. A tiny head stuck itself out of a window.

"Allo, Petite. What is wrong?"

"Nothing, Mr. D.D.A., I'm fine. . . . Just a little keyed up, I guess."

"Non. I believe not fine. Come up, please."

I expected a little tiny bed with little tiny pillows, but everything was regulation size. Except Didi, who sat like a ventriloquist's dummy in the middle of the wooden bed, under an every-colour-in-the-world patchwork quilt. He patted the bed for me to sit. Oh, pleasepleasePLEASE, I thought, please don't pervo on me in the middle of the night in the middle of the woods in the middle of fucking nowhere. I sat on the absolute edge of the bed, with my eyes on the door.

Didi sort of chuckled, a tiny noise in a smiling mouth. "Rest trankeel, Petite. Shwee payDAY."

"What?"

"I am not dangerous. I am payDAY. TaPETTE. Ohmosexwal."

"You're gay?"

"Too joor."

"Too what?"

"Yes. I am, as you say, 'gay.' I will not 'arm you. I promeez. I swear."

Because of Del, I had spent my whole life around lots of grown-up male persons. The others were all full-sized, but I seemed to know which ones were good. Some, like Marcus, could be tacky ass-holes, but even Brian was good, wonderful actually, when he was sober. Didi was sober, and everything about him said, "I may be unusual, but I am good. And kind. And not a pervo."

"I believe you. You're a very nice man and I'm sorry I woke you up."

The neat little awning-scallop smile. "It is all right. You are first night in a new plass. This bed is very grand and I am very small. Why do you not turn off the light and sleep 'ere? Wiz company. Or you can leave on the light."

Oh boy, I thought. If I was wrong about him, this could be the dumbest thing I'd ever done. But it didn't feel wrong. Not even a little bit. There was a bright red iron woodstove in the middle of the room, its stovepipe going up through the ceiling. It made the room smell like cedar. And strawberries. This really nice strawberry smell. Didi looked small and sweet in the middle of his bed. I wanted and needed very much to land, to stop circling around in the night like a grenade-evading flying starfish.

"Thank you," I said. Wrapped in my bedsheet, I climbed in under the multi-coloured quilt.

"Bon," he said. "Close or open the light?"

"Uh, close."

He turned off the lamp and lay down on his side, facing away from me. The quilt was thick, filled with feathers. And the nice roomsmell was him! Didi smelled like strawberries! I felt shy and the shyness was making me lie there rigid, staring at the shadows and shapes on the ceiling.

"You are trankeel? Fine?"

"Yes, thank you."

"Non. I can feel your ahnkyetay . . . you must sleep, Petite. 'Old on to my carapass."

My ahnkyetay? His carapass? What was a "carapass"? If it was French for dick I was definitely going to hold my breath till I died.

"Carapass?"

"My eump . . . the eump on my back. Put your 'ead eunder my eump, close your eyes . . . 'old on to the eump an' try to sleep. Yes? OK?"

"Yes, OK." What the hell, eh? I closed my eyes, nuzzled my head in under his sand dune and wrapped my arms around it. It was hard and smooth, like a Brancusi sculpture, only warmer. I loved the strawberry smell. It smelled like a lullaby sounded and I fell asleep.

Didi is one of those lucky buggers who can sleep in. Not me. I always wake up as soon as any sort of daylight comes into a room. I think it's from so much travelling. I never know where I am first thing. I need to name the place and decide if it's good or bad, so I can figure out how to handle it. Sometimes that takes a while, so I wake up early to give myself a head start.

Waking up under Didi's hump was definitely a new place. I had a scared moment of not knowing where the hell or what the hell. Then the strawberry smell kicked in and I smiled. The stove fire had died and the room outside the quilt was cold. Didi was superwarm, so I stayed holding on to him for a while. Then I decided that my life had been changing in major ways and that I needed to write it all down so I could maybe understand everything better. I slipped out from under the feather quilt, rewrapped my top-sheet nightdress and went downstairs to my room to get my journal and wordbooks. It was even colder there than in Didi's room, so I hauled the stuff back upstairs.

When I clunked under the quilt with all the books, Didi opened his eyes, sort of.

"Bonjoor."

"Oh, I'm sorry. It's really cold in my . . . the downstairs bedroom. Could I, would you mind if I stayed here under the covers and wrote in my journal? I'll be real quiet."

"PahdprobLEM. Byahnsoor."

"Is that yes?"

He smiled. "Oui, sheree, that is yes. But I sleep more." He closed his eyes, still smiling, so I figured everything was cool.

That was when I started writing all this. About Del. About Marcus. About big-handed guys and the Bend Over Thing. All of it. So I can start to figure out what's happening. So I have something to give my maybe-sister. And so that, if anything happens to me that's mega-grenade, there'll be some sort of record that I had been in the world.

Didi is walking up, so I have to stop writing now. He just asked, in this sleepy whisper, if I wanted a bool de café olay. I know "bool" from last night and "olay" from when Del was dating Julio. Mexican bubblebath. Amazing!

BONEDUNE AND BUILDINGMAN

2

Foreign Words

Chiaroscuro

Vertige

Pipistrello

Farfalla

Sizwe

Pamplemousse

Jacaranda

Iliovasilema

Mousseline

Auto-da-Fé

Bienvenue

Lavabo

Carapass?

2 Sept. 1981

On a bus and in the middle. Between midnight and morning. Between Didi-size and Pascal-size. Between Kitsilano and Ventoo Boovar. Between who I was and who I'm gonna be. There was nothing at all about the Redwood forest, or Bolinas, or the eye-food explosion of San Francisco that made me want to leave, except that I only got to stay by saying I'd be leaving. Someday, there was going to be, there had to be, a place where I got to stay because somebody besides Del wanted me to.

Del. As far as Del would be concerned, if she had any idea where I was, I was heading in the wrong direction. But here I am, with my big crush and my little budget, hauling myself south to Los Angeles. To visit Gabe. Everyone from everywhere wants to see Hollywood. Even people who don't need to stop seeing their mother's bum going up and down in the moonlight. Even people who haven't fallen in love with a bearded building who couldn't care less. So this is me, doing that. And writing about Inn Nainity, while bus people sleep and snore and turn loose their farts into Mr. Greyhound's big silver-and-blue carapass.

It turned out to be "boule" (bowl), not "bulle" (bubbles), and café "au lait"—coffee with steamed milk. Served in a big white bowl. The bowl has no handle. You cup it in both hands. Makes you feel like a little kid with a warm present. Didi has it every morning, with chewy muffins he makes himself.

After we had our muffins and bowls of coffee, Didi said we had to call Del. I told him she'd be at the college, but he said it was "Samdee"—Saturday. I did want to keep my promise to him and be honest, so I admitted that Del didn't have a Saturday class. I called Yachats. Del picked up on the first ring.

"Hi, it's—"

"Rosie! Where the fuck . . . where are you?"

"I'm fine. I'm in a good place."

"What? What 'good place'? Where?"

I wasn't sure there was any way of explaining the situation that would make sense, would make her agree to let me stay.

"Uh . . . you remember when I sent my cartoons to D.D.A., the artist?"

"The cartoonist you like?"

"Yes! Him! . . . Well, he wrote me back, remember? And he invited me to visit him. That's what I'm doing."

"You're with a man?"

"Not exactly. I mean, yes, but . . . much . . . less . . . like Clive from the Chelsea Antique Market . . . but . . . less . . ."

Didi was smiling, watching me try to figure out a polite way to say "gay dwarf." He held out his little hand for the phone. Embarrassed and spaghetti-brained, I passed it to him.

"Madame? This is Didier Rocaille. Oui, the cartooNEEST. What I believe Roanne tries to say is that I am a nain tapette, an ohmosexwal dwarf. Which is the true. She stay 'ere last night. And promeez to me that we would telephone to you today to ask if she can vizeet with me for a little time. I tell 'er she can do this if you say 'OK'. . . . Yes, of course." He handed the phone to me.

"Rosie, are you sure he's gay? Are you sure he's telling you the truth? Are you sure he's not bonkers, sure you're OK? If you're in danger, say Hammersmith. If you're OK and want to stay there, say Hampstead."

"Hampstead."

"Hampstead?"

"Yes. Definitely. Very Hampstead."

"Oh, God. . . . You have to be back here to leave for Vancouver. To go back to school."

"Yes, I know. I will be, I promise. But that's three weeks away."

"Oh, God . . . I don't know . . . I . . . give me the cartoonist again."

I gave the phone back to Didi. Del seemed to be doing most of the talking, with Didi saying "yes" and "oui" and "I understand." Then he gave me the phone again.

"Look, Rosie, where are you? Where does he live?"

"In a big redwood house. In a forest."

"In a bloody forest!? What forest? Where?"

"Please, Del, I want this to be just for me . . . just my thing. It really is super-Hampstead. I'll come back to Yachats in two or three weeks. I don't want . . . anyone to look for me . . . I just want to be here and visit, and read books, and think and draw some cartoons. Please?" There was a long silence. "Del?"

Finally, she let go this long outbreath, then said, in a really small voice, "OK."

I was babbling "Ohthankyouthankyouthankyou" when she asked to talk to Didi again. He listened some more, saying "of course" and that he understood. Then it was my turn again.

"Listen, Rosie. I'm going to trust you with this. I know that's important. But you've got to, absolutely got to, be back here before school. Understood?"

"Understood."

"And, Rosie, please stay . . . alert, you know? So you can clear off before things get bad. I'm not saying they will get bad, but they can do, and you need to be able to jump clear in time. You know what I mean?"

Now Del was babbling. I guessed it was because she was worried about me. I didn't want her to change her mind about letting me stay.

"Sure. Of course. . . . How did Jonas work out?"

"What?"

"Jonas. The guy I sent for the art class. Was he OK?"

"Oh, yes, he was fine. Super, actually. He's a lovely guy."

"A lovely guy."

"Rosie, what's the phone number?"

"Where?"

"Where you are. What's the phone number there?"

"Uh, thanks a lot, Del. This means a lot to me. Really a lot. Hampstead. I love you." I hung up.

Didi's face was soft and smiley. He made us two more white bowls of café au lait, which we had on the porch. I told him about Del's artwork, particularly the sculptures, which I've always thought were her best thing. He asked lots of questions about their size, subjects and whether she worked in wood, metal or clay. I told him all three, but mostly wood. Then he asked what gotsfaggoteurs were.

"What?"

"Gotsfaggoteurs. What are 'gotsfaggoteurs'?"

"Gee, I dunno. Why?"

"Because your mother, she say if I 'arm you, if I 'urt you, she 'ave my gotsfaggoteurs."

I laughed. "Guts for garters! She'll have your guts for garters. That's an English expression. English from England. It means she'll kill you. In a major way."

"I see."

• •

The two weeks I spent with Didi at Inn Nainity were, are, two of the best weeks of my life so far. It was, in fact, the first time ever that I was completely "at home" in a place where Del wasn't. Because we travelled so much, you could say Del was my home.

I like having rituals with people and got into some excellent ones with Didi. Mostly, but not only, about making cartoons. His last book had been a success, and he was working on a new one—*His Ass from His Elbow* (The Rude Sequel to *The Name Rings a Bell*). Both books had to do with the goofy pictures he saw in his head when he heard expressions in English. I think that's why he liked my "Moose Factory." We both drew what Didi called juh duh MOH, word games.

His workspace was on the top floor, next to his bedroom. We had a deal. He worked every day, from 2 to 6 P.M. I could work there at the same time, after our lunch, if I didn't speak to him, except in an oor-JAHNSS, an emergency. He did his drawing at a humungus wooden table, sitting on a high wooden barstool with arms. I worked on the other side of the room, sitting or lying on the floor, using my felt-tip pens. Didi gave me a large world atlas book to use as a surface, because when I tried to work directly on the floor, my pen would go through the paper into cracks between the floorboards, which made holes, and also screwed up the line.

What we were doing was similar to the "making art together" ritual I'd had with Del from as far back as I could remember. I believe there's nothing more beautiful than when two people trust eachother enough, are calm enough with eachother, to work on their individual stuff in the same room. I think this is rare. Even when both people do art stuff. Maybe especially then.

My drawings were about some of the weird slang names for women's breasts. Like "boobs," "hooters" and "jugs." "Boobs" was a naked lady with two nerdo-retardo-looking faces where her tits should be. "Hooters" was the same lady with owls for tits. The juggy one (again, same lady) had a pair of glass wine bottles with nipples and little handles.

Didi started teaching me French. On account of Boilly and Daumier.

When you move around a lot, books can be a problem. Del and I would sometimes have fights about which books we needed to throw out before each move. I'd managed to keep some wordbooks and some stories, but mostly we held on to art books. Along with visits to galleries and museums, these books were the reason I knew the names of lots of painters, sculptors and cartoonists, even when I was little. Some of these people had non-English names. I think we usually pronounced the superfamous ones correctly. Because Boilly and Daumier were early cartoonists, I knew both their names. To read, but not to say.

On this one day, it had been raining. Rainy days make me dreamy, and I'd been having trouble concentrating to draw. So I went to Didi's study, got some art books and was curled up in my corner of his workroom, reading while he drew. When he finished working, he put down his pen and looked over at me.

"'Oo are you studying, Petite?"

"French cartoonists. Boilie and Dawmyer."

"'Oo?"

"Boilie. And Dawmyer?"

He pushed with both hands on the barstool arms and sprung himself down to the ground. "Non. BoyLEE and DawmYERR are not possible. I cannot live with BoyLEE and DawmYERR. We must fix."

He waddled off down the stairs, returning after a few minutes with a large book called *Dictionnaire Larousse: Anglais-Français, Français-Anglais.* He sat on the floor next to me, sticking his baby legs out in a V and thumbing through the book. I smiled, looking at his beautiful long, thick eyelashes (guys always get the lashes!). He found what he was looking for, and pointed to it.

"Regard this word, 'bois.' It is where we are now. In the bois. In the wood, the forest. It prononces 'bwah.' You look at all this words with 'o-i.' They are all prononce 'wah.' Clair? You understand? You 'ear the sound? You can see 'ere, by the side of each word, the prononce in fo-nay-TEEK. Now, say for me B-o-i-l-l-y."

"Bwally."

I was half right. Got the "bwa," but screwed up the two "l"s which were like a "yuh" when they were followed by certain other stuff. Like a "y." But "ville" was "veel," not "vee." Then, he showed me how to do "DohMYAY," and what happened when the "ier" became "ière."

"You can take the deeksyonNAIRE to your room and look when you 'ave a French word. You can write the word in French, and then write also the fonayTEEK—the way the word is prononce. And you will learn, because you are smart. D'ac?"

"Yes, d'ac. Thank you. I like learning words."

"I know this. And I believe you will do well. Because you 'ave good hears. Some people do not. They are 'opeless."

"Hopeless."

"Pardon?"

"Hopeless, Didi—with an 'h.' Huh-opeless."

"Yes, yes, Petite. I know about the ''ash.' But it is, for a Frenchman, 'ard . . . huh-ard to make."

I picked up the dictionary and stood to go. "Uh-huh. So are Bwayee and Dohmyay for an English person. And the frog word, the word for 'frog' . . .?"

"Grenouille."

"Yeah, grun-NOOYEH. Grun-NOOYEH is a real mouth war. I'll get 'grenouille' if you'll work on 'hopeless' and 'hard.' Deal? D'ac?"

"D'accord. Deal."

I didn't miss Del. Not really. I mean, I thought about her a lot. Every day, in fact. But it was either about art stuff or just a warm thought. Or, because of why I'd left, sort of trying to figure out what we were going to do about the Guys Thing. Finally, one morning, early, while Didi was still asleep, I wrote out a basic Rules List to give Del when I got back to Yachats.

RULES LIST FOR DELORES (DEL) CHAPPELL (MOTHER) AND ROANNE (ROSIE) CHAPPELL (DAUGHTER) REGARDING MALE PERSONS.

1. ROANNE CHAPPELL will try to confine her love and sex things to guys under 30 years of age.
2. DELORES CHAPPELL will try to confine her love and sex things to guys over 30 years of age.
3. If, however, one or the other of the above-named persons (see above) notices and likes a particular male person

first (regardless of age), both parties agree to discuss the matter before either of them does any physical activities with the male person in question (including flirting, necking or holding hands).
4. If one of the above-named persons actually starts a relationship with a male person, the other above-named person will not do, or attempt to do, any sexual thing (including F, N, or HH, see above) with the male person in question.
5. Both DELORES and ROANNE CHAPPELL promise to always honour the terms of this agreement, no matter what, because they love and respect eachother.

At the bottom of the page, I made two name-size lines for Del and me to sign. I signed over my line. When Del signed hers, I'd go down to Kampus KopyKwik and make a duplicate, so we'd each have one. I put the list in my bookbag, inside my Interesting Words in English wordbook.

You've got to practice a thing to get good at it. Travelling a lot makes it hard to practice hanging out, so I wasn't very good at it. By the time I'd get past all the early-on stuff of circling around and dumb little tests to where I really had a pal, like Ti-Marie in Montréal or Squinty in Burnaby, we'd move (I don't count Brian. We got superclose, but the ending was grenade-related rather than travel-related). Of all people ever, except for Del and, in the little-kid time, Dickie Siggins, Didi was, and remains, the best hanging-out person of my life so far.

After that first night, when I was all freaky and scared, I mostly slept in my own bed. I did snuggle in with Didi a couple of times, but to be absolutely honest, it started to make me sort of horny. Not for Didi. For somebody taller and heterosexualer. Somebody like Pascal.

One morning, four days into my second week at Inn Nainity, Didi asked if I wanted to walk him out of the woods to Redwood Bob's for supplies.

"Hi, Bear," I said. It was strange seeing the Garbage Bear again. It seemed like I'd been at Didi's for a long time. Like the bear of a week and a half ago was a creature from when I was little. Pictures flooded up inside my head—not just of the woods and the moment I saw Inn Nainity, but of Del, Marcus, Geronimo. I wanted to stay "in the right now" with Didi, so I shook my head, and the kaleidoscope bits rearranged into "Didi and Roanne at Redwood Bob's Travel Necessaries."

Redwood was glad to see Didi. His big Michelangelo face went all crinkled and grinny. He came around the counter and shook Didi's hand, saying, "Well, well, well," and, "Hello, my friend." They nattered away like two different but friendly beasts in the same cage. Then Redwood noticed me, standing in the doorway.

"Well" (two "well"s less than Didi got). He scratched at his steely-coloured beard. His face crinkled again, but this time was pruney, not grinny. Slitty eyes. Scrunched nose. Pursed lips. "Hello, youngster. Still here, I see."

"Youngster." He'd called me that when I first met him. I didn't like it. Neither time. He made it sound like a cross between "little girl" and "pig slut." It reminded me of when I really was a little girl and Del would bring me to her nighttime gallery openings and somebody would say, "Should this child be up so late?" Back then, the "pig slut" would be aimed at Del. Now, Redwood B. was letting me play both parts. I guessed that meant I was growing up. "Yes, sir. I'm still here. How nice to see you again." I extended my hand. He gave it a short, sharp shake. "Lovely day," I said, smiling, using Del's "grand voice." The one she used with "tight-arsed bitches."

Most times, I just back off when people behave in an I-don't-like-you way. But I could feel Didi watching. I looked Mr. Bob right in the eye, thinking, I have a right to be here. You have to deal with me. You have to treat me as a human being.

"Bon. Why do you not look for what you need Petite, while Bob and me gather up my 'nécessaire,' d'ac?"

"D'ac."

Mr. Bob, glad to get away from the Evil Teenager, started putting stuff on the counter. Didi helped, pointing at things too high for him to reach.

There were three tiny aisles and shelves against the walls. I'd used up Didi's bubblebath, so I got some more. Mint, like before, plus something called Tropical Passion Flower (deal with that,

Deadwood Bob!). Also rubbing alcohol to dry up the zit that had arrived on my chin. Two black felt-tip pens. A small brick of cheddar cheese. Salted biscuits. I wanted some of the M&M things, but candy was too little-girly. If there'd been a candy called Dangerous, or Naked, I would've gone for it, but I felt I couldn't even be seen near the candies without losing my edge.

"Fini, Petite? 'Ave you find all you need?" R.B. was loading our stuff into Didi's two string bags ("filé," they were called. They came from France. Didi said everyone there used them. Useful things).

"Yes, thank you, Didi. Oh, except for tampons. Do you carry tampons, sir?"

Ol' Redfaced Boob looked righteously mortified. He stared down at his large, hairy hands on the countertop. "Mm. Yessadoo," he mumbled.

"Great. I'd like super, please." I didn't really want supersized tampons (they made me walk like Didi), but I thought more of a tampon made me sound like more of a woman. Redwood bunged the tampons into a filé, still not looking at me. I insisted on paying for half our purchases. No child, and no mooch either. When our filés were full, I took one, Didi the other.

"See you next month, mon ami, Bob." Bob shook Didi's hand again.

"Yep, take care." I offered my hand. Short shake. Big hand.

We were almost out the door. I looked over my shoulder. Bobbo was staring at my ass. "Mr. Bob? You have beautiful hands." Mentioning "hands" out loud was more than my bluff could hold. My face got all hot, but we were out into the cool air before the Bobber could see that.

"Your face is red, Petite. I believe you 'ave need of cool water. SweeVAY. Follow."

We went partway back along the D–rock path. Then Didi cut to the right, into the pathless redwood megatrees. "SweeVAY."

I hung onto my filé, sweevaying behind him. He was running and laughing, like it was a game. I laughed too and started to sing loudly, "Hi HO, hi HO, it's off to work we go . . ."

"Ah, bon," he shouted into the trees, "we 'ave dwarf, we 'ave sac, we 'ave forest, and La Petite cartooNEEST sees Walt DeezNAY!"

The creek was in a small, sunny clearing. Didi dropped his filé and, in superfast time, shucked off all his clothes and ran into the water. It wasn't deep, up to his nipples.

"Viens, Petite. Come and swim." He flopped onto his belly. With only hump and rump above the water, he looked like two tiny pink surfacing submarines. A "single" and a "double."

I took off my tanktop, then my jeans. When you wear really tight jeans, which I do, they make marks on your body where the seams and zippers are. The marks are a mutilation grossness, but Didi didn't seem to notice. I stuck a foot in the water. "Shit! It's cold!"

"Lash! Coward!" He splashed water at me. I waded in, splashing back. We wrestled around, laughing and snorting and having the goofies. Then Didi had me look under. Tiny shiny silvery-green fish were swimming together in a triangle formation. At the bottom of the stream were the most amazingly multi-colored little stones. Brown and white, like Indians' horses. Black and white, like Holstein cows. Rust red like barns. Gold like treasure. I scooped up a handful.

"No, Petite. Leave them where they are. They are only maJEEK where they live."

"But I can put them in a jar of water."

"No. It will not be the same. I 'ave tried. They will disappoint. Just look. Just be in the water and look. And slow you down. Rest tranKEEL." He rolled onto his back and closed his eyes. The sun was making yellow-white bolts through the trees, like corny cards about God.

We were lying naked on the sloping creekbank, eyes closed, listening to the sounds. I sensed . . . something. Opened my eyes.

The guy was standing between two trees and looked to be as big as a building. Big body, big face. Black curly hair. Black moustache and short but thick black and gray beard. Black jeans and bleached-out denim shirt. He was sort of smiling, but it wasn't a friendly smile. I wanted to scream, but that little penisy-looking thing at the entrance to my throat locked and no sound came out. Buildingman grabbed Didi by the feet, yanked him up, swung him around, then hurled him to the ground. Sweet Jesus! I still couldn't get my scream to happen, just a little gagging noise like the "ch" in German words. Inside me was filled with boomboomboom-we're-all-gonna-die-now. My eyeballs were pushing forward in their holes. Didi charged at the guy, leaping onto his chest, pounding on his back.

"No, Didi!" I said inside, still without sound. The guy threw Didi down again, and Didi leapt onto him again, making weird Chinese-y noises deep in his throat. "Hihnnngg, hihnnngg, hi-hnnngg." My scream came, filling the woods.

Didi shinnied round from the chest of the human building and onto its denim back, wrapping his little fuzzy legs around the creature. His small bearded head was now alongside the big bearded head. Both noses horse-snorted, both mouths smiled. "Petite, this is my brother, Pascal."

"Uh . . . hi." There's something about an introduction that makes you realize you're naked. If you are. Which I was.

• •

All the way back to Inn Nainity, they spoke French. I've always been quick with languages, and I'd been learning lots of French from Didi, but only for a week and a half. When two people who really know a language start to speak it together, it's like they're on the inside of a secret and you're on the outside. It sounded beautiful, but I was on the other side of the glass, and all I could do was listen. And look at their bums. The woodspath was too narrow for us to walk together. I fell in behind them so they could do their French brother thing. Didi came to a little bit below Pascal's waist. Pascal had no sand dune hump. His big legs were straight, making Didi's diamond-shaped ones even more noticeable than usual. Occasionally, Didi would look over his shoulder.

"Ça va, Petite?"

"Ça va, Didi." I knew how to do that. One person asks if "it goes," and, if everything's OK, the other person says that it does go. I felt sad in my belly, because I was outside the secret, but it would've been Asshole Central to interrupt a family reunion. It was going, and I was going along behind it.

When we got to Inn Nainity, I decided to dazzle them with my Good Girl Impersonation.

"Look, you guys are so into visiting, why don't you hang out on the porch, and I can make us all some tea and biscuits and stuff?"

"No, no, Petite. You talk with Pascal and I will fix the petit snack."

Pascal sat on the chesterfield. His black-bearded bigness looked weird against the flowery pillows. He patted a pillow for me to sit next to him and said, "Come, tell me about you." I pretended I had only heard the words, not seen the pillow pat. Hooked my bum onto the porch railing. A little snort-y laugh came out of me and I shook my head, which is something I sometimes do when I feel self-conscious and/or goofy.

"What do you want to know? Did Didi tell you anything in French? In the woods?"

"Only that you're a young cartoonist, a good one, he says, and that you're stopping with him before going back to school."

He was smiling. The sort of smile that, when a woman does it, it's to make fun of you, but when some guys do it, they may be making fun too, but it has a Sex Thing that makes you all nervous and you clench your lower holes. Was he teasing? Flirting? I knew I'd seem Not Brave if I didn't look him right in the eye, the way I'd done with Redwood Bob. So I did, but he had more power, seemed to know lots more about "I-dare-you" stuff than Redwood did. I turned my head away so fast I almost fell off the porch. Backwards. Which would've been just brilliant! I wished Didi would come back with the goddamned petit snack.

"Careful . . . why don't you sit on the furniture before you break your neck." He was still smiling that hole-clenching smile.

"No no, I'm OK. How come you don't have a French accent like Didi? My mum has an English accent, but hers is different. Hers is from London. Where's yours from?"

"From boarding schools. Snob schools. My 'mum' is a great believer in such things. Didi and I have the same mother but different fathers. Mine was Scottish."

He'd stopped doing the smile and was looking at me with intelligent greeny-grey eyes. Just talking. No teasing. It was nice.

"You said 'was.' Is he dead, your father?"

"Might as well be, I suppose. We don't see him."

"Mine too. Might as well be, I mean. We don't see him either. . . . Maybe they're somewhere together, our two fathers. Just having a beer and not seeing their kids."

"Eh, vwaLAH! Le snack!"

"Finally! We two abandoned babes are deeply hungry, are we not, Prowlet?"

Smile (him). Clench (me).

• •

At 6 P.M., Didi, who could make a fancy meal out of just about anything, decided he was going to fix le grand deeNAY. I knew what I wanted to wear. Pulled my new Deco peach jacket out of the closet. In the general zone of my right nipple was a bright red inkstain. One of the felt-tip pens must have opened when jacket and pens were in my bookbag. Apart from this yucko blotch, the jacket looked super. So I got all my felt-tips. Drew nine daisy petals around the red circle and a stem with two leaves. I colored the petals red, the stem and leaves green. Outlined everything in black. It looked a little goofy, but definitely better than the Incredible Bleeding Nipple. I was glad I'd remembered to hang up my black-and-red wide-leg pants (they wrinkle like crazy when you don't). Used an Afro pick on my hair, which made it huge. Did lips (coral), did eyes (smoky-smudgy gray liner) and ran to the loo to check myself out in the big mirror. "Yes!" I said. (I'm not the most secure person in the world about my looks, but sometimes I know when I look hot. I looked hot.)

Technically, Didi's "grand deeNAY" was scrambled eggs with stuff in them, rice with other stuff in it, and a tomato salad. That's technically. In the mouth it was pretty amazing. There were two bottles of real French wine in the middle of the wooden dining table (Pascal had brought them, along with French bread, tomatoes and fresh basil). They spoke mostly in English, said I looked pretty (Didi actually said "manyeeFEEK," magnificent, which seemed a bit of an exaggeration, but I didn't mind). They always remembered to ask my opinion of the things they were discussing, which made me feel warm and welcome. So did the French wine. By the time we came to the crème caramel, I was majorly boozefilled. Trying to hold on to their conversation was like digging my fingernails into the side of a greased mountain. I was losing my grip on the mountain. And the deeNAY. "Excuse me, mayssYERRS. ParDOHN."

I managed to make it out the door and into the trees. Megabarf! Pinky-purple megabarf of the entire grand D. Feeling shaky, I scrunched down in front of a tree, leaned against the trunk, blowing breath out, letting the night air cool my face.

"Petite? You are OK?" He was barefoot, and about to step in the mega.

"Careful, Didi. I lost dinner. I'm sorry."

He sat down facing me. "No, no, Petite. Do not be sorree. It was my fault. The deeNAY was very riche. I should not 'ave permitted you so much wine. In France one drinks wine from when one is very small. This is per'aps not true in Canada."

I shook my head. "I dunno, Didi. I've had wine before. I think there was . . . just too much stuff at once, or something. The dinner was brilliant. I hate that I didn't get to keep it."

He made a soft clucking noise. "Do not worree. I believe what you 'ave need of now is your crème caramel and a small tisane with us on the porsh."

Didi has this big crazy teapot. It's the colour of pale orangey-brown autumn leaves and has a white carved flower on each side. Each flower has a red center, raised from the surface like a button. It looks like a fairy-tale thing, like it could predict stuff, or grant wishes. It was on the little white wicker table, in front of the chesterfield rocker, in front of Pascal, who was sipping mint tea. There were two other teacups on the table, and three small white crème caramel cups, two empty and one with shiny c.c. still in it.

Pascal looked up at me. His green-gray eyes were soft. "Poor you," he said. "Come sit."

I did, looking down. "I feel like a major twit."

"Well, don't. You're not a major twit, as you put it. You're simply an amateur wino. Not a bad status to retain."

He ruffled the top of my Big Hair. I did not feel made fun of. I felt like a cloud in trouble, and let my whole cloud's body rise through the top of my head up into his hand. Big hand. Put me, I thought. Put me in your catmother mouth. Put me in your kangaroo pouch. Let me curl up in your hand. I rested my head on his chest and closed my amateur wino's eyes.

"Tyahn," said Didi (he says this a lot). Then he said something that sounded like "fay gaff, toolmond." I kept my eyes closed and fell sort of asleep.

When I woke up, it was still night, and I was in my bed, under my quilt, naked. My satin jacket and wide-leg pants were folded over the back of a chair. Rats, I thought. Pascal must've carried me upstairs,and I missed it! (I think being lifted up and carried is one of the loveliest things. It doesn't happen to me a lot, so missing it was sort of depressing.) It was sweet that he, or Didi, folded my clothes. I smiled. I knew I was having this biggish reaction to Pascal. It was sexual, but different. I didn't think we could actually fuck. Besides the fact that he maybe didn't even want to, he was too building-big. (Marcus was about as tall, but had, somehow, a more manageable-looking body.) I was pretty sure if Pascal fell on top of me, which is a known part of fucking, he'd flatten me like a cartoon cat run over by a car.

Maybe it was the wine, but the next day I woke up at noon. I wanted a bath, and to rinse the post-barf yuck out of my mouth. When I opened my bedroom door, I could hear Pascal and Didi downstairs in the kitchen. They were speaking in mostly French, and having what sounded like an argument. They both kept saying something that sounded like "zeezeezee." I didn't want to interrupt a Family Thing, so I stayed in the tub a long time. When the bubbles died, I added more and ran the water again.

As I headed back to my room, the row was still going. Didi shouted, in English, "No! She is not 'urt! She is offended, which is not the same thing!" I was dying for a café au lait, so I clunked around in my room, dropping my hairbrush and moving a chair, so they'd know there was life on the second floor. I also sang:

Dunderbeck, oh Dunderbeck,
How could you be so mean
To ever have invented
The Sausage Meat Machine?
Now all the rats and pussycats
Will never more be seen . . .
For they've all been ground to sausages
In Dunderbeck's macheeen!

They were drinking bowls of c. au l., and there was one waiting for me. Both brothers did bonjour and good morning, but they seemed separated, from eachother and from me. I wanted to make things better, but, not knowing what had made those things bad, didn't know where "better" was. Drinking my coffee and shutting up seemed like a good choice.

Didi put a plate of muffins in front of me. "You 'ave the empty stomach, Petite. You should put some of this with the café."

Pascal looked over at me. His eyes were mostly lids. "Why do you call this creature 'Petite'? It's got the breasts of a nursing mother and the hips of a miniature Clydesdale." His face had the slight smile I'd seen when he first appeared, the smile of Building-man who'd come to kill us all. And he was going to do it now. Starting with me. Grenade.

"Jesus, Pascal. Who hit you with an ugly stick?"

The eyes opened full-out and cold. "I beg your pardon? What was that?" No smile. Low, quiet voice. Kitchen so still you could only hear the appliances hum.

Inside me was *boomboomboom.* Don't panic. Don't cry. Don't run. Speak. Can't. Must.

"I . . . that's . . ." (Don't look at him. Don't look down either, 'cause it's chickenshit. Eyes straight ahead.) "That's a mean thing to say to a person." (Now you can look. Hold onto the edge of the table and look.) "I don't know what's up with you guys, but I know I didn't do anything wrong. Or, if I did, I don't know what it is. So you have to tell me."

"No, you've done nothing wrong. We're rummaging through old

baggage is all. What I said was . . . graceless and tasteless. Accept my apology?" There was no warmth in the question, but the "I can kill you with one shot from my mighty paw" was also gone.

"Uh-huh. Fine. Sure." I got up and walked to the door. "I'm going down to the creek for a while."

Strangers. They're the best because you haven't seen their worst. And the worst because you don't know what they're going to do. *Boom!* From nowhere. And your face is gone. I stuck my still-existing face under the cool water and grabbed for the wild stones, taking them up in multi-coloured fistfuls, then releasing them, watching them float back down to the creekbed. I was what I call "on the point." When you're not where you were and you don't know yet where you're going to be instead. Travelling puts a person on the point a lot. The instinct is to sort of freeze, but you know you can't stay there forever. When you get to the next thing, it's usually OK, sometimes way better than OK. But there, on the point, I am always scared.

Wanted to draw. So I climbed out of the creek, wiped myself down with my jeans, then put them, and my tanktop, on.

Pascal was sitting on the porch steps like a mammoth guard dog.

"Have a good swim?"

"Didn't really swim. Just goofed around."

"Sit and talk for a bit?"

I just wanted to draw, but I didn't want to make him go shitty and awful again. I sat, one step down and a little away from him.

"Would you like a beer?"

"No. Thank you."

"Right. Be back in a minute." He went into the house. He was wearing his denim shirt. The most perfectly faded denim shirt in the world. I'd been looking for one like that in every Sally Ann and retro store in British Columbia and Oregon. If he really wanted to apologize for making pig remarks about my body, he would give me that shirt. Or at least let me buy it.

He came back with a bottle of beer in his megapaw and sat down on the step.

"Could I have your shirt?"

"What?"

"The shirt you're wearing. Could I buy it from you? I've been looking for a shirt like that for practically ever. Really big and faded. They're hard to find."

Smile (him).

"Had this shirt for a long time. Rather attached to it. Wouldn't sell it, and can't really give it away. Sorry. I'll . . . I could, perhaps, offer you something better."

"Better than that shirt?"

"Possibly. Have you even been to San Francisco?"

In fact, I'd always wanted to see San Francisco. I'd seen pictures of it. Lots of pointy houses with neat windows full of stained glass. Some great cartoonists lived there. "No."

"Well, Didi tells me you have about a week before you return home. I could drive you down there, show you around a bit, then put you on the bus. You'd have to change buses at Eureka to get back to Oregon, but Didi says it's an easy change. He does it all the time."

"You've discussed this with Didi?"

"Yes, of course."

"And he wants me to go?" (Grenade warning.)

"No, it's not that. He just thought you'd enjoy San Francisco. It was his idea."

"I think I'd rather just stay here."

"You can't." (Grenade alert.)

"Why? I mean, why not?"

He held out two pieces of pale yellow paper. "He left you this note."

"Note? Left me? Where is he?"

"There was something he had to do."

"Had to do? Where?"

"In Eureka, I believe."

"Eureka? Will he meet us there?"

Pascal stood up. His eyes were half soft, half somewhere else. "No, I don't think so. I believe it's all in the note. Look, I need to pack my bag. Why don't you have a look at the note and then tell me what you'd like to do. I believe you'd enjoy San Francisco, but if you decide you don't want to do that, I can take you to the Redwood

Bob bus stop." (Go. Go wherever, Roanne. Just go. Good-bye. Fuck off. Grenade.) "Have a read. I'll be inside."

Chère Petite,

Something have arrived I must do. I have gone to do this. I know this is soudain, and I apologize very much. It is O.K., the thing I must do. Me also, I am O.K., so please do not worry for me. I have LOVE having you here with me, and want, very much, for you to visite with me here again. Please, leave for me your addresse on my drawing table so I do not lose you. I have propose to Pascal that he take you to view San Francisco. It is a very beautiful, very original city. Pascal have promise he will not make the monstre, he will be sweet with you. I know it is 'ard to understand my depart, but it is truly nothing of you making bad. Your visite has been very happy for me. Please accept as gift the little dictionnaire, that your French continue to grow.

Je t'embrasse, trés fort,
Didi

The second yellow page was a drawing. Didi and me, sitting at the kitchen table, drinking bowls of café au lait and smiling. Underneath the drawing, the words "notre matin." Our morning. Water-filled sobshit rolled out of my eyes and mouth. I let 'em roll.

Pascal was in the parlour, reading a magazine.

"Yes. OK, I'll go to San Francisco. I'll go pack my stuff."

"You don't sound very enthusiastic."

I couldn't get much voice out. "Please. I said I'd go. Don't push it, OK?"

He stood up. It looked like he was going to hug me. If he did, I knew I'd lose it, puddle down to nothing, become the sort of person no one wants to take on a long motortrip. I held up my hand. This little batcroak voice scracked out. "No. Don't. It'll be cool. It'll be fine. It's just . . . a lot of stuff at once. I'll go pack now."

"Very good. I'll be here."

• •

Pascal's car was burgundy, with a similar dog's-head shape to the Morgan.

"It's a T.D."

"Yes, it is. You know cars?"

"Not a lot. We, my mum and I, have a Morgan."

"A Morgan. Well." He seemed a little bit impressed, which made me feel less sad. My sense was that it wasn't easy to impress Pascal.

Redwood Boob was standing in the doorway of his store, looking on disapprovingly, as usual. I helped Pascal load our stuff into the car. Then I remembered something Del once said, when she got into this guy's convertible in Burnaby. This pissy-faced woman was staring at her with what Del calls a tight little arsehole mouth. As they drove off, Del shouted, "That's right, Mavis. I'm gonna sit on his face on the motorway!" As we pulled away in the T.D., this was what I shouted at Redwood Blob. Except I said "Redwood" instead of "Mavis." He looked really surprised. So, actually, did Pascal. "Ma fwah!" he said, looking at me. And then he laughed. A great big boomer of a laugh. I love it when guys laugh. Especially guys with low, rumbly voices like Pascal's. Stavro had a voice like that. When Del and I were living with him, I would try to think of funny things to say and do so he'd laugh. Sometimes my jokes would annoy him (little kids don't always have a brilliant sense of humour), but when it worked, and he'd laugh, it was great.

The buzz I got from Pascal's laugh wore off pretty fast, though, and I got all sad. Then I got scared. And very quiet. Pascal would look over at me from time to time as he drove.

"How are you, Miss Morgan? Are you well?"

"Yes, thank you."

"Hungry?"

"Uh-uh."

"What?"

"No."

"Right. Let me know when you are?"

"OK."

It was hard to imagine wanting to eat when I knew what I suddenly and definitely knew. Which was, of course, that Pascal had killed Didi. Didi had been so kind and generous to me, and here I was, off to see pointy San Francisco houses while his tiny, strawberry-smelling body lay broken and decomposing, stuffed in the lavabo. What sort of a suck of a friend was I? Was I willing to die for my "copain," Didi? No. No? No. Yes.

"Pascal?" I shouted over the wind and car noise.

"Yes, love?"

"Did you kill Didi?"

"What!"

"I said—"

He swerved to the side of the road, really fast, yanking the gearshift into stop so hard I jolted forward. He turned me by my shoulders to make me look at him. "What did you say?" I'd read somewhere that people shit when they died. It seemed seriously possible that they might also do that when they knew they were about to die. "Did you ask me," he began, in this really quiet, kind of angry but mostly tired-sounding voice, "did you ask me if I killed my brother?"

"Well, I just . . ."

"Look, I know people your age tend to melodrama, so I'm not going to empty you, and your gear, out here, and let you walk to Canada. Instead, we will, very shortly, have a lovely late lunch, in a pretty restaurant in Mendocino, where I will give you the longer answer to your questions regarding Didi's temporary disappearance. For the moment, however, in the interest of making decent driving time, you are going to have to settle for the shorter answer. Which is no, I most certainly did not kill Didi. Or harm him in any way. If that is not sufficient to turn you into a secure and rational travelling companion, I would be happy to leave you at the next bus stop on this route. Your choice." He was ever so slightly smiling. His eyes looked honest.

"I'll stay."

"Right."

After telling me he was definitely not a brother killer, Pascal pretty much just drove without talking, except to look over at me once, smiling, and ask if I was "quite sure" I didn't want to run for my life before it was too late. Which made me, having calmed down, feel like a jerk. Which was a less than terrific way to feel, but still better than expecting to be killed at any moment. When he asked, I did laugh. He did too.

The pretty restaurant in Mendocino was called "The Eyrie." It was made of wood, brick and stone, and was one of those health-food-for-rich-people places. "Wholesome" soups. Huge sandwiches on beige bread full of little crunchy round brown bits, with white sprouty things falling out beyond the crusts. They served no red meat, but had a long, booze-filled bar made of weathered wood, and a fancy wine list on its own separate menu.

It was still light out when we got there, but the sun had started to do its heading-into-the-sea thing, which I love to watch. Which I told Pascal, so we didn't talk until the big red ball disappeared into the Pacific. Then we ordered two bowls of a soup called "carrot & leek creamy-dreamy" and one shareable sandwich of "turkey and garden tomato with lime-cayenne mayonnaise."

We were having cappuccinos when Pascal said, "Right. I didn't read the letter Didi wrote you. What exactly is it you want to know?"

I was still feeling silly. Or like I didn't want to sound silly.

"I dunno. Why he all of a sudden took off for Eureka, I guess."

"Mm. Well, he goes to Eureka somewhat regularly. He . . . meets a friend there."

"A boyfriend?"

"No, not exactly. Let's just say an acquaintance with . . . compatible interests. I believe the gentleman in question lives somewhere in Oregon."

"So how come he goes to Eureka? The other guy, I mean."

"As I've been told by Didi, Eureka is what the other fella calls, rather wondrously, a 'layover.'"

I giggled.

"If I understand correctly, this person, who is called 'Chuck,' or 'Chick,' transports frozen poultry parts from Portland to Petaluma."

All the "P"s made it sound funny, and we both started giggling. Or, I giggled and he laugh-rumbled.

"Wait. This guy is a truck driver?"

"Yes, I believe that's true."

"And he's driving a truckful of chickens and he's called Chick?"

Louder giggle-rumbles (both of us). "Mm. Probably not. Probably he drives the chickens and he's Chuck. Unless . . ."

"He drives the chuckens and he's Chick?"

"Exactly." Giggle-rumble.

"But, wait a minute . . ."

"I'm waiting. Etonne moi."

"What?"

"Astonish me, Cocteau."

"Cock toe?" I started a whole new giggle.

"No, not feet and willies. A Frenchman. Jean Cocteau. *What* is your question?"

"My question . . . my question is, how did Didi, who draws cartoons in the woods, meet an Oregon chickentrucker in Eureka?"

"He does leave the woods from time to time. They met in a bar, I believe."

"A gay bar?"

"I'm not certain. Probably."

"So, this Chuck guy is a gay chickentrucker?" I had a full-out gigglefit at this point, and Pascal waited for me to pull it together (he was no longer in out-loud laugh mode, but he was smiling).

When I had it together, he said, "I would doubt that. I reckon our Chuck would at least *seem* quite hetero. Without betraying family confidences, I believe Didi prefers heterosexuals."

"But, if chicken-man is straight, how come he's, you know, with Didi?"

"Ah. This I cannot tell you. Because I do not know." He took a packet of cigarettes out of his shirt pocket. It was a hard pack, with a design I'd never seen before. Blue, white and black, with a silhouette of a lady holding a tambourine over her head.

"Are those American?"

"French."

"Ghee-TAYNE?"

"Jee-TAN. Means gypsy."

"I don't remember seeing you smoke at Inn Nainity."

"I did at night. On the porch. Didi's quit. He'd also smoked Gitanes, but it was too difficult to keep supplied at Inn Nainity."

The waiter brought our bill, which was pretty big for two soups, two cappuccinos and a sandwich. I offered to contribute, but Pascal said that wasn't necessary and I didn't argue. He gave the waiter a credit card.

It did sound like Didi was very much alive, and having a fine time. There was still one thing I didn't understand, though.

"Why couldn't I stay at Inn Nainity while Didi was in Eureka? And why did he take off so fast, without saying good-bye?"

Pascal smoked, took a deep drag on his cig and blew smoke out through his nostrils. "That's a bit complicated. It has to do with our mother. Seeing Chickie-Chuckie at precisely this time has the added benefit of Didi not being at home when our mother telephones, and . . . look, it's been sweet and uncomplicated dining and laughing with you. Discussions concerning chère Maman are not, never have been, either sweet or uncomplicated. So, would you mind terribly if we put off discussing the maternal aspects of all this for another time?"

Would I mind? He put it as a question, the way Del did when she'd say, "I am very interested in what you have to say, Rosie, but would you mind telling me about it later, because I'm working now?" These are not real questions and, unless you're what Del calls "a major barbarian," there's only one acceptable answer.

"Sure. OK. As long as Didi's fine."

"Didi's fine. We're all fine. and if you're fine, I think we should get back to the car and continue our adventure."

"Sure. Let's. Thanks for the food. And the sunset."

"My pleasure."

His pleasure. Our adventure. Pascal could be a major charmer. When he wasn't being a big black-bearded building with a grenade in it.

• •

There are things that only your deepest-inside self knows about a person. These deepest-inside things have nothing to do with logic. They're about essences. I knew Pascal and Didi had different fathers and the same mother. My information mind knew this. In my essence mind, though, Didi did not have a mother, was not born in a regular way. As sometimes happens with deep-inside stuff, I didn't consciously realize I thought this until Pascal connected "a mother" with Didi's taking off. My absorbing this Didi-Mum connection made the brain-info collide with the essence-info. Which was that Didi was born from his sand dune. The hump appeared first. A strawberry-smelling mushroom-cap-shaped bone. In a French forest. Small, skin-covered, growing out of the green ground. Then came the legs. Then the arms. Then the face formed, under the ground, and when this little face couldn't breathe, the tiny legs and arms started to scratch and kick and push like crazy until the little head popped out of the earth, panting and spitting dirt, alone in the forest.

As I rode beside Pascal on the road to San Francisco, all this below-the-brain info rolled up into where I could see it and feel it in my upper self. And, no matter what I now knew, or might find out, Didi the self-birthing bone mushroom was still more real than Didi the dwarf with a mother.

"Do you know blinis?"

"Yes. Del, my mother, makes them."

"Makes what?"

"Blinis. Little rolled-up Russian pancakes with cheese and jam in them, right?"

Pascal laughed out loud. "No, daffy, not 'blinis.' Bolinas."

"Oh. What's 'Bolinas'?"

"It's where we're going to spend the night."

It being dark, the M.G. being a sportscar, and the Mendocino-to-Bolinas road being mostly alongside the sea, it got to being majorly cold. When he asked, I told Pascal I was OK, but my face and feet were icethings and my nipples were hard as pebbles. He pulled the car over and we put up the black canvas tonneau top. This helped, but it also made Pascal better able to hear me sucking in my breath. We stopped again and he went round to the trunk, returning with a big white Irish sweater and a humungus beige-and-white sheepskin jacket. He pulled the sweater on and handed me the jacket.

"Put that on."

"I can wear the sweater."

"Not without climbing in from underneath and pressing against my body."

"No, I meant—"

"And then you'd likely suffocate, unless you put your head through the neckhole, and then your head would make it impossible for me to see where I was . . ."

"Oh, come on, Pascal, it's your jacket, eh?"

"Right. So I can do what I wish with it. And what I wish, Roanne, is for you to stop martyring yourself and put the damn thing on. All right?"

"Yes."

"Good."

"Thank you."

"You're most welcome."

The jacket was all big and superwarm. Being inside it made me smile. All the way down to Bolinas, though, I kept seeing myself climbing inside Pascal's Irish sweater. Which made me feel hot. And made me want to giggle. Each time this happened, I'd shoot my tongue out and press it over my upper lip to keep the giggle from becoming an out-loud thing. Pascal was busy watching the road (which had gotten seriously foggy) and smoking his strange-smelling gypsy cigarettes, so I don't think he saw this. Or knew what I was thinking. Two things. One, that we'd each said the other one's actual name for the first time. And two, that maybe I could be OK with his weight on top of me. If he asked. He'd have to ask. No way I was going to offer, and have him laugh at me, or say something mean and awful.

• •

Dark as it was, I could still see, in the light from a sliver of moon, that the house was small, square, with a pointy place above the door, and made of old, unpainted wood. "I'll let you in," Pascal said, "then I'll get our things from the car."

It was, or looked to be, just one large white room, with dark-wood ceiling beams. The kitchen space had lots of copper pots and pans hanging from one of the beams. There was a white stone fireplace in the middle of the room, with wood and newspapers stacked alongside it. One whole side was glass doors, facing out into the blackness. Against the left wall was a large white chesterfield with a long, low, dark wood table in front of it. Across the room was a king-sized bed, covered by a white duvet. The only decoration on the walls were framed black-and-white photographs.

"Do you know how to make a fire?"

"Sure. All Canadians do."

He handed me his lighter. "Right. You do that, then. I'll get the gear."

The photos were amazing. A long, thin, beautiful, naked blonde woman lying draped round an equally long alligator. Beautiful naked black children sitting outdoors in a circle, eating goop from bowls. Another circle of old, tight-faced English women sipping tea. An elegant-looking middle-aged woman with fierce, pale eyes, bare shoulders, pearls, slight smile, wonderful cheekbones. A black woman's beautiful bum with sand on it. Didi, naked, sitting yoga-like on the floor of the Inn Nainity porch, licking a vanilla-coloured ice-cream cone.

"I thought you knew how to make a fire."

"I'm sorry. I do. I just got hung up looking at the pictures."

He dropped all our bags on the floor, took the lighter from me, crouched down in front of the fireplace and set about building a fire. "Ah, yes, the pictures. Do you like them?" His back, hunched over the fireplace, was so big, so beautiful. Stavro had a back like that. I would jump on it and then Stav would stand up and walk around the house with me hanging on. I was little then, and Pascal would probably think I was a jerk, or at least a nuisance, if I jumped on his back. Or he'd think I was attacking him and, not understanding that I just wanted to play, break me in half.

"Yes. I think they're super."

He laughed, a short "Ha! 'Super,' is it? You sound like the girls I knew at school." The fire kicked in. He turned to face me, sat on the floor. "I'm glad you like them. They're mine."

I looked at them again. "Yours? Wow. Photography is what you do, eh?"

He lit a cigarette and grabbed an ashtray from the low table. "To the extent that I do anything, yes."

"I love this of Didi."

"I'll print you one."

"Really? I'd really like that."

"Well, then, I'll really do it. Really print you one."

He was making fun of me, making fun of my "really." I didn't want him to think I was too stupid to know that. I looked him right in the eye. "Really? Well, that would be really great." He tilted his head, raised his eyebrows, sort of smiling. I walked to the glass doors. "What's out there?"

"The beach and the Pacific."

"Really? I mean, just outside the doors?"

"Mm-hmm. Really just outside the doors."

"Wow! Can we go? Go out and look at it?" He laughed his "Ha!" laugh again and shook his head. "You're a lot younger than the rest of us, Prowlet. You go. I'll make us a warm tisane. You'll need it when you come back, it's bloody cold out there at night. Go on. Have a look."

I did wonder, had been wondering since Inn Nainity, what the hell a Prowlet was. Wanted to ask. Was afraid to. Did not want, if everyone else in the universe knew the answer, to look stupid. I slid open the glass doors, could smell and hear the sea. I ran down to the water's edge. It really was right there. The house really was right on the beach! Amazing! I took my sandals off, felt the cold water on my feet. Looking back at the house, I could see Pascal making our tisane.

There are moments, little perfect eggs of time, that you'll always remember, because everything, absolutely everything is exactly the way you'd have everything be if you had control over how everything was. For me, that moment on the beach at Bolinas is one of those. I lay down on the cold sand, stretched my arms out like Jesus and looked up at the low-hanging stars and the white crescent moon. "Our adventure," Pascal had said. No. My adventure. And I could feel myself having it.

There was something under my right hand. I sat up to look at it. It was hard and round, almost flat, with little nubblies on it, and a hole in the middle surrounded by a propeller-like design. I stood up, a little bit chilled.

I saw through the glass doors that Pascal had taken the phone receiver from the kitchen-space wall and was talking, smiling. He didn't see me approach and hung up just as I was sliding the doors open.

"Hi."

"Well, look at you. Liked it out there, did you?"

"It was great. Found this thing."

"Sand dollar. There are lots of them in the area. Type of shell."

"Pretty."

"Mm-hmm. Are you ready for your tisane? Afraid I've nothing to offer with it. The tea is jasmine."

"Oh, I used to have that when I was little. A friend of ours drank it. Dickie Siggins."

"The pop star? I *am* impressed." He didn't look all that impressed. Curious, more like. He put tea things (white Japanese-y teapot with two tiny matching cups) on a black tray and carried it to the low table. I scrunched into a corner of the chesterfield, leaned over and filled our cups. He took one, thanked me and sat down on the floor, sort of at my feet.

The minute I tasted the jasmine tea, I was three years old and back in Dickie's London house. I said this to Pascal.

"Madeleines," he said.

"Who?"

"Madeleines. Proust."

Proust, Madeleines, Prowlet. Stuff I didn't understand was starting to pile up. I thought I'd sound less stupid if I asked about them over a period of time. One later, maybe, and two more the next day, in San Francisco. At that moment, though, what I mostly wanted to know about were our sleeping arrangements.

"Should I sleep on the chesterfield?"

"Are you tired?"

"No. I was just wondering."

"Well, wonder no more. No, you don't have to sleep on the chesterfield, as you call it. Or on the beach. You shall sleep in the bed." The insides of my crotch leapt up into my chest.

"But where will you sleep? The chesterf—"

"I'll be sleeping in Sausalito."

The leap reversed and my heart dropped into my crotch. "Where?"

"Sausalito. A few towns down the road. I've a friend there. It seems this friend expected to see me two days ago and is now rather cross about that. As I should like to keep her friendship, I think I'd better do a bit of damage control. Don't look so worried, I'll be back in the morning for our trip to San Francisco. I'll also make sure you're comfortably settled in here before I go. The place is quite quiet and safe."

I was grinning like a frozen idiot mask. "No, no. It's OK. I've stayed by myself a lot. Sometimes in really dangerous places. And I'll get to wake up tomorrow right on the beach, eh? May I take a bath now?"

"Afraid not. No tub. The shower's quite good though. Lots of water pressure. Come, I'll show you."

And when I stood up, I knew, in a flash, the deeply gross and hideous truth. The thing that had roller-coastered through my body wasn't my heart, or my crotch. It was my period.

The first thing I did, after Pascal showed me where the light switches were, produced a radio, kissed me on top of my wet head and left, was to check the chesterfield for bloodstains. None. Proving that there was some sort of God in charge of preventing total humiliation.

The second thing I did was notice that, while I was in the shower, Pascal had taken down the photograph of the lady with the pearls and bare shoulders. I slid open the wooden doors of the clothes closet (where he'd gotten the dark blue terrycloth robe I was wearing) and there it was, facing the wall. I turned it around. Fierce pale eyes looked at me as if I were lower than wormshit. It was her. I was sure. The mum. I could see why he took her picture down. What I wondered was why he had put it up.

I decided I'd better protect myself from yucko (I mean, the whole entire house was white!). Did a ladyplug, and two pairs of panties, then climbed into bed, under the white sheet and equally white duvet. Pascal had left a large book on top of a pillow. It was called *Yoruba: Textures of Nigeria. Photographs by Pascal Douglas.* It had the lady's sandy bum and the little kids in a circle, plus lots of other wonderful pictures of people and things. Colour as well as the black-and-whites. The white driftwood-and-alligator lady was not in the book, even though her two wall pictures looked like they were also taken in Africa.

Was the alligator lady his Sausalito "friend"? If she was, I had been a major jerk to think he'd want to sleep with me. He was being really nice, but why would a guy who could pull beautiful, skinny models want to do it with a big-titted, big-assed kid? I mean, lots of guys wanted to do it with me, had since I was nine or ten. But international sophisticated glam guys like Pascal? No way. I mean, I did pull Marcus, but Marcus was what Del called "a male bimbo." He'd go with anybody. By now, I thought, he'd probably done everybody from Eugene to Yachats except Geronimo. Marcus and Pascal were very different. They were both tall, had great cars, gave me their jackets when it was cold on the road, but that's where the similarities ended. Marcus was a slut and Pascal was a sometimes scary but very nice man who was taking a kid who was a friend of his brother on a two-day outing. A kid. Did he know how old (young) I was? Did Didi tell him? I fell asleep, with the photo book, wondering about that.

I dreamt Didi, Pascal and I were all living at Inn Nainity. There was a terrible clangy shrieky war being fought in the redwood forest. The three of us stayed inside, drinking warm things and watching the fighting. The warriors were male and female, mostly naked. Some had feathers stuck onto them here and there. They had swords and shields. Their scream-cries were high and horrible. We watched from the porch windows. All the Inn Nainity lights were on, but the warriors either didn't see us or were in some other time zone.

I woke up early because light was flooding the room. The clock on the kitchen-space wall said 6:20. The electric baseboard heaters Pascal turned on before leaving had eaten the air, and my nose and mouth felt closed. I got out of bed, after checking it for bloodnasty (none), and opened the glass doors.

Sea sound. Sea smell. And, bonus, daylight! I took another

shower, did a new plug, got dressed. Pascal had taken his big jacket, so I got a humungus black turtleneck from a shelf in his closet and pulled it on over my tanktop. Took a beachwalk/run. Found two more sand dollars and a triangular piece of bleached seaglass. Dark pink. No. Pale red.

• •

"I haven't the machinery here for a proper café au lait, so I'm doing cocoa. Cocoa and croissants. With jam. Will that do? Did you sleep well?"

He said all this with his back to me, fussing with breakfast stuff. I couldn't tell whether he didn't want to look at me or was just busy like Del is when she bungs out information without looking.

"Fine. Yes. Fine to cocoa. Fine to did I sleep well."

He looked over his shoulder, smiled. "Good. That looks well on you."

"Oh. Do you mind? My wearing it, I mean. It was too—"

"Not at all." His back was to me again as he stirred cocoa in large yellow mugs. "In fact, keep it with you for San Francisco. It can be quite cold there until the fog burns off."

I knew what this was about. He was acting exactly the way Del did when she'd had what she called "a bummer evening with a tits-for-brains super dickhead." I was pretty sure it had nothing to do with Pascal's being remotely interested in possessing the blood-filled bod of Titsy the Killer Teen. (Brian sometimes called me that. Only he said "tot," because I wasn't a teen yet.) But I was still sort of gladdish that Sausalito had been unfun.

"Wanna see my piece of glass?"

He turned all the way round. "Your what?"

"This. Found it on the beach. I've got other ones in a jar in Vancouver, but not this colour."

He rubbed my cheek with the back of his hand. "It's pretty. So are you. Let's eat."

Heading to San Francisco, we passed through two great-looking little towns, Mill Valley and the dreaded Sausalito. I asked if we could stop and have a look around, but Pascal said that if I were to have "a proper dekko in San Fran" there wasn't time. So I rode facing backward, until the Golden Gate Bridge, to see as much as possible.

San Francisco was the best-looking city I'd ever seen in North America. Up to then, it had been Montréal. San Francisco was best because of the surprises. Lots of wonderful-looking places that looked different from the last wonderful-looking place. There were killer hills to climb, though, and I had no traction on my elfboots, so Pascal walked right behind me and held onto the sides of my upper arms to keep me from falling. The hilly streets had pastel clapboard houses with windows shaped like the mirrors in department stores when you're seeing if your ass is too big in a bathing suit. And there was a great Chinatown where he bought us sugar-coated strips of coconut. And we visited an art gallery where someone Pascal knew had a show on. The artist wasn't there. The paintings were huge abstracts full of red and brown. I didn't like them much. Pascal asked why not. I told him that there wasn't enough happening to justify the size of the canvas.

"I see," he said, and asked how come I knew so much about painting. I said it was because I'd been around art all my life.

"Indeed. Well, I bow to your superior knowledge . . . and I agree with you."

By mid-afternoon we'd been all over the place. I was feeling it in my plugzone and the backs of my legs. Pascal, being older, looked pretty wasted.

"Hungry?"

"Yes, please."

We went to a touristy-looking but nice water's-edge area called Fisherman's Wharf and had great bread and a bright red fish soup called "cioppino." Then we drove over to North Beach, which wasn't a beach at all but a district full of people with from-all-over-the-world faces, wearing mostly black clothing. There was a boutique there with a black-lacquered mannequin in the window wearing a silky sort of oversized crocheted sweater that fell off one shoulder. It was Deco peach. I screamed, "Oh, God, I have to!"

"Well, then, I think you should."

Pascal wanted to buy me the sweater, but I wouldn't let him. It cost $125.66 (!!!), but I was cool for money, and Del had taught me, when I was little, not to hustle presents from guys (after she heard the eight-year-old me working Stavro for a bicycle). She said not "working guys" was about "belonging to yourself, and about being able to leave." I didn't really understand what she meant, but she said it was important, and Del was usually right about stuff.

We were having cappuccinos and little custard-filled pastries in a tiny place with posters of Italy on pale green walls and a silver espresso machine shaped like a huge dick with a brass eagle on top when I asked about the picture.

"Was the woman in the closet your mother?"

"The woman *where?*"

"The picture. It was on the wall but you put it in the closet."

He sort of smiled and sort of snorted. "Smart little detective, you are. Yes, that's Zizanie."

"Zizanie?"

"Mm-hmm. Her name at birth was Chantal, but everyone called her Zizanie. It means 'discord.' Mother was a difficult child."

"People actually call your mother Discord?"

He laughed. "No. The world at large usually calls her Zizi, but it comes from Zizanie."

Zizanie. Zeezeezee. That was the sound that Pascal and Didi kept making when they were having their fight at Inn Nainity.

"Why is it in the closet?"

"Because it . . . stares a bit."

"Then why was it on the wall in the first place?"

"Because she had been visiting. One of her pilgrimages from Paris to the Heathen New World to visit her spawn, socialize in San Francisco and shop for ultrasuede." I asked if she had visited Didi too. Pascal said she wanted Didi to meet her "in a city," because the woods trail "played hell with her shoes." Didi had said "No," but she was due back soon, and that Didi was dealing with it by "running away from home." To Chickenchuck. He said they had "this debate every time" and that "Didi usually won."

"Oh." I had started to realize that there were lots of different kinds of weird families (not just Del and me). And that our kind, Del's and mine, even with the Guys Thing, was one of the better ones. I mean, I always thought we were better off than the "normal" ones. I had thought, though, that one day I'd find this band of other weird family people and we would all be proud of our differentness together. Watching Pascal's eyes cover over with shutdown, I wondered whether that band was out there at all.

He paid the bill and said it was time to take me to the bus station. It was my turn to be sad. I had really been enjoying "our adventure," and wanted it to continue. At the bus station, I took a shot at making that happen.

"Listen, Pascal, I don't actually have to be back in Yachats until next Monday. Could I go back to Bolinas with you and hang out for a few days? To see Sausalito and Mill Valley and stuff? You won't have to play with me like you did today or anything."

"Oh, dear. Listen to me. It's been a delight playing with you, as you put it, but I'm not going back to Bolinas. I'm heading down to my main house, in Malibu. The Bolinas place is an escape space. I've a photo shoot to start for a film company in two days. But should life take you to Los Angeles some day, I'd love to see you." He took two business cards out of his billfold, asking me to write my address on the back of one and keep the other. I said that Del and I might be moving, that we tended to move, but that we'd leave a forward at the post office. I wrote out our address ("Good," he said. "I will send the print of Didi I promised you") and looked at the front of the other card.

P. DOUGLAS, PHOTOGRAPHER. "EVIL OWL HOUSE"
33457 MALIBU COLONY RD. MALIBU, CAL.
TEL: 213-457-0956

"Evil Owl House?"

He took my pen, turned the card over, saying, "It's a Didi Joke," and wrote, "Mal Hibou."

I felt sick to pukepoint about saying good-bye, so I asked Pascal to split. Which he did, after kissing the top of my head and telling me to "keep communicado," blah, blah, blah.

• •

The bus station was really scuzzy. Dirty floors, pissy smells. Lots of druggies, drunks and general burnouts. I'd given Pascal's sweater back to him, so I put on my denim jacket, asked a normal-looking old couple if they could please watch my stuff for a moment and queued up to buy my ticket. Suddenly, I really wanted, before going home, to see L.A. I mean, *most* people want to see L.A., and it was so close to where I was. Just for a few days. I had no idea how to do this. I mean, I was pretty damn sure Pascal's invitation wasn't for a few hours later, or even the next day. Then I remembered. "Gabe!"

Gabriel Dobson and I became buddies in Vancouver last summer. His parents, Rex Dobson and Mara Lane, had been cowboy picture movie stars in the 1940s. They were retired from that, and ran some sort of Christian religious centers. They were in B.C. to set one up in Vancouver. Gabe was into athletic things (running, parallel bars, pole vaulting, etc.) and could also juggle. We met in this clown workshop a friend of Del's was doing. Gabe was this really beautiful 18-year-old-blond guy, with an incredible bod, who was really shy, really sweet and not all that bright. We were clown partners. Our clown names were Potsie and Patootie (I picked the names, because his clown suit had a padded belly and mine a padded bum). Gabe's Not-Bright Thing was a problem for conversation sometimes, but sweetness ran so deep in him it was like being blessed. Everybody in the workshop (all the girls, plus a few guys) was trying to get him to do kissy-touchy-feely with them, but I (being mostly attracted to older and/or smarter guys) wasn't. Just liked him as a pal. He liked me as a girl, but, being Gabe, didn't push it. When the workshop ended, he said to please come visit him sometime. This, I thought, was that time.

"H'lo."

"Huh?"

"Gabe?"

"Uh-huh."

"It's Patootie."

"Huh?"

"Roanne. Roanne from clown school?"

"Roanne from Canada?"

"Right."

"Oh, hi!"

"Hi."

"Hi. Are you here? In L.A.?"

"No, but I'm gonna be. Tomorrow. Morning. Ish."

"Oh, great. Great!"

"Can I come visit? Say hi?"

"Yah. Sure. Great!"

"Where are you?"

"At home."

"Right, Gabe, I know that. Where is it, though? What place?"

"In the Valley? The San Fernando Valley? Where will you be?"

"I don't know exactly. Hang on." With all the crazies mooching around, I didn't want to leave the phone receiver dangling. The ticket people were pretty far away. So I bellowed. "EXCUSE ME! CAN YOU TELL ME THE LAST STOP ON THE BUS TO L.A., PLEASE?"

Just about everybody in all the queues turned to look at me, plus a number of assorted winos and scuzzballs. An Asian ticket guy shouted, "FIFTH AND HIRR."

"Gabe? Fifth and Hirr."

"Hirr? Hill, probably. Why're you going *there?*"

I could tell by the "there" that Fifth and Hill was less than terrific. "It's where the bus stops."

"You're taking a bus from Canada?"

"No, from San Francisco."

"Can you scream again and ask if the bus makes a stop in the Valley?"

"Sure. EXCUSE ME AGAIN! DOES IT STOP IN THE VALLEY? THE L.A. BUS?"

The Asian guy shouted back, "YES! VENTOO BOOVAR."

"Gabe? Ventoo Boovar?"

"Ventoo Boovar? Oh, right, he probably means Ventura Boulevard. Is the person you're asking Japanese?"

"Something like that."

"Yah. Our yard man is Japanese. He says 'Ventoo Boovar' . . . V.B. is perfect. It's really near where we live. I can pick you up if you want. What time?"

"I'd rather not shout again. . . . Could I call you when I get to that boulevard? Or maybe you could call the Greyhound terminal in L.A.?"

"For the time you get in, you mean?"

"Right."

"Sure. OK. That's what I'll do. And I'll pick you up."

"That would be great, Gabe. Thanks a lot. See you tomorrow."

Del always says be as inconspicuous as possible in creepy places. As I walked to buy my ticket, it was clear that I had blown that behaviour option. When I took my place in the ticket queue, this really drugged-out skinny young guy, with major dead-animal body odour, in dirty jeans, no shirt, long stringy honey-coloured hair matted like the hair under a stray dog's asshole, started sort of lurching around me, shouting, "ARE YA GONNA BUY YOUR TICKET NOW? ARE YA? ARE YA?" I was saying, probably too softly, "Please, please leave me alone . . . please go away," when he just fell down on the floor. And stayed there. I thought he might be dead. It's probably a flaw in my character, but I didn't supermuch care. I was just glad he was out of my face. A short black guy, who was equally fucked up, sort of dragged him over to the waiting area and propped him up against a bench.

The ticket cost $20 U.S. ("Full fare." They were having a "Back to School Special" for people my age, but you had to have proof that your school was in the place your ticket was sending you.) I put my ticket and money pouch in the inside pocket of my jacket and went back for my stuff. The old couple were looking at me like I'd disgraced the family. I said I was sorry. They looked away, without even grunting. I said, "Thanks for watching my things," and dragged it all to the next bench over, so they wouldn't have to sit near the gross noisy scumbucket they'd definitely decided I was. The L.A. bus left at midnight. Five hours to wait in the Hieronymus Bosch Bus Terminal.

MACKALAHOOPOO IN TARZANA

3

Foreign Words

Chiaroscuro

Vertige

Pipistrello

Farfalla

Sizwe

Pamplemousse

Jacaranda

Iliovasilema

Mousseline

Auto-da-Fé

Bienvenue

Lavabo

Carapace

Sausalito

10 Sept. 1981

I'm here! Mal Hibou! In a guesthouse that sees the sea. The guesthouse of His house! And about to have the first of what could be lots of sweet 16 parties. Without even having to be 16! Amazing!

I've also seen my first actual dead person. I mean the first one in Regular Life (as opposed to film or television). It's more about skin when it's real.

Even though it was absolutely what I had to do, I feel shitty about leaving Gabe. He's not good with complicated things, and taking care of Mara definitely qualifies as complicated. No way I could stay, though. Truly. Not with my own megapile of mother stuff to work out.

I've now fully blown the deadline for going home before school starts. Del still has no idea where I am. And if she's going to fuck an enemy of our family, or even let him into the house, I'm not ready to tell her.

In the night like this, I'm not even sure I know. It seems to be lots of fancy houses right on the beach. Very different from Tarzana and the Christian Rebirth Center. I keep seeing that little gray ruggy rat floating at the top of the pool. Mara screaming wine-drunk glosso in the lanai. Gabe holding her in some sort of tender Nelson, saying, "Mama, Mama, it's OK, Mama," when, whatever it was, OK definitely wasn't it. Matthew, Mark, Luke and John, out of their cages, flying freaking and screeching, dropping major doveshit on the terracotta tiles. And me, in Little Pam's big pink swimsuit, holding this humungus pizza box while Jesus waits for his tip.

By the time I boarded the bus, it was all new people, so none of them knew me as the Screaming Idiot. It wasn't crowded. I sat next to the window and put my bookbag on the other seat. Partly to use my wordbooks and look in the French dictionary, but also to keep any possibly awful people from sitting next to me.

After looking up "Mal Hibou" (Mal: evil, ill, wrong, harm, hurt, mischief. Hibou: owl), I fell asleep. Dreamt I'd gone to Inn Nainity to make sure Didi was OK. The porch was being guarded by about ten owls, brown or black, all as big as Didi. Their faces were pinched, beaky, mean looking. They spoke a screechy, jabbery language, and would hiss and make pecking motions every time I tried to come up the steps. Some of them had flown onto the hanging paper lanterns, clawing and pecking until the paper tore, making the naked bulb light blindingly bright.

If you're not used to it, L.A. sunlight tears your eyeballs out. Superbright and superwhite. Being "natural," it's not as bright as fluorescence (which, in addition to tearing out eyeballs, turns white skin the color of scrambled eggs and can cause barfage). The light yanked my eyes open and the killer owl army disappeared. I grunted, moaned, covered my face with my hands, peeking out between my fingers. Palm trees. Shopping malls. Fast-food places. I pulled t-brush and t-paste out of my bookbag and headed for the loo at the back of the bus.

The smell was truly G. and D. (gross and disgusting). Disinfectant, Kool-Aid, piss and shit. I breathed through my mouth and managed to brush my teeth (much harder to do than with nose breathing). Peed. Washed hands and face.

In the loo mirror, I'd noticed I had the twelve-year-old-kid-with-tits look, so, back in my seat, I put on mascara, lipstick and cheek blush, using the little mirror in the "Desert Peach" blush compact.

Even in a crowd, I think a person would spot Gabe's lemon yellow hair. With only six or seven people waiting to meet the bus, it was a cinch. He saw me too. Waved and grinned.

"You look great, Gabel!"

"So do you."

"Yeah, sure."

"No, you do."

"Amazing. Nothing like sleeping in your clothes to improve your appearance, eh?"

Gabe really did look incredible. All tan and healthy. In Vancouver, I thought Gabe Dobson was the healthiest-looking person I'd ever seen. It was still true. And his arms, legs and chest were all sculptured and muscly looking. "Definition," he called it. Said you got it from working with weights. The clothes helped. Faded, shredded, cut-off shorts. Bleached-out pale orange tank top. Yellow rubber thong sandals. A black shoelace around his neck with a key hanging from it. It was fun to watch all his stuff happen while he loaded my gear into the back of a big white American station wagon. There were three bumper stickers: JESUS SAVES, THIS CAR BRAKES FOR GOD and LIE DOWN WITH THE LAMB.

Gabe opened the passenger door to let me in, then got behind the wheel and rolled the Yank Boatcar out of the parking lot onto "Ventoo Boovar." The light was still majorly blinding. Gabe didn't seem bothered by it, but he was wearing wraparound sunglasses. If I was going to stay in L.A. for more than overnight, I'd have to get some serious shades. Mostly to ease my eyes, I decided to study Gabe's arm. A truly Michelangelo thing. The upper part was all that definition stuff. Two bulges, stacked like tan ice-cream scoops, the biggest one at the top. Below the elbow, he had lots of soft-looking shiny golden-yellow armhairs. Holding the wheel made his arm-veins move. Hands, good. Not as big and sculpted as Marcus the Boy Bimbo's, or as powerful looking as Pascal's, but big enough. Very clean (which I admire. I can't seem to keep crud from getting under my fingernails, no matter what I do).

Gabe's neighborhood was called Tarzana.

"Like Tarzan?"

"Uh-huh."

"Of the Apes? That Tarzan?"

"Yah. Lots of places in L.A. are named after movie people and things. I went to high school with a Disney and his house was on Disney Drive."

"Is your house on 'Dobson Drive'?"

He laughed, a shy little "hee." "No. Nothing like that. We're on Brewster."

"Named after people who make beer, right?"

"Huh?"

"Nothin'. Canadian joke."

"Oh." He grinned. Gabe was willing to support a joke he didn't get.

Tarzana was the least jungly place imaginable. Flat, with large houses, all different styles. We rode down one street that had a cottage straight out of what Del calls "Ye Olde Englande" right next to a huge gray concrete thing, all rectangles, upside-down triangles and big cylinders, like giant toilet paper rolls, with windows like pregnant portholes. Neatly trimmed lawns. Some with trees and/or flowers. Some with high hedges or fences. One house had a family of gnomes on the lawn, another, a family of ducks. Then there was a humungo beige-y stucco house with arches and a beautiful roof of bright orange tiles. It looked like a picture Del has of a house in Sardinia. She had stayed there a long time ago. Before I was born.

"Holy shit!" On the lawn of the Sardinia-type house was a huge cement sculpture. Botticelli's Venus on the Halfshell talking with the Virgin Mary.

Gabe hee-laughed. "That's Mr. Delvecchio's house."

"Is he a sculptor?"

"No, he's a gangster. At least that's what Rex says. Rex says Mr. D.'s the secret owner of the biggest hotel in Vegas. And all the jukeboxes in America. Rex says the guy having Our Lady on his lawn is a sacrilegious offense."

"To God?"

"Yah. And to Rex. Rex was gonna go to the Chamber of Commerce and demand that the statue get removed. Mara talked him out of it. She said that if Rex ticked Mr. D. off, he'd get guys to shoot off Rex's kneecaps. So Rex passed. He's already got bad knees. From when he fell off a horse in *The Man from Cimarron*."

"What do you think? About the sculpture?"

"I dunno. Maybe Mr. D. just wants to say hi to God or something. So he won't be in Dutch so much later. When he dies, I mean. I know his son. He's a good guy."

"You mean Jesus?"

"No, Donato. We went to high school together. He's an ace football player. Quarterback. Got a gym in his basement. Weights, machines, running track. The whole enchilada. I used to use it sometimes. Didn't tell Rex and Mara."

"Do you still go there?"

"Uh-uh. Donny's gone. Got a football scholarship to Princeton. I think he'll turn pro."

In Vancouver, during the clown workshop, I don't think Gabe ever said more than ten words in any ten-minute cycle. And here he was nattering away. I had pretty much no idea what he was talking about, but that was OK. It's fun to hear new stuff. It all rolls into your head, then it rolls back out later as cartoons or answers to questions. I liked the sound of Gabe's happy babble as we drove through his L.A. burb-y jungle village. His voice was breathy-husky. Soft, but very guy.

The Dobson place was surrounded by a fence made of old, weathered barn wood. The entryway was a pair of fat logs, about two tall-people high, with another big log across them at the top. Hanging from this top log was a carved wooden sign: CASA DEL CIELO/CHRISTIAN REBIRTH CENTER. Underneath these wood-burned words was a horseshoe pointing upward. In the center of the U was a shiny bronze cross. Gabe got out, undid a chain across the logs and we drove through, up a long pebbled drive to the house, one of those sprawly one-story things. There was a horse, colored like a calico cat, in the field. There seemed to be lots of land.

"Rex and Mara are leading a tongues meeting up north. They'll be back tomorrow. They know you're coming, though. Said you could sleep in the pool house. Oh, listen, when you meet them, don't say 'holy shit,' O.K.?"

I was a little bit insulted, not having been, as Del would say, "brung up as a bint." "I never say 'shit' when I meet people's parents, Gabe."

"No, not the 'shit' part, the 'holy' part."

"Oh. OK."

At the door, Gabe leaned forward and tilted his head to the right, so he could turn the key that was on the shoelace around his neck. I giggled.

"Wouldn't it be easier to take the necklace off?"

"Shoelace is too short. Won't go over my head."

"Oh." I didn't ask about the possibility of untying the shoelace. Maybe he'd tied the knot too tight and would have to wear the key for the rest of his life.

"Listen," he said, the key in the lock, him still bent over, "don't say the 'shit' part either, OK?"

"G-a-a-a-be!"

"Huh?"

"I won't say the 'shit' part! The 'shit' part was the part I knew not to say!"

I really wouldn't ever say "shit" (or "fuck") to people's parents, but it did seem like you should be able to say pretty much any damn thing to people who were "leading" something called "a tongues meeting." What, I wondered, was "a tongues meeting" when it was at home? I hoped it would be cool if, when I met the famous Rex 'n' Mara, I just shook hands.

The main visiting parts of the house were all open and doorless, with a pretty rust-coloured tile floor and little steps up or down to its various sections (two steps up to the big, fancy kitchen, which had copper pots hanging on the walls. Three steps down to the eating section, with its long wooden table and eight chairs).

The living room area was the largest part, and had lots of Indian (as in cowboy and) rugs on the walls and floor. Against one wall was a stack of large bright-coloured pillows, and two little tables, with lamps that had bases made of wagon wheels. A strange rolling, gurgling sound was coming from this megabig wrought-iron birdcage, painted white, with four doves in it. "Hi, guys," I said, sticking a finger in, to be play-nibbled, like with Cliff, Arabella's budgie, at Le Temps Perdu. No takers, and one wing-flapping freaker.

I withdrew the scary finger and flopped down on a large beige leather chesterfield with a big multi-coloured striped blanket over the back. It faced an enormo gray boulder fireplace. There were trophies, plaques and a big gold-colored Bible on the mantel. Above the mantel was a giant oil painting (I think the style's called photographic magic realism) of Jesus. He, Jesus, had his arm around a good-looking silver-haired guy. Silver Man was wearing a white cowboy hat, yellow-beige western shirt, brown suede-y jeans and black cowboy boots. A tall, beautiful blonde, in a pink-and-white checked western dress, was standing off to the side, smiling at the guys. She had a really tiny waist.

"Is the cowboy Rex?"

"Uh-huh, and the other man is—"

"I recognize the other man. The woman is Mara?"

"Yah."

"She's pretty."

"Yah. She's still real pretty. You'll see when you meet her. Adelita, our housekeeper, made us lemonade and chicken tacos. Want some?"

The tacos, all white meat (yay!), with lettuce, tomatoes, cheese and a spicy red salsa, were brilliant. There was also guacamole (double yay!!) and corn chips, and more salsa in a little tan bowl with red flowers painted on it. Mexican food had recently come majorly to Vancouver, and was/is one of my absolute favorite things in all of life. The lemonade was pink. Not homemade, like Didi's, but just fine after a long bus trip.

After eating, I thought I'd better change ladyplugs.

"Where's the loo, please?"

"The what?"

"Washroom."

"Bathroom?"

"Right."

"Behind you, straight down the hall to the end."

"Ta."

The loo was small and basic. There were about fifty framed photographs on the walls. Most of them were "Rex and . . ." Rex and three different American presidents. Rex and three different preachers (two white, one black). Rex and three different horses (two white, one black). Rex and film stars. Rex standing between a big-haired woman in a wheelchair and a woman in a ruffle-sleeved sort of bra thing and a humungus turban hat covered with what looked like fruits and vegetables. He was in his cowboy clothes for all of them, except two of the president ones. In the third, the prez was in cowboy clothes too.

There were four pictures of Mara. One with Rex (both of them in western gear, both smiling, Rex's arm around her tiniest-in-the-whole-world waist). Another on a golden beige-y horse. One sitting on sand, with the sea behind her and a pretty baby Gabe standing on fat wobbly little legs. And a "draw me and win" profile picture. Mara had the same little nose, the same perfect skin and angel face as Del's "draw me and win" girl. Del still had that drawing. The one she did when she was 17.

She'd entered this contest, advertised in a London magazine. It was for a scholarship to the South Kensington Academy des Beaux Arts. You were supposed to draw your interpretation of this pretty woman with a tiny nose and wavy pale yellow hair ("No tracing permitted," the rules said). Del did the girl in soft pastel colours, with bluebirds and winged flowers flying out of her profiled open mouth. When you looked very closely, you could see "help!" written on some of the petals, some of the wings. Del won. When she went to the South Kensington Academy to collect her prize, she discovered her "scholarship" meant she'd have to pay £1,000 a year instead of the £2,000 normally required to study with Mad Jack Aspinall in his heat-free, housekeeping-free old madhouse. Del was, she said, angry at being scammed, but she also knew that John Aspinall had been a brilliant magazine illustrator whose drawings of London's "Bright Young Things" from the 1930s still brought "a pretty penny" at auction. And she needed a place to stay, having "split from where I was crashing" due to something she called an "orifice crisis." So she told Mad Jack she'd clean up the mansion and get wood for the fireplaces (the broken and end bits at the picture framing shop where she was working) in exchange for a free room and lessons ("the mad old bugger knew absolutely everything about color and line").

The "mad old bugger" was also spending almost his entire pension on gin. For months, Del would come home from the frame shop, make a fire in the largest room and sit in front of it with Mad Jack, both of them wearing lots of socks, sweaters and scarves, and draw until two or three in the morning, when Mad Jack's head would drop onto his drawing pad. Del always stayed with him until this happened to make sure he didn't fall into the fire. She lived there until the album cover jobs started really happening, and she moved into Dickie Siggins's Hampstead place. She continued to look in on Jack a lot, arranging for one of his three other students, Fouad from Algeria, to live there. Del sent funny presents to Mad Jack Aspinall, and visited with him, until he "cirrhosified" and died three years later. He left her the house (the South Ken Ack des Bozoes). She sold it and, between that and her album covers, had lots of money for the next five years of her life, which included the first four of mine.

And here I was, in the mini-loo of Gabe's house, in the middle of a nowhere named after an apeman, looking at the Born Again Draw-Me Girl who was Gabe's mum. Did this mean anything? Was it what Brian called a Young Ian's sin crony city?

My sleeping place, the "poolhouse," was a large, pale blue room with motel-y furniture and another tiny loo.

When it got dark, Gabe defrosted a pepperoni pizza. We ate at a candle-lit umbrella-covered white metal table on the large, half-awninged patio called "the lanai." It, and a huge swimming pool, separated the Big House from the poolhouse. I told him about my Yachats summer, saying nothing about Marcus, Didi or Pascal. Or about the biting of my mum's bum. Then we swam in the pool. I didn't have a suit, so I wore panties and a tanktop. When I got out, I could see that I'd become a nipplefest. Gabe could see this too, but being the sweet non-slimeball he is, only did a quick, smiling blink. Then he said good night, and that I should come for breakfast in the Big House, and that it was "really neat" that I'd decided to visit. We hugged. Then I went into the poolhouse, took off my wet gear, hid behind the door, wrung the water out of tank and panties and hung them on the outside doorknob to dry. As I'd be sleeping naked (my "things to buy" list was growing—sunglasses, bathing suit, nightie), I closed the curtains and crawled under the Mexican blanket. The sheets were cool and the color of Gabe's hair. I fell asleep right away.

I dreamt Gabe and I were in a rodeo. He was riding the calico-coloured horse. It was bucking, but Gabe stayed on. I was riding on Pascal's shoulders. He was bucking. But I stayed on.

• •

Even with the curtains drawn, the killer California light needle-probed its way under my eyeballs, and I woke up super-early. Washed, toothed, plugged, jeansed, tanktopped and headed for the Big House.

She had her tall, tiny-waisted back to me. Her long silky robe was the colour of champagne, and the morning sun was angel-haloing that amazing mother-and-son hair.

"Hi."

She gave a little gasp and turned. "Oh. Hello, dear. You must be Roanne. Welcome to Casa del Cielo. Gabriel is mucking out the stables, and his dad's still asleep. We're the early birds. Would you like some breakfast?"

It was all absolutely welcoming. Except that her soft, breathy voice was barely above a whisper and her eyes looked like she knew for total fact that I was there to cut her throat. Huge robin's egg blue scared eyes. The scared look went away on about the word "breakfast." It was replaced by something that looked like I felt when I was real little and Del would leave me with a new baby-sitter. Still scared, but being brave. And sad.

I thanked her, saying I didn't usually eat big bacon-and-eggy breakfasts. She smiled her pretty perfect please-don't-kill-me smile and said she didn't either. She brought a glass of milk and wonderful little muffins (carrot-apple-walnut. "Adelita's best," she said) to the wooden table and gestured for me to join her there. She was sipping one of those coffees with brandy flavouring. Or maybe rum. I liked the smell, wanted some, but thought it was important to seem like a proper milk-drinking young person.

"So, dear, when is your mother arriving?"

"In a few days. She has this number. She said she'd call and let me know. Her exact arrival time, I mean. Thank you very much for letting me stay."

"Oh, we're delighted to have you. Gabriel is terribly pleased. We keep him rather busy here at the center. It's good for him to be with people his own age. How old are you, dear?"

"Sixteen. Next week."

Mara jerked her head and upper body, just a little, and made a tiny "Oh!" noise. I looked where she was looking.

"Well, well, well! And who have we here!"

I had figured the whole family had these soft, breathy voices. Rex Dobson's boomer of a bass baritone could fill a concert hall. Without a mike. He stood in front of the fireplace, just under the painting of Rex/Mara/Jesus, wearing a bleached-out flamingo pink western shirt, black neckerchief, faded jeans and high-heeled scaly gray boots. He reminded me of Lloyd Williams, the rich Calgary oil guy who bought lots of Del's sculptures (even after she wouldn't marry him). Lloyd had a bad hairpiece too. Not as bad as Rex's. Rex's looked like a small silver-gray dog had collapsed on top of his head. Splat. Little furry dead dog. Del said she couldn't understand why "these geezers with absolute pots of money couldn't commission a decent rug."

"So! *This* is Roanne!" he boomed, heading straight for me in three great strides. "This" stood up like a jack-in-the-box, threw its shoulders back in its best "stand up straight, Roanne" posture. He grabbed my hand and pumped it up and down in his two large enough but slightly pudgy paws. The doves' cage was swinging back and forth because all four birds were hopping all over the place, cooing like crazy.

"Hello, darlin'. Welcome to the home the Lord shares with us. Mara, has this young lady been fed an' watered?"

"Yes, Rex."

Rex looked at the plate of muffins. "Hmm, not a very hearty . . ."

She had come in so quietly. Short and round, with curly-frizzy shoulder-length black hair and skin almost as coppery as the terra-cotta tile floor. Round, black, superkind eyes. Sweet, sweet smile. The kind of eyes and smile that made me want to say, "Hey, I've got a mother I really love. Who really loves me back. But would you like to be my other mother? You could hold me when I'm sick. Hold me when I'm scared. Sing me to sleep with Mexican songs when my mind's all wired and hyper. Like the song on the speakers in Carlito's Enchilada Palacio in Kitsilano—'CucurucucOOOO, Palo-o-omah . . . '" It's extremely rare that I flat-out love somebody on sight. I loved Adelita like that. Without even remembering that she could also make tacos.

"Good morning, Adelita. This young lady is Roanne . . . Campbell?"

"Chappell."

"Chappell! SUPERB! What a FINE name for a visitor to the home we share with the Lord Jesus (praise his name). Chappell! Oh, that's very fine indeed! Miss Chappell is a friend of Gabriel's. She's staying with us, out in the poolhouse (so, please tidy up the poolhouse, Adelita darlin', and put some fresh flowers in there). Her mother will be collecting her in a day or so, but in the meantime, we WANT her to FEEL like a MEMBER of OUR FAMILY."

All the while that Rex was doing his Glory Hallelujah nut, Adelita and I didn't say a word, just stood there, pinned eyeball to eyeball, grinning like curly-headed bookend gypsy fools. She knows, I thought. She knows I love her. And she loves me too.

"I think we can clear these breakfast things, Adelita." Rex yanked Mara's coffee cup out of her hand as he said this. Mara blinked once, the way Gabe sometimes did—a little baby's blink thing. Her eyes were wide, wide, wide, but seemed to hold no thought, like she was pretending to be some other place. She pressed her palms against the sides of the table, then curled her fingers up onto the tabletop, lightly, very lightly, scratching her fingernails back and forth on the wooden surface. Rex put her cup in the sink, Adelita following silently. He smelled the coffeepot, emptied it into the sink, turned to face us.

"Well, Mara, shouldn't you be dressing, darlin'? We don't want to be late to the prayer meeting in Petaluma."

"Of course, dear. I'll change tootie-sweetie." She smiled her sad perfect smile at me as she stood up. "Lovely to meet you, dear. We'll see you this evening." She headed off down the hall.

Petaluma? I wondered if she knew Didi's friend Chuck the Chickentrucker, but decided this wasn't the time to ask if they knew a guy who sometimes fucked a French dwarf.

I looked at Rex, who was smiling at me with his mouth closed. "Something's happening. What is it?" my eyes asked him. "None of your business, darlin'," his eyes answered. And in came Gabe, smelling seriously terrible.

"Jesus, Gabe, you smell like horseshit!"

Gabe went rigid. Amazing! I thought. I do not believe it! I did it! I actually said "Jesus" *and* said "shit!" I was so mad at myself that I followed "shit" and "Jesus" with "damn!" Brilliant or what, eh? Three for three. Like, tell us, Roanne, while you're standing there having fuck-up of the mouth, is there anything you'd like to say about the Virgin Mary giving blowjobs on Ventoo Boovar?

Gabe said it wasn't major. That it would've been better if I hadn't said Jesus. And shit. And damn. But that Rex and Mara were used to forgiving thoughtless blaspheming by the unknowing so it would probably be cool. And that he would be happy to drive me to the Van Eyes Mall to buy my travel necessaries.

• •

I'd wanted to do all three—sunglasses, bathing suit and a nightie. Then I counted my money, $509.49. I still needed to make sure I was "always responsible for myself" (Del) *and* get my bus ticket for Yachats. Besides, all the bathing suits I tried on, particularly the black just-below-the-bellybutton bikini with tiny white stars (the one I looked best in), didn't seem "Jesus worthy." They were also, for little bits of fabric, majorly expensive. If I was going to spend major money, I *had* to have these big black movie star shades that were from Italy and would keep me from going sunblast blind. Also, a plain white cotton floor-length nightie that was on sale.

A strange thing happened in the nighties ("Sleepwear") department. There was this girl. She was with her mother, who sort of had a face like a large cinnamon bun. She, the girl, was pale, with blondie-brown long straight hair, held out of her face by two plastic barrettes of little blue and red birds. She had no stuff. No boobs, no bum, no lipstick. She looked about ten. I knew she wasn't. I knew this baby child person was my age. She knew it too. We eyelocked, looked really hard at eachother, each one thinking the other was the strange thing in the fishtank. Her cinnamum bought her a pale blue nightie that was covered with doggies. Not dogs, doggies.

After buying the shades and nightie, I had $363.38. And nothing to swim in except my tanktop and panties. I figured I'd be going home in a few days and could always swim late at night, after Rex 'n' Mara were asleep. Or not swim at all. I mean, I'd managed to live my whole life without a pool outside my door without feeling majorly deprived. It's tricky about fun stuff, though. Once you do something you like, you want to do that thing again and again and again. I suppose it would be easier to just never do anything. Easier, but seriously, even tragically, boring.

Gabe asked if there was anything else I wanted to do. I wanted to go back to Casa del Cielo. I wanted to see Adelita, maybe talk to her.

No luck. When we got back, she'd already gone to where she lived, in a little cottage at the far end of the fenced field. It didn't feel right to ask if we could visit her there, so I let it pass. There was a wonderful spicy smell in the Big House kitchen. She'd made a big pot of chili. Chili is one of the world's great foods. Adelita was definitely a Special Person.

I wanted to draw, and asked Gabe if he'd mind my cooling out alone in the poolhouse for a while. He said no, that he had gymnastic things to do, and that he'd knock on the poolhouse door when it was time for "supper." (Del hates it when people call dinner "supper." She says "supper" is a late, light meal. I thought it would be showoff to tell this to Gabe.)

There wasn't any sort of proper table, and the carpeting made the floor lumpy, so I pulled the rocking chair over to the dresser and wedged my wordbooks under the rockers so I could draw a steady line. I thought it would be interesting to try some California place names. Tarzana, Van Eyes (Van Nuys), Christian Rebirth Center and, of course, Mal Hibou.

I'd done a pretty good basic drawing of a demento-looking killer owl when suddenly I got hugely sad. That happens sometimes, where I'm fine, fine, fine, then whammo! from out of nowhere, Big Sad. Can't always figure out why, but this time I could. All at once I was missing Del like crazy. Maybe it was because I didn't get to see Adelita. Or I wanted Adelita because I was missing Del. I decided to call Yachats and tell Del I'd be home in a few days. The call changed everything. Changed my whole life.

"Hullo?"

"Del?"

"Rosie?"

"Uh-huh."

"You lied to me, you little shit!"

"Did not."

"Did, dammit, did! You said you'd be here—"

"In two or three weeks. I've got—"

"You've got sweet Fanny Adams! You're pushing all my bloody buttons, you are. You know bloody well that I don't want to call the law, and you expect me to just let you—"

"Del, please! Stop freaking and listen to me."

"I'll have your mad poof frog dwarf up for—"

"Del, stop! I'm not there, I'm not with Didi. I'm—"

"You're what? You're not—"

"I'm not there! I'm somewhere else!"

"Somewhere else? Where else? Where the fuck are you?"

"It doesn't matter. The point is—"

"Doesn't matter!? Doesn't fucking matter?! Bloody 'ell!" Del's phone receiver clunked onto the floor. Then . . .

"Roanne? Rosie?"

"Who is this?"

"It's Marcus, Rosie."

I got as quiet as the end of the world. Stopped breathing.

"Listen, Rosie, your mother is really worried about you. She—"

(Whisper) "Put my mother on the phone."

"She's really upset . . ."

"PUT HER ON THE PHONE, YOU DICKHEAD!"

I could hear mumble, mumble, mumble, then . . .

(Real quiet voice) "Rosie?"

"How could you let that slime in the house?"

"I . . ."

"How could you? How can you fuck a guy who bet on us?"

"Rosie, it's not like that . . ."

"Oh, sure. He's just there because he absolutely had to hear Eric Clapton sing 'Lay Down Sally.'"

"The Morgan's in the shop . . . he's giving me a ride to Eugene, Rosie, I wouldn't—"

"He called me Rosie! That fucking pervo called me Rosie!"

"Rosie, please . . ."

"If that fucking scumball ever calls me Rosie again, if he ever calls me *anything* again, if he even tries to *talk* to me again—*ever*—I'll hit him with a fucking brick and tie his dick to a tree and leave him to be eaten by fucking cougars! I'll—"

"Rosie . . ."

I hung up. Hard. I wanted to scream. Wanted to barf. Wanted to break things. But it wasn't my place, wasn't my stuff. I put on my denim jacket and went to look for Adelita.

From behind the poolhouse, in the almost-dark, I could see lights on in Adelita's little house at the end of the field.

I knocked. The door opened, and there was that sweet, smiling round apple-doll face. "Hi. May I . . . come in for a minute?"

She was still smiling, not saying anything. Maybe she didn't speak English. When Del was with Hoolio the Foolio, he taught me to say "My name is Rosita" in Spanish. Something about a llama. Usually I'm good with remembering language things, but I was too freaked to put it together. "I . . . wanted to visit you . . . I . . . do you speak English?"

She reached up, put her warm little copper hand against my cheek. She opened her mouth, pointing inside. No tongue. Adelita had no tongue. I turned and ran.

• •

Sometimes there gets to be Weirdness Overload and you feel dizzy and nauseous and falling. Sometimes, growing up with Del and all, with all sorts of "interesting people," I'd get to craving ordinary, less interesting people, and I'd go looking for them. But they didn't like me. If they were my age, sometimes they'd like me, but then their parents didn't like me. These same people didn't like Del either. Del said this was because they thought we were "getting away with something," that we were having some sort of good time that people weren't supposed to be having. Del said this was probably true, but that the good time was a "trade-off." That you gave up some things to have other things. She said there was no way to explain this to the less interesting people without making it worse. That it was "best not to struggle with it." Best to go where you're welcomed, she said, or stay by yourself. Well, here I was, majorly By Myself, scrunched up in the dark, on the ground, pressed up against the side of the poolhouse, wanting to pack my gear and go, but not knowing how to get to anywhere from where I, in the dark, was.

Thought a shower might help. Got up and walked round to the poolhouse door. Saw the station wagon in front of the Big House. Saw the lights on in the big room. Saw Rex shaking Mara. Looked up. Moon was full. Maybe that was it.

"Aahh! Jesus, Gabe, you scared the shit out of me!" Then I laughed. "I can't seem to stop saying 'Jesus' and 'shit,' eh?"

Gabe snort-laughed and got up from next to the dresser, where he'd been sitting on the floor. "Sorry, Roe. Didn't mean to scare you. Came to hang out with you. Rex and Mara are fighting."

"Yeh, I saw. What's up? Is it about me?"

He shook his head and sat down on the bed, looking bummed out. I sat next to him, asked if he wanted to talk about it. He said no. Then he said Mara had smuggled booze in her purse, and that she'd "killed a bottle" in the "john" on the plane, so when they got to Petaluma for the prayer meeting she was pissed and kept saying Jesus wanted her for a sunbeam. Gabe said Mara had gone away for treatment three times, but kept going back to drinking. She and Rex and the Rebirthies had "prayed over it," but nothing seemed to work for very long. I told him about someone I knew in Kitsilano who had a Booze Thing. He shaved his head, changed his name to

Dharuma and went to live with monks who made bread. It turned him sort of boring, but he didn't drink anymore. I said maybe Mara could try that. Without shaving her head, because her hair was so pretty. Gabe said it wouldn't work, because Rex and Mara believed other religions were "part of the Antichrist." He got up and peeked through the blinds. I peeked too. Mara was sitting on the chesterfield. Her head was bowed. Rex was standing over her, gesturing and looking like he was shouting.

"Does he hit her?"

"No, never. . . . Well, once, when I was little, but never again, I don't think."

"Before, he was sort of shaking her."

"Yah, he does that sometimes. But no hitting. Mostly yelling. And going through her stuff. And locking her in her room. I wish things could just be nice."

"Yeah, Gabe, me too."

"You hungry?"

"I dunno. Maybe."

He unzipped a little red gym bag. "I thought it might be better if we ate here." He took out plastic plates, paper napkins, some lumps wrapped in foil and two small bottles of bile-green Gatorade. There were chicken breasts covered in brown goop, corn chips and salsa, fresh pineapple slices. The chicken goop tasted weird.

"What's this stuff on the chicken?"

"Molé."

"What's that when it's at home?"

"Chocolate."

"Chocolate chicken? Yuck." I ate some of the other stuff, mostly the chips and salsa, and drank some Gatorade, which tasted like bubbly lime-flavoured mucilage.

"What happened to Adelita's tongue?"

"She was born without one."

"So is that what a 'tongues meeting' is, a meeting of people without tongues? Are there lots of people in California without tongues?"

"Uh-uh. Adelita's the only one I know. A tongues meeting is people doing glosso."

"Glosso?"

"Glossolalia. Speaking in tongues. It's when you speak words you don't know, in a language you don't know. It's a gift from God. The Rebirthies do it in the pool."

"So Adelita couldn't be a Rebirthy because she doesn't have a tongue?"

"I think she could be one anyway. Not everyone has the gift. Don't tell Rex, but I don't have it yet. I kinda stand at the back of the group and make up words."

"Like what?"

"Mackalahoopoo."

"Mackalahoopoo?"

"Yah."

"Great word."

"Yah."

We shouted it together, "Mackalahoopoo!" And we larfed. It was good to larf.

"So Adelita is a Rebirthy too? She does silent mackalahoopoos in the pool?"

"No. She *is* Christian. Catholic. She's got the Lord on a cross on her wall. Doesn't do Rebirthy nights, though. I think it's because Rex and Mara need her to serve food and clean up and stuff. I dunno. Never asked her."

"How could she answer if you did? Ask her, I mean."

"She writes notes. Keeps a little pad and pencil in her pocket. Doesn't use it much. Just if it's really important, or if she wants to cheer you up. Sometimes she draws."

"She draws? Cartoons?"

"I dunno. Little drawings."

"Do you have them?"

"Yah, some. She always does one for my birthday. And she did a really fun one of me when I won the high school pentathlon. She came to that."

"Could I see them sometime?"

"Sure. If you want to." He scrunched up all the aluminium foil bits and pitched them across the room into a little woven waste-basket.

"So, how did she come here?"

"She's Carlos's sister. Carlos was Rex's stand-in and stunt double. He broke his neck when they used a tripwire on a horse, to make the horse fall. In *Durango Sunset*. The horse broke his leg and Carlos broke his neck. They shot the horse."

"What happened to Carlos?"

"He died right away when his neck broke. After Carlos died, Rex brought Adelita here to be our housekeeper. It was all before I was born. Adelita's been here my whole life, like a member of the family."

I started to cry. No noise, just water.

"What's wrong? Did I say something bad?"

"No, Gabe. It's me. I did something bad. To Adelita."

"What? What did you do?"

"I went to visit her. In her little house. Because I really like her, and I was sad. And she opened her mouth and showed me where her no tongue was and I freaked and ran away. It must have hurt her feelings."

"Oh, it's probably OK. Adelita's kinda used to people being a little nutso. I mean, Rex shouts at her a lot of the time, and she cleans up when Mara wets her bed and like that."

"Still, I want to apologize. It's important not to be mean to people when they're different."

"You can tomorrow. I'm sure it's OK, though." He peeked through the blinds again. "The lights are out. They probably went to their rooms. If I cut the pool lights, you wanna swim?"

"Yeh. Sure."

• •

We were under the water, and came up to the surface together. Gabe kissed me. After, he was just looking at me with those wide baby eyes. Eyes like Mara's. I could see that he wanted to do it. Not in a letchy way. Like a newborn baby would want to do it if babies did it. I could also feel that he had a grown-up boner. His voice was all breathy-husky. "Can I stay with you?"

"I dunno, Gabe . . ."

"We don't have to do anything . . . we could hold eachother. We're both sad . . . it could be nice . . ."

"Yeh, it could . . . yeh, OK, sure."

"Thanks."

"You're welcome. Let's get out of the water, I'm freezing my nubbies off."

I took off my wet clothes, towelled dry and got under the covers. "OK, you can come in." I'd turned off the bed lamp but could still see him in the dark, taking off his wet jockeys. Even without light, his bum showed really white against his tan. Round, with indentations and dimples. The absolute best type guybutt.

"Brrr," he said and pulled the covers over him. We pressed hard against eachother. Body heat, skin and some sort of woodsy oil. We were kissing and rolling around and rubbing up on each other, and that lifetime key on the leather thong around his neck was cold and pressing between my tits and I was all of a sudden really hot and really happy and laughing and he was inside me and it was easy and it was good and it was over.

"I'm sorry, Roe. I wasn't going to . . ."

"Yeh, you were. Don't worry, it's cool. Stay. Stay on me, OK."

"Aren't I heavy?"

"Uh-uh. You're warm. I love your skin."

"Really? You love it? My skin?"

"Yes. It's beautiful."

"My skin?"

"Your skin. Don't you know that?"

"Uh-uh. I've only done this one time before, well two, but with one person. She didn't say anything. About my skin, I mean. You're not mad?"

"No, Gabe, I'm glad. Glad you're here."

"Me too. I'll have to sneak out, though. Before Rex and Mara get up."

"Can we sleep for a while, together?"

"Uh-huh. I've got a beeper on my watch." He got up. Put his watch on. Set his beeper. Got back in bed. Put his arms around me. I fell asleep, smelling his woodsy self and sort of sucking on his shoulder.

In the middle of the night he was inside me again two more times, but each time it was over before I could do anything with it. He fell back asleep and I lay there, thinking about the Coming Thing. Wondering if I could ever get fast enough to catch it in time.

Gabe's beeper went off. I was really sleepy. He kissed me on my cheek and my mouth and my shoulder and said he had to go. I said OK. He said, "I love you." I said, "Thanks, Gabe," because I was half asleep but I did recognize it was a nice thing to say. He said, "Would you like to marry me and go live somewhere?" I said I didn't think so. He said, "Could we talk about it again sometime, when you're more awake?" I said sure. He said, "Thanks." I went back to sleep.

When I woke up for real, I was thinking of Adelita. I had a Gabesmell on me. I liked it, but thought I'd better shower. I wasn't sore, like with the Roadie, or bloody, like with Mucus, but did feel sort of crotchraw because my jeans were so tight. Put on black tank and wide-leg pants. Better. My hair was seriously huge from swimming and rolling about, so I made one big braid down the back. Didn't have an elastic band, but there was a red twist-tie on the floor, from the corn chips. Used that.

• •

Adelita was sitting on the horizontal log that made the top part of the entrance gate to Casa del Cielo, wearing a long red Mexican dress with a square neckline full of embroidered flowers (Del has one like it, in yellow). She had a big silver plate of tacos in her lap. The tacos had wings, and were flying down to Rex, Mara, Gabe and me, who were standing on the grassy ground, with our arms reaching up to catch. I finished colouring it in and wrote, in big, black letters, "YOU ARE A VERY SPECIAL PERSON. I AM GLAD TO KNOW YOU. I AM SORRY I WAS RUDE LAST NIGHT (I WAS HAVING PERSONAL PROBLEMS). Yours Sincerely, Roanne Chappell."

I figured she wouldn't be there, but knocked anyway, because you're supposed to. No answer. I went in.

It was one room, like the poolhouse, only bigger. There were lots of bright-coloured little rugs scattered about on the tile floor, and a twin-sized bed, covered by a red and orange spread. A crucified wooden Jesus hung on the wall above the bed. Under Jesus was a woven diamond of different colored wools, with a red or purple tassel at each diamond point. Against the opposite wall was a sink and a tiny fridge (the kind Trish McPhee had in her basement in Burnaby, in what she called the "rec room." I thought she was saying "wreck"—a place you could go to smash stuff up when you were freaking. My first time there, I asked Trish what she had that we could wreck. She looked at me like I was a major Mars Person, and never invited me there, or anywhere else, again). On top of the fridge was a two-burner hotplate, with shiny copper pots and pans on the wall behind it, and some shelves for plates, glasses, cups, etc. There was a happy-looking wooden chair, painted glossy yellow, with red and blue flowers. The whole back wall was filled with paintings and drawings. People, animals and one amazing gray-green face with a sexy mouth and a bright red feather growing out of it. I wanted to study these, but didn't feel right about being in somebody else's place without being invited. Especially when I'd been so awful the night before. I went to leave my drawing on a little table next to her bed, and saw the photographs, in their silver frames. One of a much younger Rex and Mara. Another, a great big head of a beautiful baby Gabe. A Mexican-looking woman and two little girls. A handsome man with slicked-back black hair, a beautiful nose and major cheekbones. Carlos? I left my drawing between Carlos and Gabe.

Rex, Mara and Gabe were seated around the big wooden table, eating pancakes. Adelita wasn't anywhere in sight.

"Hello there, darlin'. You sleep well?"

"Yes, thanks, Mr. Dobson."

"Rex, please. Mr. Dobson's my daddy."

"Well, actually, Mr. Huckabee's his daddy. The late Mr. Floyd Huckabee. Senior."

"There you go again, Mara, darlin', bein' literal. Mara's real literal sometimes. Her mama taught school. I've been Rex Dobson for a very long while now, Mara, dear. What I'm trying to say, Roanne, darlin', is that we're all on a first-name basis here, and I'd be mightily pleased if you'd call me Rex. You been fed an' watered?"

"I'm not superhungry, thanks. Are there any more of those little muffins?"

Gabe leapt up so hard I thought there'd be a floorful of pancakes. "There's some in the cookie jar. I'll get 'em."

Mara asked if I'd like some milk. Gabe said he'd bring it. What I truly craved was a café au lait, but was still afraid asking for coffee might not seem "age-appropriate," even though they did think I was almost 16, so I had the milk and muffins.

"Gabriel tells us he's going to take you riding this morning."

"Riding? On a horse?"

"Well, we sold the cattle." Rex laughed at his own joke.

"I dunno, Gabe. I haven't ridden since I was 10. I've only done it a few times, ever."

"Don't worry, Roe. You can ride behind me, in the same saddle." He was looking at me with such a sweet face, I couldn't say no.

The saddle was "western," completely different from the kind I learned on. You had to lean back, instead of forward, and there was this little leather dickthing sticking up in the front of it. Gabe was really good at riding, though, and the horse (Star of Bethlehem) galloped superfast, with me hanging onto Gabe from behind, and, loving guys' backs anyway, I was bouncing up and down, screaming and larfing and forgetting about how fucked with soreness I was probably going to be as soon as I got off that horse. Gabe kept asking, "How you doing?" and I kept saying, "I'm great! Perfect! Brilliant!"

The chapel was one of those White Christmas-card-looking ones with a pointy steeple. It had beautifully carved wooden pews and a huge stained-glass window that was exactly the same as the painting of Jesus, Rex and Mara. I wondered how come it was a sacrilegious offense for the gangster guy to have a statue on his lawn of Venus on the Halfshell talking to the B.V.M. but it was cool to have a church window of God hangin' out with a pair of western movie actors.

"Pretty church."

"Yah . . . Roe, can we talk for a sec?"

"Sure. About what?" (I knew about what.)

"About what I asked you this morning."

I didn't want to make it harder for Gabe, but I guess I even more didn't want to talk about what he wanted to talk about, so I did this awful slut bitch thing. "This morning? When?"

"In the poolhouse. When you were asleep."

"When I was asleep? If I was asleep, how am I supposed to remember what you said?" (I truly hate it when girls do that sort of shit, and there I was, doing that sort of shit.)

"You don't remember what I asked you?"

"Uh-uh. I'm sorry." (You ought to be, you rotten slag.)

"About us . . . I asked if . . . if maybe you'd like to get married . . . with me, I mean, and we could go live somewhere?"

There it was. Right out in the middle of the road, where I'd have to deal with it. And, even though I definitely did not want to get married just then, it was a Big Thing. My first marriage proposal. When you grow up sort of different, you get used to the fact that things that happen to the more like-eachother people don't much happen to you. Like the prizes given to the hundreds of Heather MacWhatevers in your school. Girls with white blouses that stay clean, girls with no crud under their fingernails, with plaid skirts in the family tartan. Girls who get up and thank their one-of-each-sex parents and their no-sex church. Those prizes are not going to be given to you. Not when your science project was to do rude (and very well drawn!) cartoons of all the planets, especially Uranus.

Marriage is one of those sorts of prizes. And, like the dumb-looking trophy they gave as the science prize, the one everybody called the Silver Tit, you may think it's nerdy, but you want it offered, because it means some of the Majority People said "yes" about you.

And here was this really sweet guy, this really good-looking guy, the sort-of-looking guy the Heather MacWhatevers wanted to pull, and he was asking me, with my un-Heather looks and my un-Heather life, to marry him. And maybe, if I didn't say yes, nobody would ever ask me again. And ten years from now nobody would believe that anybody asked me, ever.

So there I was, staring at the polished wooden floor in the Chapel of Saint Rex 'n' Mara, thinking all this, when a miracle of sanity happened. I mean, I remembered I was 14. And that in ten years I'd only be 24. And that probably at least one more person would ask me between now and then.

"Gabe, I can't. I'm not ready. I'm too young . . ."

"Come on, Roanne, that's not it. . . . It's that you don't love me, right?"

"Aw, Gabe, it's not . . . it's not about that. It's about the world. I want to do the World Thing for a while. To see what's out there. I'm too young to love anybody in a marriage way yet. So are you. We both need to sort of wander around on our own first. You should take off. By yourself. Get out from under Rex." He turned his head away from me, looking really sad. He wrapped his arms around himself and just sort of sat there, rocking.

"I . . . don't like being by myself."

"Nobody does. Not all the time. It's scary in lots of ways. But it's also exciting. I'm doing it."

"No, you're not."

"Am."

"Uh-uh. You're just here with us until your mom comes down, and then you'll get to do stuff with her again. I remember, when we were in clown school, you saying how you and your mother were both artists. How you drew pictures together and travelled around together and all."

What Gabe was saying was making me majorly miserable. He didn't know how fucked my situation was right then, and I didn't want to bum him out worse than he was already bummed out. "But you do lots of stuff with your family."

He jumped up off the pew where we were sitting. It was the first time I ever heard Gabe Dobson yell (it may have been the only time he ever did).

"No! It's not the same! You and your mom like to draw and travel and stuff. Mara and me, we only get to do what Rex likes! It's not the same. It's not! . . . Lookit, I wanted to go for the Olympics, OK? There were people who wanted to sponsor me, pay all my training and travel expenses and everything, OK?! But Rex said no. He said I had to stay and do the Lord's work. To bring people my age into the Christian Rebirth Center."

"Do you believe in God?"

He blinked, looked at me like I'd asked him if he believed in breathing. "Sure."

"Well, tell Rex that. Tell him, if you love your God, sports can be the Lord's work too."

"Oh, sure. Easy for you to say. You can talk to your mom, and she listens."

"Not always. There's . . . stuff you don't know. And I don't really want to talk about it, because it's between Del and me. But I will tell you we're in a mess right now. Majorly. And I don't know how, or when, or even if it'll get better. And I lied. I *am* on my own. She's not coming here. She doesn't even know where here is."

"You mean you ran away from home?"

"Not exactly. I just took a time out, because a bad thing happened. And then the bad thing rehappened. So I'm having to take a longer time out. I'm not really ready to say anything else about it right now." I stood up and hooked my bum onto the back of the pew in front of us. "Look, Gabe, I'm really grateful you let me come visit you. And I think you're a supergreat guy. I just think I need to not be a heavy girlfriend with anyone right now. And I still think you should split. . . . Look, if you're scared, I'll walk you to the corner and stand there until you can't see me."

"What does that mean?"

"It's a thing Del, my mum, and I used to do (I didn't say 'when I was little'), if I had to do something scary by myself (I didn't say 'like go to kindergarten'). Del would walk me to our corner. And she'd stand there while I walked away from her. And I'd keep turning around to see if she was still there, and she would be still there, and she'd wave and smile and wave. And I'd wave back. And keep turning around, and she'd be still there, waving, until I'd get too far away to see her anymore. And I'd have my phone number in my pocket, in her handwriting, and something small that belonged to her, that smelled like her, a scarf, or a hanky. And I knew I could call if I got supersacred. Or I could smell the scarf. If you want, we could do that. We could go to Ventura Boulevard together, and I'd give you something of mine, and I'd stand there, waving and smiling like crazy, until you were really on your way, and . . ." And we were hugging and kissing and crying buckets and we did that until our crying places were empty. Then we held hands and walked Star of Bethlehem back to the stable.

I wanted to give Gabe my body. For the skin of it, but mostly because he was so sad and I thought it would cheer him up, but he had to go with Rex and Mara to talk about Jesus at a high school. It was also Adelita's day off (Gabe said), and she was wherever it was she went on days off. Gabe thought she visited a sister in a place called Loss Feelers. I went to the poolhouse. Called Didi. No answer. Looked at Pascal's Mal Hibou card. Didn't call. Wrote new words in wordbooks (Glossolalia, Mackalahoopoo). Tried to draw, but nothing good came. Called Del. No answer. Took off all my clothes and crawled under the covers. Too mind-wired to sleep. Did Brian's sleep trick where you visualize an animal and keep adding different parts from different animals until you fall asleep. Snakeface/elephantears/giraffeneck/squirreltail . . .

When I woke up, the room was dark and I had major puppy-breath armpits. Got out of bed and showered. While I was doing that, I heard this growly noise. It was my stomach. I'd gone the whole day on early-morning muffins, and was what Joe, the guy who fixes our sink and toilet in Kitsilano, calls "hungry enough to eat the ass end out of a hedgehog." Put on wide-legs and black tank. Gabe was tapping on the window. I gestured for him to come in.

"Casa del Cielo is full of Rebirthies. I forgot to tell you, on Saturday nights we have this 'glosso in the pool' thing. Rex said he'd be pleased if you'd join us."

"Oh, God. I mean, oh, gee, I don't know anything about—"

"You don't have to know anything. Or do anything. Just be in the pool. Rex just wants you to feel the celebration, he said. I'll be right next to you."

"No suit."

"What?"

"I don't have a bathing suit, remember?"

"Oh, yah, right. We have a half hour or so, I'll get you one of Mara's."

"Ga-a-be!"

"Wha-a-t?"

"Mara's waist is the size of my arm."

"Nah. Your arm is smaller than her waist."

"Not by much."

"I dunno . . . I'll see if I can find something. Some of the Rebirthies leave suits here sometimes. I'll be right back."

"Gabe?"

"Yah?"

"Food? I'm starving!"

"Oh, yah, right. Pizza?"

"Brilliant."

"OK. I'll call Hey Sooss."

"Hey who?"

"Hey Sooss. It's Jesus in Spanish. He's the delivery guy from Valley Pizzarama."

"And it's cool to say his name?"

"Yah, because he's a person. You just can't say it in general."

• •

It was like one of those movies. *Invasion of the Jesusfreak Pod People.* Rebirthies were pouring out of the Big House, heading straight for where I was standing, next to Gabe, in front of the poolhouse door.

There were three kinds of light. Moon, Big House, and four tall lamps around the pool. Surrounded by endless welldigger darkness. There seemed to be about 40 of them, all ages, sexes and sizes. All in bathing suits. All singing "Amazing Grace." Rex, in shiny white bathing trunks, with a big gleaming silver cross on a chain around his neck, was leading them. Mara, in a long white dress, her hair moonyellow, walked beside him, carrying the dove-filled birdcage.

"Here they come."

"No shit."

"Roe!"

"Don't worry, Gabe-o, I won't . . . but here they sure as shit do come."

"You OK?"

"Uh-huh. You sure this bathing suit belongs to someone called 'Little Pam'?"

"Yes."

"'Big Pam' must be bigger than a bus!"

Gabe got the giggles, but swallowed them down to nothing as Rex reached us.

"Welcome, darlin', to our Saturday night celebration of the Lord Jesus (praise his name). Gabriel, why don't you and Miss Chappell find a place in the water."

The still-singing Rebirthies were climbing into the pool. Mara hooked the birdcage onto one of the lanterns, then stood beside it, her hands folded in front of her. Rex climbed the ladder to the diving board. When he got to the board's edge, he spread out his arms toward the black sky. For an old guy (Gabe said Rex was lots older than he looked), he had a good bod. Little fat-pooches at the sides of his waist, but no more than lots of younger guys.

When Rex did the Arm Thing, everybody got completely quiet. His voice boomed out into the sound-empty night.

"Matthew! Mark! Luke! John!" The four doves started cooing like crazy. A megabig sound, like each dove was the size of a bear.

"Wow!" I whispered.

"They're miked. There's a microphone attached to the lantern." Gabe whispered back.

"Amazing!"

"Matthew, Mark, Luke and John, doves of peace! Bless this assembly, in JEEEZZUSSname!" In the megadovecoo, everyone in the pool, including Gabe (but not me, because I didn't know you were supposed to), shouted, "PRAISE HIS NAME!" Then Rex extended his arm out toward me!

Oh shit, I thought (but did not say it), please don't single me out, I'm scared of crowds, and I'm in a majorly ugly two-sizes-too-big hot pink bathing suit!

"We have a guest with us, brothers and sisters. Miss Roanne Chappell, a friend of Gabriel's."

They were all looking at me, smiling. "Welcome, in Jesus' name, Roanne!" they shouted, all at the same time.

"Hi. Thanks," I said, thinking they must've practised in the house or something, because no group of people has ever gotten my name right like that.

"LOVE SPLASH!" Rex shouted, and everybody, especially this

grim skinny kid with a face like a fist, started splashing water on me, something only people you know you like have a right to do.

I swung my hand up and out. Gabe grabbed it.

"Don't splash back. It's a blessing. It'll stop in a minute."

"Promise?"

"Welcome, Roanne. Jesus loves you, and we love you. Now everybody, feel the spirit, listen for the spirit inside you, let the spirit move through you. Let the spirit speak through you . . ."

People were sort of jumping up and down in the water, making moaning or gurgling sounds.

"FEEEL the SPEERIT, LISSSEN for the SPEERIT, LET the SPEERIT MOOOVE THROOO you, let the SPEEERIT SPEEEK THROOO YOOOOOOAGGADA BRAGGADANANANANAN-AAA . . ."

The Rebirthies were jumping or swaying, their heads turned up, chins pointing at the sky, eyes closed or bugging, big glossowords here and there. "Flibbidum." "Nakalono." "Brammmesskaaa." I looked at Gabe, reached for his hands, shouted, "Mackalahoopoo!"

Rex was definitely the Biggest Glossolaliac of them all, his arms outstretched, his bass voice cutting through everything. "AG-GADAMANADAFLASSSANAKAAAFAAA . . ." and he pitched forward into the pool.

"Gosh, he never did that before," little Fistface said.

"He can't," Gabe said, "because of his hair."

And Mara screamed and Rex's rug floated to the surface like a gray rat, and now everybody was screaming and two men with beer bellies were trying to haul Rex up and the doves were out of their cage and Gabe was out of the pool trying to hold onto Mara who was screaming and clawing with her long white arms and a short Mexican-looking guy was standing by the poolhouse door holding a large pizza box. Jesus.

TIGERS ARE WHO'S HERE

4

Foreign Words

Chiaroscuro

Vertige

Pipistrello

Farfalla

Sizwe

Pamplemousse

Jacaranda

Iliovasilema

Mousseline

Auto-da-Fé

Bienvenue

Lavabo

Carapace

Sausalito

Jeu de Mots

Gitane

Mal Hibou

Glossolalia

Mackalahoopoo

Fellatio

Oct. 1981

Beautiful things. Major weirdshit.

That could be how life has to work. If you want to be out where the wonderstuff is, there's also got to be more ripping and tearing, more grenades. Maybe the only way to live a grenadeless life is to run a laundromat like Midge's mother in Kits. Dick-all happens in the Green Machines Biodegradable Laundrette, but Mrs. Newsome, Midge's mum, has the calmest face I've ever seen on an undrugged person over five years old. If those are the choices, then there's been, grenade-crazy and all, way too much magic for me to choose anything but this. It started with Didi, and certainly with Pascal. But the explosion into where you're way high up, and flying and falling at the same up and down weaving time—that definitely started with Gilbey.

I woke up at dawn. In the poolhouse. Wonky. It was too early, but the Los Angeloid white-bright was still winning that war. When L.A. sunlight wants you up, up you get.

I packed. Everything. Folded things that weren't mine (towels and Little Pam's swimsuit). Pulled on my jeans. Looked at the tanktop I'd laid out. Black, because somebody died. Yuck. I was bored, bored, bored with tanktops, tanktops, tanktops. My satin jacket and new cotton sweater were too dress-up. Gabe had left a faded denim shirt hanging on the loo door. Not as brilliantly, perfectly faded as Pascal's, but pretty damn good. It didn't seem quite right to take shirts from someone whose father just kakked forever by flopping wig-first into the pool. But Rex was dead, and he did have denim shirts out the wazoo. Now all those shirts belonged to Gabe, Son of Cowboy Movie Star (funny how you can find a really solid reason for doing what you want to do). I put the shirt on. It was soft and had a nice Gabesmell.

Casa del Cielo was quiet. Two women, one the exact miniature of the other, were sitting silently on the chesterfield, small, pudgy hands folded, Good Little Girl style, in their bathtub-size laps. The Pams. Had to be. Their skins were part pink, part pale, like the inside of conch shells. Soupbowl-cut black hair. Both wore thin sleeveless sundresses. Big Pam's was cream yellow with little red and blue flowers, Little Pam's, baby blue. They were barefoot. Leg flesh rolled over their anklebones. Round little feet with fat pink toes. Their perfect-circle, coral-cheeked faces were so full that it squinted their eyes, making them look like parade float-sized versions of those dashboard stick-on dolls with the bobbing heads.

When they saw me, they smiled, quick and frozen, like a group painting by Hanna, Barbera and Botero. The bigger one stood up, hands pushing herself free of the chesterfield.

"Hello, darlin'. I'm Big Pam. This is my daughter, Little Pam."

"I'm Roanne."

"Yes. We saw you . . . last night. With Gabriel."

"Where is . . . Gabriel?"

"He's in with his mother, dear. Everyone else from the C.R.C. went home. We said we'd stay. We slept out here, on the sofa."

I looked at "the sofa." They must've taken turns. Otherwise there was no way, unless they stacked themselves like fireplace logs. Or soft lumber. Seriously soft lumber. The thought made me want to draw, want to giggle. I fought it down, hoping my smileflicker-twitch looked like friendliness.

"We've made flapjacks and bacon, dear. Would you like some breakfast?"

I was hungry, but it didn't feel right to be filling my face if Gabe came out. "No, thanks, I'll just have a muffin." I lifted the cookie-jar lid. Two tiny muffos were in there from two days earlier, hard as little brown doorstops.

"Roe."

Gabe looked wasted. Wasted and lost. I wanted to hug him, but felt self-conscious in front of the now-standing-side-by-side Pams.

"I borrowed your shirt."

"Sure."

"Is Mara OK?"

"Yah. She is now. Dr. Baxter came. Gave her something so she could sleep. It took a while. She was . . ."

"Freaked?"

"Yah. Screaming, crying and laughing. Finally, she got real quiet and we put her to bed. Then we were all out here trying to figure what we were supposed to do and somebody called the Blessed Shepherd Funeral Home and Rex was lying on the floor and Darlette Hanson had his hairpiece in the palm of her hand and was blow-drying it. Then Mara was out of bed, in the little john, smashing pictures and singing 'OH-klahoma, where the sun comes right behind the rain,' like she used to when she'd take me on her horse when I was little, and . . ." He was getting all gulped-up, swallowing too much air.

"Easy, Gabe. It's OK. . . . Pams? Could I talk to Gabe for a minute, just by ourselves, please?"

"Of course, dear. We'll sit with Mara."

"Don't wake her."

"We won't, Gabriel. We'll be quiet as mice."

They waddled off down the hall, rumps rolling. I took Gabe's hand and guided him to the chesterfield. Sat him down. Sat down beside him, rubbed his cheek with the back of my hand. He stared at his knees for a while. Then he looked at me with that open babygaze, and said, "I don't know how to do this."

"Nobody knows how to do this, Gabe-o. You're doing fine. And you've got all the Rebirthies to stay and help, and . . ."

"Will you? Will you stay and help?"

I knew it was coming. Knew it had to come. No guts, me.

"I'll try, Gabe, for a while."

He was crying and hugging me and saying, "I love you, Roe," and it was like I was in a vat of yellow-green hair gel that was reaching past my mouth to my noseholes and then there'd be no breathing places. None at all. And he didn't love me, not like he thought. He loved me best of what he had to love. I was what Del called "the only game in town."

• •

Dear Gabe,

You're a very special person. One of the kindest, sweetest and special-est I've ever met. In my whole life. I want to keep knowing you, I really do. And I feel like a major suck leaving. But I have to, Gabe. I really do. I've got my own shitstorm to get through. My shitstorm is at the same time as your shitstorm. There's nothing worse than simultaneous shitstorms, but that's what we've got. And it makes me pretty useless. Even for my own stuff, let alone yours. You need a grownup. I need a grownup. What I think you should do is stay here until you're sure Mara's OK (but not longer than a month or two), and then go. Go find your grown-ups. Go find your dreams. I don't want to say bad things about the dead, but you did tell me Rex was sitting on you, sitting on what you wanted to do. Now you can do those things. I don't know where I'm going to be, exactly, but when I do, I'll find you. Like I said in the chapel, I'm not really ready to be a "girlfriend," but I would like to be your FRIEND-friend, forever. Forgive me for leaving in this chickenshit way, but I couldn't find the guts to say it in the house.

Your friend,
Roanne

I put the letter in an envelope, wrote "Gabe" on it and propped it against the mirror of the poolhouse dresser. I leaned my gear against the wall and went to find Adelita.

I was hoping she would be in her little one-room house, so I could see her alone. No luck (but I was happy that she'd put my drawing of her and the angel tacos on the wall, with her other paintings and drawings).

She was in the Big House, stirring a big pot full of spicy-smelling brown stuff. Chili, I figured.

"Hi."

She turned, saw it was me, smiled a real smile. She gestured for me to come into the kitchen, pointed into the pot, then at me.

"No thanks, Adelita. I'd love to. I mean, it smells great. But I have to leave. . . . Where's Gabe?" She put her palms together, tilted her face and rested her cheek against them. "The Pams?" She made a shooing motion. "Home? Went home?" She nodded, smiled again, took a little yellow notepad out of her apron pocket. Wrote, "Thank you for the beautiful picture. You are good." I didn't know whether she meant I was good at drawing or a nice person. Either was fine. I thanked her. She touched my cheek, tilted her head in a small nod.

"Adelita?" I was whispering, realized I'd been whispering since I came in. "I need to go. Right away. Do you know the number for a taxi?" She pointed to a paper taped next to the wall phone. Doctors, pharmacies (Drugstores), people's initials, taxis (Cabs/Limos)—Ventura, Valleywood, All-Star, Yellow Valley, Celebrity. I chose Yellow Valley, because a valley all different shades of yellow was a bright, sunny picture. The guy who answered said "driver 327" would "be there in fifteen to twenty minutes." I told him I'd be at the main gate, the one with the big logs. I hung up, I whispered to Adelita that I was really glad to meet her, that I hoped to see her again, that I'd left a note for Gabe on the poolhouse dresser. We snortsmiled at eachother and I thought I might blubber (something about Adelita always made me teary. It wasn't the tonguelessness. I'm not usually oogus-boogus about most things, but it was like we knew each other, in some very intense way, from another life). I thanked her, touched her face real quick and took off for the poolhouse.

A knock. "Shit," I thought, "I can't fight about this." But it was Adelita. She held out a supermarket bag with little containers in it. Red plastic fork and spoon, paper napkins. I took it. Said she didn't have to. That I was glad she did. Said thank you, again. She held out her copper-brown open palm. In it was a small green stone carving. A face, with the full, curving open lips of the sexy-mouthed painting I'd seen on her wall. With that mouth, its almond-shaped eyes and flaring nostrils, it looked like a cross between a cat and a baby. It was truly beautiful, had what Del called "major mojo" coming off it. Adelita ran a dark leather thong, like the one for Gabe's lifetime key, through two little holes in the catbaby forehead. She fluttered her hands up-up-up and I held my hair off my neck. She went behind me and knotted the thong. Catbaby rested in my throat dent, like it had always lived there. The stone felt cool.

There was honking. "The taxi! 'Bye, Adelita. Thanks again. I think you're really super! Tell him about my letter, it's over there, tell him I really had to . . ."

More honking, and I've slung all my gear over each of my shoulders, and I'm running and clunking past the pool and across the field to the gate, to the man from the Yellow Valley, and he wants to know if I want to put my stuff in the trunk and I'm saying no that's OK, and I'm in the taxi, which is bright yellow, and Gabe comes running out of the Big House and I hear myself say, "Go! Go NOW!" and the taxi is charging down the bumpy, dusty road and Gabe is still running. He's running after the taxi, and I actually think he's going to catch us, on account of his being an award-winning runner, and I'm watching through the back window, my hands pressed against the glass, like I'm trying to push him back, and I say, "Can you go faster?" and the driver says, "Don't worry, baby, we got it aced," and I keep looking and Gabe is there and there and there until the cab is driving through the streets of crazy Tarzana houses and Gabe isn't there anymore.

"Bad scene back there?"

"No. Well, yeah. I just had to go, is all."

"Yeah. OK. Do you know *where* you have to go *to?*"

I fumbled for the card in the side pocket of my bookbag. "Three thirty-four fifty-seven Malibu Colony Road."

"The Colony. That's a ways away from here. It'll cost."

"How much?"

"Forty, fifty bucks or so."

"That's OK."

"You got it."

Gabe had been nothing but good to me. He'd been stuck with the care of Mara, who was a sweet but very strung-out lady. And there was I, who he at least thought he loved, taking off like a hit-and-run. I couldn't stop seeing Gabe, racing, barefoot, after the taxi. And I knew he'd see it for a long time from his end. His bad rotten friend picking up speed and getting gone. In his denim shirt. I could've, should've, at least given back the shirt. "You're a scum-sucking bitch pig."

"What?"

"Nothing. Just talking to myself. Do you mind if I eat chili in your taxi?"

"Go ahead on. You can throw a party back there, baby, long as the neighbours don't complain."

• •

Malibu Colony was right on the beach. It was, always is, magic-happy to see the sea. The taxi pulled up alongside a skinny white guardhouse, shaped like a giant pencil. Inside the pencil sat a large man with a big, reddish face. A German shepherd next to the guardhouse had stood up out of his lie-down and was looking at me.

"Yes?"

"Hi. I'd like to see Pascal Douglas, please."

"Mr. Douglas. Right. Is he expecting you?"

"No, sir. But we're friends. I was in the neighbourhood and thought I'd say hi."

"'In the neighbourhood.' I see. Just a moment. Your name?"

"Roanne. Roanne Chappell."

He picked up a phone receiver, pressed three digits. "Mr. Douglas? It's Murph. There's a Miss Chaplin here to see you."

"CHAPPELL. ROANNE CHAPPELL."

"Sorry, miss. It's 'Chappell,' sir, Miss Roe Anne Chappell. Right. Very good, sir, will do. You can go through, miss. Turn right at the end of the drive here. It's the third house down."

All of a sudden it was real. I hadn't phoned or anything, and felt squirrelly about barging in with all my gear. I asked the guardhouse man if I could leave my stuff with him. He said sure. The taxi meter read $47.80. The driver got out, opened the back door, passed my two bags to Murph, who put them under a tiny table attached to the wall. The dog was snurfling me in a friendly way.

"What's his name?"

"Grady."

"Hi, Grady." Grady let himself be petted, licked my toes.

"Well, that just about gits it, baby. You gone be OK?"

"Yeh, I think so."

"Well, if you ever need a getaway cab again, here's my card."

I looked at him for the first time since we charged out of Tarzana. Super-skinny, tight black T-shirt, tight jeans. Black straight hair, combed back into a low ponytail. Thin walrus-type moustache, and an amazing red-and-black tattoo running from above his elbow almost to his shoulder. A snake eating a bear, ass-end first. The head and furry neck of the bear stuck out of the snake's mouth. The rest of the bear bulged inside the snake.

"Great tattoo."

"Thank you, ma'am."

I gave him $55. He flicked his index finger off his forehead, got into his taxi and drove off. I headed down the laneway toward the houses and the sea.

Crazy mix 'n' match California houses again. An almost gingerbread Hansel-and-Greteloid number, then a big creamy stucco with those pretty orange roof tiles, then Pascal's. Two-story white clapboard. And big old Pascal standing out in front of it. In navy sweatpants and that killer denim shirt. Smiling. Smiling full-out. Yay.

"Hello, Prowlet."

"Yeh, hi. I hope it's OK, my coming by? Without phoning and all?"

"And all. Yes, it's fine. It's lovely to see you. You've come, in fact, at a perfect time."

"I have? How come perfect?"

"Come in and you'll see. Don't be frightened, I'm right beside you."

Frightened? Why was I supposed to be frightened?

Zizanie was why. She was wearing a white suit and there wasn't a single smudge or spot on it. I want so much to wear white clothing without getting grunge on it. But I can't. Neither can Del. We always say the marks are artstuff—occupational hazard, Del calls it. But most of the time it isn't artstuff at all. It's pizza or chocolate or like that. Me and Del have the grubbies. We can't stay clean. Our bodies, yes. White clothes, no.

And here was this lady, old enough to be my mum's mum, all in white, and absolutely clean, with beige slingback high-heeled shoes, great legs, cute little bubble-butt, and able to look good in a straight skirt. A straight *white* skirt. Her face was scary, though. Scary like in the picture at Pascal's Bolinas house. Her wavy rich-lady hair was sort of Queen Elizabeth. Not the colour. The colour was a combination of caramel and gold, and looked glazed, like the Della Robbia ceramic painting kit Brian bought me for my sixth birthday. And those pale eyes. Eyes so light it was almost Little Orphan Annie Time. Those long eyes. Eyes that forgave nothing, forgave nobody. Zizanie's eyes said, "You are already in trouble for things you haven't even done yet, but will probably do between now and your death." And her lips were waging a big war. The lower lip was full, wide, made her look like the world's oldest Hot Chick. But her upper lip was thin and tight. Like it was the monitor in charge of keeping her lower lip in line.

"Zizi, this young lady is Roanne Chappell. A dear friend of Didier's and mine. A rather celebrated Canadian cartoonist. Didi framed one of her works and put it on his wall, before they had even met. What is that cartoon called, Prowlet?"

"Moose Factory."

"Yes, exactly. 'Moose Factory.' Roanne, may I present one of the treasures of liTOO Paree, indeed one of the treasures of liTOO damn near anywhere she chooses to hang her custom-made shaPOE. My mother, Madame Chantal 'Zizanie' Douglas-Hyde."

"That is quite enough, Pascal. You are frightening her. Hello, my dear." The eyes studied, studied, studied. Never gave an inch. Del's famous "Ice in Winter." The mouth did a closed, slightly up-turning thing. Smile-oid. It had nothing to do with happy. Or friendly. The Queen smiling, pre-apple, at Snow White.

When I'm scared, weirdshit rolls out of my mouth. Always did. Probably always will.

"So, you're married to Pascal's father, eh?"

"Actually, no, my dear. Not any longer. My present husband is called Yoop VanderHayden."

"Yoop?"

"VanderHayden."

"'Van Der.' That's Dutch, eh? I went to school with a Nancy VanderLinden. She was Dutch. That's how I know Van Der is Dutch."

"I see."

"She had a nose like a whole garlic, Nancy did." Pascal walked away from us, into the big kitchen that was sort of part of the big living room.

"Do you have a son with him too? With Mr. VanderHayden?"

"Why no, dear. We had . . . wanted a child, of course, but my husband was . . ."

"Shooting blanks?"

When I said this, Pascal, who was walking toward us holding a bowl of mixed nuts, dropped the bowl onto a curly white rug. Nuts went everywhere. Even if he hadn't done that, I knew "shooting blanks" was about as far from "appropriate" as it gets. I knew this even as it was going from mind to mouth to world, but by then I was pumping too fast with goofbabble to put the thing into reverse. I tried to dig out. "That's an expression of my mother's. For when a guy is—"

"Prowlet, would you like to help me pick up nuts?" He was squatted down, facing away from me, denim pulling across his big back. I practically dived into the rug, grabbing handfuls of nuts, putting them into the bowl, white rugfur and all. We eyelocked.

Pascal's whole big face was beaming at me. "It's all right, Prowlet. It's better than all right, it's bloody marvellous!" he said in a whisper. The bowl was now full of nuts and rugfuzzies. He stood up. I did too. A little too fast. Got dizzy (that always happens when I stand up too fast). Lost my balance. Fell back onto my bum on the rug. Pascal laughed. It wasn't a mean laugh. A horn honked outside. "Well, here's your taxi for the airport, Zizi. Roanne, I'll see my mother to her cab and then we'll get things together for the party." He offered her his hand, which she used to pull herself up out of the big, phlumphy white chesterfield.

"Oh. Sure. Nice to meet you, Mrs. VanderLinden . . . Hayden," says I, still sitting where I had fallen. Zizanie made a quick, closed-lips tight smiley mouth. She tilted her face slightly to the right, closed her eyes, nodded once, turned her back to me and headed for the door like a well-dressed knife with a cute ass. I decided that Zizi's ass was the friendliest, happiest thing about her. Probably because it was behind her, where she couldn't sneer at it or tell it what to do. She and Pascal were just outside the door, speaking French. I couldn't understand, except for "see voolGAIR!" I'd never heard "voolgair" before, but I knew what it meant, and knew she meant me.

Pascal stood in the doorway, shaking his head and grinning. "Nothing stops her. Absolutely nothing. She's like a bullet train. But you did it. Stopped her dead in her shining silver tracks. Bless you for it. Bless you forever." As he was blessing me, he wrapped me up in this big wonderful hug. He smelled like limes and I thought, Let me stay here. Inside Pascal's hug. Let me just stay here, without having to figure out all the What the Fucks, Where the Fucks and How the Fucks of my life. He released me. Rumpled my hair, grinning still.

"Party?"

"Hmm?"

"You said something about a party."

"Ah. So I did. As it happens, there's to be a party here this evening. For a young friend of mine. A sweet sixteen party. Her actual birthday was sometime last week, but tonight was the best time to let her use this place."

"Oh, I'm 16 next week." (I was starting to actually believe I was going to be 16 in September instead of 15 in December.) I watched his face to see if Didi'd told him my real age. Didn't look like it.

He nodded. "Ah. Perfect. We'll make it a party for you as well, then. I'm sure Gilbey won't mind. She's a generous-hearted creature in her way."

"Is she your girlfriend, this Gilbey?"

"Good lord, no. She's a chum, our Gilbey. Models for me on occasion. Uses this house as an emergency landing strip. I think you'll like her. Lots of energy. Funny. Quite good-looking. And, seemingly, has no petty jealousies about other women. That's unusual in this town. Very. And commendable."

As he told me all this "Gilbey stuff," Pascal was taking prepared munchfoods out of a huge black fridge and then sorting out boozes at a black-and-white bar that was angled in a corner by the glass doors that faced the beach. Everything was all in one big undivided space. California people were definitely not into rooms with doors and walls. Canadians had rooms. Oregonians had rooms. English people always had rooms. But Californians, at least the ones I'd met so far, had "spaces." Like art galleries do. Or airports. Or waiting rooms. California had these big, expensive-looking waiting rooms. In colours that would get dirty if they were mine. Or Del's.

Pascal lit one of his short fat French gypsy cigarettes. "I've not had a chance to ask you, Prowlet, what exactly are you doing here? In Los Angeles."

"Uh. Waiting. For my mum."

"Oh? Didn't you say you were meeting her in Oregon? Washington?"

"Oregon. Yeah, that was what was supposed to happen. But this L.A. art dealer wants to talk to her, see her portfolio. So she said she'd pick me up here. In the Morgan. And we'd drive back to Vancouver."

"I see. And when is this happening? This 'pick up in the Morgan'?"

"Next week. She said next week. Thursday."

"That would be next week and a half. Don't you have some sort of school to be attending?"

"Yes. Canadian school starts later. In October."

"Aha. And where are you staying? While you wait for Mother and Morgan?"

"Uh, I hadn't sorted that part out. I was wondering if . . ."

He sat in a corner of the megachesterfield, put out his cig. "If you could stay here? Is that what you were wondering?"

I was sweating under my tits. Like I always do when I'm nervous. Not under my arms. Never my pits. Always my tits. I wasn't going to beg. Begging is scuzzy. "No. Not . . . necessarily. I know this other friend of my mum's I can call and—"

"Easy, Prowlet, easy. Sit." He pointed, with his head, to the other end of the chester. I sat. "Of course you can stay here. For a few days, at any rate. There's a little guesthouse. That's not a problem." He got up and walked to the glass doors. Turned round to face me. Sighed. "The problem, the concern, is about your age. The Yanks have some very peculiar notions about age and womanhood. I don't know if Canadians have these notions as well. In any event, we're not in Canada. And I do know that your mother has some very definite ideas about where you are and why. Didi told me about the phone conversation at Inn Nainity. He said she was quite angry. I try to lead a reasonably calm and uncomplicated life, Prowlet. I'm . . . pleased to see you, but I do not need to have some crazed mother descend upon me screaming rape, statutory or otherwise. Do you understand?"

Did I understand? Understand what? That he wanted, oh pleasepleaseplease, to sleep with me? That he was afraid of Del whether he slept with me or not? What did rape have to do with it? What was "statutory"? My face felt hot. I stood up. "Look, Pascal, why don't I just take off? I just thought I'd say hi. I can stay—"

He crossed the room, took me gently by the shoulders. "Oh,

dear. I didn't intend this to become so . . . grave. It's a rotten way to begin a celebration of one's seventeenth year on earth. Why don't we, for the moment, just have our party. You are most welcome to stay the night here. We can sort the rest of it out tomorrow. How would that be?"

"Good. It would be good."

"Good." He laughed. "That it would be good is good. Now, then, don't you have any gear?"

"It's in the pencil."

"Pencil?"

"The guardhouse thing. Murph's got it."

• •

Pascal's guesthouse was a sweet space. A small room, all white (again) except for deep blue floor-length curtains on both windows, one of which faced the sea. Kitchenstuff was built into the wall (sink, electric range, white fridge). The queen-sized bed was "wrought iron" painted white (like Del's), with a white patch quilt that had a red star in the middle of each patch. There was a white wicker bedtable. On this table was a white globe lamp, and an ashtray shaped like a whale. A teeny-tiny telly (what Del calls a "belly telly"—Stavro had one) sat on a wooden dresser that had an oval mirror attached.

In a wicker magazine rack, next to the dresser, were fashion and photography mags, a six-month-old French newspaper called *Le Monde* and something called *The Hollywood Reporter.* After I hung up the really few possibilities for party clothes (all wrinkled to ratshit—I pulled on them for a while, then put them on hangers and hoped for the best), I took a look at the *Reporter.* It was all about how much money movies cost, and how much they made (amazing amounts. Enough for lots of people to live on from what Del calls "womb to tomb") and who was hired for different films. I recognized some of the movie star names. There were also weird-sounding jobs. Grip. Gaffer. Best Boy! What the hell did a "Best Boy" do? Was he really a boy? Who decided he was the best? Best at what? I had to ask Pascal. And I definitely had to ask him what a "prowlet" was.

Pascal had said the party would start "about eight." I decided to go there about nine, because roomfuls of strangers are scary. It's easier to slip in when they're all there and nattering. I had lots of time. Wrote and drew for a while, which helped cool me out. A little.

I took a long bath, using the tiny plastic bottle of orange bubblestuff in the guesthouse loo. Decided not to think about what I was going to say or do when morning came, or what Pascal might say/do. My peachy satin jacket was still too wrinkled to wear anywhere, except maybe in a roomful of blind people (and even they'd be grossed out if they felt me). Decided to try the off-one-shoulder crocheted sweater I'd bought in San Francisco. Retied Adelita's catbaby around my neck for luck. Put on white panties and, my best thing, the white Victorian petticoat. Still a bit wrinkly as well, but the layers of old lace ruffles made the wrinkles look *almost* like they were supposed to be there. Put on the sweater. Nipple crisis! I could see, through the open crochet, very clearly, two pinky-brown nipples. Took off sweater. Put on black tank. Didn't go. Needed a belt. Looked majorly like shit. Decision required. Shitty Outfit or Visible Nips? No contest. Took off tank, put sweater back on. Nips did look sort of hot—I just didn't want Pascal's friends, or Pascal, to think I was a slut-bimbo. Or nudge eachother and whisper, point and laugh. Like at school.

The gray flatstone walkway leading to the glass doors was lit by little black metal lamps stuck into the ground on either side of the walk. The big room was jammed with bods. I deked to the left of the glass doors, so I could peek in without being seen. Most of the girls/women, some of whose nips I could see (good), were younger and prettier than any roomful of women I could remember ever being in. And most of the men were older and uglier. I could see about seven young, nice-looking guys, but at least three of them were serving drinks and munchfood. A lot of the old guys were bald or balding. Most were short, and tan. One was tall and had no headhair at all. Bald as the guesthouse lamp. Very tan. He was goodlooking, in an old richguy sort of way. One tiny (but not dwarf) old guy was sitting in the big leather chair by the fireplace, wearing a black velvet suit. He had rings on almost every one of his delicate fingers. His silver-gray hair was combed like in pictures of

Napoleon. Each arm of his chair had a great-looking girl sitting on it. One of these girls had long blonde hair. And Visible Nips. Pascal had said the Gilb had long blonde hair. Actually, there were lots of could-be-Gilbeys. Most of the women were blonde. I counted. Fourteen. Two brunettes. One very thin cutebum Asian wearing a pale green sarong with big-ish cream beige flowers. Shiny straight black hair almost to her waist. The other had black curly hair (shorter and neater than mine) and was wearing a just-below-crotch short white dress with thin straps. She was tan, had lots of makeup on. Gooey-shiny coral lips. Major black eyeliner. High, round cute boobs.

Fu-u-uck! I thought, these people are *so* pretty. Seriously glam. Roanne, go back to the guesthouse. Before anybody sees you. Take out your dictionnaire. Try to read *Le Monde*.

Then, I noticed something above my head, screwed to the clapboard. A painted wood sculpture. From naked tits to top of head. Tits full and round, just like mine. Long neck and strong clavicles, like me. Face almost exactly like mine, with a less fat nose. Eyes like mine. Mouth like mine. Crazy-curly black hair. Just like mine! I knew all at once, the way you sometimes do. This was Prowlet. And Pascal thought she was good enough to live attached to his house. Every day. All of a sudden it was cool. I was cool. I could do this. "Thank you, Prowlet," I whispered. And slid open the glass door.

Pascal, in his silky white shirt, white pants and skinny black belt, was at the kitchen counter, talking to an older woman (there was one, after all). She had short, shaggy pale blonde and gray hair and wore a loose-fitting man-type white suit. No shirt or blouse. Tanned skin. No makeup. Thin gold chain around her neck. Major cheekbones. She looked super. Pascal grinned, waved. "Ah. At last, one of our birthday girls has arrived," he said, moving towards me.

There was soft, flute-y music, but some of the others heard the greeting and looked at me. Like when there's an ambulance and police, more others noticed the first group looking and they looked too. Pascal put his arm around my shoulders. I was wishing he'd've just let me hang out and arrive slowly.

"This is Roanne Chappell everybody. A dear friend of my brother's . . . a fellow cartoonist. And, like the late, the very late Gilbey Tarr, about to be sixteen." Some people said "hi" or "happy birthday." Others smiled and went back to their conversations. "Not knowing everyone in the room, I won't attempt introductions. This is Roanne's first night here, so don't run at her, but do make her feel welcome. Want a glass of wine, Prowlet?"

I didn't really like wine, but didn't want to look like a little kid on my bogus almost-sixteenth birthday. "Yeh. OK, sure." He walked me over to the kitchen counter, where the wine bottles were lined up.

"Red or white? Roanne, this is Corie Layton."

"I dunno. White, I guess. (Less likely to be clumsied all over my white petticoat, I figured.) "Hi, Corie."

"Hello, Roanne."

"Great suit." (That's it, Roanne. Jump in. Make conversation. And it *was* a great suit. A great look. I've always figured I'd know I was truly on the road to Grownup when I knew what "my look" was. Mostly, so far, I just try, when I remember, to not look like shit.)

Corie Layton made a little "hhn" laugh, then smiled a full-out major white teeth smile. I'd already noticed, after Pascal's Birthday Girl announcement, that a lot of these people had terrific teeth. Mine were pretty good for whiteness, but one of the two front ones was slightly farther forward, and one of the side-lowers chipped when I was eleven and punched Anton the Asshole in the eye and he punched me in the mouth.

"Thank you, Roanne. Glad you like it."

"Corie Layton. I know your name. . . . Did you write a book about single parents?"

"Yes, I did. *Creative Solo Parenting.*"

"Right! My mum has it."

"Oh? Did she like it?"

"Yes, a lot. Especially the part about how too much television stops a child from making her own images. I get three shows a week. Actually, she still has that book. We travel a lot, so we're only allowed to keep seriously favourite books."

"I'm pleased. Are you travelling now?"

"Sort of. I mean, *I* am. She's coming down to pick me up. She's an artist."

"Oh. What kind?"

"Painting and sculpture. Her most famous thing is album covers. Mostly in the 60s and early 70s. But she did one last year. For *The British Blues Retrospective.*"

"Sounds interesting."

No, it didn't. I could tell. She was being really nice, but I knew. I was glad when Pascal handed me the glass of white wine.

"Yuck." It tasted sour and nasty.

"Yuck! What do you mean, 'yuck'? I'll have you know, Prowlet, that you've bestowed your 'yuck' on a quite expensive Montrachet."

"I'm sorry."

"Don't be. I prefer red myself. Want to try my very upmarket plonk rouge?"

"Yes, please."

He emptied the white into the sink, rinsed the glass and poured in some red. Better. Tasted more like food. Liquid food. I looked at the label. "Aloxe Corton. 1964!"

"This wine was made in 1964?"

"Mm-hmm. A year before you were born."

I almost said, "No, I was born in 1967." Caught myself. "Wow! Amazing! It hasn't gone off."

The little man in the velvet suit was D'Artagnan. He was "seventy-six-and-a-half" years old and his mother had named him for one of the guys in *The Three Musketeers.* He said my petticoat was "a very good example." He collected period clothing and invited me to visit his house in Hollywood to "talk and play." He gave me his card—was very pleased when I identified the card's colour as "ashes of roses." It said he was "D'Artagnan Roland—student and aesthete."

The two girls bookending his chair were sisters. Ashleigh (she spelled it) and Deleese (she spelled it). They were models and Deleese was studying acting with someone who'd once roomed with Marlon Brando. She'd had one job, an "under five, in a bathing suit," on *Hollywood Detective.* She was 19. Ashleigh was 17. They called D'Artagnan Dart and said his house was filled with f-a-a-bulous things. The tall, rich-looking, head-shaved guy was a producer named Kurt Hubscher. He had a Euro-accent—Brit mixed with something else. He kissed my hand. There was something creepy about his eyes. He was asking me if I was an actress, when all hell broke loose at the front door.

When we lived in Burnaby, and other kids were treating me like a hamster pellet, I started having this fantasy. I'd walk into a room at the school, like the gym, or the auditorium, with a Really Famous Person. All the kids I knew would be there, and they'd look all "duh"-mouthed and stunned. Finally, someone would say, "F-u-u-ck! Check this! It's Weird Roanne!" Then another duh-face would say, "With Queen Elizabeth!" Or whoever. And they'd start being all friendly, to show the Queen they were cool, because they knew me and all, but there'd be guards and stuff to separate the Mean People from the Nice and/or Famous People, and the N. and/or F. People would like their lives enough to be able to also sort of like me. Just me being Roanne, without having to figure out what other people wanted me to be.

Del's London rock 'n' roll people were like that. With Del. With the three-year-old me. With eachother. Then we came to Canada and it was never like that again. For either of us. Del says Americans think everyone in America can be famous and Canadians think no one in Canada can. Del thinks that only "Old World countries" understand that famous is "neither a requirement nor an embarrassment," just a "talent that got noticed." She says that while you're working hard, and not knowing what will or won't get noticed, it's really great to stand in the middle of a group that has "nailed that," because those people don't usually mind if something nice happens to someone else.

I had been happy nesting inside that sort of group, in London, when I was little. And here I was. In the New World. Surrounded by these perfect-looking people, and PASCAL!, when it happened again. When I got to feel something other than "wrong," in a roomful of strangers. And one of the ones who had done it in the London "then" was the one who did it in the Malibu "now." It began when Gilbey Tarr, the real sixteener, and her party, arrived.

There was this megabig, weirdassed car in front of Pascal's house. It was white and looked like somebody'd cut a tiny bit off the back of one car, and a tiny bit off the front of another car, and then glued the big parts of the two cars together. The driver, in a chauffeur outfit, opened a door and all these rock 'n' roll people got out. Five wiry little guys in jeans or supertight black stretch-velvet pants. Tight T-shirts, mostly black. Some rings, some bracelets, some earrings. Scarves. One or two black leather jackets with chains or silver studdy things on them. Shaggy hair. They had to be Brits. More style. More perfume and sweat smell, instead of the perfume and piss smell the Yank and Canadian rockers have (it would be good if rock guys bathed more, but, if that's not gonna happen, sweat is better than piss). And not one of 'em was taller than me. Yankanadians are bigger.

In the middle of this crazy bouquet of tiny rockers was a tall, majorly blonde, long-haired goddess with clear, pale skin and bright shiny red lips. She was wearing a mustard-gold satin slip and a silver metal shoulder bag that looked like a bottle. I could see her pelvis bones. No panty line. No panties. And, most amazingly, she was balanced on these superhigh-heeled gold strappy sandals that I couldn't walk in for ten steps without breaking both legs.

Some of us, including Pascal, Corie Layton and me, had gone outside when the big car rolled up, because it was horn-honking, looking for the house. There, in the light from Pascal's lamppost, the goddess stuck her hand out to me.

"Hey. I'm Gilbey. You must be Roanne."

Must I? I thought. You're so amazingly, dazzlingly, all-the-guys-in-the-world-are-going-to-howl-at-once beautiful, couldn't I please be someone else? I mean, Roanne just isn't going to cut it here. Couldn't I be Dominique, the French movie actress whose picture is part of the Beautiful Humans collage inside my closet in Kitsilano? Or Botticelli's Venus on the Halfshell? Or the one who plays Georgina on *Upstairs Downstairs?* Or the lady in the David painting who glows like she's lit from inside? Could I please, please, PLEASE by any of those?

That's what I thought. What I said was, "Uh-huh." Then she hugged me, nailing me in the belly with her killer pelvis bone, looking and smelling like she wouldn't be dirty even if you threw mud at her. Even if you could see the mud. It wasn't Perfect Order, like Zizanie. It was about glowing. It was celestial!

"Well, hey, Babygirl, happy birthday to us!" Her accent was like the taxi driver who rescued me from Casa del Cielo. Some sort of American southern. The really pretty girls I'd known at school were always such stuck-up, packrunning shits, but Gilbey seemed so friendly. Maybe it was because she was running with a pack of guys, which is, I think, less competitive.

Whatever the reason, the Gilbey Goddess was being friendly and happy and beautiful all at once, and perfectly pleased to let me be in the world with her. Then the really amazing thing happened. The front door on the passenger side opened. And. Out. Walked . . . Dickie fucking SIGGINS!

"Dickie."

"That m'name."

"It's Roanne."

He squinted, even more than usual, Dickie having slits for eyes anyway. "It's who?"

"Roanne. Rosie. Rosie Chappell."

"Del's Rosie?"

"Right."

"Not true! I don't beLEAVE it!"

And he was laughing and hugging me and saying how amazingly great this was and explaining about how I was like his baby sister or his daughter and how my mother was "like blood" to him, and all these people, these Malibu people, these people with perfect teeth and perfect tans, were looking at us and grinning and I was all warm and filled with lovegift and smack in the middle of my Queen Elizabeth fantasy, only bigger, better, because rock stars are more flash than even royalty!

So, there's me, being kissed up on by Dickie Siggins, International Pop Idol, and being introduced to the other guys in the Yobs, one of the three or four most famous rock bands in the whole world, and feeling like Cinder-fucking-rella. Stop time now! I thought. Let me stay in this moment. Let me live here, in this moment, and be safe. Why safe? Don't know, except that if Dickie Siggins and his hot band and his golden girlfriend and his driver and his big stupid car can't get safe, well then, nobody can, and at least it wasn't just me and Del having to solve the tightrope spooky every day, day after day, from womb to tomb.

The carry-on finally cooled out, and we all trooped back inside Evil Owl House, and the music kicked into high gear. Trevor Doone, the Yobs's keyboard guy, started playing heavy-duty rock blues on Pascal's piano. Dickie and Gilbey did this majorly sexy dance, featuring their lower bodies. Gilbey's sun-butter blonde hair flying and glowing under Pascal's fancy ceiling lights. People were clapping in rhythm, and Kurt Hubscher, the shave-headed tan old slicko, was looking at Gilbey like she was dinner.

Dinner. Suddenly I was seriously hungry. Ate six or seven smoked-salmon-on-biscuit things, and three or four of what tasted like either clams or garlic-flavoured elastic bands. Washed this down with a glass of Pascal's upmarket plonk rouge. Drank it too fast, because I was drinking for wash-down rather than for booze-up. Felt a bit wonky. And there was Dickie, asking if I remembered any of the songs he taught me when I was little.

"Yeh, sure. Like what?"

"Dunno . . . 'My Old Man'?"

"Yeh! Yeh, I do. Sang that in the woods about a month ago."

"Did ye? Wanna try it now?"

"Alone?"

"No, wit' me."

"OK." So we did. We sang "My Old Man" together, dancing and pulling faces and carrying on like a pair of old music hall looners. And everyone loved it and cheered and applauded and stuff, and then we sat down on the floor and did this blues thing he had taught me when I was nine and he visited us in Vancouver.

Up on Black Mountain,
Li'l chile will sla-ap yo' face;
I say, up on Black Mountain,
Li'l chile will sla-ap yo' face.
All the women chew rusty na-ails,
An' all the bi-irds sing bass . . .

We did six verses of that, with Trevor Doone playing piano, and Neil Campbell, the Yobs's drummer, beating the shit out of the top of the bar, and Charlie Fields, their bass player, singing "*bom-bom-bom-BOM*" over and over.

"In-bloody-credible," Dickie said when we finished, and everyone was, amazingly, cheering again. "You remembered that thing all this time!"

"I remember every word that was ever said to me by someone I care about. And most of what anyone else says as well."

"Amazing."

"That's what Del says."

"Del. Where in hell is Del anyway? I tried to ring from Devon to tell her we were coming over."

"Oregon. North of here. Teaching a summer art class for grown-ups."

He pulled me into a corner, turning his back on the others and leaning in, in that way that tells people you're having a private conversation.

"You're here alone, then, Rosie?"

"Roanne. I use Roanne now. No, not really alone. I mean, Del is coming down here next week. To do some gallery business. And then take me home. To B.C. To Kits. We still live there. I'm in high school now. Second year. I don't know what that is in the U.K. It's a little scary. I mean, I was going to this smallish 'alternative' school before. The high school is this truly *huge* building, and they ring this really loud bell between classes and thousands of people pour out of everywhere all at once."

I was full-out babbling and pretty sure Dickie knew I was talking through my ass and covering like crazy.

"Where are you staying?"

"With Pascal." I gestured with my head.

"Black Bart? Huge fucker, innee? A friend of Del's, izzee?"

"Uh-uh. Friend of mine. The brother of one of my best friends, actually."

"Mm. Does Del know him?"

"Not really. It's cool, Dickie, really. Everything's O.K. It's just for a week. It's not a sex thing or anything. It's really cool. Please don't blow my cover."

"Your cover?"

"Yeh. I'm having this great superamazing time! One of the best times of my whole entire life . . . and they all think I'm gonna be 16 next week and if you say anything they'll all get nervous and suspicious and pissed off and everything and it'll all turn to ratshit." (I whispered this last part, the age part, into Dickie's ear, so that nobody could hear it, though I'd been saying all the rest of it pretty softly too.)

"I dunno, Ros—Roanne. The band's playing Vancouver in a fortnight's time. What am I supposed to say to Del?"

"I'll be back by then. Home. With Del. It'll all be cool. We can check with eachother then, you and me, OK? Please."

"Oh, gawd. Teen shit. All right, love. I'm awfully glad to see you, and you look bloody great and happy and all, and I don't want to bugger up . . . what promises to be the first of many sweet sixteen parties over the years." He laughed, showing his big, white, rabbity teeth, his squinty eyeballs disappearing. I hugged him and kissed his cheek. "Easy, baby," he sort of shouted, laughing. "Between you and Gilbey, I'm gonna get busted in the colonies without ever gettin' off!"

Gilbey heard her name and swung over, sucking from her silver purse. It wasn't a purse that looked like a bottle. It *was* a bottle. What she called her "ancestral flask." It had belonged to her grandfather, and had his initials "R.L.T." carved on it in curly letters. "Hey. Sumbuddy here lookin' to get off? That what I heard?"

"Stay calm, baby, just a figger of speech," Dickie said and tugged on her hair in a friendly way. Then he said he needed to libate. "You birthday girls hang together for a moment. And stay out of trouble. Fat bloody chance."

He headed for the bar, and his hole in the picture was immediately filled by a fat reddy-gray-haired guy with a bushy moustache and major Death-Breath. I mean, the worst, shittiest-smelling breath I had ever inhaled. He was chatting a streak, flirting like crazy. I was breathing through my mouth and smiling and trying not to gag. Gilbey was doing the same thing, and wanting, I could tell from her eyes, to burst out laughing. Finally, she said, "Hey, Roanne, you ever gonna show me your new dress?"

"My dress? Oh, right. Yeah, sure, follow me."

Pascal, standing by the glass doors, talking with Corie and the Asian skinny-sarong lady, said, "Where are you two off to?"

"My room. To look at something."

"And a joy to look at it will indeed be," he said, or some tangled-up sentence like that, and he snortlaughed, and Corie gave a little "Ha!" It wasn't mean or anything. Just slightly higher on the mountain than where Gilbey and I were. A little cold, but mostly about being older, I think.

When we got to the guesthouse door, Gilbey let her breath out, going "Poooh." We both giggled and ducked into my little room.

"That guy, eh! What a smell! Megabarf! You've got to wonder what the hell he's eating!"

"That's Ernest. He's a producer. Everybody talks about the breath mess, but nobody says a mumblin' to him about it. Because he's had these hits. Action hits. 'Big Dumb Guys with Fast Fists and Feet' hits. *Tokyo Deathgrip* was his. And the *Crusher Jones* films."

"I've heard of those. Never saw them. And it's no excuse anyway. Nobody's got a right to smell like that if they plan to breathe out in front of anybody else's face." I was so pissed at the guy for smelling so gag-making that Gilbey laughed at me, which made me laugh too.

"Yeah, yeah, I know. My daddy says a small animal crawled up between his dentures and his gumline and died there . . ." I could see this teeny-tiny furry creature doing that, and the picture gave me another gigglefit, and me and Gilbey fell onto the bed, larfin'. She held out the silver flask, still giggling. "Here, have a shot. It'll chase the smell away."

"What is it?"

"Rock 'n' Rye."

"What's that?"

"Booze, Babygirl. Candy-coloured 'shine. A white-trash delicacy. Take a swig. It'll warm the ice ball."

"What ice ball?"

"The ice ball in the center of the whole damn thing. Go on, Birthday Buddy. It's a birthday bond. Two on a flask." Her incredible pale perfect face and soft brown eyes had gone all serious, like my drinking from her flask was a Really Important Friend Thing. I wanted to be her friend. I was thrilled all to hell that she wanted to be mine. I drank. It was sweet and strong at the same time, and burned my throat. Didn't much like it. Didn't much like any of the boozes I'd tasted so far in my life. Did like the ritual of drinking from her flask, though. I grinned at her like a goof. She grinned back.

"You're all right," she said.

Someone knocked hard on the door. I jumped up and screamed.

"Are you two decent?"

"No way, 'Scal. We're havin' a big ol' dickless frenzy in here."

Pascal opened the door, pretty much filling the whole space, smiling gently, shaking his head. "I dunno about this duo. In any event, this is your joint—"

"JointLESS."

"Ssh. Gawd, they'll let anyone be a debutante in this country. . . . As I was saying, this is your joint birthday party, and it's time to blow—"

"Oh, blow, blow, blow. Duddn't ennybody cuddle ennymore?"

"To blow out your 16 candles. Up we go." And he yanked Gilbey onto her feet. She looked in the dresser mirror, combing her hair with her fingers.

"You can use my brush," I said.

"Naw, it's cool. This your lipstick? Can I borrow?"

"Sure. It's not red."

"'Pale terra cotta.' Nice colour."

"Thanks."

"It's not that this isn't fascinating, girls . . ."

"Yeah, yeah, OK. Let's do it. Birthday girls together. Teen queens against the whole damn world!" She hooked my arm and up the lane we went in the nighttime sea air, Pascal bringing up the rear, muttering about what he could possibly have been thinking when he agreed to this.

The cake was perfect. Big, round and whipped creamy. A pair of yellow roses, and, in the center, two girlfaces, one with long straight yellow hair and another with curly dark-chocolate hair.

"Wow. How'd you get this? With Gilbey and me on it, I mean."

"Described the two of you on the phone to the baker, Hollywood Hot Cakes."

"Wow."

"Welcome to Howling Wood, Prowlet, where anything you can

describe can be yours. Especially if it's edible. Which, of course, everyone is." He sounded sort of quietly angry, but I was flying too high to stop and check on his bummer.

We blew out the candles (I did most of it, Gilbey being, by this time, pretty drunk). Then Dickie sang the Irish Happy Birthday song, the one Brian used to sing.

Why was ye born so beautiful?
Why was ye bo-o-orn atall?
Yer no fuckin' use to annyone,
yer no fuckin' UUUSE atall!

About half the people had left, including (yay!) Ernest Death Breath. Corie Layton and the sarong lady were also gone. D'Artagnan Roland, Ashleigh and Deleese were leaving. D'Artagnan said, "A very happy birthday to you both. You have my card, dear. If you'd enjoy seeing my clothing collection, do phone, and we'll arrange a visit. Gilbey knows how to get there. As does Pascal."

"Thanks. I'd love to. I will."

Dickie stood in front of me, grinning. With his suntan, his streaky blondy-brown hair and the deep creases in his face, he looked like a cross between the Dickens porcelain urchin from my room in Kits and the tiny old aboriginal shaman from the film they showed at last year's Save the Earth Festival. He took my face in his hands. "Happy, happy birthday, luv," he croak-whispered. "I'm going to go as well, I'm shagged. We're on a plane at the crutch of doom. Playin' the Cow Palace tomorrow night."

"The what?"

"Cow Palace. It's a big arena in San Francisco."

"Hey! I'm goin' up for the show. The guys have their own plane, a charter. There's plenny of room. Dickie! Can Roanne come too?"

"Sure, Gilb. Sure, if she wants to. You want to?"

"To see the Yobs live? I haven't done that since I was nine! Yes! Big yes! That would be great! If you're sure it's cool."

"Of course it's cool. It's done. We're all crashing at Gilbey's tonight. You have to be there at 8:30 A.M. That's in six and a half hours. Can you cut that?"

"Sure she can. We're young an' strong. You're the old guys."

"Any more of that, Blondie, and you can run behind the limo all the way to the airstrip."

"How do I get to the house?"

"It's just down the beach. 'Scal can point you there. Hey, 'Scal! Can you tell Roanne how to get to my place tomorrow morning?"

Pascal was across the room, saying good night to some people who were leaving via the beach. "Don't bellow at me, Aphrodite," he shouted, "it stands your beauty on its head." Kurt Hubscher, who had joined our clump of humans, said that Gilbey's beauty would be "spectacular" standing on its head. Gilbey laughed, and said something that began with "hey," and Dickie ruffled my hair, kissed my nose, said, "Eight-thirty sharp" and "Let's go, group." The group went.

And there I was, wondering if I'd imagined the whole magical perfect thing. Then Kurt Hubscher said, "So. Where do you live, my dear? May I offer you a ride?"

"I'm staying here. In the guesthouse."

"I see." He said this in a low, almost catpurr rumble, like whatever he "saw" was sort of pervo-creepy. I said "good night," and that it was "good to meet" him (because I was brought up to say that when I was leaving a new acquaintance), headed for the guesthouse (I needed an alarm clock, but figured I could ask Pascal for one once Kurt had split).

I took off the white petticoat. Two tiny wine stains and a yellow-brown bit of foodgunk. For me, not bad. Kept the silky sweater on. I'd been having such a super time I'd forgotten all about my Visible Nips. There they were. "Hi, guys," I said and lay down on the floor to zip up my jeans. Got up. Looked in the mirror. "Huhn. I'll be damned." I thought I actually looked pretty. I almost never think this. Figured it was something that happened when a reasonably non-ugly person was happy.

I turned off the lights and peeked out the guesthouse door. I could see Pascal fussing about in the kitchen. Couldn't see anybody else.

"Can I help?"

"Just about done, Prowlet. Going to make a small tisane and turn in. Interest you?"

I figured he meant the "tisane," not the "turning in," but my face got all hot. "Yes, please. I've been invited up to San Francisco for the Yobs concert tomorrow. In a private plane! It's in the cows place!"

"Cow. Singular. Are you going to go?"

"Oh, for sure! GOT to! It's kind of a once-in-a-lifetime thing, eh? We have to leave at 8:30 in the morning. Sharp, Dickie said. Can I borrow an alarm clock?"

"Of course. How will you get back from San Francisco?"

"Shit. Don't know. Didn't think of that. With Gilbey, I guess. I mean, I suppose she's coming back. If not, Dickie would probably lend me some money. He's sort of like family."

Pascal poured our tisanes into bright yellow Japanese-y cups and we both flopped down onto the big chesterfield. "Yes. I saw that. Kids are always saying they know pop stars, but you truly do." Kids. I stretched both arms above my head, pretending to yawn. See my Very Adult Boobs.

"Tired?"

"Not as much as I should be. I'm not gonna get much sleep."

"True enough. With all the flash, you probably won't sleep properly until you're back here. Of course, your family friend, Mr. Siggins, could also send you home. To Vancouver. But I suppose that won't work if you're supposed to wait here. For your mother."

Eyelock. Big, deep eyelock. He knew. Just like Dickie knew.

"Look, Pascal, I will clear off. As soon as I get back. I don't want to take advantage or anything. I'd just like to stash my gear here until after the Yobs gig."

He was still looking at me in this intense way, but he didn't seem angry or anything. "Don't worry, Prowlet. It's all right. It's fine. We'll sort it out when you return from your adventure. Now, I'll get you that alarm clock."

In my guesthouse bed, between cool sheets, breathing sea air and watching the shapes and shadows on the ceiling, I knew I should go to sleep, but was megawired with all the stuff that had happened and couldn't turn off my mind.

Gilbey. Nobody like that had ever chosen me for a friend before. Nobody like that had ever even appeared in front of my eyeballs before. Corie Layton. A whole other kind of "glam." I didn't know quite what it was but I could tell it was some sort of major. The painted wooden Prowlet lady. Pascal. Dumb crush? The Big L? Something completely else? Did it make any damn difference? Dickie. Dickie! Everything about reconnecting with him was super-perfect. How it happened. Where it happened. The fact that it was still happening. And, finally, Del. I'd been ducking Del all night, but she was there, there for the whole thing. I mean, if it weren't for Del, the whole Dickie Siggins Malibu Miracle would not, could not have happened. Dickie's whole feeling for me, a feeling everyone at my "sweet sixteen" (!!!) party could see, existed because I was the daughter of someone he'd loved like a sister for a very long time, someone he'd been through a lot of Life Stuff with. Someone I'd loved all my life. Still loved. I flooded up with Del-Roanne sweetness, so strong it made me cry. It was like, in one night, at Evil Owl House, major things had changed. I mean, I still didn't want to go home. More than ever, I didn't want to, but for a whole pile of new and different reasons. I mean, the Marcus thing was still a piss-off, and Del and me, Del and I, had stuff to work out in the "guys" zone, but even that wasn't the Big Thing anymore. The Big Thing was that the world was full of these amazing people, these amazing places. Learning was great, the Best. But school was a Big Fuckin' Drag. The Worst. Teenagers, "ordinary" teenagers, hated me and made fun of me all the time. Gilbey was a teenager and she liked me . . . but Gilbey was the Teenage Goddess from Outer Space. She probably liked me because she recognized another, much less beautiful, space case. No matter how good people are at being on their own (and Del and me were really good at it), they still want to, maybe even need to, have "their group." Del, and some of the Del-people, had been my only group. Now, for the first time ever, I felt like I might be able to build my own group. Roanne People. That feeling, the wonderful night and all the new possibilities, made "school in Kitsilano" sound like three more years of feeling freaky and afraid, of eating wormshit and pretending not to mind.

Del, who was pretty loose about most things, had this obsession about my going to university. Because she had wanted to, but couldn't. So university was Del's dream for me. What was my dream for me? To be a professional cartoonist, with books of my stuff, like Didi. To travel. To meet lots of interesting people, and to have those people like me, because I was pretty sure that less interesting people weren't going to (they hadn't so far). To learn how to stay clean for longer than two hours after I bathe (especially hands, feet, neck). To not say dumb things in public, or what Del called "invasive things," things that aren't dumb but that people don't want to hear out loud. To make great love with Pascal. Without bleeding on him. Or getting crushed.

Could I explain this to Del? Could I say it right, so she'd understand? Trying to figure out how in hell to do this turned my wire to mush, and I fell asleep. I didn't dream anything and I didn't wake up until the alarm went off three hours later.

The taste in my mouth made me wish I'd remembered to brush my teeth before crashing. Wine, birthday cake, smoked salmon and those little lumps of garlic-flavoured elastic made Morningmouth from Hell. Ernest Death-Breath II. But I hadn't barfed. Not once. Even mixing all that stuff. Almost always, ever since I was a little kid, when I'd get really excited, it would cause barfage. Not this time. Maybe I was growing up. Grown-ups could get excited and not barf. I'd seen them do it. Maybe that was what being grown-up meant. Having lots of exciting things happen and also getting to keep your food.

What were you supposed to wear to a rock concert in a Cow's Palace? My travelling clothes were getting to be seriously limited. And, after seeing Malibu Gear, seriously boring. There wasn't time for pissage and moanage about it. Black tank, denim jacket, sandals and tighter jeans for the show. Plus drawing pad and felt-tips, in case inspiration hit.

• •

Before going to sleep, Pascal walked me out onto the beach and pointed toward Gilbey's house. He said I couldn't miss it, that it was a large white southern Gothic pile with doric columns fore and aft. He also called it a Frank Lloyd Wrong. He said that Gilbey's dad was an international real estate type with dodgy associates, and that

Gilbey's mum was dead and that Johnny, her dad, was married to an ex-tennis player who spoke babytalk.

I was trying to picture all that as I trudged, hauling my army bag, up the early-morning beach. A man and a woman, with excellent bodies, jogged past me, but otherwise the beach was deserted except for Grady, the guardhouse dog, with a driftwood stick in his mouth.

"Hi, Dogstuff," I said, taking the stick and throwing it into the sea. He went bounding after it, brought it back to me. We did this dance all the way to Gilbey's, where the game was interrupted by my announcement. "Holy Fuck!"

Pascal was right. I mean, I know bugger-all about designing houses, but this one was, to quote Zizanie Rocaille Douglas-Hyde VanderHayden, "See voolGAIR!"

First of all, it was this Humungus Thing that had totally nothing to do with what was around it, which was a beach and an ocean. Two, it was, except for a humungo glossy black door, Very White, which made it, in the L.A. light, which was also Very White, totally blinding! I pulled the movie star shades out of my army bag, plunked 'em on, marched myself up between the pairs of columns and knocked hard on the big black door. Which was opened by a big black human.

She was almost as tall as Pascal and half as wide as Pascal was tall. Her face, though, wasn't fat. It was a shiny, dark, copper brown, with cheekbones that looked like someone had cut a rubber ball in half and put each of the halves under the skin of each of her cheeks. Her mouth was sexy, like the picture Del had of the statue of the Emperor Hadrian's boyfriend. Her eyes were warm and careful at the same time.

"Good mohr-nahng." An accent like Didi's. A black lady with a French accent?

"Good morning. I'm Roanne Chappell. I'm supposed to meet Gilbey and Mr. Siggins. To go to San Francisco?"

"Yes, Miss Rwan. Please enter. They are all in the ah-tree-ewm. There is brake-fast."

The "ah-tree-ewm" was an all-glass room shaped like a carousel, filled with flowers and hanging plants. Everybody was sitting sprawled around a large, food-filled glass table, looking like what Brian used to call "the fellers that lost the fight."

Except for Dickie, who jumped up, shouting, "Hail gorgeous Rosie . . . ROANNE. Roanne, Roanne, Roanne. I'll get it, love, I promise . . . me mum still calls me Rich."

"That's cuz y'are, mate!"

"Belt up, Trev. Have a jam botty and a cup o' rosie for the road, love, I'm off to wake the dead." He kissed me on the nose and took off up the big fancy stairwell in the center of the main hall.

I figured "the dead" was Gilbey. Trevor started pouring tea for me. Tea was one of those substances that produced the non-grown-up food-release when I got excited.

"Is there coffee?" There was. Neil put a buttered and jammed piece of bread on the little plate in front of me.

"So, your mum is Del Chappell? I never knew 'er. I joined the band about a year after she took off for Canada. But I love the Yobs covers she did. Brilliant. Especially *Red Eyed Dogs and Jungle Queens.*"

"Yeh, Neil, you met 'er. She came to the big Vancouver show in 'seventy-six. Good looker. Red hair. Great Bristols. Had a little kid with 'er, and a guy with a moustache."

"That was Stavro, the guy with the moustache. I was the little kid."

"I thought so. Do you remember me?"

"Yeah, you're Trevor. From Dickie's house in Hampstead. You had a moustache back then, a walrus-y one."

"Thass right."

"And rings, silver rings on all your fingers except the thumbs. And your wife was Fiona, right? Are you still married to her?"

"That's what she tells me. She'll be pleased that y'remember 'er. You'll see 'er in San Fran. She went up two days early to spend some of me money. She's earned it, puttin' up wit' this circus all these years."

Dickie said, "Ladies and gentlemen, I give you Miss Gilbey Tarr," and Gilbey, too tall to rest her head on Dickie's shoulder, but trying to anyway, said, "Aaarrgh." She still looked beautiful, because it would be almost impossible for the Gilb to look anything else, but she was super-pale. "Co-o-f-f-eee," she groaned. Dickie sat her down, poured coffee and sort of fed it to her. Charlie offered bread and jam. "Pukey," she said. "Charming," Dickie said. "Hi," I said. She looked at me. Blinked. "Roanne," Dickie said, "from last night." "I know," she whined, making a pouty mouth. "Hey, Babygirl."

"Eef I have to dreenk any more of thees rotten Amereecan coffee, I weel sheet!" Another Goddess entered. This one was tiny. About five feet tall, with round Christmas ball boobs and round honey dew melon buns. Her waist looked to be about ten inches around. Short jet black supercurly hair. Round eyes, round nose, round mouth. She looked almost exactly like the doll in Arabella's retro store window, back in my previous life. Betty Boop. She wore supertight faded jeans. I no longer wanted to wear supertight jeans at the concert. Not unless I was going to the Cow Palace as the official Palace Cow.

"This is Silvia," Charlie said. I felt like the reproduction on Del's worktable at home. A lumpy little goddess from the beginning of time.

"Hi," I said. "I'm the Venus of Willendorf."

• •

The weirdassed white limo took us to the L.A. airport. ("LAX," Dickie said. "That's what they call their airfield. Does not exactly fill one with confidence, do it?") Instead of sitting in waiting rooms and queuing up and stuff, weirdass drove right out onto the tarmac. A big jetplane, with the word "Ascentair" written on it, was waiting for us ("Bloody well hope so," Dickie said, "I'm bloody well not boarding a plane called 'Descentair'!").

Two big guys, one white, one black, wearing black satin bomber jackets (with globes of the world on them) that said YOBS! PLANET EARTH TOUR! 1976 hauled our gear onto the plane (I asked to keep my army bag with me). Silvia, coughing and declaring that the L.A. air was like "sheet," headed up the stairs and into the plane, teetertottering on her white high heels. Neil, watching her ass, said, "Oh, it's grand how cheering Silvia is when she is walkin' away from ye. Fills my heart with joy." "That's because yer heart's in yer pants," Trevor said. "Oi!" Charlie said. "Sorry," Trevor said, and we all boarded.

We were greeted by a tallish, plumpish, pale orange-haired man in a too-tight cream-coloured suit. His pointy-collared shirt was silky, and the same colour as a cat's tongue. There was a shiny gold chain around his neck. Trevor put his hand on my shoulder.

"Roanne, this is Derek Rubin. Captain Yob. Our manager, mother and nurse. Der, this is Roanne Chappell, Del's daughter. She's coming to the gig. Please make sure her hotel is sorted and that all the clearance people have her name."

"Certainly. Pleasure to meet ye, treecoo. 'Ow is your muvver?"

"She's good."

"Lovely to 'ear it. Give 'er my best. Welcome aboard the Yob Express."

"Huhn. Your watch has no numbers on it."

"It's a Movado."

"Oh. I thought it was a watch."

The seats were way bigger than on a regular plane. Like plush little single beds. They went all the way back into a bed shape.

"Hey, Dickie, mind if I crash?" Gilbey asked.

"Fine, if you put it some other way."

"Oh, right. Sleep. Mind if I sleep?"

"Do it."

"Wake me fifteen minutes before we land."

"Done."

I took a window seat, and Trevor buckled up in the seat next to me.

"It is a watch."

"What?"

"Derek's Movado. It is a watch. 'Movado' is the name of the company."

"Shit."

"Don't worry about it. Derek's only known it was a watch for about six months longer than you have."

"Where is Derek?"

"In the big bed. At the back. He can take these little catnaps, ten, fifteen minute things, anytime anywhere. Says he wakes up 'fresh as a daisy.' That's what he says, 'Fresh as a daisy' . . . a real phrase-maker is our Derek."

"How come he wears his hair like that?"

"The comb-over? It's called a comb-over. You take all the little hairs inside yer ears, grow 'em long and pull 'em over the top of yer head."

I giggled. "It looks weird."

"Der thinks it looks like 'normal' hair."

"Really?"

"Mm-hmm."

"Amazing"

"Truly."

Across the aisle, Silvia complained to Charlie about how she'd left the shoes that went with her "outFEET" for the "geeg" at her "seester's." Charlie said she could buy shoes in San Francisco. "Ah. Good. OK," Silvia said, and stayed quiet for the rest of the flight, reading a big magazine that had three blonde women in very tiny bikinis on the cover. The magazine was called *Oggi.* I asked Trevor how that was pronounced.

"Rhymes with 'podgy.'"

"Not 'froggy.'"

"Nope."

"Ta."

"Anytime . . . I'm gonna kip for a bit. Long day ahead."

"OK . . . I'm gonna draw." I pulled out pad and felt-tips and lowered the serving tray. Drew a castle. At the top were the battlements, which had eight sculptured, upside-down udders. Under each udder was a big hole, with the front of a cannon showing through, with lots of explosion gunk and comicbook stuff (*!@'BOOM!#;@*KER-BLAMMO!!!@#*!) showering out. There was a coat of arms down below, one on each side of the humungus wide-plank castle door. A big pink-tongued, white-faced cow. Huge eyes, long lashes, crown on her head. Wearing a necklace of red roses, yellow star earrings, a gold ring through her nose. I knew, from Del's book of family crests, that the shields needed a motto, but I was too sleep-goofed to think of one. I drew Dickie, and the rest of the Yobs, on the battlements, singing and playing their instruments, behind Holstein bull soldiers, who were kneeling on one knee, firing the cannons or shooting arrows. A great big flying banner said THE YOBS! LIVE AT THE COW PALACE!

• •

The sillycar waiting next to the plane in San Francisco was black. Running down the stairs, Derek's comb-over got caught in the breeze and flipped the wrong way. His gold-and-diamond pinky ring glittered in the sun as he tried to hold onto this long thing of hair. "Rapunzel," I whispered." "Ssh," Trevor said, squeezing my hand, "be cool."

At the hotel there were skeighty-eight hundred people behind blue wooden barricades ("Sawhorses," Trevor said. Saw horses! Cow palaces! Cat. Ass. Trophies! Don't people see what they're saying?) There were fans and photographers. Television people, radio people, guys in uniforms, guys in jeans, guys on horseback, guys on foot, guys in Yobs jackets, guys in dark suits talking into their hands, men and women talking into microphones and lots and lots of female members of My Peer Group screaming their guts up, faces all red. Gonna barf, I thought, gonna make themselves barf. Not me, though. I'm with pals. I'm safe. Safe people don't barf.

Dickie nested in the middle of us like a raisin in a muffin, and, surrounded by Yobs Security, we moved to the top of the hotel's vanilla-fudge marble stairs, where he spun like a musicbox doll whose light just went on, tossing his hair back and grinning like it was Christmas morning.

"Hi!" he shouted, and some of the microphones, shoved through holes in the security wall of bodies, picked up the sound so it bounced. "H-I-I-I-I!"

"WE'LL SEE YOU GUYS (uys . . . uys . . .) AT THE CONCERT TONIGHT (i-i-ight). IT'S GREAT TO BE BACK IN SAN FRANCISCO! THERE WILL BE A PRESS CONFERENCE. AT THE COW PALACE (alice-alice). DURING OUR REHEARSAL THIS AFTERNOON. SEE YOU THERE. Let's move!" Dickie's face-light, the one he could stop and start from someplace inside, shut off, and his wanting to go was so damn strong that we all turned, like a robot centipede, and headed for the lobby.

Hotel people were all waiting to take care of us. The lobby was majorly Cinderella beautiful, with a huge crystal chandelier sparkling way high up in the most faraway ceiling I'd ever seen. There were little palm trees and marble columns and polished wood furniture and old red velvet and pale flowered upholstery and wonderful mostly deep red multi-coloured rugs.

Derek said Gilbey and I would share a room. I'd figured she'd be sharing with Dickie but was happy to have her as a roomie. There were all these questions, and I didn't want to ask them in front of the whole Yobs Army.

"Let's hit the mini-bar."

"Not me, Gilb. You go ahead."

"Don' hafta drink, Babygirl. They's candy an' Cokes an' stuff too."

"No, uh-uh. Not now. I wanna check out the room."

It was bigger, this room was, than the living and dining rooms (both together) of our Kitsilano house. I was beginning to get it: there were people in this world who weren't cramped, crowded or sweating the rent. There were people in this world who didn't steal bologna from Mac's Milk stores. Fuck, there were people in this world who didn't even *eat* fucking bologna!

At that moment, in the big, beautiful room that went on forever and had more than one shape, I was trying to memorize everything. In case I died the next day, in case I was never allowed in a room like this again, in case it was all a dream and I woke up as an 11-year-old in the middle of Shoppers Drug Mart in Burnaby and Marcy She-Who-Shits-Roses Halloran is buying barrettes with fucking cats on them, and she says to her slave, Sheila the Zit Farm, just loud enough so I can hear it, "Oh, yuck, gag me, it's Roanne the arTEEST and she's wearing a red velvet pillowcase!" Well, check this, Marcy! I'm travelling with the Yobs and Dickie Siggins is my friend, and my roommate is so beautiful she makes you look like your face was hit by a car, and we're in this room that's the size of a house!

On a low marble table, there was this huge bowl of fruit. Free fruit! Including a whole ripe pineapple and fresh peaches that ran juice down your chin, and chocolate (chocolate!) on the pillows. Also free. And towels the size of bedsheets and white bathrobes made of towel, and two woven baskets with shampoo, thread, needles, buttons, bubblebath and bodygoo. And a telephone next to the toilet (!!!).

I wanted to stay living in this world. I wanted Del to live in it too, so she could always buy exactly the art supplies she needed, so she could just do her work and laugh and talk and think and have terrific boyfriends and be beautiful. Without having to worry about what she called "Roof 'n' Rosie." Not to mention "Morgan Maintenance."

But how? How did a person, even if she was really sixteen, get all this? Without Dickie Siggins? As one's own personal accomplishment?

Gilbey was kneeling on the thick pale green carpet looking at eight or ten little bottles, one of which was open and emptied.

"Hey, Babygirl, which one should I drink?"

"Looks like you did that already."

"That's Baileys. Irish Cream. It's candy, duddn't count."

"Oh."

"So pick one."

"I dunno, Gilb. I dunno anything about booze. . . . Is there gin? My mum drinks gin."

The Gilb laughed and shook her head. "Your mom drinks gin! My momma *was* gin. I'm named for what she was drinkin' on the night I was born. My daddy didn't want to do it, to name me that, but she was a Thibodeau and he'd married up out of a family of lintheads, so he did what Momma wanted."

"Lintheads?"

"People who work in the cotton mills. That's what he comes from. Money's all his now, but it was Momma's daddy's cash he needed to get started, and, like he says, you go along to get along an' you don't send a message till you got the power to back it up." She stood up, long and tall, holding on to this baby gin bottle like King Kong holds the tiny lady in the poster from the weird old movie.

"Then . . ." She opened the bottle and chugalugged the gin. "Then, when you got the power . . . you take the sumbitches off at the knees! That's what my daddy says."

I felt nervous, like I used to with Brian. I mean, I didn't know Gilbey well enough to tell her what to do, but I didn't want her to get all pissed so early that I wound up having no one to play with.

"So, 'Gilbey' is the name of a kind of gin?"

"Uh huh. Dickie says I should be named for this one. Beefeater."

"How come?"

She laughed, dropping the bottle onto the thick carpet. "You know," she said, "BEEFeater." She pinched her fingers together and shoved them into her mouth.

I knew about this. Sort of. It was what Kirby Ross made Kimi Watanabe do to him in the gym last year and Kimi's family tried to send Kirby to juvie jail but he only had to do community service. Maybe it's because I can't even stand to have the doctor use the tongue depressor, but I couldn't imagine somebody agreeing to do that without being threatened. Besides, Kimi said it tasted like rancid fish-glue.

"Oh. That. You're good at that, eh?"

"Brilliant, Dickie says."

I smiled, but the smile felt goofy on my face, like I wasn't in control of my mouth. I wanted to change the subject before she asked if I was good at beefeating and I had to either lie or tell my new friend that something she was good at would, probably, if I had to do it, make me orally return lunch to the floor for a week and a half. "How come you're not sharing with Dickie? I mean, I'm buzzed that it's us and all, but, if you two—"

"Legals and personals. He can't shack with jailbait, which is what we are, you an' me. Don't they have those laws in Canada?"

"I dunno. Don't think so. No one's ever mentioned it."

"Yeah, well, they got 'em for serious in the U.S. of A. And Dickie's also got a regular lady he lives with in London, a costume designer. They been together a long time. And when they're separated, when the band is on the road, Dickie does what he does, an' sometimes what he does is me."

"How long for?"

"Oh, sometimes for hours and hours, unless it's a concert night, an' then I'm lucky if he duddn't fall asleep after—"

"No, I didn't mean it like . . ."

Gilbey giggled. "I know, Babygirl, I'm just funnin' with ya. I met Dickie two years ago, when he was in L.A. to open the *Live from Planet Earth* concert movie. We hang out when he's on the coast, or when I can get to where he is, which only happened once, when he was in Rome and Daddy was puttin' together this resort in Sardinia, an' I told him a girlfriend was in Rome with her folks and could I go up. It ain't a big thing, Dickie an' me, but he's real sweet an' kind. He's a good guy. What about you? You an' 'Scal a thing?"

"No, he's a friend. I met him through his brother."

"The fag dwarf?"

"The cartoonist. The great cartoonist. . . . Yeah, the fag dwarf as well."

"But don't you think 'Scal is hot?"

I knew what colour my face was, because I felt the heat change. I laughed, looked down. "Yeah, Gilb. I think he's hot. But he's real old."

"Forty-two. Two years younger than Dickie. I did 'im once."

Heartslide to belly. "You did?"

"Mm. And I would've again, but *he* wouldn't. Said it was a bad idea. He's a good friend, though, I model for him sometimes. And he's always been there for me. 'Scal's m'pal."

"Allora! Who ees ready to go show-peeng?" Silvia looked great, in pink silky hip-rider wide-legs and a pink-and-white crocheted crop top. And she actually looked happy.

We took off for this big expensive department store Gilbey knew.

"I can't do this," I said. "I don't have a lot of cash with me."

Gilbey yanked on my hair. "No sweat, B.G., we'll put it on my daddy's plastic."

And we did. I got this black jersey halter-tie wide-leg jumpsuit, with the back cut to almost the start of my bum, and big silvery hoop earrings like the ones Silvia was wearing (only hers were real silver), a little black shoulder bag with a silver star buckle and a pair of black suede platform slingbacks that I wasn't sure I could walk in, but Gilbey said, "We'll have the limo all the time. You'll just have to stand around lookin' hot an' havin' fun."

I also scored a black two-piece bathing suit ("modified bikini"—that means your belly button shows but most of your belly doesn't). It was on sale for only $25 (reduced from over a hundred), but I was still going to pass. Because of the Pubes Thing. My pubes were overflowing both sides of the suit's crotch like two little furry black animals. Gilb said, "Don't sweat it, Babygirl. When we get back to the Colony, I'll take you to Ilona of Malibu."

"*Who* of Malibu?"

"Eye-lona. She's a Ezz-thet-tishun. Removes extra hairs from all over the place. She does my daddy's back. And Clarissa's cute l'il moustache."

There was a humungus cosmetics section. About ten counters' worth. Gil and Sil bought tons of stuff, and I had a "makeover," which is where they take the blank wall that's your face and turn it into a movie star with enormous eyes, heartbreaker lips and cheekbones like a model. "I don't fu . . . I don't believe it! You're a genius!" I said to the lady who'd made me over.

"You helped, Roe," Gilbey said. "You've got a real pretty face."

I did feel weird letting Gilb's father, who I didn't even know, pay for all of it (over $500), which was more than the entire rest of my travelling gear, even with the crocheted sweater, which was the most expensive thing I'd ever bought with my own money, but she said, "Don't even think about it, Babygirl. My daddy's got so much guilt happenin' that I could outfit all of Malibu Colony an' he wouldn't say a mumblin' . . . unless sumbuddy said the clothes looked ugly an' that Johnny Tarr bought 'em."

When we hit the street, Silvia started doing her "I weel sheet" coffee thing.

"I know a place that has real coffee. Italian coffee." I didn't remember the name of the place, but the neighbourhood was North Beach, so that's what I told the cab driver, and the Caffè d'Abruzzi was easy to find. Silvia totally blissed, chatting away with the waiters in Italian and being a Beautiful Cuteperson, drinking "doppio" espressos and eating hard little crescent-shaped biscuits. Gilbey thought the guy working the espresso machine had "incredible arms" and "primitivo sexy lips," so she was happy too. Me, I loved being, for the first time ever (and in a very flash group), the One Who Knew Where the Good Place Was.

• •

Carrying on in the shop, cheered on by Gil and Sil, I had thought my half-naked black jumpsuit looked great. But that night, in our room, looking over my shoulder at the mirror, my ass looked like a big black bowling ball.

"Gilb! Does my bum look too big to you?"

Gilbey came out of the loo, all blonde, in what looked like gold silk pyjamas. "Your what?"

"My bum."

"Your butt?"

"Yeah."

"No, it looks great. You look great."

"I feel fat."

"Oh, God . . . wait a minute." She went to the closet and pulled out a long black glittery fitted jacket. "Here. Wear this until you feel cool. It won't close over your tits, but it looks better open." It was perfect. And my makeup, which the Gilb had done almost as brilliantly as the cosmetics lady, was amazing. Gilbey put a white plastic pass, on a long chain, around my neck. "Don't lose this, no matter what. It's your clearance to be everywhere. And always stay with one of us, 'cause it gets really crazy. We have our own limo, you, me and Sil. We'll meet the guys after, back here at the hotel. Now, I've gotta do my face. You look beautiful, Babygirl. Honest. You want one of these?" She had five or six of those little bottles in her hands.

"No. Yes. Any more of those Irish Cream things?"

"Yeah. Two. In the bar."

She was right. Two. I drank one. Right again. It did taste like candy. Put the other one in my new evening bag. Fluffed up my hair in the mirror. "Wow!" I said. Gilbey was three for three. It might never have been true before. It might never be true again. But at the moment, jolted by a sudden hot bellyful of candy-coffee booze, Babygirl was beautiful.

• •

"There's a puppy in here!" There was. On the backseat of the limo. A shaggy little sheepdog puppy, waggling his bum, pink tongue hanging out.

"Oh, he's Oddie's. Oddie breeds them. He came up here early, with Fiona Doone, to try and buy one."

"Eet weel peess! I know eet weel peess! Theess dress eess seelk! Eef eet peesses, I weell—"

"We know, you'll sheet. Get in the car, Sil, an' hand me Furface. I'll give 'im to the driver."

When we got near the Cow Palace, everything was seriously thick with cars and people and police. The driver showed his plastic passcard (we three did too), and we were waved into a lane that was being kept open.

The C.P. was just a big light-colored building. Not a king, a queen or a cow in sight. Not that I ever saw the front of it. The limo pulled into a dark grubby alley that smelled of piss and Dumpsters. There were lots of police and guards and cars and limos. We gave our names, showed our passes again and went through a red iron door to an ugly gray basement corridor. Then up in an ugly gray elevator to another ugly gray corridor, which led to a big booth with all sorts of switches and phones and colored lights and television screens and guys wearing headphones with little microphones attached. And Derek Rubin, comb-over in place, in white suit, black shirt, white tie, white shoes.

"Good evening, dazzlers! Welcome to Command Central, the throbbing, pulsing nerve center of this entire bloody circus!"

What we were in was a black glass cube on top of a tower and just under the majorly high ceiling of the Cow Palace. We could see out, in every direction, but nobody, even if they felt like staring straight up, could see us. Way down below, the thousands of Yobs freaks packing the place to the walls were just little blobs of colour. The stage, a square arena, white, edged in zigzags of glossy black glitter, looked like an Art Deco poster with amps, drums and a bright red electric piano.

You could see this stage, from different angles, on three of the telly screens. Others showed the lobby, the alley, different parts of the audience, and one showed a bearded guy with a beer gut. Derek was talking to him through a tiny black machine in his hand.

"Oi! Rog! Can ye 'ear me?" Rog nodded, saying something we couldn't hear. "Right! I can't 'ear ye personally, mate, but Marty's got the phones on. I can see ye on the screen. Everything's cool here. Everything copacetic back there?" Rog nodded. "Ye check the rope?" Rog nodded again, holding up four fingers, mouthing the words "four times." Derek said, "Right! Tell Dickie that, an' tell 'im the girls 'ave arrived." Silvia jabbed Derek with a tiny, shiny perfect fingernail.

"Dereek, tell Rog to tell Charlie 'Nel' boca del' lupo!'"

"Uh, Silvia says 'Nellie boca . . . ' Yeah, what she always says. Tell Charlie."

Marty, the "sound engineer," said, "He's gonna go do final checks on the mikes, headsets and amps now, Der, OK?"

"Yeah. 'Ave 'im do the bleedin' rope one more time."

• •

"Go sound! Go stairs! Go ringrope!"

Supershiny black stairs burst through the floor of the white arena. On those stairs, in a black suit, black shirt and red tie, stood Oddie Ogden, lead guitarist of the Yobs, playing this loud fat rock 'n' roll chord. At the same time, a thick, shiny white rope with a black metal ring on the end started lowering from the ceiling. Holding onto the ring, in a white suit, red shirt, black-and-white striped tie, with a really loud major-echo mike that must've been up his ass or somewhere else hard to see, was Dickie Siggins, singing, "Ain't . . . comin' . . . down, bay-bee, NE-VER CO-MINN' DA-OON!" On four screens and all over the entire Palace of Cows, the entire wriggling multi-coloured megablob of audience went crazy screaming nuts.

By the third song ("He's Gone, She's Sad, Too Bad, I'm Glad"), Derek had stopped jumping up and down and was doing this Head Counsellor at Camp Cow Palace thing, passing around "champers and nosh," which was Derektalk for sandwiches and champagne. There was a tall skinny guy at the back of the booth, talking into a little recorder and writing stuff down. None of us looked like eachother, but this guy had his completely own look. Baggy beige cotton suit. Pale yellow shirt with button-down collar. Little knitted striped tie. White running shoes. No socks. He had big teeth, a big nose, big nostrils and bright blue eyes that looked surprised the way babies do when they burp. He had baby hair too. Soft, sandy blond, fine, and long, straight, blond eyelashes, like a pig's. His face, up close, was weird. It had lots and lots of very fine lines but seemed just-born. His name, he said, was Carter Endicott Junior. He said he was writing a chapter on the Yobs for a book on "pop as sociocultural anthropology."

Gilbey laughed. "Thass great, baby," she said. "Have some of this jetfuel gingerale and a cracker fulla fisheggs."

Red, white and black balloons had been released from fishnets in the ceiling, the guys were singing their third encore ("Too Good for Good-bye"), and the whole audience was waving its arms in the air, from side to side, imitating Dickie, when, as Gilbey put it, Derek's little white pills kicked in and he jumped up out of the chesterfield.

"Right! Everybody what's going to the 'otel 'as to go to the alley now, or we'll have a bottooneck!"

"Thass us, Babygirl." Gilb stood up, ruffling Carter Endicott Junior's fine, peachfuzz hair. "Come on, Junie, you're with us. Grab a bottle an' try t'keep up."

The puppy was superglad to see us. Figuring I was in black, and how much could a puppy who'd had four walks in an alley "peess" anyway, I offered to sit in front with dog and driver so that Carter, who had legs forever, could sit in the back. Carter, looking at Gilbey like he was willing to do all her math homework for the rest of her life, said, "Thank you, miss, thank you very much."

Puppy wanted to lick my face, which is normally something I love, but, not knowing how to fix it, and figuring Gilb wouldn't have the time, I didn't want him screwing up the amazing makeup, so I took off the platform sandals, which was a relief anyway, and gave him toes to lick.

I was looking forward to seeing the beautiful lobby again, but, because of all the crowds in front of the hotel, we were driven around to the back where there were more security people, and took a freight elevator up to the twenty-third floor, where we showed our passes and were escorted by a walkie-talkie guy to a suite of rooms that took up practically the whole floor and had a great view of San Francisco. The minute I put Puppy down, he pissed.

Derek and the guys weren't back yet, but there were lots of serving-people, in white shirts and black pants, and served-people, in every getup imaginable, eating, drinking, nattering. An older woman—shoulder-length dark blonde hair in a low ponytail, gray sweater, gray, red and navy plaid skirt, pale gray tights, flat shoes—was heading straight for me.

"Rosie Chappell?"

"Fiona Doone? Wow. Hi. You look . . . like I remember you."

"Oh, I couldn't possibly, but it's a lovely thought. Now, you definitely do not look as I remember you. You're a beautiful young woman. How old are you now, love?"

"Sixteen. This week." (Well, I thought, this week I *am* sixteen. Who knows what age I'll be next week?)

"Sixteen! That doesn't seem possible."

"I know what you mean."

And in came the guys, dragging a monumungus crowd in front of them, on each side of them and behind them, including a woman with white-white skin, red-red lips, black ruffled dress, red rose in her slicked-back black hair and tons of diamonds all over her ears, wrists, fingers, neck.

"Crikey!" Fiona said. "The world's richest Spanish dancer!"

The Spanish dancer, according to the short bald guy with the nipple-shaped wart in the middle of his forehead, who was explaining her to Carter Endicott, was called Jan something. She was an art collector who "endowed things," and her family, if I heard Nipple-head right, invented white sugar.

Jan had Dickie seriously cornered, and she kept saying, "Everything is so ephemeral." She also said, again over and over, that the scene at the Cow Palace was "utter mayhem," but that Dickie and the band had been "utterly brilliant."

I thought, That's it!

When you're trying to find someone in a major mobscene, it helps if they're very tall and very blonde. "Gilb, do you have our room key?"

"Sure do, Babygirl. What's up? You in love?"

"No, nothing like that. Just need to go there for a minute."

"You fall off the roof?"

"What?"

"You got the curse?"

"No. It's cool. Everything's cool. There's just something I've got to do."

"Go for it, here's the key."

• •

I pulled the drawing pad out of my army bag, turned to the drawing of the Yobs Live at the Cow Palace and, on the two shields, wrote the motto "Udder Mayhem! Udderly Brilliant!"

I stayed in our room for a while, putting finishing touches to the drawing. Then I had to call the front desk, because the elevator wouldn't go to the Yob floor without a clearance and a security guy escort. So, by the time I got back there, things had thinned out a little, which was good.

Derek was sitting on the chesterfield, being nattered at by the Jan woman. A boy, looking about 16, with suntanned skin and curly black hair like Silvia's, was on the floor between Derek's legs, receiving a neck massage. His eyes were closed. He was saying, "Mmm, mmm, mmm." He had those superlong eyelashes that girls always want and boys always get. In another corner, Gilbey was also on the floor. With Carter Endicott. She was making hand gestures and he was laughing like Gilb had the funniest hands in the world. Oddie, Trevor and Fiona were sitting on another Chester, talking about sheepdogs, while the puppy slept in Fiona's lap. Charlie was jamming blues with a shave-headed black guitarist who had a tattoo of an alligator on his cheek. Silvia was sitting on the arm of Charlie's chair, studying a possibly broken fingernail. The person I was looking for was nowhere in sight.

"Hey, Gilb. Hi, Carter. I've got something for Dickie. Do you know where he is?"

"In his suite, changin' clothes and havin' a breather. I c'n phone 'im." She picked up the phone on the lamp table. "Yeah, hi, Front Desk. This is Miss Tarr, T-A-R-R, from room . . . whassit say on the key, Babygirl?"

"2307."

"Room 2307. Will you put me through to Mr. Siggins in the Presidential Suite. He expects my call. Yeah, I'll hold. . . . Hey, baby, I'm with Roanne. She's got a present she wants to bring you. Now. Great. Yeah, it's windin' down. . . . That's Charlie, jammin' with Crocodile Crane. Yeah, she's still here, talkin' Der's ear off. . . . He's rubbing Carlos's neck . . . his *neck,* I said. Yeah, yeah. Talk to you later." She replaced the receiver. "It's cool, Babygirl. He said to wait ten minutes so he can tell security, and then come up. It's one floor up."

"Great, thanks. Is Derek gay?"

"Does the Pope shit in the woods?"

"What?"

"You know, is a bear Catholic?"

"Oh."

Dickie was lying on his bed, barefoot, in jeans and a long, silky cream-coloured shirt, drinking white wine. "Hullo, miss. Want some wine, or would you rather have a soda?"

"Nothing, thanks, Dickie. I brought you something silly . . . something I made."

"Great!" He sat up, patting the edge of his very, very large bed. "Come sit an' let's have a look."

When I sat, I noticed that there was a smallish green stone statue on the bedtable. This one was a whole body, with a bald head, chubby little arms and legs, but it was the same face as the Adelita Catbaby on the thong around my neck. "Hey, you have a catbaby. Like mine. See?"

"Where did you get this?"

"A Mexican woman gave it to me. As a present."

Dickie fit his hand under my catbaby, studying it, pursing his lips. "This is a good piece, Rosie. It looks authentic."

"Authentically what?"

"Olmec. Jaguar god. Pre-Columbian Mexican art. I'll bet Del doesn't have it insured."

"Uh, no."

"Well, she should. These things are rare. And pricey. It's lovely. You be careful with it. And if you want to sell it, sell it to me."

"Sure, Dickie, but I don't want to sell it. It's my mojo."

"Gotcha. Did you have fun tonight?"

"Oh, yes! Thanks, Dickie. Thanks so much for everything. The last two days may've been the two best days of my whole life!"

"Really? Whole life been a bummer, then?"

"No. Not at all. There's been lots of neat stuff. But this, this has been . . . I dunno, more mine."

"Did you like the show?"

"It was brilliant! The songs and the show were great. It would've been neat to be able to see it from in the audience, though. From inside the glass cube, with Derek and the sound guys and all, it was a little, I dunno . . ."

"Less like music, more like Mars?"

"Yeh. Exactly."

"I know. That's the problem with these extravaganzas. But you've gotta do 'em. For credibility an' all that. What you've got to hear is one of the one-night surprise gigs we do in clubs. Those're just about the music. They're the only gigs Fiona Doone will come to. Didja see her? Fiona?"

"Yeh. She remembered me and everything. She's great."

"Yes. She is. The only grown-up in our whole crew, I reckon. Too bad she and your mum never got on . . . I think they would now."

"How come they 'didn't get on'?"

"Young stuff. Bloke stuff. . . . So, what's this present Miss Gilbey says y've got for me?"

I held the drawing pad to my chest, feeling suddenly supershy. "Oh, it's just a silly thing. A drawing. About the Yobs. I started it on the plane. Then I finished it after the show, in my room. Put Derek in it. Changed the clothes to be like the Art Deco stuff you're wearing. But the rest isn't Deco, it's sort of medieval, and—"

"Crikey! You gonna tell me about it or show it to me?"

I opened the notepad.

Dickie looked. And grinned. And grinned more. And laughed out loud. "It's super! I fuckin' love it! This is great! Ha! Look at Der's fuckin' comb-over flyin' in the breeze. And there's you an' Gilbey an' Sil lookin' out a window. Oh, no! With a sheepdog puppy! Has Oddie seen this?"

"Uh-uh. Nobody has. Just you."

"And I can keep it? For me very own?"

"Sure."

He leaned over and kissed my forehead. "Well, bless you, my child. I shall treasure it always. Truly . . . how'd you know the style thing we were doing was Deco?"

"Artist's daughter. I know a lot of art stuff. It's pretty much the only thing I do know a lot about. Been looking at art books since I was two or three. . . . Well, I should go back to the party. I've got our room key, and you probably want to rest and—"

"Rosie?"

"Mm?"

"She's one of my best friends. When I get up there in two weeks, I'll have to tell 'er."

"I know."

And I did know. I'd known pretty much from the beginning. And even if Dickie didn't say anything, Fiona, or Trevor, or Derek were bound to. Of all the people I might've run into, Dickie Siggins was the one who could make the most magic happen, but he was also, of pretty much anyone in the world, the one who would most lead right to Del. When I got back to the party room, I grabbed the nearest phone and went through the security natter.

"Dickie?"

"Could be."

"It's Rosie."

"Yeh, love, what's up?"

"When you see Del, when you talk to her, could you tell her I look happy, and healthy? And that I'm not being a jerk and that I love it here?"

"Sure, love, I will. I'll do that. Promise."

"Thanks."

"Sure, love . . . where are you now?"

"Party room."

"Perfect. Can you put Gilbey on?"

I looked around. "She doesn't seem to be here, unless she's in the loo. Or she may've got another key and gone down to our room."

"Well, when you find 'er, would you tell 'er I'd like to say good-bye. We fly back home tomorrow, the band does, at sparrowfart."

"Sparrow? Fart?"

"Very early in the morning. So I want to say good-bye. Could you find her for me?"

"Sure, Dickie, I will . . . and good-bye from me, and thanks again, for the whole thing."

"Anytime, love. Great to see you. Take care of yourself, all right?"

"Yep, I will. And I'll go find Gilb."

"Ta."

• •

The chain was on the door. "Gilb? Gilbey? You in there?" Whispering. Giggling.

"Hey, Babygirl . . . yeah, I'm here. Could you come back in ten, fifteen minutes?"

Showed my pass again, went back to the party room. Jan's rose had wilted and she was telling Trevor and Fiona that everything was "so-o-o ephemeral." Silvia was gone. So were Derek and Eyelash Boy. Charlie and Crocodile Crane were still jamming, and a woman with matted hair and a missing front tooth was singing that she was "a windin' boy." The room smelled of smoke and mixed perfumes. I was asking the bar guy for a ginger ale when I was grabbed by the wrist.

"There you are. I wondered where you disappeared to."

"You did?"

"I did."

He had one of those wide-forehead lionfaces that some gray or ginger cats have. Lionhair, as well. Gold-red, straight, falling over his eye. Mucus Willoughby hair. And, when he smiled, this great dimple. Definitely a cute guy. I mini-giggled, shrugged.

"Well, here I am."

"So you are. This is good. I'm Adrian."

"Hi. Roanne. Roanne Chappell."

"Adrian Mills."

"Adrian *Mills?*"

"Mm-hmm. Do we know each other?"

"You're English."

"I am."

"You write songs."

"I do."

"You were my mother's boyfriend in London when I was three."

"Oh, dear. I was?"

"Uh-huh. Del. Del Chappell."

"My God. Extraordinary."

"Yeah."

"Well, why don't we have a quiet nightcap in my room, fill in the lost years?"

"Uh . . . no, I don't think so, Adrian."

"Why not?" He ran his finger back and forth over the back of my hand, dimplegrinned like crazy, tossed his hair out of his eyes. A really cute guy. "I don't bite . . . unless asked to. I think you're very lovely."

"I can't handle this."

"Of course you can."

And I lost it. "No! No I can't! Don't tell me what I can handle, OK?!!" I pulled my hand away and people were looking and Fiona Doone was walking toward us and I ran out of there, showed my pass, and hoped to Christ Gilb was done beefeating or whatever the hell she was doing in our room.

Gilbey was stark naked, in the loo, brushing her teeth. I did and did not want to know why.

"Sorry, Babygirl. It got a little crazy here for a minute."

"Who was here?"

"Junie."

"Carter?"

"Uh-huh." She wrapped herself in one of the big white towel bathrobes, sat on the edge of the bed, lit a cigarette.

"Do you like him?"

"Who, Junie? Not in the way you mean. He's sweet. It didn't take much time, an' it made him so happy! You shoulda seen his face. Looked like he died an' went to heaven. . . . Didn't do him for me. Did 'im for my daddy. He's always sayin' how hard it is to get next to Eastern Establishment money. Well, Junie's this millionaire from Connecticut who likes playin' journalist, an' I have his card an' his private numbers an' everything."

"Dickie's looking for you. He wants to say good-bye."

"What did you tell him?"

"That I'd find you."

"Right. Thanks. I'll call 'im." She did the security thing. "Hey, baby. Yeah, she did. I really needed a bubblebath. . . . Well, I smell real good now. How do *you* smell? Well, take a damn shower, I'll be up in two minutes." She hung up, went back in the loo, threw some stuff into her gold bag and headed for the door.

"You're going like that?"

"Uh-huh."

"In your bathrobe?"

"Uh-huh."

"What'll the security guys think?"

"Like I give a damn? See you later, Babygirl."

I walked across the room to the bowl of free fruit, picked up a banana. Put it in my mouth, skin and all. Moved it in and out. Wasn't too bad as long as I didn't go too far back. Did this for a while, staring at the full-length mirror, trying to look happy. Shit, I was happy. It was the two best days of my life. So why the fuck was I crying? Ate the chocolate mint on my pillow. Ate the chocolate mint on Gilbey's pillow. Called downstairs. Ordered six more chocolate mints. They came, in a little woven basket. Ate those. Stole the basket. Stole the bath and sewing stuff from the baskets in the loo. Stole those baskets. Ate the banana. Barfed.

When I opened my eyes, I had that thing like during those three years when Del and I kept moving house. Didn't know where I was. Looked around. Saw all of Gilbey's hair. Figured her face was somewhere under it. Knew we were in the hotel I had wanted to live in forever. Didn't think I wanted that anymore. Wanted to see Pascal.

"Gilb? Gilbey?"

"Mmmh."

"Are we going back to Malibu today?"

"Mm-hmm."

"When?"

"Later. Sleep now."

We wound up running like hell for the plane, which Dickie had paid for, but it wasn't a charter and wasn't going to wait for us. Mostly our being late was Gilbey, who couldn't or wouldn't get her shit together, and kept saying, "Chill out, Babygirl. We miss this one, we can take another one on my daddy's plastic."

As soon as we were settled and the seatbelt sign went off, Gilbey was pressing call buttons and craving something called a Ramos Fizz. She settled for a rum and tonic, drank it really fast and then fell asleep. She could do that. She knew where she lived and her cover wasn't about to be blown all to hell.

In the taxi, on the way to Malibu Colony, I had an idea.

"Gilb, you busy tonight?"

"Uh-uh. Wanna do somethin'? If there's a good band, we could hit Red Rocket or Decadence."

"No way. I'm boogied out. What I need to do, if it's cool, is to talk to you about something."

"Sure, Babygirl. You got it. Let's just hang out. We could do eachother's nails or somethin'. Nobody home but me an' Donnie."

"Who's Donnie?"

"Our housekeeper. You met her when you came over. Her name's really Dieu-Donné. It means 'gift of God' in Haitian. In French. Idd'n' 'at a trip! But my daddy can't pronounce it to save his ass, so we call her Donnie. She makes this great food. Creole. We don't get to have it when Clarissa Cunt is in residence."

"Clarissa Cunt?"

"My wicked stepmother. She thinks if she eats what she calls 'Third World food,' she'll turn coloured or poor or somethin'. She's with Johnny in Sardinia. He's opening this enormous rich people's resort there, so it's just me an' Donnie . . . an' you. Yeah, definitely come over. We'll eat chicken with rice an' peas an' I'll show you how to do your face. 'Kay?"

"Great. Thanks."

When we got to the guardhouse, Murph said that Mr. Douglas had left a house key for me and that he'd be back that night about ten. I got out of the cab, patted Grady, took the key and told Gilbey I'd come to her place after I dropped off my stuff.

I was disappointed. I'd been looking forward to seeing Pascal. Partly, it was that I wanted to tell him about the whole San Francisco trip and everything. It was also, though, that I just wanted to see him, wanted to be where he was. At some point during the plane ride back, I realized, admitted to myself, that the crush, or whatever, was HUGE.

• •

The Creole food was great, but I had a problem.

Donnie was really nice, but I had a question.

I did want to learn how to do my face, but I had a plan.

"Gilb?"

"Hey."

"Could we hold up on the face painting? I've got to talk to you about something." We were both lying on her bed. Looked like it slept six, and, what with Gilb's lots-of-guys beefeating thing, I suppose it might've, at least once.

"Damn! I'm sorry, Babygirl. You said you wanted to talk t'me about somethin'. Whassup?"

"Well . . . it's about going in once you've been out."

"Uh-huh. Could I maybe have a li'l bit more information?"

We both laughed. "I'm getting there. It's new stuff, shy stuff. Takes a little time to spit it all out."

"Thass cool. I'm good till the booze runs out. Or till I pass out."

"Oh, shit, don't pass out, I really have to—"

"Take it light, B.G. I'm just funnin'. Ain't gonna pass no out. Takes a lotta this stuff to do me in . . . so tell me."

"You know Dickie Siggins knows my mum?"

"Uh-huh."

"And that the Yobs are gonna be in Vancouver, where she lives, in two weeks."

"Uh-huh . . . oh, I get it. She don't know you're here, right?"

"Right. Dead right. And I really want to stay. I mean, my mum is this really amazing lady—"

"Yeah, Dickie said."

"Yeah, well, Dickie's right. She's smart and hot looking, and makes this amazing art and I love her, but . . . here with you . . . and Pascal. And all these amazing people and this beach, it's like . . . like I'm starting to make my own world. Roanne's world. With Roanne's people in it. And if I go back to Kits, or to wherever Del wants to land up next, I'll go back to being this . . . this piece of Del's life, this 'and' thing. And I can't do that. Not anymore. Like I'd rather hide inside one of the iron beach pipes for five years until they get tired of looking for me. Don't laugh, I mean it. Yeah, OK, laugh. It's your house. But I really do mean it. I would take stuff to draw on, stuff to draw with, and I'd stay in the fucking pipe as long as it took, and then I'd come out, put on my San Francisco jumpsuit, maybe without the platform shoes, head up the beach looking for you guys, and just continue my life. The Roanne life."

"There's gotta be an easier way than stashin' yourself in a runoff pipe."

"Yeah, there is. I think there is. I'm just using the pipe to show how big this is for me. The thing is, when Del, my mum, finds out I'm here in the Colony, it's gonna be a problem, 'cause she's got this school thing. It's also gonna be a problem because of Pascal. He already doesn't want me staying with him much longer, on account of he thinks it'll get him some sort of busted, and besides, Del'll take one look at him and she'll fuck him or kill him or both and—"

"Why don't you just stay here? With me?"

"That's the one. That's what I was going to ask."

"Shit, baby, you do go the long way round. Why'n't you just flat-out ask?"

"Because I'm Canadian. We don't like to bother people."

"Ain' no bother. It'd be great to have you here. Shit, I always wanted a sister. Even a half sister. Ain' no way that's gonna happen on accounta C.C., that would be—"

"Clarissa Cunt?"

"Thass the one. Anyway, she don't wanna give Johnny no babies on account of her tits'll droop, or get little wormy-lookin' marks on 'em . . ."

"What about Clarissa? And your father? Wouldn't they mind some stranger staying here?"

"No way. Johnny has for-fuckin'-ever wanted me to have a best friend, someone to play with who wuddn't a guy his age who led with his dick. Naw, he's gonna love this. Love it a lot."

"What about C. the C.?"

"In this house, she does what Johnny says. Most people do what Johnny says, wherever they're livin'. Besides, have you any idea how big this house is? Shit, there's eight bedrooms an' about 12 other rooms and four full baths an' two half baths, an' that's not countin' the poolhouse where Donnie lives. Look, I never want to see C.C., and she never wants to see me, and for months at a time, with both of us here, we don't. It'll be cool. It'll be great."

"Yay."

"Yeah, yay." And we hugged, and I didn't want her to know I was crying because crying was so uncool and Gilbey was so cool and then this tear that wasn't mine hit my shoulder so maybe crying was cool after all if it didn't happen in front of enemy types.

I didn't want Pascal to worry about where I was, and I wanted to tell him what I'd done to show him that I'd sorted myself without waiting for him to do it. And I needed my stuff. Gilb gave me a pair of keys ("Front door, back door") and showed me how to work the alarm. Numbered buttons to press every time I left or came in, if no one was home, or everyone was asleep ("It's big-time important, Roe. Forget, and we'll be up to our ass in guys with guns"). I told her I'd be back in an hour or two, and took off for Evil Owl House.

He wasn't there. All the way down the beach I had practised ways to be and things to say and it didn't matter. No Pascal. So I went upstairs, just to be sure. Still no Pascal. Went to his study, where there were floor-to-ceiling bookcases. Found the Didi books, most of which I'd seen before, and a big photography one from

Paris. Hauled 'em downstairs, made a ginless, rumless tonic with lime and, after I checked my face for not-ugly, curled up, barefoot, on Pascal's big white Chester to read and wait.

Didn't have to wait long. Key in front door. In he came. Big. Beautiful. In the denim shirt, black cords, sandals. He grinned. A little too goofily. Buildingman was, I was pretty sure, pissed drunk.

"Ah, Prowlet, triumphally returned from the epicenter of Rock 'n' Roll Valhalla."

"From where?"

"De rien, ma biche, de rien."

"Bitch?"

"'Beesh.' Means 'deer.'"

"Like 'darling'?"

"Like Bambi."

"Pascal, you pissed?"

"Pissed? Pissed, ye say? Well, yes, Prowlet, I believe I am. As you say, pissed. Piss-ed. Piss-ed to the tits."

"You drive like that?"

"Ah, Little Mother. Yes, dear heart, I did indeed Drive Like This. Just like this, all the way from . . . from quite a distance away. And lived to tell it. And I'm touched by your concern." He banged his big paw three times over what was probably his heart place. "Genuinely."

"Want me to make some coffee? I know how."

"Myth. Doesn't do a thing. Sleep. Best thing I could do now would be shower and go to bed. I imagine you could do with a bit of kip as well . . . unless the Benzadrine Botticelli has you wired for the week."

"Gilbey? No. We, I, haven't done any pills. But there's something I do have to tell you . . ."

"Tomorrow, Prowlet. I'll hear about all your adventures tomorrow. For now, I must bid you good night." Then he sort of bowed, sort of blew me a kiss and sort of lurched up the stairs.

It wasn't the adventures. I mean, I did want to tell him about the adventures, but I had to tell him I was moving in at Gilbey's. If I didn't tell him, he'd wake up in the morning and think I left because I was mad at him for being drunk. Like Brian did when I was a kid and ran away the first time I saw him majorly drunk. I've thought about it since, and I'm pretty sure that was why I went up the Mal Hibou stairs.

The shower was running and he was singing, or mumbling. I knocked. "Pascal?" Nothing. "PASCAL?" Still nothing. I opened the door. The whole black-tile room was a shower, sink and toilet all in one, with a long shower attachment in the wall that you could hold in your hand, as opposed to the Yankanadian thing you had to just stand under. There was a big drain in the middle of the floor.

Pascal's head hair, beard hair, arm and leg hair were all gleamy and wet. His chest hair was like a comic-strip balloon you write words in, all full around his guytits, then tapering down in a line of hair to his Thing. Around his Thing, like on his arms and pits, was lots of soap lather. In the middle of the Thing lather was the Thing. It was peachy-pink, hard as a cat's scratching post, and pointing right at me. I wondered if he had been doing Onanism, like Mrs. Ross in grade five said Bobby Keating wasn't supposed to. I hoped not, because Mrs. Ross said it was really risky, and I didn't think there could be a blind photographer.

Pascal was smiling slightly, but he looked tired, and sort of sad.

"You OK?"

"Mm-hmm."

"Great shower."

"Mm-hmm." He reattached the shower sprayer to the wall, stood under it, water running down his body. He was looking at me. No smile. Not mad. Not anything. Just looking at me, his gray-green eyes almost as dark as the slate tiles down to the guesthouse. It was like he was waiting for me, me, the amateur, the 14-year-old 16-year-old, to do something so he wouldn't be accused of raping a statue, or whatever the hell that American bustable was. Beefeating was out of the question. I mean, I really felt like I loved this person, but rancid fish glue?

It was good that he wasn't jumping me or smirking or anything. He was just looking. Deeply looking. This was my shot. I knew if I didn't take that shot there might not be another one. I was looking back at him, trying to be as no-blinky as he was. Trying to show I was brave. I was all gulped-up inside and poundy and breathing through my nose so I wouldn't sound like a telephone pervo. My fists were clenching and unclenching, just like my lower holes. I wanted to scream or laugh or do something noisy that would turn the eyelock into some sort of celebration.

"This is a bad idea," he said, very softly.

"Is not," I said.

He laughed, just one small "Ha!" He held out his hand to me like God in the Vatican ceiling. I grabbed onto it with both hands. He pulled me to him and I was hugging him and kissing his wet chest hairs, soaking wet in my jeans and black tanktop (later he said I was "suckling," sucking on his nipple. I don't remember doing this).

He unzipped my wet jeans. I sat on the tile floor and pulled them off, threw them into a corner. Stood up. He took off my tank. I was reaching up to put my arms around him, to hug him, to hold him, to kiss him.

"Easy, Prowlet. Slippery. You'll crack both our skulls. Hold still." He soaped me, all over, tits, lower-hole zones and all, then rinsed me with the shower thing. Wrapped a blanket-sized black towel around his shoulders and dried me with the other. It was nice, and, for a minute, softened my crazyhot into something about safety. I thought, amazingly, of hot spiced milk.

Then he dried himself. I watched, all full of happy. He looked really incredible. "I think you're beautiful," I said very quietly.

"And I think you're beautiful." He took my hand. "Come."

He let go of my hand to light two fat white candles on a table next to his huge bed. (As thumpy and pumpy as I was, I still wondered if anybody in Malibu Colony had your basic double bed. Probably not. I was trying to remember if, before I took off from Yachats, I'd ever seen a bed bigger than double. Didn't think so.) He lay down, on his back, on the bed. Even with the candles, it was pretty dark, but I could see that his Thing was pointing toward his chin. He just lay there, didn't reach for me or anything.

"I . . . I don't know what I'm supposed to do."

"What would you like to do?"

"Be next to you."

"Please. Please be next to me."

The bed was higher up off the ground than shorter people's beds. I climbed onto it and scootched over next to his body, pressing myself right next to his skin. It was hot, his skin, like the blood under it was shining through, like when you hold a turned-on flashlight behind your closed fingers. His arm had muscles. His body hair was soft. He smelled like limes and wood. Next to his skin was the best place I'd ever been. I was kissing and biting and licking his arm and then I shinnied up higher and kissed his mouth and he kissed me back and we were both using our tongues and it was, maybe because I loved him so much, the best I'd ever done that.

We were on our sides now, looking at eachother. I'd gotten used to the light and could see his shiny eyes and friendsmile. I smiled back, tongue-kissed him again, to prove to both of us that I could do that twice. It was time, whether it crushed me to death or not, for him to climb onto me, to be inside me. But he didn't. He was still really hard and I was wriggling all over his side and sort of humping his leg like dogs do and kissing his arm, his neck, his face, and I knew I was really wet inside because I could feel my own goop on his leg.

Then I remembered, not in a bad way, Del and Marcus. She had been on top of him. I hadn't known, before biting my mum's bum, that there was even a position with the girl on top. I climbed onto Pascal, sitting on him, just below his thing. "Can I? Can I put. Your thing. Inside me?"

"Mm-hmm."

But when I started, he swung his hands up to my shoulders, holding me away from him. "Slowly," he said, "very slowly."

I did "slowly" for as long as I could stand it, then sank down onto his belly, his thing all the way inside, bumping up against the bottom of the inside of my belly so it would almost hurt if I wasn't really excited. I said "Oh!" and "Ooh!" and "Ah!" and was wriggling around against his skin like something itched like a throat tickle inside my stomach and his big hands were in my hair and he was softly laughing and wriggling and pushing up into me and saying "Mm-hmm" and then I was screaming and exploding inside and hanging on like he was a mountain and I was going to fall off and I didn't want, really didn't want to fall off. Not now, not ever, and this exploding was so huge, so everywhere, it was all of the happiness in all of the world and I was saying, "Wait! Wait for me! Please wait!" but I wasn't stopping, wasn't waiting and neither was he, and when I thought I was slowing down, floating down, and knowing all at once why there was a rock band called the Sweet Jesus Parachute, the whole amazing thing started again! Laughing, screaming, afraid he wouldn't wait, even though he said, "I'm here, Prowlet, I'm with you." Then he exploded too, in the middle of my second one and I finished my second parachute float before he did, but I shoved both my hands under his bum and jammed myself onto him as hard as I could so he could have his own explosion, which was the least I could do for a man whose thing made my entire body, brain and heart explode in a yay hooray that probably caused people all over Malibu to sit up in their humungus beds and say, "What the hell was that?!"

Nothing smelled like limes, wood and soap anymore. More like sweat and, yeah, fishglue. I was lying froglike on top of Pascal, giggling "tee" and shaking my head because I was still surprised and amazed. Pascal's hands were playing with my sweaty hair, rubbing my head, massaging my neck.

"Was that the first time?"

"Fourth. But first time the . . . exploding thing happened."

"I thought that might be true. I'm honoured."

"You should be." Then I realized how that might sound, and sat up. "I didn't mean you should be like 'you bloody well ought to be.' I meant you did an amazing thing and should feel honoured that you're able to do it."

"A lot of people have that . . . skill, Prowlet."

"Really? People you know?"

He was laughing, holding my hair out of my eyes. "Yes, Prowlet, people I know."

"People *I* know?"

"I should think so. If you like, we can try ringing them up. Sample three or four of 'em before sun-up."

"Oh, no! I didn't mean it like that, I just meant—"

"It's all right. You're full of wonder and joy and it's lovely. I was just . . ."

"Takin' the piss?"

"Yes, my lyric young love, takin' the piss . . . which, if you would be so kind as to dismount, I desperately need to do now."

"What?"

"Take a piss."

I climbed off and Pascal headed for the loo. As soon as I separated from the plug of Pascal's thing, major more-than-ever-before bodygoop came out of me and onto Pascal's white bedspread. White on white. Not so bad, but definitely more gross than not-gross. I wanted to clean it up. Pascal, proving he was a psychic genius, returned with a yellow towel. "Is that for goop?"

"Goop?"

"I gooped. Lots of sticky stuff came out of me. Here. See?"

"Goop tends to happen. Here, put this between your legs. It's the traditional goop catcher. Or better still, go have a wash."

While washing face-pits-crotch, I remembered Gilbey. She was probably waiting for me to come back to her place. And I hadn't told Pascal that I'd arranged to stay there. Now, I wasn't sure I wanted to tell him. What if he liked the explosion as much as I did and wanted me to stay at Evil Owl House? He did say I was beautiful. He did call me his "lyric young love." Just thinking about it made my face go all hot and red. It was too much to get my mind around. I needed more information. I needed to keep the magic of the right now for a little while longer.

Pascal had blown out the candles and turned on a little lamp shaped, at least to me, like an Art Deco dick. The shape made me laugh.

"What's so funny?"

I pointed at the lamp. "Art Dicko."

He made his "Ha!" noise, shook his head. "Oh, gawd, I've created a phallomaniac."

"What's that?"

"Dick worshipper."

"Cartoonist."

"Oh, right, cartoonist. I'm surrounded by bloody cartoonists. And they're all dick worshippers. Now, are you going to stand there all night like September Morn, or would you care to join me under the covers?"

"All night? Can I 'join you' all night?'"

"You make me feel like a john. Or a trollop. 'No, gimme twenty quid, luv, an' I'll be off 'ome to buy milk for our kid.' Of course all night."

"Great. Super. I need to call Gilbey first, though. Told her I'd come over. She could be waiting up."

"Sure. Use this phone. Unless you need privacy," (he said "privvy," like Del sometimes did).

"Uh-uh. Don't know the number, though."

"It's in the book. The dark red one."

There were two small leather address books next to the phone. One was racing green, like the Morgan. The other was burgundy, and on the front it said, in gold, NORTH AMERICA/U.K. I looked under "T." "Tarr, Gilbey" was just above "Townes, Ashleigh." I wondered if that was the Ashleigh I'd met at my bogus birthday party. The Ashleigh with D'Artagnan Roland (unless L.A. was up to its ass in Ashleighs, it sort of had to be). I wondered if she modelled for Pascal. I wondered if he'd given her an explosion too. I knew he'd given Gilb one. Were all the names in the book explodees? I wanted to look through and try to figure it out, but couldn't very well do that with Pascal in the room. I got under the covers, turned toward the phone, pretended not to realize I was pressing my bum against his body-warm leg. I pressed Gilbey's numbers.

"Oh, hi, Donnie. It's Roanne. May I speak to Gilbey, please?"

"Oh, allo, Mamzelle Rwan. Mamzelle Geelbay is not'ere. She leave a note 'ere for you. She say she see you in the mornang."

"Oh. OK, Donnie. Thank you. I'm staying with a friend too. See you tomorrow." I hung up. "Gilb split."

"She doesn't like being alone. She's been alone too much, that one."

"Do you think she's doing . . . what we just did?"

"Gilbey? Damn near a dead certainty. Though probably not as brilliantly. And it's almost a full moon. Makes people randy and foolish."

"Foolish?"

"Bloody ridiculous. Now, turn out the light, light of my life. Old people need sleep."

I'd never actually slept, as in sleep, with a man I'd also slept, as in fucked, with. I had thought it would be a huggy sort of business, but when I put my head on Pascal's chest and reached to hold him around the neck, he said it was impossible, and he taught me a two-people sleeping position. Well, not exactly taught. It was the spoony one I did with Del, except that I could feel his soft thing between the cheeks of my bum, and he didn't so much hold me as fling one big hairy arm over my body. He murfled something with "Prowlet" on the end of it, moved my hair, like Del always did, out of the way of his face. He kissed my back two times and then was, *bam!* asleep. I knew because I said his name, twice, really softly, and he didn't answer. I was glad his arm was over me, so entirely happy that I thought only the arm's weight was keeping me from float-flying straight up and disappearing into the sky way too soon in my life.

I woke up first. Pascal was over on the other side of the bed. I moved a bit closer, leaned up on my elbow and looked at his big black-and-gray bearded face. His eyebrows looked bushier when his eyes were closed, and his eyelashes seemed longer. His nose, which I hadn't particularly noticed before, was beautiful. Straight and strong, like Nevin, the Shakespeare actor from Stavro's theatre company. His mouth was sort of a rectangle, but full, sexy. There were little lines, down-turned indentations, beginning on each side of his lower lip. A few lines across his forehead and a frowny pair of vertical ones between his eyebrows. There was a tiny scar on his right cheek, like an animal had scratched him. There was a little black zit on his other cheek. When Del got those on her back, she'd let me squeeze them. I was pretty sure if I woke Pascal by doing that, he would be annoyed. Angry, even. Definitely did not want that. What I wanted was to pee, but was afraid that if I left the bed, somehow I would not be allowed to return to it. I knew this wasn't logical, but felt it so strongly that I stayed there, doing my famous Camel Thing.

When Pascal was almost awake, he reached for me, pulled me close. The Wonderthing was up, so I tried to climb on top. "Mm-mm," he said, getting out of bed and leaving the room. His bum was whiter than the rest of his skin. When he came back, Wonderthing was soft.

"Did you Onanize?"

"Did I what?"

"Um . . . wank?"

"Ohmigawd, such elegant discourse, Prowlet. No, I did not, as you so endearingly put it, 'wank.' What you were trying to mount, however, was not, despite your extraordinary desirability, a proper erection. It was, to describe it in language similar to that of whomever has taught you English, a 'piss-hard.' On the other hand, if one may risk even mentioning another hand so soon after one has been accused of wanking, this glorious priapism you see growing, even as we speak, is all for you."

It's not just fucking and beefeating. There are parts of one person's body that can be put together with the most amazing collection of another person's body parts in order to make an explosion. The explosions are, in fact, what Del called "coming." And it truly is as superamazingbrillianterrific as Del said it would be. It can also be called, if you want to be really grand and all, "achieving orgasm." In Brit slang, according to Pascal, it can also be called "spending" or "spunking." It genuinely surprised me when he said lots of people could do it. I mean, I didn't think we invented it or anything, but it seemed to me that if something was so amazing, people would be talking about it all over the place. Pascal said it was in books and films sometimes, but that it was probably a good idea not to try talking about it at parties and stuff, because it was a personal matter and would probably make people feel uncomfortable as a social discussion subject.

He kept saying he was "on deadline" and had to get into the darkroom, but we stayed in the *QE2* (that's what Pascal calls his bed, which is actually bigger than a regular king-size) all morning, while I climbed all over him, laughing a lot and figuring out different ways to explode.

Finally we had to stop because I was really sore and a little swollen. Pascal, laughing and holding me, said, "Bloody good thing too. I do not wish to deny you, Prowlet, but if we keep swiving at this rate, dear heart, there will be nothing left of this old satyr for the days to come." I didn't understand all the words he was using. Satyr? Swiving? Priapism? Pascal, like Jan, the "ephemeral" woman in San Francisco whose family invented sugar, has a lot of big fancy words. This was, I thought, good. I liked looking up words. I told him what Dickie said about Gilbey and asked him about "beefeating." That really made him laugh, which was also good, because he tended to hug me when I made him laugh, which was majorly good, especially when there was naked skin in the hugging. I mean, all hug is good, but naked hug is the best. He said one could do beefeating without having to swallow goop and that it wasn't called beefeating, and yes, it could be called "a blowjob," "going down" or "giving head" (the terms I'd heard at school and around), but its real name was "fellatio." Fellatio. Sounded like a great Italian painter. I said it was funny, considering what the word meant, but that the word was beautiful in the mouth. That made both of us laugh, getting the joke at the same time (I love it when that happens. Especially with older people. Most especially with an older person you love, which Pascal, that morning, definitely was). Then he flipped me off him, where I'd been frog-hugging. He said he had lots of wonderful new words for me, but that they'd have to keep for next time, or some woman called Ghislaine ("Spell that," I said. He did.) would have him shot for missing his deadline.

Right. He said I was beautiful. He said I was desirable. He said we'd learn more words "next time." He let me stay in his bed all night. He seemed really happy exploring explosions with me. So, where was I? What was my situation? Where did I live? Fucked if I knew.

I heard the shower, got out of bed, went down the hall, opened the loo door.

"No," Pascal said, holding up his hand, "do not come one step closer or this day is lost."

"But . . ."

"No, Prowlet, not 'but.' Please, if you care for me, return to the bedroom, return to any room but this one. Until I've finished showering. Once I have vacated this room, you may shower. Now, go!"

I went. Pascal's darkroom was in the basement and, no, I couldn't watch him develop pictures. There were starting to be a lot of "no's" (OK, only two, but it was beginning to feel like a trend). I was flooded up with questions. I really wanted to ask some of them, but for as long as I didn't, there was less possibility of "no." So I stayed shtumm and drank my bowl of café au lait at the kitchen counter, while he wandered about with his bowl, talking on a long-cord telephone.

"Yes, Ghislaine, I know. This afternoon, by courier or in person. . . . Between three and four . . . yes, love, I promise. 'Bye." He washed out his coffee bowl, looked over at me, smiled. "So, we need to . . ." He walked to the chesterfield, sat, patted it for me to come and sit. I did. He put his hand on my exposed knee. (I was wearing one of his short black cotton Japanese robes. A jacket on him, on me it was full length. My jeans and tanktop were still wet from the night before, and he'd thrown them into a dryer, also somewhere in the basement.)

He smiled his friend smile. His eyes were also friend. "Oh, look at you. You look like I'm going to do something hurtful . . . and perhaps I am." (Oh, God, I thought. Do. Not. Cry.) "Look, Prowlet, you have a wonderful . . . aliveness. . . . Your joy is . . . well, a joy. It seems clear that it's, if not a good idea, certainly a lovely idea that we . . . spend some time together." (Do not panic. Do not cry.) "And I want us to do that. But I'm a 42-year-old man and you are . . . an underage girl. With what I have been told is a fierce mother. So I would like you to be . . . a part of my life, but I do not, under any circumstances whatever, want this fierce mother to be a part of my life. You do understand this?"

"Yes" (gnat-sized voice).

"Good." He got up, walked to the glass doors, turned round to face me. "And, as we discussed when you arrived, this is not the ideal place for you to be staying." (It is for me! It is for me!) "I don't know when your mum is arriving to collect you, and I'm not entirely certain you do either. What I do know is that you should be my visitor, not my guest, and that, for everyone's sake, something needs to be arranged, as soon as possible, concerning where . . . oh, God, don't cry." He stayed where he was. I stayed where I was. I turned my face away from him.

"I'm not. OK, I am, but it's cool. I mean, a lot of stuff has happened and I'm . . . I've already done the 'place to stay' thing. I'm going to move in at Gilbey's."

"You are? When did this happen?"

"We agreed on it last night."

"Are you making this up?"

I leapt up. "Fuck you, Pascal! You can't fuck me like I'm a grown woman and then talk to me like you caught me cutting class or something and if I'm crying it's because I have feelings, which maybe old guys don't, and no, I'm not making any fucking thing fucking up and I was coming back here last night to pack my stuff and tell you I was moving over to Gilb's and that's what I'm gonna do now, and if you want to see me or whatever, you can call me, it's in your North America/U.K. address book next to Tarr, Gilbey, on the same page as Townes, Ashleigh, and all the other 'T' people you stuck your thing into!"

"Penis! Cock! Dick! You want to be a bloody 'grown woman,' you cannot keep referring to my member as my 'thing'!"

"Whatever! I'm gonna go pack!"

Hauling all my gear, stomping up the beach to Gilbey's in the late morning, screaming, "Willy! The fucker forgot willy! His member? Member of what? If his goddamn peniscockdick is a member who else is in the goddamn club? Everybody in his fucking phone book! Both phone books, I'll bet!" (Later, when I told Gilb about my beach-rant, she said, "That's one of the great things about the Colony. Everybody's so damn rich you have more room to be crazy. Unless you're wavin' a gun around, people just kinda look the other way when you lose it.")

Donnie opened the door, scooping up my shitload of gear like it weighed zip. She said Gilbey wasn't back yet but that she'd show me to my room.

It was a sweet room. White, with yellow-and-white checked curtains and the first double bed I'd seen in ages. What with all the stuff that had happened, both brilliant and fuckin' awful, I was supertired. Lay down on the white-and-yellow quilt, still wearing the black cotton robe that smelled like Pascal, and fell dead asleep.

It was still daylight when I woke up. I was hungry. Went downstairs, looking for food and for Gilbey. Donnie was shelling peanuts in the kitchen. She said she was "worray."

"Mamzelle Geelbay do whatevair she wan' about 'ome—not 'ome, but she 'ave tol' me sure she be 'ere in mornang to meet you. Also, when she decide to stay out long time, she always tellayphun becauzat is rule of M'sieu Tarr."

Donnie said there were special "saycooreetay" police for the Colony, police who kept people's names out of the newspapers and stuff. She wondered if she should call them, should report Gilbey missing. I knew how freaked I had been, how freaked I still was, about the possibility of Del doing that.

"I dunno, Donnie, she's only a few hours late. Gilb sort of zones out when she's having fun. Let's wait a while, I think." Donnie still looked "worray," but agreed to wait until dark. She said she was going up to the Colony supermarket to get some stuff. And "Oh, M'sieu Pascal was 'ere while you sleep. 'E say you forget some of your clothang at 'is pool'ouse."

There in the kitchen, on a chair, neatly folded, were my jeans, my black tanktop. And Pascal's denim shirt! Sitting on top of the shirt was a little white envelope with "Prowlet" written on it.

I heard the front door close and was glad to be alone because, the minute I saw that shirt, eyeblubber kicked in hard. I tore open the envelope, tearing a piece of the note as well. I held it together and read.

My dear Prowlet,

Happiness can be overwhelming to those who do not often witness it. Please accept this gift in lieu of the many things I can neither give nor be. You are not a "grown" woman, nor should you be, just yet. You are a wondrous young woman, and I'm very pleased to be your friend. If I still am? Telephone me? 453-2271,

Affectueusement,

P.

I had my hand on the phone when it rang. I picked up. All I heard was breathing. "Hello?"

"Hey, Vavygir . . ." It sounded like she had hot mashed potatoes in her mouth. "You lyuh?"

"What?"

"You 'lone?"

"Yeah. Donnie went to the Colony market. You sound awful. You drunk?"

"No. Can't talk. Clease, cong geck ee! Clease!"

"Come get you?"

"Yes."

"Where?"

"Ge' keng. Wri'."

I grabbed a pen and notepaper next to the phone. It took a while because Gilbey's speech was so weird, but I got the address down. "Where is that?"

"Vel Air."

"Bel Air? How do I get there from here?"

"Taxi. I pay. Non't tell ayvuddy, 'kay?"

"'Kay. I'll be there fast as I can."

Taxi. Yellow Valley. Card. I ran upstairs, emptied out my bookbag. There it was, Yellow Valley. Ray Flynn.

"Hello, I need Ray Flynn, car 327."

"Where are you phoning from?"

"Malibu Colony."

"327? One moment . . . 327 is in West Hollywood now. We don't normally send specific drivers, we can send—"

"No! It has to be 327. I'll pay double."

"Are you a regular client?"

"Yes. Casa del Cielo."

"In the Valley?"

"Yes. I'm in the Colony at the moment. Look, it has to be 327! Can I give you my number? Can Mr. Flynn phone me? It's superimportant!"

"That's OK, Mrs. Dobson. Just give me the address and number, and I'll get Flynn out to you A.S.A.P." I gave him the info and hung up. He thought I was Mara! Probably thought I was pissed! Didn't matter what he thought. Only mattered that I got to Gilbey before whatever was wrong was wronger. Ran back up to my room. Put on jeans and Pascal's shirt.

Donnie:

Gilbey telephoned. I've gone to pick her up. We'll see you later. Don't worry.

Thanks,

Roanne

I put the note on the kitchen table next to the bowl of shelled peanuts. Ate a banana and a cinnamon roll. Drank half a bottle of Perrier. Doorbell rang.

"Figgered it was you. Wassup?"

"Dunno, Ray, but we've got to go fast."

"Damn, baby. You ever get to go slow?"

"Not a lot lately. Here's the address."

"Bel Air? You rich people do get to get in trouble at some fine addresses." It was weird. It was Del's voice that came out of me, in Del's way.

"Listen, mate, I'm probably the least rich bloody person you get to drive about. I've a friend in trouble is all, and I need to get her and I'm trusting you to help me. OK?"

"Absotively."

"Can I sit in front with you?"

"It's against the rules and 'course you can."

They wouldn't let us in. Guard guys, like in Malibu Colony, but no dog and nowhere near as friendly as Murph. Their pencil house was gray and stony and they, both of them, were gray and stony too.

"Where do you wish to go?"

Ray read out the address.

"Mr. Hubscher? Mr. Hubscher is out."

Hubscher? Who he? Then I remembered. Kurt, the shave-headed old guy who offered to drive me home at the birthday party. Gilbey knew him. "We're here to pick up his houseguest. Miss Gilbey Tarr. She expects us."

The fat one looked in a big notebook. "Tarr? T-a-r-r-?"

"Yes, that's right."

"We'll have to call. What is your name, please?"

"Roanne Chappell. C-h-a-p-p-e-l-l."

"One minute." He dialled a number, listened to it ring, hung up. "No answer. Sorry." He wasn't sorry. He didn't give a damn. He turned away, expecting us to just bugger off.

"Please, could you try one more time? She may be having a bath." (Or a shit, I thought, but knew it wouldn't help to say it.) He dialled again, waited, then, "H'lo. Izzis Miss Tarr? There's a Miss Chappell here in a taxi. Says she's supposed to—very good. Next time, miss, if you're expecting guests, tell Mr. Hubscher to leave word at the gate, please. Will do. Good night." He looked at Ray and me like we were Wormshit Central. "You can pick up your friend. Fifth house on the left. It shouldn't take too long. Mr. Hubscher is out and he didn't leave any names."

"Thank you, sir," I said. "I hope a whole family of starving scorpions nests in your fat ass," I thought.

• •

When I was six, Brian went crazy-drunk-grenade on St. Valentine's Day. He beat Del really badly. I kept running at him to make him stop, and each time I'd get close enough to tug on his shirt, he would throw me against the wall, and Del would scream, but she couldn't get up, couldn't protect herself, couldn't protect me.

They had rowed before, but it was, as far as I knew, all mouth. They both had a lot of mouth, and mostly used it to make eachother think, make eachother laugh. Del has always said they really loved eachother. I believe this is true. I also believe they both loved me. The thing was, Brian was two guys, Sober Bri and Drunk Bri. Sober, he'd make jokes about Drunk Bri, call his drunkness the Irish Flu.

When he saw what he'd done, he was completely freaked and cried and begged and pleaded and had a sorry the size of the world, a weepy sorry so big it made his nose run and his whole face blur.

And it didn't matter. "You hurt my kid, you bloody bastard. You're gone." Her voice was quiet. "We're going to leave now. We'll be back, with friends, or police, or whatever it takes to get you out of here. That clear?"

"Please, darlin' love . . ."

"No. No please. No darlin'. No love. Gone. You have to leave." She was holding me in her arms. I was a little bruise-y and sore, but not seriously hurt. Del had taken the worst of it, by a lot. I didn't know what to feel. I loved Brian. We had fun. He taught me songs and poems, sometimes making them up on the spot, just spinning them out from nothing. Hitting, or any other physical bad stuff, had never happened before. As I thought this, it was like I sent the thought to him.

"Delora, please, nothing like this ever happened before, and I swear to you, it'll never, never happen again, hand to my heart!"

She stood, slowly, painfully, still holding me. "No, Bri. I can't. I swore too. Swore that this child would never see this sort of . . . madness in her home. This is her home. Our home. You are a guest here. I'm sorry. I truly am, because . . . no, the because doesn't matter. There is only that you've got to go. Now. Tonight."

He held out a hand to her, palm up. "Is there nothing I can do to change this? To stay?"

She sat me in the soft wine-coloured chair. Her eyes were weird, in a way I'd never seen on her before (or since). Like the Reeses' dog from up the street, the one they kept in a big cage. Shiny eyes, and, like Brian said in the letter he left, "cold and sure as a knife." She walked really close to him, looked up at him, stood right in his face, with those eyes and her broken lip. "Yeh, Bri. You can kill me."

We didn't have to go get friends or police or anything. Del carried me upstairs and bathed me, with lots of bubbles, in our clawfoot tub. No speaking. No singing. Just this deep, hot, silent bubblebath. Then she dried me and ran the same sort of bath for herself. I lowered the toilet seat, sat down, watched her bathe. There were baboonybum bruise marks all over her body, all over her face. She washed cut-lip blood off her jaw and chest. We could hear Brian packing, hear him crying. Del dried herself, put talc on both of us, braided my hair, then hers.

We stayed in the loo until the door slammed downstairs. Then Del took my hand and we went to the kitchen. She cooked us a pair of baked potatoes.

We never saw Brian again. Maybe he left the province. Maybe he went back to Ireland or England. When I was eleven, I tried to find him. Sometimes I would look for his name in poetry magazines. Nothing. It was like he vanished off the earth. None of Del's guys after Brian had the Irish Flu. None of them ever hit Del, or me. Stavro was good to us, and fun to know, but I don't think any of them loved us as much. Or had Sober Brian's huge, magical poet's heart. But, like Del said, if the poet-hearted guy has a demon inside, and the demon could do you serious harm, you simply have to do without and hope for a demon-free poet in the future.

He took all his stuff that night, except for the two poem books he'd made us for Christmas. Handwritten. One for Del, one for me.

• •

I took one look at Gilbey and asked Ray to please wait for us in the cab.

Both her lips were smashed up, and the lower one was swollen like mad. So was her left eye. There were teethmarks in her shoulder and her little black spaghetti-strap dress was torn and hanging by one strap. There was a baboon bruise on her exposed left breast and all over her arms and neck. I figured she'd showered because her hair was wet.

"Hey, Vavygirl."

"Jesus, Gilb."

"Genng outta here." When we were in the cab, she said she couldn't go home. "Iss'l scare shit outta Donnie. Don' think she'll tell Daddy i' I ask her not to, 'ut need to get nyself together a li'l. Diver, you know a quiet li'l hotel?"

"You look pretty chewed up, babe, you need to clean up before you go where they's people."

Cut lip and all, Gilbey smiled (all her teeth were OK). "Hey, Vuvva! Where you from?"

"Valdosta, Georgia."

"Hey, Cracker!"

"Hey yisself, girl. You?"

"Charleston."

"St. Cecilia's Cotillion?"

"My momma. Daddy cons fun lintheads."

"Aw-right."

"You gotta hohn, Cracker? C'd I clean ut there?"

"I gotta be outta my mind. Yeah, sure. White trash solidarity."

It was supergood to hear Gilbey laugh. It didn't make anything less serious, or less horrible—just a little less sad and scary.

Ray's place was in West Hollywood and looked like a two-story motel. It was called Levinson Lanai. The only other time I'd heard "lanai" was at Casa del Cielo, and I wondered if it was some sort of Christian glosso. Ray said it was a Hawaiian word, but that the Levinsons weren't Hawaiian. He said there was a Rancho Rabinowitz around the corner and Logan's Lagoon two blocks away. "It's an L.A. thing," he said.

• •

The floor-to-ceiling glass doors of Ray's "studio apartment" faced a courtyard. There was a blob-shaped swimming pool and some umbrella tables and chairs. Nobody was in the pool. He put his baffed-out brown leather jacket around Gilbey and we walked her inside, as fast as possible. I was glad it was dark.

"I can't say hap my damn consonants. You call Donnie, Vavygir. Te'r I went to 'Arm Strings."

"Arm Strings?"

"Think she means Palm Springs," Ray said, pouring Jack Daniel's into a juice glass and handing it to Gilbey. Then he gave her a facecloth to put over her lower lip so the booze wouldn't burn as much. Gilbey nodded.

"Palm Springs. OK. With who?"

"Hubscher."

"The fuckhead who did this?"

"Uh-huh. He ain' gonna deny nuthin' vout no 'Arm Strings. If Johnny finds out what he did, he'll shut his 'uckin' lights out! An' Kurt damn knows it. He went to get his damn doctor . . . vastard's scared." She chugalugged the whole glass in one shot, then held it out for Ray to refill. He did. Gilb wrote out her phone number.

"Donnie. Hi, it's Roanne. Everything's cool, everything's fine with Gilbey. She asked me to call you because she was . . . running . . . to catch a plane. Kurt Hubscher, a friend of hers, was taking a group of people to a birthday party in Palm Springs. She said she'd be back . . . in a few, in three days . . . she . . . call you from under. From down. Down THERE. Me? Later. No, don't go to any trouble with dinner. I'm not sure how late I'll get back to Malibu. Thank you, though. Very much. 'Bye."

When, while trying to interpret Gilbey's hand signals, I said "three days," Ray looked a little, even borderline a lot, worried. The Gilb, wedged in the corner of his beige-y chesterfield, said, "Ve cool, Vuvva. I'll get to a hotel. Like you said, though, need to look nore together firs'. You got a tencil and tafer? Thanks." She wrote down a bunch of stuff, reached into her little gold bag, pulled out a little gold plastic card. Handed them both to me. "Vavygirl (her lipcut was starting to close with scabby blood. Her "L"s were stronger) you go in the taxi to these tlaces, vuy these things, OK?"

I looked at her chickenscribble.

The Max—owner Carlo. Rodeo Drive, just n. of Wilshire—Long midnight blue jersey dress with tutleneck, long sleeves. Designer Mira DiNovi.

Beverly Hills Chemists, Wilshire—Derm-Efface creme coverage. Shades. Peaches 'n' Cream and Alabaster.

"Gilb, I can't pass myself off as you. I'll get busted."

"Don' 'orry. I'n gonna call the stores now. Tell 'en you're conin'. They know ne an' I'll descride you."

Gilbey didn't realize how late it was. The Max was closed, so she called the Carlo guy at home. Amazingly, he agreed to meet Ray and me at the shop. The Derm-Efface place was open until midnight. Ray said he'd "run a tab" and we took off.

Carlo had the dress all ready, in a shiny black shopping bag full of hot pink tissue paper. We thanked him. "Any time. Miss Tarr and Mrs. Tarr are very valued customers." Then we got the makeup and headed back to West Hollywood.

Gilbey was sound asleep under a blanket on Ray's chester, hair all wild and Botticelli. Face still pretty fucked-up. We tiptoed around, figuring she could use the sleep.

I took the dress out of the tissue paper. Laid it over the back of a chair. The makeup label said Derm-Efface was for "maximum coverage. Ideal after surgical procedures." Had Gilbey ever had "surgical procedures"?

"Listen, Roanne, yer buddy here's hadda helluva a time. Whyn't you just let 'er sleep it off. I c'n bring 'er to the Colony tomorrow. The tab's covered. I c'n take you there now an' then go back to work. My shift is until four."

"Ray, I don't know a lot about it, but I think her father knows these gangsters an' stuff. If you touch her . . ."

"You think I'd do that?"

I looked at him. I didn't. Shook my head. Smiled. He smiled back.

It was 1:30 in the morning. Donnie had to be asleep. I took the keys out of my shirt pocket, opened the door, opened the hall closet, pressed all the buttons, 22342. The red light turned green. I would not, at least on this particular night, be up to my ass in guys with guns.

There was a covered clear glass bowl on the kitchen table. Chicken with rice and peas. I was too weirded out, too still-seeing Gilb's bruises and smashups, to even think about food, but I did think about how great Donnie was. How great Adelita was. All these rich kids with insane family stuff were lucky to have these sweet women worrying about them, feeding them, loving them. And I was luckier because I had Del. Did I still have Del? She was probably seriously mad at me by now, I thought, but yes, I, for sure, still had Del. I would always have Del. Did I still want Del? Yes, yes, definitely. Always. But not so close by. At least not for a while.

Gilbey had truly become, in a fairly short time, very special to me. There is no other possible explanation for the fact that, from the time she phoned and asked me to come get her, I had not thought once of Pascal's shirt, of Pascal's note, of Pascal. As soon as I was safe, and knew Gilbey was safe, he was my first thought. I pulled his note out of his shirt that was now, amazingly, my shirt, and went to the phone in the hall. Dialled. No answer. Probably just as well. I was punchy with tiredness.

Donnie had been sweet enough to leave food out for me. I didn't want to insult that, so I hauled the glass bowl upstairs, figuring I'd eat it in the morning. Needed a bath. Took a bubble one, in Gilbey's fancy marble sunken tub. I was still very slightly sore from where I'd been exploded. That made me smile.

Had a dream. I was at Pascal's and there was blood shooting out of the bright red sunset into the sea. Pascal wasn't around. Just outside the glass doors, the beach and sea were full of tigers. Tigers everywhere. Sleeping tigers, tigers playing with a beachball, tigers fighting, tigers eating people, tigers eating people's pets, tigers cleaning eachother with big pink tongues.

There was this loud, steady, growling purr that went on and on and on. I was wearing Pascal's shirt. I took it off. I was naked. I opened the glass doors, then closed them behind me (so tigers wouldn't get into Pascal's house and make a mess while he wasn't home). The tiger lying just in front of the door, paws in front of him like a Mytho-God, licked my bare feet. It felt good. I let him do that while I looked around.

There were browny-red bloodstains all over the sand. I started to walk toward Gilbey's house. Two really big tigers came and walked with me, one on each side. They were purring, and it didn't seem like they would hurt me. I was scared, but I was also buzzed, pumped. There were body parts, an arm here, a thigh there, a toe with a red-varnished nail being batted back and forth by a pair of tiny cubs. There was hair (and hairpieces). A half-eaten skull under the paws of a dozy tiger, his face all bloody.

"Prowlet! Prowlet!" Pascal was screaming in a voice so loud it cut through his glass doors and made some of the tigers look up, look toward Evil Owl House. He was gesturing really hard for me to come back. I wanted to know if Gilbey was OK, but I wanted to please Pascal more, so I headed back, just walking, because I thought if I ran it would make the tigers attack (like Del once told me about bears when we were in the woods in B.C.). When I got to the glass doors, Pascal pulled me inside and locked the doors. "Are you completely insane! What in God's name possessed you to go out there?" He spun me around, hard, to face the beach, and pointed. "Look! Look, dammit! Can't you see the tigers, you stupid cow?! Can you not see all the blood, all the torn-up people?! What in hell were you trying to do, get yourself killed?!"

The sky and sea were full of blood and the tigers were getting majorly crazed. Charging around. Dragging bloody bodies. Bounding and leaping up in the air, all fangs and teeth. Except for "my" two, who seemed to be just waiting for me. I was sure these two tigers were friendly. I wanted to let them in, to demonstrate their friendliness to Pascal, but I was also sure that if I even suggested this, he would go ballistic. I turned to face him, looked up, looked him in the eyes as strongly and calmly as I could.

"I was lonesome, Pascal, OK? I was bored. I wanted to go for a beach walk. I wanted company. I wanted to be with . . . with whoever was here. Tigers are who's here."

When I woke up it was 10 A.M. and tigerless. The bowl of yesterday's Haitian dinner on the dresser was a really gross first-thing-in-the-morning food idea. I went to Gilbey's room, telephoned Pascal.

"Thank you for the shirt, Pascal. I love it."

"I hoped you would. I stopped by last night. Dieu-Donné said you'd gone off to fetch Gilbey somewhere. Is everything all right?"

"Sort of. May I come over? Just for coffee?"

"Of course. Are you all right?"

"Yes."

"Is Gilbey?"

"May I come over?"

"I see. Come ahead. I'll start the coffee."

• •

"Shirt looks good on you. Very large, but very good."

"Thanks . . . could you, would you mind . . . just holding me for a minute?" He did, and he's so wonderfully big it was like being inside a one-room house that smelled really good and I cried and he didn't panic and he didn't let me go.

I don't think it lasted all that long, probably no more than a minute and a half. When I stopped he gave me a Kleenex and a bowl of café au lait. I sat on the Chester, sipping foamy coffee.

"Right. What's up? Is this about us, about me?"

"No. The note was . . . I was, I am, very glad about the note."

"Good. Is this about Gilbey?"

"Yes."

"She get beaten up?"

"Yes."

"Kurt Hubscher?"

"Yeh! How'd you know?"

"Kurt's kinks are well known in the Colony, as are Gilbey's. She'd been playing at some sort of game with Kurt for a few months. Some of us, myself included, had warned her that he was well beyond 'spanky-spanky,' but Gilbey is not known for taking advice."

He went around behind the Chester, massaged my neck and shoulders, rubbing my arms, kissing me once on the top of my head. "How bad was it?"

"Very."

He came back around, sat down. His eyes were sad, serious. He put his big paw alongside my cheek, the way Del does. "Oh, Prowlet, I am sorry. Is she at home now?"

"No, not quite. She's with . . . a guy I know, actually. A very nice guy. A southerner too. They get along. He's bringing her home today."

"You trust this fella?"

"Yes."

He took one of his French gypsy cigarettes out of the pretty blue-and-white packet on the counter, lit it, shook his head. "I dunno. Must be phases of the moon. Do you know where I had been the other night when I stumbled in here and you asked if I were pissed? Eureka. Eureka, California. Rescuing Didi. The chicken-trucker had beaten the hell out of him. It's all right, he's been seen to, and he's fine. He's back at Inn Nainity, drawing pictures, finishing his book. And he specifically asked me not to tell you."

"I won't say anything."

"Thank you. It's happened before. Our sainted mother, whom you have met, trained him from very early on in self-loathing. 'Ugly little dwarf' and all that. It made . . . look, how would you like to go for a drive? Santa Barbara and back?"

"Yay! I'd fucking love it!"

"Me fucking too. C'mon."

• •

It was perfect being in Pascal's shiny burgundy M.G. The wind in my face helped blow out some of the ugly, and there was the happy thing of just being with him. He was driving too fast, which was also good because fast driving was a Family Thing for me. We drove inland for a while, through a canyon with vegetable gardens, winding roads, funny little houses and an African-sounding name (To-pan-ga).

"Pascal?"

"Mm?"

"Do you know how to do four-wheel drifts?"

"Drift turns? Sure. You want drifts, do you?"

"They scare me a little, but yeah. It's a buzz."

"Buzz. Right. Hang on."

Actually, Pascal's drifts weren't as good as Del's, but they were heartgulp good in the same way. I screamed and laughed. Pascal laughed too.

In Santa Barbara, a small, pretty rich-people's town right on the water (like the Colony, but more of a real place—sidewalks, people, shops), I had my ears pierced. The earpierce guy said I needed to have "studs to keep my holes open."

"Studs to keep my holes open?" I repeated, and then got the giggles.

Pascal put his hand over my mouth. He said, "You must excuse my niece, she hasn't been entirely socialized." He was laughing too, sort of. Smiling, anyway.

I only had a twenty-dollar bill (and all my money wouldn't have been enough anyway), so Pascal bought me the studs, gold and amethyst. The amethysts reminded me of Clyde's Rock House, but that was cool. Marcus seemed in the faraway past. I wasn't even all that mad at him anymore. I mean, if he had been the one, I wouldn't be with Pascal, who was the one. He might even stay being the one. As long as I never mentioned it to him.

Driving back, there was more traffic, so the driving was less flash but still good. I watched Pascal moving the stickshift around. Like Del, he did this without thinking about it, like he was born shifting gears.

"I wish I could do that."

"What?"

"Shift gears. Drive."

"Well, you can, now that you're 16." (Yeh, right.) "You can probably learn at school." (Yeh, right.) "Or your mum could buy you some lessons." (Yeh, right.) "Where is your mum? Isn't she due to collect you about now?"

"Mm. Any day now."

"Yeh, right."

I looked over at him. Was he invading my mind and taking the piss? He was looking straight ahead, watching the road. Get out of my head, Pascal, I thought. Then I remembered this expression from school: "And into my pants." That gave me the giggles. Again.

"All right. Now what's funny?"

"I was thinking about . . . having a stud to keep . . ."

"Oh, gawd. Hopeless. She's hopeless." He sighed, but he was also smiling, and touched my cheek just before he geared down and turned off for the Colony.

I knew I should call Donnie, or Ray. Contact Gilbey. It was just that there'd been this energy between Pascal and me all day, and everything was still so new and so amazing.

We explored and exploded until it was dark outside. Between explosions, I would sometimes say, "I should call Gilb," and Pascal would say, "You will," or "Donnie knows you're here. Gilbey has the number."

Eventually, I got to being too sore to do anything about anything. Only problem was Pascal's member was still doing Small for a Baseball Bat but Big for a Thing.

"I . . . I can't anymore."

"Sore?"

"Yes."

"Understood . . . wonder what I should do with this" (pointing at the mini-bat).

I wrapped my hand around it. "Teach me to drive."

"What?"

"Del, my mother, says a stickshift is like an 'H.' Where's reverse?"

• •

I left a message for Ray at Yellow Valley. When he called he said Gilbey was at the Beverly Wilshire Hotel, "on her daddy's plastic," and that she wanted me to phone her there, room 704.

"Hey, Babygirl. Whey izz you?"

"At Pascal's."

"Yeah, that's what Donnie thought. I didn't want to call there an' interrupt anything. You two got stuff I could interrupt?"

"Yes."

"Yes? You say yes?"

"Yes, that's true."

"Well, all right!"

"Yes, I think so."

"You happy?"

"Yes, there's an amazing amount of that. Just about everywhere."

"He lookin' at you right now?"

"Yes."

"Yeah. You're talkin' in what Johhny calls Teenybopper Phone Code. I wanna hear the real deal. Can you come over?"

"Yes, I think so."

"Listen to you. 'I think so.' I ain't gonna keep you all night. You can go back to Bigstuff. Or you can bring him. Just call Yellow Valley. I'm runnin' a tab. Write this down. 'Worldcard, number 233-43-1256.' Names on it, 'Mr. John Tarr' and 'Miss Gilbey Tarr.' Expiry date 22 November 1981 . . . oh, an' can you get me some shoveruppers? I fell off the roof."

"What were you doing on the roof?"

She laughed. "No, goofball. Toldja in 'Frisco. Means I got the curse. You can get the shovers at the same drugstore where you got the Derm-Efface. It's next to the hotel."

"Got it. OK. You sound good. See you 'bout an hour, hour and a half."

Pascal was lying on his back, pillows under his head, stickshift all small and relaxed. He said my end of the phone conversation had all the subtlety of a wet T-shirt contest, but that Gilbey was, "for a variety of reasons," one of the few discreet people in the Colony. I said I was going to visit her, asked if he wanted to come. He said no, that he needed "a short kip," being older than I was and all. He said to give his love to Gilbey, and that I should come back later, but not too late, if I'd like. I said I'd like, took a shower, called Yellow Valley. They said it would take an hour, because they were "at peak and it was the beach." Pascal was "short-kip" unconscious. I gave Gilbey's address. Went over there. Wrote in my journal while eating amazing Donnie food.

WHAT IS THIS PUMPKIN? WHO ARE THESE MICE?

5

FOREIGN WORDS

Chiaroscuro

Vertige

Pipistrello

Farfalla

Sizwe

Pamplemousse

Jacaranda

Iliovasilema

Mousseline

Auto-da-Fé

Bienvenue

Lavabo

Carapace

Sausalito

Jeu de Mots

Gitane

Mal Hibou

Glossolalia

Mackalahoopoo
(not real word, but great to say)

Fellatio (Latin)

Mov

23 Nov. 1981
Evil Owl House

What Gilb said was that here, in the Colony, everybody is so rich that, if you're not waving a gun, you can run up the beach screaming all kinds of motherfucker and everybody will just look away. Well, there's too fucking much looking away in the fucking Colony. This is what I very deeply think. Even so, if the scream hits the mouth-hole while I'm here, scream is what's gonna happen.

Right now, I feel bone-frozen. Can't draw. For the first time ever in my life since age four. Except eyes. Can draw them. Nothing else comes. Just pages full of eyes.

Getting lots of words, though. By themselves and in groups. Besides, backward, even with its seriously creepy places, is easier to do, to understand, than Freaky Fucking Forward. So I am going to bring my journal up to right creepy now. Dead babies and all. I will try to get every moment down because once the scream gets here, I'll have to stop.

Sometimes you just suddenly know a thing. You're in the middle of other stuff, not even thinking about that thing at all, and then there it is, the thing you know.

At the checkout counter of Beverly Hills Chemists, waiting to pay for Gilbey's shoveruppers, *bammo!* I knew one of those type things. Unless all the exploding had burned my body bloodless, I was what Del called up the spout. Pregnant. This thought punched a huge hole in my happy.

It could've been the Derm-Efface, or maybe the Gilb was just a quick healer (Lucky. When I get a mark it stays for like ever before fading), but she looked great. She was wearing a silky wide-leg pantsuit with a black-and-white diamond pattern, and her hair was a long blonde braid down her back. Even though I'd wanted to stay in bed with Pascal, curled up against his body heat, I was really glad to see her. We did hugs, then she held me away from her tall self and looked at my face.

"Awright, Babygirl, where's the orgasmo glow? You're supposed to have this goddamn glow."

"There was a glow, Gilb. There still is, but there's also a thing, a problem."

"What's up?"

"I think I'm pregnant."

She laughed. "You can't be pregnant. Not by 'Scal. 'Scal's had a vaso."

"A vaso?"

"Yeah, vasectomy. They went up into his balls and tied his baby juice in a knot. Something like that."

"Yuck. Who went up into his balls, his mother?"

"Uh-uh. Doctors. Last year."

"So Pascal can't ever have a baby? I mean *make* a baby?"

"Nope."

"Forever can't?"

"I think so. I think it's forever."

"Why would he want to do that, to not have kids forever? Because of his mum, I bet."

"Dunno. A lot of guys in the Colony get vasos, so girls can't sue them for lots of money by saying they're the father of their kids an' stuff. So you can't be pregnant."

"Yeh, I can. Not from Pascal. From somebody before. Somebody in Tarzana."

"In the Valley?"

"Yeh."

"They fuck in the Valley?"

• •

I drank some "Pouilly-Fuissé," a fancy French white wine, and told her about Gabe, about Rex and Mara and the Casa del Cielo. I also said how I was afraid that if Pascal found out, he'd be annoyed, think I was too much trouble.

Gilb did a shooing thing with her hand and said, "No sweat, Babygirl. You won't even have to tell 'Scal about it. I'll send you to Norrie and he'll take care of the whole thing. Norrie's great. He was President Kennedy's gynecologist."

"President Kennedy had a gynecologist? What's a guy need a gynecologist for?"

"For his girlfriends. Almost all the L.A. girlfriends of every famous person in the damn world use Norrie Denbaum. He's my gynie too. Since I was 13. I've had two A.B.s with him."

"A.B.s"

"Abortions."

"Two? Wow."

"Before I got my pills. He'll check you out. If you're pregnant, he'll do your A.B. and then he'll give you pills, an' checkups to make sure everything's cool."

"How old do you have to be?"

"I don't think there's an actual age. I mean, eight or nine would be weird, but I think it's up to the doctor. We're both covered, though. Norrie won't do an under-sixteen without a parent signing. To avoid a publicity thing, I guess. But with us, all we need is 'emancipated minor' papers. Any 16-year-old can get them."

So I told her about my bogus sixteenitude. About Del and Marcus. All of it.

She was a little surprised by the age part, because of our shared party, and Dickie Siggins not telling her anything. "Huhn," she said. "I used to look real older at your age, when I wanted to. Norrie won't do you, though. Not without the papers or a parent. He'll give you the test, but for the A.B., you should do Lopez-Garcia."

"Lopez-Garcia?"

"Gynie. In Mexicali."

"Where's that?"

"Baja, Mexico."

"Mexico! Jeezus, Gilb, that's a whole 'nuther fuckin' country!"

"Easy, Babygirl, don't panic. Mexicali's just across the border. Lots of people use Lopez-Garcia. He's clean and he's quick. I have the address and number. So does Pascal."

"How do you know Pascal has the number?"

"Because I gave it to him. Last year. For a friend of his."

It's amazing how quickly a really happy person can be, all at once, majorly bummed out. I did and did not want to know why Pascal needed the phone number of a Mexican doctor who depregnanted people under the age of 16 (and whether this was before or after his knotted balls). Mostly did not. I drank more wine. Gilbey said Dr. Denbaum's office was a few blocks away from the hotel, that I should stay with her, see Denbaum in the morning and then we could go back to the Colony together.

Not being a major drinker, I was already more than a little drunk. "Great," said I. "Got any bubblebath?"

I think guys are wonderful in lots of ways, but they can also be really offpissing. There I was worrying about hurting Pascal's feelings because he'd invited me to spend the night with him, and I was going to stay in Beverly Hills with Gilb. I rang Evil Owl House. Nobody was home.

Gilbey'd arranged for the hotel operator to wake her up first thing in the morning so she could get me an appointment with the famous Crotchdoctor to the Stars. My appointment was for 11 A.M.

"If he's looking into the lower holes of all these film stars and politicians' girlfriends and stuff, how come we could get this last-minute appointment?"

"He likes me."

I added this announcement to the suddenly growing list of things I didn't want to know more about.

• •

When I was nine and we were having a broke time, Del raised a bunch of money by doing weirdass drawings for a rich Swiss pervo. The drawings were of curly-haired naked ladies in creepy machines. Del called them Aubrey Beardsley meets Tomi Ungerer. Gynecology is a lot like those drawings. You lay on your back, on a high skinny table, a sheet across your belly (when your belly isn't even the body part you're shy about), knees bent, legs apart, naked heels in these shiny steel things.

Dr. Denbaum seemed like a nice man, with a mellow-sexy voice and Humphrey Bogart's face. He said that, because I was a first-time patient, he'd do a general gynie as well as the pregnancy test. His fingers were very long. He put them into my lower holes. (Fortunately not all at once. One of the things I'd just recently found out was that going into both holes at the same time caused this really noisy explosion.) He asked if I "had protection."

"You mean birth control?"

"Yes. Are you using anything?"

"No."

"Why not?"

"I . . . I guess I didn't expect to be . . . doing anything."

"How old are you?"

"Sixteen."

"Mm. Well, Roanne, any pretty girl of 16 should *assume* she's likely to be doing something. When we get your results, we should also discuss birth control."

"Oh. OK. Thanks."

"No thanks necessary. It's my job." He said all this while scraping out a couple of goop samples, saying he'd have my results the next afternoon. While I was pulling my jeans up, he asked how Gilbey was, and asked me to ask her to give him a call.

I recognized two actresses in his waiting room. Bibi Drake and Michelle Sorenson. Bibi Drake has one of those great bums, the kind you can set a glass on. (I've always wanted one like that. Can get it when I clench, but can't walk clenched. I always mean to practice this, but I get busy with other stuff and forget.)

Maybe, I thought, maybe I was being jumpy-crazy. I mean, I wasn't totally certain I was pregnant. I would know the next day. I was pretty sure, though. And even surer that if I said anything to Pascal, I'd get sacked as his not-girlfriend-Prowlet-thing, due to being a major pain in the ass. And there was the kid. Inside me. All eyes, mouth, fingers and toes was what I imagined. Freaking and silent screaming as this big dickthing blotted out the light outside the vadge-hole as it came straight at him-her. "I'd rather not go to Pascal's until I know what's happening with the pregnant thing. Would it be cool if I stayed at your place until tomorrow night?"

"Whatchoo mean, my place? Your room is there. It's your place too."

"Thanks, Gilb."

"I wanna stop at Dart's before goin' back to the Colony. You cool with that?"

"'Dart'?"

"D'Artagnan Roland. You met him at our party."

"Oh, right. The little Napoleon-haired man who brought Ashleigh and Deleese."

"The Braindeath Sisters. Yeah, that's Dart."

"Yeah, I'd like to go there. At the party, he invited me to see his retro clothes collection."

"Cool. I'll call a cab."

D'Artagnan Roland lived in a pointy little house on stilts that sort of hung over a cliff on this tree-filled hill in another one of the canyons (Laurel). Gilb said the house type was called "A-frame." There was so much stuff, leaning, stacked and standing, in every possible corner, on every piece of wall, hanging from the ceiling, it made Del's and my whole life of crazy places look like the empty rooms of really clean people (what Del calls "the Swissoids"). Daylight was kept totally out by floor-to-ceiling dark heavy velvet drapes on wooden rings and rods. There were wonderful lightbursts, though, from all sorts of different-coloured glass lamps on little carved one-of-a-kind tables.

In the middle of the books, sculptures, lamps, dolls, drapes, tassels and lots more of whatever else, wearing a shiny black robe with a multi-coloured mandarin collar and matching cuffs, Dart Roland sat, in tiny delicate amazingness, smoking a cigarette that was crammed into a long bright red holder that had little rhinestone-eyed flying black birds on it. He looked, he was, so totally the only person like himself in my life so far that I gleed up with the gift of it and forgot for a while about what might be growing inside me.

"Hey, Dart, you 'member Roanne?"

"I most certainly do. The wonderful petticoat at Lord Large's in Malibu. Hello, dear. Welcome. And hello long blonde beauty who fails to return phone calls." Gilbey laughed, kissed him on top of his thinning white forward-combed hair, saying she'd been "into some sorta hairy stuff," but that "evvything is cool now."

"Oh, dear. This young woman is a significant avatar of the death of the English language. I hope you're not following her example, dear."

"C'mon, Dart, gimme a break. Ashleigh and Deleese don't exactly talk brilliant."

"*Lee,* dear, brilliant-*lee*. Speak, not talk, brilliant-*lee*. And, in fact, both Deleese and Ashleigh rarely speak at all."

"Yeah, well, whatever. Anyhow, Roanne 'speaks' great English. Her mother is from actual England, so Roe knows all kinds of big words and fancy sentences an' stuff."

"Excellent. Perhaps, for a change, you've selected a companion who might ameliorate your already abundant beauty and charm with the verbal virtues."

"Could be. Got any beer?"

"Beer! Barbaric. Beerbaric. The girl knows we don't stock beer here, dear. Only asks to vex me. I am abstemious. There is, however, a bit of plum wine in the cobalt blue decanter on the kitchen table. You may help yourselves."

The wine was bellywarming and boozy-lemony. I drank a shot of it out of a tiny blue glass. Gilb sucked her gulping wallop straight from the decanter.

"Don't tell Dart. He'll think it's gross." She giggled. "It *is* gross."

Dart had this huge room with nothing in it but clothes racks, closets and mirrors. It was filled with all sorts of clothing, mostly women's, from all over the world and from practically back to the cave years. He said we could try stuff on.

"But remember to be careful. Some of it is, as you know, Gilbey, quite fragile."

"Yessir," she said, rubbing his shoulder.

Gilbey is always beautiful. No matter what she's wearing, what she's doing, the time of day, whatever. Even when her mouth starts to slant a little down on the right side because she's overboozed, the Gilb could not be anything but beautiful. Despite knowing that with my forever heart and soul, I stood there open-mouth amazed at how she looked in the flapper dress. The whole thing was made of tiny metal bits! Air-light metal bits, like they were spit out by butterflies. These bits were shaped like little hearts, in silver, gold and black. The dress was sleeveless, with armholes almost to the waist, and a drapey V neck just about as low. The bottom, just above her knees, was all triangular points. There was a matching floppy beret. Gilb shoved most of her hair into it, threw her arms into the air. "Whatcha think?"

What came into my head was, I am so lucky to get to look at you, but that was way too sappy to say out loud. "It's beautiful, Gilb! You look super!"

"It is a f-a-a-bulous dress. Now you pick one. Wait, try this."

It was see-through black gauzy chiffon, with lots of little red or yellow carnations that had green stems and leaves. The top part had long, floaty sleeves and side-zippered, tightly but smoothly, down to a triangle point just above my belly-button. Then it flare-floated all the way to the ground, where it had a ruffle that was longer at the back. You could sort of see my stuff through it, but, being black and all, it wasn't too porno. It had a matching sash with yellow-and-red fringe. Gilbey tied it into my hair, arranging my crazy curls this way and that. She called Dart to come look.

"Ah! Wondrous! An Erté and a Bakst! Would you two care to accompany me next month, thusly attired, to Venice?"

"Venice, Italy! Where the houses come right out of the sea?"

"Uh-uh, Babygirl. Venice, California, where the roller skaters get right in yer fuckin' way."

"Language, Gilbey, please. Yes, dear, the Venice where the houses rise out of the sea. Have you been?"

"No, sir. But my mum's got this book of paintings by Canaletto that's really amazing, and I've always wanted to go."

"Well, splendid, dear. So you shall. The end of October. A special screening at the Guggenheim Palazzo. I am, at my advanced age, going to be a movie star!"

"No shit!"

"Gilbey!"

"Sorry. I meant, 'Oh, my, how come?'"

"Aidan Marney's made a film about the silent-movie era. The William Desmond Taylor killing. I play an old movie queen, emphasis on the latter. It was rather fun. And now Marney wants to do a charity benefit in Venice for restoration/preservation, et cetera."

"It's really sweet of you to invite us, Dart, and we'd love to, but how come you're not taking Ashleigh and Deleese?"

"Well, Miss Deleese has gotten herself a running part on one of those all breasts and no brains television series, and Ashleigh won't travel without her."

"And we're the B-team."

"Not at all. You are a delightful alternative. So, get your passports in order."

"Right."

I had absolutely no idea how a fourteen-year-old Canadian was supposed to get a passport in California. Gilbey said that it wasn't a problem, that she'd take me to Buffalo.

"Buffalo, New York?"

"Buffalo on the beach. Buffalo Bevilacqua. Lives in the Colony. Mob guy. He gets phony papers for people."

• •

I woke Pascal.

"Mm-hmm."

"Hi. It's Roanne. I'm at Gilbey's. It's her first night back, and I thought . . ."

"Fine, Prowlet, not a problem. Ring tomorrow. Late afternoon."

"OK." (Boo? Bow?) "Beau rêve."

He laughed a little. I was v. glad I remembered Didi's "sweet dreams" thing.

"Toi aussi, petite amie, bonne nuit."

"Right."

"Hey, Babygirl, you get 'im?"

"Uh-huh. It's cool. I'll call him again tomorrow."

"Dyno. I'm gonna bag it, I'm wasted. See you in the morning. What time does Norrie get the news?"

"Dunno exactly. Afternoon."

"Don't worry. Whatever happens, I'm witcha."

"I know. Ta. Beau rêve."

"Huh?"

"It's 'sweet dreams' in French."

"Oh, yeah? Bo rev. I like it. 'Night."

"'Night."

I knew who Erté was because Del had a book of his drawings. Didn't know Bakst. D'Artagnan had lent me a book ("Fail to return it and you'll be plagued by the Bitch's Curse"). I couldn't sleep. Sat up in bed looking at the pictures. Léon Bakst designed costumes for Russian ballets. The costumes did look like my Dart dress, and the girls did look like me. I was starting to find my type in the world. And, once I was away from kids who made me feel like "what the fuck is that?" then it was, I was, an OK type. There were people, strangers, some of them very smart, with wonderful faces, who actually wanted this type, this person, around. I was still v. scared about the maybe-baby, but Bakst was a big help.

• •

Yep. Tiny creature growing inside. A Gabelet. A Rosielette. A Rosielette? What if Del had done what I was going to do, what I had to do? Gilbey said be cool. I said I'd be cool, but that first I needed to freak and scream and cry. Ran into the sea. Freaked. Screamed. Cried. Swam back to the beach. "Right. Can we go see the Buffalo guy?"

I thought Buffalo might be a name in Italian, the way Jesus was in Spanish. The minute I saw him I knew that wasn't it.

He was a biggish blocky guy with bulgy muscles, like he worked out a lot. His brown hair was shaved close on the sides and in very tight curls on top of his head. He had a big flat nose with superwide flaring nostrils. He looked just like a fucking buffalo!

"Hey, Buff, this here's Roanne."

"She's wet."

"Yeah. We can stay out here. She needs a dead baby passport. As fast as possible. I'll bring you the cash later today, OK?"

A dead baby passport? Like the woman in Margaret Campbell's grade nine book report who had an "A" burnt into her body because she fucked? And how much "cash" was involved? I was afraid to ask.

It turned out a "dead baby passport" was a passport in the name of a baby who died before a certain age. There was a record of the birth but not of the death. Apparently mob guys had a business getting these passports for people. I thought I might be able to get one soon enough for Norrie Denbaum to de-baby me, but Buffalo said it would take at least three weeks. Dr. D. said I should decide what I was going to do and book as soon as possible. I didn't tell him about my real age. Said I would call him in a day or two.

We were on Gilbey's bed and she was painting my fingernails bright red ("It'll cheer y'up t'look at 'em"). She said there was no point in her asking Dr. D. to do me, that he had all these famous people and wouldn't chance it. So I'd probably have a passport for Venice, but the right-away thing was Mexicali.

Mexico? "How do we get there?"

"I can drive us?"

"You have a licence?"

"No, but I know how to drive."

"Really?"

"Really. I drive real good. When I'm sober" (giggle).

"Gilb, it isn't funny."

"I know, Babygirl. But I do drive real good. Do it all the time."

"What do you use for a car?"

"One of Johnny's. They's three of the suckers in the garage."

"Does he know?"

"He ain't here."

"What if we get stopped?"

"We won't."

"What if we do?"

"I'll blow the cop."

"Seriously."

"I *am* serious."

• •

Gilbey called Mexicali and, in English, booked me in with Doctor Lopez-Garcia (I supposed he was a doctor. For all I knew, he could've been an auto mechanic). The next day, 3 P.M.

It would cost $150. Gilbey said she'd pay it. I was getting seriously uncomfortable about not having money. Dart Roland had offered me a "jobette," alphabetizing and itemizing his books and possessions. I told Gilb I'd pay her back out of the first Dart cheque. She argued, but, when she saw it was important to the already weirded-out state of my head, agreed. She showed me the cars. I picked the bigger one, in case we hit something. Called Pascal, feeling majorly wormshit, but managing to sound cheery. He said he was finishing up in the darkroom and invited me over for high tea.

He'd fixed these little tiny sandwiches. There was something sweet about such a big guy making such a small sandwich. He asked how Gilbey was. I said fine. He asked how I was. I said fine. He said I seemed upset. I said no, I was fine. He put his hands on each side of my face. He said, "Look at me." I lost it.

What came out was something like "I'm pregnant and I don't have ID so President Kennedy's gynecologist can't do me so Gilbey's gonna drive me to Mexico and she doesn't have a licence but she can blow the police officer and I don't want you to think I'm too much trouble and I can do this because Gilbey is with me and we'll—"

"Stop! Just STOP! Let me understand this. What you are telling me is that you are pregnant, and what you plan to do is have yourself driven to a Mexican border town by an underage, alcoholic teenager, who does not in fact have a driver's licence, and, once you get there, if you get there, you will have internal surgery performed on you by somebody or other?! Are you completely insane?!"

"That's exactly what you said in the dream."

"What dream?"

"*My* dream. About the tigers." And I told him about the tigers on the beach, which gave me a chance to stop crying, to stop pumping so hard. It also gave Pascal a chance to stop shouting.

"Oh, Prowlet, I didn't mean to bellow at you. I'm sorry."

"It's OK." (Actually, it was sort of neat that he got so angry. Del always says she only yells when she thinks I'm gonna get hurt, because she loves me. Del doesn't yell a lot, and I had a hunch that Pascal hardly ever did.) "You know him."

"Know who?"

"The Mexican doctor. I think he's a doctor. Lopez-Garcia."

"I see. Yes, I do know him. He is a gynecologist. But the two of you cannot go lurching into the grottiness of Mexicali on your own, with Gilbey pretending she can drive, which I have seen her do, and which is deeply terrifying. So I shall drive you. We will have to leave at about six in the morning. Do you want to sleep here or at Gilbey's?"

"Here."

"Fine. I'll ring Gilbey and tell her she's been retired as a chauffeur."

"OK."

Funny. Once I'd gotten everything out and he called Gilbey, everything was way better than I would've ever expected. That night, in fact, was one of the best times together Pascal and I ever had. He'd always made such a thing of how he wasn't my boyfriend and that he wasn't responsible for me, and how teenage females were some sort of risky problem. Now, here I was in the middle of a supernuisance megamess, and he was taking really good care of me, without seeming to mind at all.

First, we had a really soapy shower. Then he wanted to do a bed thing, and I told him about poking the kid in the face with a dick and blocking out the porthole vadge-light. This cracked him up laughing, and I could see what he saw and I started laughing too, and then he said the kid wasn't a kid yet and he/she was in a different room from the dick room and I felt like the girl he was loving and not just the car he was driving and it was great. Then, because he was being so terrific, and I wanted to say thank you, I decided to try beefeating. I asked him not to explode down there while I was doing beefo. He gave me his word, which he kept. It wasn't my favourite thing, but it was all right, and sort of like a gift from me to him. We finished together, in the him-inside-me way that I liked way better.

After, when I was curled up next to him, I said, very softly, "You're really being very nice to me," and he said, "I'm the son of a woman who never took care of anyone. I am more like her than I think is good."

"You take care of Didi."

"Yes, I do. I try to. Didi is . . . a complicated creature."

"Complicated how?"

"Too long a story, Prowlet. We have to be up at five in the morning. Let's try to sleep."

• •

When Pascal called Gilb they had this huge debate about whether she could come with us to Mexicali. She said she had to because she was my pal, and he said Mexicans had a blonde thing and that she'd make the locals randy and crazy, and that he'd have to fight our way out of there, and she said she'd put her hair under a hat and wear baggy clothes and no makeup and I said I'd like her to come and Pascal said she'd have to sit in the jumpseat.

Except for the bright red fingernails (same as mine), Gilbey arrived completely without makeup. All her hair was shoved into a stretchy thing that looked like a navy blue supercondom. She wore dirty white running shoes and a very baggy gray sweatsuit (probably her father's). Because she couldn't help it, she looked great.

"See, I'm on time," she said, climbing into the jumpseat behind Pascal and me. There wasn't really a place for her long legs. "No sweat, I'll just put 'em over 'Scal's shoulders."

I hated this idea. "Uh-uh, you'll put 'em over *my* shoulders."

"Whatever," she said, flinging one leg over each of my shoulders. And we were off.

Mexican customs was easy. Pascal said we were just going to "see the sights." There really weren't any "sights," and the customs guy probably figured out why we were there. Pascal said Lopez-Garcia was "one of Mexicali's growth industries." He drove straight to where the two-story motel-y gray building was, having been there before, for reasons I still didn't want to know about. He said he would wait, with Gilbey, in the car. Gilb said she'd come with me if I wanted her to. I said I was cool on my own, but could they please not go anywhere. They said they wouldn't. I crossed the street, read the name "J. Lopez-Garcia, 104."

I gave the name Gilbey had used on the phone, Lucinda Thibodeau (Gilb's dead grandmother). The nurse or receptionist person didn't have my appointment written down but said it was "no a pro'leng." She took me into a very small pale green room, sat me in a brown leather chair, hooked a humungus paper towel around my neck.

Then Dr. Lopez-Garcia came in. Tall and skinny. Black-and-gray hair. Big bald spot on top. Skinny moustache. White doctor shirt. Nice smile. "Hello," he said.

"Hello," I said.

"Please open your mouth very wide," he said.

"You can see the baby by looking down my throat?" I asked.

"Baby?" he said. Then he laughed. Then he told me he was a dentist. He said the Dr. Lopez-Garcia I wanted was his brother, Miguel. He was Hor Hay. Brother Miguel's office was on the second floor. I said I was sorry and he said this happened all the time. I thanked him and ran up the stairs, hoped I wasn't late.

The nurse asked for the money ("Cash only, yes?" "Yes."). Then she told me to go into a cubicle and undress. I did. She gave me a paper wraparound gown, brought me into a green room exactly the same as the one downstairs, only with a stirrup table like Norrie Denbaum's. The right Dr. Lopez-Garcia, who didn't have a bald spot but otherwise looked a lot like his brother the dentist, came in. He examined me inside. He said not to be scared, that it was "an easy procedure" and that it wouldn't hurt. He said he would give me an injection so I wouldn't feel or remember anything about the procedure. He asked me to count backward from a hundred.

"One hundred, ninety-nine, ninety-eight . . ." The last thing I remembered was a yellow-haired baby being pulled out through my mouth.

When I woke up I was woozy, thirsty and alone. "Hello . . ." The nurse lady came in. She had my clothes. She asked if I had a skirt, because my jeans would be too tight. I said no, but that my friend downstairs, in the dark red sportscar, was wearing baggy sweatpants, and that maybe we could trade. I asked if she could go get my friend. Then I thought it could scare Gilbey, and Pascal, if someone other than me did that. I was really rocky and when I tried to climb down from the table I felt, then saw, the sanitary pad that had been taped to my body.

"Is the baby out, gone?"

"Gong, sí," she said. Then she crossed herself. Dr. Lopez-Garcia came in. He said the procedure went "good," but that I might bleed a bit for a day or two. He said I could not have anybody "in there" until after my next period. He gave me a small jar of pink cream, to use if there was "itching from the stretching." He also asked about a skirt. I told him about Gilb. He said to put my arm around the nurse lady's shoulders. She walked me to the window. I could see the M.G.

I really did know the baby hadn't been removed orally, but I felt sore at both ends. My voice didn't want to come out. After a couple of croaky tries, I managed a biggish "GILBEEE!" She and Pascal looked up. "Everything's fine. Come up, please?"

"Wha . . . at? You OK?"

"Yes. Come up."

"Come up there?"

"Yes."

"Gotcha."

I think I'd hoped Pascal would come up with her, but he told her to explain that he had to stay with the car to protect the hubcaps (so at least he'd thought to come up, which was good).

We swapped pants. My jeans were too big and too short on Gilbey, but the Gilbaggies were superroomy. Dr. L.G. said good-bye and that he and the nurse lady had to go to another room for another procedure. Gilb said it was cool, that she could get me downstairs. I washed my face in the tiny sink, looking into the mirror above it. No makeup. Looked 12. Otherwise, fine. Didn't look at all like a person who'd just had a person removed. Not that I knew what that would look like.

• •

"I want to buy something. A souvenir."

"Aren't you a bit shaky, Prowlet?"

"Yes, I am, but I want something from here. I've never been to Mexico before."

"This isn't Mexico. It's the border."

"I don't care. I want to buy a souvenir."

"Right."

I bought a small stuffed doll. A girl doll in a red-and-yellow Mexican dress. Her curly black hair felt like the nasty spunstuff some people put on Christmas trees, but it looked shiny and nice. She had a redlip smile and round button eyes. I was getting wobblier, but wanted to look around more. Pascal said no. He was right. When I got into the car, where Gilbey was waiting, I sat down sort of just before I would've fallen down.

There really isn't anyplace to lie down in a sports car. I wanted to put my head in Pascal's lap, like I sometimes did in the Morgan with Del. He said we had to clear the border cops first.

"Why?"

"Because, if you look sick, they'll stop us."

"An' you'll look like you're givin' 'im head."

"Gilbey!"

"Am I wrong, 'Scal?"

"Not entirely."

I turned to face the jumpseat, which was slightly puke making. Gilbey put lipstick and cheek gel on me. Pascal said to look "jolly."

Buildingman, Jolly and the Tall Blonde in the Short Jeans made it through U.S. customs without anybody being busted or shot. I put my head in Pascal's lap and just about immediately fell asleep.

At some point, somewhere or other, I opened my eyes. Pascal's thing was hardish (probably because I had my face on it and may have been squirming around in my sleep). I was still groggy, so putting it in my mouth was a major gagger idea. He looked down. I whispered and gestured that I could try to do something with my hand.

"It's a lovely and generous thought, Prowlet, but no, thank you."

"Whut's a lovely and generous thought?"

"Never mind."

"Bet I know."

"Bet you'd hate having to walk all the way back to the Colony."

"Oh, boo on you, 'Scal, y're no fun."

"This is frequently true."

I went back to sleep.

We were about a half hour outside Malibu when I opened my eyes again. Felt more awake, sat up, looked at my little doll.

"What're you gonna call 'er?"

"I dunno. Adelita." Then I remembered. "Gilb?"

"Uh-huh?"

"Would you feel in my jeans pocket."

"Which one?"

"Don't remember. Front ones."

"Empty."

"Back ones?"

"Empty too."

"For sure?"

"Uh-huh. What's up?"

"Oh, shit. Oh, shitshitshit! We have to go back!"

"Back? To Mexicali? Why?"

And I told them about Adelita and that she'd given me the little green stone head when I was leaving Casa del Cielo. Because I was going to Mexico, and because I was scared, and Adelita was Mexican, and the catbaby was Mexican, I'd put him in my jeans pocket for luck. And now he was fucking gone. And I wanted to get him.

Pascal pulled the car onto the side of the road. "We can't, Prowlet, we can't go back."

"We have to, he's my mojo, my good luck charm!"

"I understand, and he probably brought you good luck in your operation. But now he's lost—"

"Or stolen."

"Gilbey, do not participate in this."

"I'm only sayin'—"

"You're only sayin' absolutely nothing. Prowlet, if it fell out of your jeans in the office, I will ring them tomorrow, and I will ask if they have found it. That is all we can do. It's dark. It's well after office hours, even Mexicali office hours. You need food, rest and sleep now. Nothing else can be done until tomorrow."

"Could it be stolen?"

"Yes, of course. Anything lost can be stolen."

I couldn't help it. I was tired and full of stupidjuice medicine. I started to cry. Pascal rubbed his face with both hands. Then he took my hand.

"Right. Listen to me. If it's lost, if it fell out of your pocket and they can find it, we'll try to get it back. If it's stolen, there is no way we'll get it back. The theft will be unprovable. Understand?"

"But . . . they seemed . . . like . . . nice people."

"I think they probably are. I also think your little catbaby may be valuable. Do you remember Corie Layton?"

"The writer in the white pantsuit? At our party?"

"Mm-hmm. She thought the head looked authentically pre-Columbian. Which means it's also probably Mexican. Which can mean, if they found it, there's no way, culturally, that they will feel any compunction about keeping one of their ancient artifacts rather than return it to a briefly pregnant teenage 'gringa' who blew in and out of town with two pals in a red sportscar."

"But Adelita gave it to me!"

"This is not working. Look, we're going home now. We will deal with this in the morning."

"But—"

"No. Not 'but.' Not another word on this subject. We have all had a long day. A day in which the eldest of us could have been various sorts of arrested. Therefore, we drop this subject until tomorrow or you're on your bloody own."

"Hey, c'mon, 'Scal—"

"I wouldn't, Gilbey."

She didn't. Nobody did. Not a mumblin'. I knew where I wanted, needed to sleep that night. Thought I'd better protect my choice. Asked if I could put my head in his lap again, try to sleep some more. He grunted a sort of yes thing.

When the car stopped in front of Gilbey's, I pretended to be asleep. Pascal petted my hair, whispered, "Prowlet?" I kept my eyes closed, made a "murfl" noise. Gilbey said, "She probably wants to stay with you." (Right on, Gilbey!) Pascal said he'd planned to bring me to his place. (Yay, Pascal!) Gilbey said she'd check in by phone in the morning. Pascal said, "Fine. And please bring some of her things over tomorrow." (Nice, I thought. He knows I'll want to change.) Gilbey untangled herself from the jumpseat and climbed out of the car. Little Red chugged slowly down the road to Evil Owl House.

Yeah, we'd all had a long day. A day in which the youngest of us killed something and lost her mojo. So, this youngest of us wanted something to happen. Not a big thing. Not a difficult thing. Just a rare and favourite thing.

And it happened! I kept my eyes closed. Pretended to be deep asleep. And he did it. Picked me up and carried me to the door.

"Prowlet?"

"Murfl?"

"I have to put you down for a moment. To open the door. Just lean on me." I did. He did. "Can you walk?"

"Mm-hmm."

He snortlaughed. "You look like you're developing."

"Developing?"

"Mm. In the darkroom. Not quite a picture yet." I held out my arms to be picked up again.

"I see. How long do we plan to be carried about from place to place?"

"Just tonight?"

"I suppose we can manage that. Come on."

He carried me to his room, lowered me onto the *QE2*.

"I can't . . . we can't . . ."

"I know."

"Oh, right. You've done lots of this."

"No, I haven't 'done lots of this.' And don't be brittle, it doesn't suit you. Makes you sound like you're playing dressup."

"Oh, fuck you, Pascal."

"Now, that sounds like you. Want some ice water?"

"Yes, please."

"Good. Gilbey gave me this bag from the doctor's. Clean yourself up, put on one of my shirts and get under the duvet. You shouldn't shower, but have a wash and do get out of those clothes. You smell like Gilbey, which confuses me, and might eventually confuse you."

I truly didn't want to know what that meant. He went downstairs and I went off to the loo to try and smell like myself.

• •

"Not that shirt."

"You said 'one of my shirts.'"

"Yes, but the one you've chosen is normally worn with a tuxedo."

"Oh. I suppose I could put on a tuxedo."

"I suppose you could. How has this happened to my life? How have I let this happen to my life? Come here. We sleep now."

The things you suddenly know. Like when I knew I was pregnant. Like lots of things, ever since I was little. In the dark part of early morning, just before the gray light, I knew something. I wriggled out from under Pascal's arm. My body ached in a hollow sort of way, but I could walk OK. Went downstairs and out to the car. The air smelled of the sea and felt great on my skin. I put my body over the front seat. Hurt a little. Felt around on the floor of the jumpseat. There he was! I shouted "Yes!" over and over and laughed and cried and grinned and giggled. Then I ran back in and up the stairs.

"Pascal!"

"Jesus Christ! What? What's wrong?"

"Nothing's wrong! Everything's right! I've got him! I've got my catbaby!"

"That's wonderful, Prowlet. Terrific. May I go back to sleep now?"

"Don't you want to know where I found him?"

"I know where you found him."

"Where?"

"In the car."

"Yeah. How did you know that?"

"I'm a visionary. Now, if you watch very closely, I am a sleeping visionary."

When I woke up again, it was 10:22 in the morning. My catbaby was on the bedtable, looking at me. Pascal was clattering around downstairs. I closed my eyes, heard him coming up the stairs. "Café au lait, mademoiselle?"

A bowl of coffee and a croissant, on a tray, brought to me in bed? This was not Pascal stuff. Didi, yes. Pascal, no. I was about to be some sort of sacked.

"Good morning. Thought you might enjoy a bit of breakfast in bed."

"Thanks."

"Gilbey's downstairs."

"Oh, yeh?"

"Yes, she's brought you fresh clothes and some of your things." I grabbed the catbaby, tied him around my neck, double knot. Pascal put the tray on the bedtable, sat on the edge of the bed.

"You want me to leave."

"Only for a few days, Prowlet. How did you know?"

"I'm a visionary."

"Right. You probably are a bit, actually. What's happening is this. Zizi is returning. Only for a day or two. There are family papers of some sort to deal with. There's no way I can have you both here. Trust me on this, Prowlet, you'd hate it as much as I would."

"So I go back to Gilb's?"

"Empty Manor? No, I don't think that would be much fun for you just now. Besides, Johnny Tarr and his ditsy little wife are due home at any moment, which might also be a bit . . . complex."

"So where do I go?" (I told myself that if I cried, I was lower than wormshit and deserved to die at once. It worked.)

"That's the good news. I think. I hope. I know you liked the Bolinas house. And Gilbey's never been there. So I can drive you both up there and then, after Zizi's gone, pick you up and bring you back to the Colony. I might also be able to bring Didi."

"Didi!"

"Charming. I chauffeur the creature hither and yon for hours and hours, wait on her hand and foot, bring her breakfast in bed, and the only damn thing that gets a rise and a smile out of 'er is a possible visit from a fuzzy little dwarf."

I couldn't help it, I laughed. He was right. He had been amazing. Gilbey too. I'd had a major hairyassed crisis and they were both there for me. Expecting him to share Evil Owl House with his snobby mum and a "voolGAIR" post-abort teenager would not be fair. Bolinas House was beautiful. And I'd be with Gilb. We could both just cool out. I could cartoon, which I hadn't done since the Yobs concert. "It's good, Pascal. It's great. I'd love to do that. Thank you. For everything. I'll get dressed."

Dunderbeck, oh Dunderbeck,
How could you be so mean
To ever have invented
The Sausage Meat Machine?
Now all the rats and pussycats
Will never more be seen . . .
For they've all been ground to sausages
In Dunderbeck's macheeen!

Pascal said "One Hundred Bottles of Beer on the Wall" was unacceptable (we were at eighty-seven bottles), so I tried teaching them some of the music hall and pub songs I'd learned from Del People. It was just Gilbey and me on "Please Go Easy, for I've Never Been Done Before" (the Gilb had a soft, sweet voice), and just Pascal and me on "The Ball of Ballynoor" (Pascal's voice was more loud than good). After those two megahits, Pascal taught us an excellently filthy little song.

> *Asshole, asshole*
> *A soldier I will be.*
> *To piss, to piss,*
> *Two pistols on my knee.*
> *Fuck you, fuck you,*
> *Fu' curiosity.*
> *To fight for the old cunt,*
> *Fight for the old cunt,*
> *Fight for the old countreee!*

"Great song, 'Scal."

"Ta. Learnt it at me mother's knee."

"Really?"

"No."

• •

Some houses never look familiar, even if you actually live in them for a while. Others are like old friends, even if you've never seen them before. Bolinas House is one of the old friend ones. I could tell this wasn't just my thing. As soon as we were in the doorway and Pascal hit the lights, Gilbey blissed out.

"Whut a sweet li'l playce!"

"You don't see it as a toolshed?"

"Naw, 'Scal, it's great!"

It had taken us about eight hours to get up there, so there was no way Pascal could just turn around and drive back to Malibu. It was late. He put together some canned Scottish soup.

"Cockaleekie."

"'Scal, you made that name up!"

"Did not."

"Did too!"

"He didn't, Gilb. It's a real soup. We have it in Canada too."

"There. Now, Miss Tarr, might you get your mind out of the dustbin and eat?"

Bolinas House being one large room, there was this big debate over who'd sleep where. Pascal said he'd take the chesterfield ("I can sleep on the couch"). Gilbey said she'd take the chesterfield ("Whut, the sofa? I kin sleep there"). There was no way I was going to take the chesterfield. Gilbey said she insisted. I said Gilbey insisted. Gilbey said, "OK, you guys, let's shave, shower, shit an' rack it." Pascal said, "Charming."

The clock radio's buzzy alarm went off at 6 A.M. Pascal got up to make coffee. Gilbey, asleep under a white cotton quilt, her arm over her eyes, long hair all over the place, looked like an illustration for Rapunzel. I guess Pascal thought so too. Motioning for me to keep quiet, he grabbed a camera out of his bag and took a few shots of her. I understood why he'd want to do that, but also thought, He's never done that with me.

When breakfast was ready, he woke Gilb. She got up really fast and took off for the loo. I knew she was my friend, and that Pascal truly didn't seem to want her "that way," but still wished she'd had on a shirt or panties or something.

After breakfast, Pascal sat us both down on the chester. He stayed standing (what Del calls the power position).

"Right. Here's how this needs to work. You, Roanne, are to rest, relax, not lift anything. The larder is reasonably stocked for a few days, but there is also a small grocer's for milk, fresh bread, that sort of thing, just down the road. The owner's called Fred. Nice old bloke. You can put what you need on my tab. I believe you can safely have a 'whole body' shower starting tomorrow. This music system plays both records and cassettes, which are all on this shelf. You have the Malibu number if you need me. Please don't throw anything but paper in the toilet, and throw nothing into the sink, or you'll bugger up the septic tank. I'll be back to get you in about two days, as soon as Zizi leaves. I'll ring first.

"You, Gilbey, are not to make fires or set the house alight. Don't giggle, I'm serious. I've watched you play at building fires. It's very worrying. This is a wooden house. Roanne is a Canadian. Fire-building is, I'm told, an ethnic talent in Canada. She builds the fires. Now, there is booze here. If there weren't, you'd wander up the road looking for it, which would be worse. Please try to ration it, to pace yourself. I know you can do this, because I've seen you do it. Just make believe Johnny's watching. And do not get Roanne pissed, she's healing."

"'Scal, I'm not—"

"Let me finish. Neither of you is to invite any playmates here. Fred checks on the house in the evenings, but there's no point in your showing putative burglars around. I expect you, Gilbey, to respect every aspect of other people's property. You do understand?"

"Uh-huh."

"Good. Any questions? Yes, Roanne?"

"What's 'putative'?"

"'Potential.' Something that could happen."

The lecture being over, he grabbed his gear and headed for the car. I followed. He bunged everything into the jumpseat, asking if I had the housekey. Yes, I said. As he was straightening up, I put my arms around his neck and kissed him, majorly. He kissed me back, also majorly. He laughed, shook his head, ran his big hand around my face, got in the car, took off. I guess he figured I was watching, because, a little way up the road, without turning round, he waved. I was pretty sure Pascal didn't love me like I loved him, but it was putative.

I was cool until I walked back into the house. As soon as I closed the door, I felt this total Pascal-lessness. Gilbey was in the loo doing whatever. I looked at the Pascal pictures on the walls. His scary, beautiful mother. The black lady's perfect bum. The tall, thin, naked blonde lady in Africa, and on the beach in what was probably in Malibu. Gilbey came out of the loo.

"Great pictures, huh?"

"Is that you, the blonde?"

"No, that's Ditta. She lived with 'Scal for about a year. Never said much. Real pretty, though. Went back home to Sweden or Norway. 'Scal said it was cool between 'em."

Gilb's known Pascal a long time, I thought. I could ask her things.

"How long have you lived in the Colony, Gilb?"

"A little over three years. When Johnny started doing all this real estate in California, we moved up from Charleston."

"Was Pascal already living here?"

"Uh-huh. That's when he was with Ditta."

"Pascal says Johnny's coming home any day now. Are you happy?"

"Yeah. Superhappy! I talked to Johnny a few nights ago. He said something about our moving to Europe. That would be really great! I could hang more with Dickie and other European guys I know. Most Malibu people are stuckup and lowclass all at once. If we do Venice with Dart, you could come live with us after. I know Johnny'd be cool with it. Like I told you, Johnny's always wanted me to have a pal my own age. A girl. And you're my best pal ever!"

She gave me this humungus hug. I felt a little closed in on. I mean, Gilbey was my best pal as well, but I didn't necessarily want to live Somewhere in Europe as a guest of the Tarr family. I hugged her back, but then sort of changed the subject. "How come you didn't mention Johnny was coming home? I mean, while we were driving up?"

"I dunno. Wanted to keep everything mellow, I guess. Johnny an' 'Scal hate each other."

"They do? How come?"

"I dunno. Johnny says 'Scal thinks he, Johnny, is white trash."

"What does Pascal say?"

"He says Johnny's white trash."

• •

I've always admired people who could do French braiding. Gilbey had put her hair into these perfect French braids. I asked if she'd do mine, and while she did I told her all the different meanings of "plait." When she finished, we looked at ourselves in the loo mirror.

"Which one of these people looks like an illegal Mexican housekeeper in Malibu Colony?"

"An' which one looks like a Swiss yodeller?"

"You don't look like a Swiss yodeller."

"An' you don't look like no Mexican housekeeper."

"I like Mexican housekeepers. A Mexican housekeeper gave me my catbaby."

"Groovy. You still don't look like one. You look like a beautiful gypsy."

"Like on Pascal's cigarette packet?"

"Beautifuller. The lady on the cigs doesn't have a face."

"Ta."

"Ta. That's weird. Is it Canadian for 'thank you'?"

"Brit. English."

"Is 'chesterfield' English too?"

"I don't think so. I think chesterfield's Canadian. Not sure. I'll ask when I'm back there."

"When do you think that'll be?"

"Dunno."

"Do you want to go back?"

"No. Not for a while."

"Then don't. Come with Johnny and me. They'll never find you in Europe."

Gilbey wanted a drink. Drunks are no company. I reminded her of the promise to "pace" herself. She asked when I thought she'd be "paced" enough. I said, "When it gets dark." We settled on sunset gray, because we could watch that from the beach.

Bolinas House has a basement, a raw concrete floor thing. There were tools, a fire extinguisher, some broken chairs, boxes, suitcases. In one corner, next to a big cement double sink, was a darkroom setup. Shelves with pans and bottles of liquid. Against that wall were stacks of matted or framed photographs. We sat on the concrete and went through them. There were three of Gilbey. One sitting on the beach, in profile, wearing a big black sweater. Another straddling Grady, the world's friendliest guard dog. In the third photo, she was standing next to a tall Asian-looking man. They were both wearing false eyelashes, lots of makeup, high ponytails and glittery versions of what Del called a little black dress.

"Wow! Who's that?!"

"Faboo Balang. He's great! He's one of the best hairdressers in probably the whole world. Been written up in lots of fashion mags. He's really fun. We're good pals. He's off doing hair for the 'Divine Goddesses' tour, but when he gets back, I'll ask him to do you. He does lots of Pascal's models. He's Ditta's cousin. They came to the Colony together."

"I thought you said she was Swedish."

"Uh-huh."

"But he looks Chinese."

"Filipino. His mother was from Manila. His father was Ditta's uncle. I think they met in Sweden. Ditta said they never married, but that her uncle took care of her and Faboo. Fab's real first name is Thor. It's pronounced 'Tor,' but people kept doing these dumb jokes about how his name was 'thore,' you know, 'sore' with a lisp, so he changed it to Faboo, which is short for 'fabulous.'"

"Does he always wear dresses?"

"No. We were just goofin'. He does do a drag show sometimes. At this little club in West Hollywood. He lip-syncs to Shirley Bassey records."

"Are there any kids our age in the Colony? You know, kids who just, like, go to school and stuff?"

"Not a lot. There are some kids who are away at school someplace. The only ones like that I can think of who're actually *in* the Colony are Jeffrey Kronfeld, whose father produces *The Law of the Street,* and the Corrigan twins, Alice and Mary Kate."

"What're they like?"

"Boring. Bad clothes. No makeup. No tits. Except for Jeffrey."

Later, while Gilbey was showing me exercises that "help keep y'r bod from headin' for y'r ankles," I asked her about Pascal's houses and stuff. I'd been wondering, ever since Inn Nainity, if cartoonists and photographers could make so much money that they didn't seem to have to worry about it. She said she didn't know much about Didi. That Pascal did OK, but that his "big" money came from "his grand-daddy's camera part."

"Camera part?"

"Yeah. I don't know if I remember this exactly right, but he told me that his French grandfather, his momma's daddy, invented this really tiny dingus inside movin' picture cameras, an' like no camera, right up to right now, can run without this thing, an' so the family, him an' his brother, an' their momma, get these big cheques from all over the world every year. I think him and his brother get pretty good money for their work on top of that, so everything's like supercool for cash."

"Amazing! I wish I could do that, invent some tiny thing that everybody had to use for something."

"Maybe you can."

"I don't think so. All I know how to do is see what I hear and draw pictures of it."

"I think that's great. I can't even do that."

"What would you like to do, I mean if you could do anything?"

"Have Clarissa killed an' have them not be able to trace it to me."

"I'm serious."

"You think I ain't?"

"OK, what else?"

"I dunno. Have fun. Buy clothes. Go places. Dance. I guess my favorite thing is hangin' with Johnny. Wait till you meet him. You'll see. He's so fun to be with! I think the sun's startin' to set. I gotta have a drink."

"And a beachwalk?"

"And a beachwalk. I'll grab the bottle."

The beachwalk didn't really work. We'd both put on some of Pascal's sweaters, but Gilbey kept bitching about how she was "freezin'-ass goddamn cold!" and sucking on the bottle of red wine. "I gotta keep warm." I was afraid she'd drink the entire bottle and pass out on the beach. Pascal said I shouldn't lift anything, and that sure as hell had to include Gilbey, so I suggested we go back to the house, where I could build a fire and cook us a meal.

There were cans of chicken stew. There was rice. There wasn't any bread, but the Gilb was already seriously bombed. I knew that if we went to Fred's, there'd be some sort of problem. I also knew she wouldn't let me go alone. The third thing I knew was that she was too blotto to care whether there was bread or not.

I think growing up is not so much about learning to lie, which little kids start to figure out at age four or five, but how to lie better. Maybe not so much "lie" as say things in the way that gets people to do what you need to have them do, or at least to *not* do what will cause a major fuckup. So I told Gilb I wanted us to eat on the big bed because my insides were sore (which they weren't), and because I was bleeding heavily again (which I wasn't). My real reason for our eating on the megabed was that, when she passed out, I wouldn't have to carry her anyplace.

She did pass out, in the middle of telling me how "dumbass Clarissa had this friggin' nosejob one time, made 'er friggin' nose so friggin' small it was just nostrils, just friggin' holes, man, so they had to do the whole friggin' thing over, right, just to put back some friggin' nosemeat and she . . ." I took the food off the bed, got the clothes off the Gilb-lump, put her under the duvet. There was a bit of wine in the bottom of the (second) bottle. I drank it because I'd friggin' earned it. Then I did all the washing up, took a few puffs on one of Pascal's gypsy cigs, coughed, put it out, built another fire. I wanted to call him, but he'd said "if you need me." I was pretty sure the way I needed him wasn't what he meant.

Went to the loo. I was still bleeding, but not as much. Had one more pad. Figured that would get it. Wanted to be padless as soon as poss, so I could get out of sweats and wide-legs and back into my jeans. I "abluted" (could hear Del's voice: "Rosie, time to ablute and go to bed"). Put on a Pascalsmell white thermal shirt. Thought I'd sleep on the Chester, but there was the good old "possible bleeding on the white stuff" problem, so I climbed into the bed, which was big enough to sleep six anyway.

In the middle of the night, Gilbey snuggled up next to me. "Oh, God," I thought, "I do love this person, but not 'that' way . . . please let this not be a problem." No problem. Just a warm, drunk friend-sister body. I fell back to sleep with the Gilb holding on.

When morning came, I woke up wanting to draw in the way Gilbey sometimes wanted to drink. Had to draw. Untangled from Gilb, who was asleep to the point where there wasn't even a "murfl." Found some mint teabags, made a tisane, got drawing and writing gear out of my army bag. The warm teacup brought my hands to life while the new fire started to do its thing.

I was drawing a cartoon of Zizanie, based on Pascal's photo, when the phone rang. Gilb slept on. I picked up.

"Good morning, Mr. Douglas-Hyde's northern beach house."

"I think just 'hello' should suffice."

(All lower holes clutch.) "Oh, hi. You got back OK? Safe and all?"

"'And all.' Quite safe, thank you. How're things up there?"

"Good. House fine, fires fine, food fine, beach fine."

"And that job in Mexico, it concluded well?"

"Your mum is watching you?"

"Yes."

"Well, the job in Mexico seems to have been OK. I've almost stopped bleeding."

"And the Tarr project? How goes that?"

"That is sound asleep. She got pretty drunk last night, but everything's cool. When are you coming back up?"

"Actually, that's what I'm ringing about. I've quite a lot of driving to do today and this evening. I should be there quite early tomorrow morning. Before first light, I expect. If you could have everything ready for an early-morning meeting, that would be super."

"Will do. You want us dressed and ready to roll?"

"Uh, no . . . leave the Prowlet lined up in a prone position, so I can check the fit on the large frame."

"Does that mean what I think it does?"

"I believe so, yes."

"Shit, Pascal, you speak better Teenybopper Phone Code than I do."

I finished the drawing of Zizanie. Put Pascal and Didi in it. Pascal was twice her size. Didi came up to the top of her knee. She stood between them, looking like an angry mother lion. The caption was "Look, God," (what is this in French?) "couldn't you do me one between these two extremes?!" I liked it, but wasn't sure I'd show it to Pascal. Gilbey woke up.

"Did I sleep in the bed?"

"You slept in the bed."

"Did we dyke?"

"Uh-uh. Do you dyke?"

"Not usually. Never sober. Did only once really, with Corie Layton."

"Corie Layton? She a dyke?"

"Yeah, mega. She lives with this neat lady, a painter named Bedo. From one of those vakia-slavia places. Thick accent. She did a dyno painting of me. Johnny has it in his office."

"Could I draw you?"

"Now?"

"Uh-huh."

"You'll have to make my head real big. And green. I feel like shit."

"It's the wine."

"You ain't woofin', it's the wine. Guess I din't pace myself too good."

"I'll make some coffee. Why don't you take a shower?"

"Yeah, shower." She stumbled out of bed. I wondered if the Gilb would drink so much if she wanted to do something like I wanted to cartoon, if she wanted to be something. Something besides her father's girlfriend. Her father's girlfriend? Fuck! I didn't even know I thought that. If I knew who my father was, would I want to be his girlfriend, want to have Del killed? No way.

After coffee and some chocolate biscuits ("'Cookies,' Babygirl, cookies. 'Biscuits' are a whole 'nuther thing"), and a short walk in the sea air ("It is fuckin' FREEZING-ASS out here! Why are we doin' this? You could hang Christmas balls on my nipples!"), she felt at least a bit better and agreed to be drawn. She was just wearing a gray sweatshirt and black button-fly jeans, but I drew her in lots of Art Nouveau and pre-Raph gear. Long gauzy dresses, leafy garlands of flowers in her hair. Rabbits, birds and butterflies around her. No captions. I pulled out the colored felt-tips and we both did some colouring. Gilbey had already started sucking on a bottle of tequila, the only booze left, but she did a really good job of staying inside the lines. Better than me, actually.

"Gilb, how come you don't have to go to school?"

"'Emancipated minor.' Once you're 16, if your parents sign these papers, you don't have to go if you don't wanna."

"First you have to be a real 16—and an American."

"Buffalo Bevilacqua can probably get you phony papers. Shit, Buffalo can probably get you phony parents!"

"I don't want phony parents. I love my mum. I just don't want to go to school."

"How come? I mean, I know why I don't want to go. I'm school-stupid, an' I get bored. But you seem real smart."

"Thanks. I do love learning stuff, but I'm learning tons more these days than I was in school. And, when I'm sorting Dart's books, plus going to Venice, I will learn amazing amounts. Anybody would."

"Even me, huh?"

"I didn't mean it like that."

"Have you learned anything from me?"

"Yeah, lots."

"Like what?"

"Like hair. Like makeup an' clothes."

"Yeah. Faboo says I could be a makeup artist. In movies, even. He offered to train me once, but he was really stoned at the time, so I wasn't sure I should bring it up again."

"I think you should."

"Yeah? Maybe I will. . . . You know what?"

"What?"

"I have gone a whole day without buying a damn thing. Let's hit Fred's!"

I tried explaining to her that Fred's was probably just a convenience store and that there wouldn't be anything interesting to buy there.

"Betcha I'll find something."

And she did. Little black sea pods. You empty them into a glass of water and little dots turn into black sea horses the size of exclamation points. She got really happy with it. "Look, look, look! I love stuff I've never seen before!"

"Yeh, me too."

"Like Venice?"

"Like Venice."

"Here's to Venice!" And she took this monstro swig on the tequila. I asked if she'd mind sitting on the Chester.

"How come?"

I didn't want to mention passing out or heavy lifting, so I said the light was better, that I wanted to draw her some more.

If you ask enough questions, eventually you'll find out something you don't want to know.

"So Corie Layton's a dyke, eh?"

"Yeah. Evvy now 'n' then she does guys. I think she . . . never mind."

"What?"

"Nuthin'. I'm thirsty. Want some Co'-Cola?"

"Uh-uh. That shit takes rust off cars. You think she what?"

"Nuthin'."

"Fucked Pascal?"

"Yeah."

"When?"

"I dunno. Whenever."

"Before I came to the Colony?"

"Yeah. Not a lot. They're, like friends. It's a buddyfuck thing. I don't think it means diddly-squat as a man-woman thing. I think, and I'm not just saying this because I'd like to get out of discussing a yucky subject, which I would definitely like to get out of doin', but I think 'Scal likes you more'n I've ever seen him like anybody. There's somethin' special between you two."

"Special how? What's different about it?"

"Dunno. It's hard to explain. I just absolutely do not believe he'd drive a knockup that wasn't his fault all the way to goddamn Mexico an' risk getting busted an' evvything, if that person wasn't real special to him."

"He wasn't doing the operation. What could they bust him for?"

"Takin' an underage girl across a state line. Out of the country too!"

"Under what age?"

"Eighteen. Don't you have that in Canada?"

"I don't think so. Don't really know. I never heard a Canadian person mention it. I don't think most people who live in British Columbia want to leave."

"Oh yeah? How come?"

"Probably 'cause the weather's better than anywhere else in Canada, if you don't mind rain . . . and there's lots of fresh food."

"We got good weather an' fresh food all over California, but people still get knocked up."

"I'm sure people get knocked up in Vancouver too. And maybe go with older guys to doctors in Alberta, which is the next province over. Do you think he's still fucking her?"

"I dunno, Roe. Doubt it. When would he have the time?"

"Now."

"Now? With his bitchy mama there?"

"How do we know she's there?"

"Oh, sure. He's gonna haul both of us up here to a freezing-ass-cold beach house in the middle of East Pissant just so he can have a buddyfuck with Corie Fucking Layton! Forget it, Babygirl, let's paint our toenails Fred Red."

"You go ahead. I'm gonna have a beachwalk."

• •

Gilbey didn't come out and say I was acting like a major asshole, but it was pretty obvious that's what she thought. Walking along the beach, watching the big red sunball get swallowed by the sea, my hands jammed way deep into my jean jacket, I sort of thought so as well. I mean, no matter how much I liked Pascal, and even if he liked me too, we were not a declared couple. Whatever he did with Corie, or anybody else, before he met me was certainly cool, even if we were boyfriend/girlfriend, which we weren't. Gilb was definitely right about Pascal not going through all the hassle of stashing us in

Bolinas just to have a one-nighter. All he had to do was send me to Gilbey's, where I was supposed to be living anyway. Or take Corie somewhere else. They both had enough money to do that. So why was I thinking all this stuff?

Back at Bolinas House, Gilb had done a fine job of totalling the tequila and was solidly asleep on the Chester. I woke her, asked one stupid question ("Are you hungry?"), got her undressed, into a sweatshirt and under a sheet and blankets. Was bored with building fires, so I just turned up the electric heat, abluted, put on the thermal shirt, grabbed a book of photographs by someone called Diane Arbus, poured a glass of milk, opened a bag of pretzels and got into bed.

Arbus was out of the question! I mean, the pictures were brilliant, but really twisted. I drew for a while, just scribbly animals, and one of somebody who looked sort of like Brian, with wings, flying over the sea.

In my dream a group of majorly deformed people with pointy teeth were running down the beach in the Colony. They had Gilbey, they were holding her above their heads. They were hurting her. Biting. Tearing her clothes, burning her hair. Laughing. She was laughing too, saying, "Don't bother me none!" I knew she was only saying that to not give them the satisfaction of knowing they were putting her in pain. I couldn't get into Evil Owl House because the sliding doors were locked. Pascal and Corie Layton were fucking on the living room floor. Corie was on top. I knocked on the glass. Corie didn't look up. Pascal did. He mouthed, "Not now, Prowlet." I wanted to tell him it was important, it was about Gilbey, but Gilbey and the laughing monsters were getting farther and farther away. I had to run after them. I was running and running. I had a stitch in my side. I kept running until the door of Bolinas House opened and woke me.

"Prowlet?"

"Pascal?"

"No, Bonny Prince Charlie. Shh, go back to sleep. I'll be there in a minute." There was a lot of shuffling, stuff hitting the floor, doors closing, water running, then he was naked and warm next to me. There was also this wonderful smell in the room. Strawberries!

"Didi!"

"Salut, Petite."

Pascal turned on the bedlamp and sitting on the bed, fuzzy-faced, bowlegged and barebum naked, was my friend and cultural hero.

"Yay!" I shouted, hugging him, waking Gilbey.

"Wass happenin'?"

"Didi is happenin'! Didi, this is my best friend, Miss Gilbey Tarr, of Charleston, South Carolina, and Malibu Colony, California. Gilb, this is Didier Rocaille, also known as the great cartoonist D.D.A., and also Pascal's brother."

"Hi," Gilbey said, squinting, turning on the floor lamp next to the chester. Then she squinted some more. "You're Pascal's brother? Fuck, you guys, don't your momma make any normal-size kids?"

"That's my cartoon!"

"You 'ave make a cartoon of Pascal and me?"

"Uh, sort of."

"I want to see."

"Well, I dunno . . . it's not really—"

"It's all right, Prowlet, I can take it, whatever it is. Let's have a look."

I dug the drawing book out of my army bag. Gilbey stumbled over and sat on the edge of the bed. I showed everybody my drawing. They all laughed, really liked it a lot. Didi gave me the French for the caption: "Alors! Écoutez-vous, bon Dieu! Pouvez-vous me donner un enfant entre ces deux extrêmes?!"

Then Pascal said "Right!" and explained that he'd been shuttling people places for what seemed like weeks, and that we should sleep "until we naturally awaken," and that we'd stay at Bolinas House until "after the high-traffic evening hours." At that point we'd head south in the car, dropping Didi in San Francisco. This meant he'd drive all night.

"Is that all right for you, Prowlet? How're your insides?" I told him my insides seemed really good. "Excellent. I then propose that we all get some sleep."

Amazingly, everybody in the room had, at some point, slept in the same bed as everybody else in the room. Except Gilbey and Didi. So, when Gilb asked to sleep with the rest of us, it was the only "next to" that was even a little bit acceptable to me (and I wasn't crazy about that). It wasn't a "sex thing" in the regular way (in that "regular way," I couldn't do anything until my next period. And, if Gilbey even started offering to "help out in the meantime," I would have been, to use Brian's expression, "compelled to do her an injury"). It was just that she said she'd feel left out if she was the only one sleeping on the Chester. I could see where that would be true, and I think feeling left out really sucks.

Pascal thought it was funny when I started assigning places.

"OK, I sleep next to Pascal, Didi sleeps next to me and Gilb sleeps next to Didi, OK?"

"It is all splondeed, Petite, I believe. We are all veree ti-red, and I believe that I should make myself clean and then we all fay dodo, d'ac?"

"Fay dodo?"

"Make sleep."

So we did, and the sleep we made was warm and good. Full of love and totally unweird.

When I "naturally awakened," I was alone in the bed. I could see the Gilb and Didi goofing on the beach. They were both doing cartwheels! Amazingly, she was doing this without puking her guts up. When I went to the sink for water, I could see Pascal outside, loading stuff into a four-door American car.

"New car?"

"Rented. We had to drive Zizi to the San Francisco airport. Didi wanted to see you. It also seemed that driving even a short distance with all this gear, Gilbey's legs over your shoulders and Didi on your lap was a bit much, even for this group. Walk with me a bit, Prowlet? I have some information."

The "information" started fairly easy. Johnny and Clarissa Tarr were back in the Colony. Johnny was looking for Gilbey. Buffalo Bevilacqua was looking for me. Said he had good news. Donnie, the giver of all this information, also told Pascal there was a phone message for me. From my mother.

"Del? Is she in the Colony?"

"No, she left a number. Wants you to ring her. As soon as possible. Donnie said she sounded tray jhontee."

"Gentle?"

"Gracious."

Gracious. Gracious was good. If Del had left a screaming freaking guts-for-garters message, Donnie would've told Pascal and Pascal would've told me.

I recognized the number. Our place in Kitsilano. I dialled. It rang and rang. No answer. I was nervous, disappointed and relieved all at once.

Had to be Dickie. When the Yobs played Vancouver, Del and Dickie for sure saw eachother, and he told her where I was. I pretty much knew he would, knew he'd have to, knew that whatever was going to happen now had to happen eventually. I hoped he also told her I was cool, was covered, was happy.

In came Gilbey, with Didi on her shoulders. "We're hittin' Fred's, see what they've got for food. Wanna come?"

"No, ta, it's my turn on the beach." What was really happening with me, apart from being really twitchy about Del, was that Gilb didn't seem to know that her family was home, and I didn't feel ready to tell her. Too many families, too much family stuff. I felt swamped.

I was beachwalking when Pascal called out, "Prowlet!" I turned around. He snapped my picture.

"It's about time!" I shouted.

"What?"

"I SAID, IT'S ABOUT TIME YOU TOOK MY PICTURE!"

"OH, I'VE PICTURES OF YOU!"

"YOU DO NOT!"

"YES, I DO!"

"YOU DO?! FROM WHEN?!"

"VARIOUS TIMES!"

"AREN'T YOU TOO FAR AWAY? NOW? TO TAKE MY PICTURE?"

"ZOOM LENS!"

"OH!"

• •

I figured I might not see Didi for a while, so said I'd sit with him in the backseat until San Francisco. I wondered if the neighbourhood we were taking him to was named after the president of Cuba, which would be weird, given how pissy the Yanks always were about Castro. Didi was going there to meet Chuck the Chicken-trucker. I almost said, "The guy who beat you up?" but remembered in time I wasn't supposed to know that. What I did do was ask, "Is he nice, this guy? Do you like him?"

"We 'ave known each other for long time. 'E is an old friend."

The Castro neighborhood looked like fun. Cafés, shops, lots of good-looking guys hanging out together. I figured it was the gay district, like English Bay in Vancouver. Didi told me to write and to send him a copy of the Zizi cartoon. I said, "Hey, you can have this one." Pascal said, "No. He has enough cartoons. I want that one." I filled with major glee, promising to make a copy for Didi. We did the French both-cheek kissing thing, he said it was "soo-pair" to "review" me.

"Bye-bye, Sondreeyohn."

"Sondreeyohn?"

"Cinderella."

Then he bounced out of the car into the crowd of guys. Gilb and I traded places, me settling in next to Pascal, who was looking a bit grimmo.

I thought maybe Didi had told Pascal my real age. "Are you mad at me?" I asked.

He looked straight ahead. "Everything isn't about you, Roanne."

Gilbey had been very quiet, which was deeply un-Gilbey-like. I'd seen Pascal talking with her on the beach while I was packing the last of my stuff. Figured, even though she hadn't said a word about it, that he must've told her the Tarrs were back. Suddenly, she spoke, a bit too loud.

"I think he's great, Didi! Fabulous! Really fun! He's a famous cartoonist, huh?"

"Superfamous. He's brilliant. Has a couple of books out. I have them in B.C., but he's even more popular here in the States. Is there a bookshop in the Colony?"

"Yeah, Malibooks."

"Well, we can probably get Didi stuff there. Or order it."

"Great! He's a really neat li'l guy."

"He's a damn fool!"

Gilb and I went shtumm, knowing that when Buildingman did his black-cloud thing, it was better to just keep your head down.

As we swung onto the open highway, Pascal seriously picked up speed. Usually I like fast driving, but this was different. Del always says don't drive fast when you're driving angry.

When he spoke, it was out of nowhere, into the silence. "That 'really neat li'l guy,' that 'adorable wee person,' that 'superfamous brilliant cartoonist,' whom, I would venture to say, I love rather more than anyone else in this great American petrol-devouring pig of a car, is trying his damnedest to get himself killed! And would anyone here care to venture a wee guess as to why?"

"Because he's a dwarf?" Gilbey ventured in a really tiny voice.

"Interesting guess, Gilbey, but it was a rhetorical question, actually, so do shut up, all right?"

"Damn, 'Scal, how the fuck was I supposed to know it was a retronical damn question?!"

"Right. I'd failed to take into account the stupidity factor."

"Jesus, Pascal, cool out! You're not the only person in this car!"

"Well, fine, Roanne, we can *certainly* change *that!*"

"Great! Fine! Terrific!" I said. "Stop the damn car and we'll let you be alone with your own rotten company."

He ran one hand over his face, from forehead to chin, then shook his head. "Sorry, kids, bad form. I think I'll stop being a prat now and just drive the car. But I do need silence for a bit."

Except when someone was thirsty, or needed a pee break, Pascal pretty much got his silence. In Santa Barbara, in the middle of the night, while Gilbey was having both a pee break and a Coca-Cola run, he turned to me. His voice had a slightly broken sound I'd never heard him make before.

"I am truly sorry about earlier, Prowlet. My behaviour was, at the least, unacceptable. You know about Didi and Chuck. Chuck is a very small part of a very old story. The problem is that my brother, this gifted, wonderful little man, has spent most of his life trying to get someone, anyone, to kill him . . . because . . . because, from early on, it has been his belief, his understanding, that the woman he worshipped as a child wanted this of him. When we were children, he'd run at me and run at me, and pound and pound on me, in hope that I'd do the deed, so there would be some love in it."

"Like at Inn Nainity, when you found us in the stream?"

"Exactly. And the sex he has is terrifying. Unbelievably violent. Do you know what fisting is?"

"No."

"Just as well. Suffice it to say it turns this tiny person into a wrist ornament, into a fucking bracelet! And, one of these days, one of these beer-gutted redneck closet cases he fancies will break him in half, and there is fucking nothing any of us can do but wait for it!" He was holding tight to the steering wheel with both hands. He wasn't crying, but his eyes, in the gas station fluorescence, were all liquidy.

I reached out to touch his face, but he shook me away. "I'm really sorry, Pascal," I said, thinking, Boy, is that ever not enough.

Gilbey, her hands full of liquid and solid junkfood, took one look at us and announced that she was going to have a nap in the backseat.

I was tired as well. Wanted to curl up with my head in Pascal's lap, but figured that was risky. Turned away from him, pulled my legs up, put my head against the seatback. Closed my eyes. Pascal tapped me on the shoulder. He sort of smiled, patted his thigh, made a "come over" move with his head. I smiled back, lay down, fell asleep.

• •

It was morning when we pulled into the Colony. There was Murph's guardhouse. There was Grady. There was the Morgan.

"Hello, Rosie. It's all right. I'm not going to kill anyone. Unless there proves to be a very good reason for so doing."

What do you say? You could say what I said.

"Hi. You look great. Guys, this is my mum, Delores Chappell. Del, these are my friends, Gilbey Tarr, whose house I'm staying at, and Mr. Douglas-Hyde."

Gilbey put out her hand. Del shook it. Gilbey said, "Real pleased to meet you, ma'am."

Del looked good. Her Irish-setter hair was all tied up in a yellow chiffon scarf. She was wearing her nubby black caftan and a huge red leather bomber jacket that I'd never seen before. It almost matched her red elf boots.

She sounded weird. At first I thought it was just that we hadn't talked to eachother for a while. Then I got it. She was doing the absolutely grandest of her Grand Voices—Mrs. Miniver, the woman who saved English people from Hitler in that old black-and-white movie she liked to watch on telly in the middle of the night. Del sometimes used this voice with my teachers, and with receptionists in big buildings. I thought it sounded silly. I wanted her to sound like herself, so I could introduce a real person to other real people. Saying any of this was massively out of the question.

"Yours is the house I rang? The number Dickie Siggins gave me?"

"Uh-huh. Yes, ma'am."

"And you, sir? How do you know my daughter?"

"Roanne is a friend of my brother. And now of mine as well."

I saw a place where speaking up might be cool. "Mr. Douglas-Hyde's brother is D.D.A., Del, the cartoonist I'm so crazy about, the one who invited me to visit, where I spoke to you from, and told you how Hampstead it was. This is all Hampstead too!"

"I see. Do you think we might all continue this discussion somewhere where there's a lavatory and a shower. I've been driving all night. I'm frightfully tired."

"As are we all, madam. Utterly shagged. Follow me." Gilbey and I sort of stood there. "Roanne, go with your mother. Gilbey, come with me."

Delface, Delhair, Delsmell. I was all *boomboomboom* inside, but also really glad to see her. I said, "I'm really glad to see you."

"Mm," she said, kicking the Morgan into gear and following Pascal.

"May I get you a drink? Coffee?"

"Coffee would be lovely. Loo?"

"Large one upstairs, small just here."

"Small will be fine."

When Del was out of earshot, Gilbey whispered, "She's real pretty, your momma."

I mouthed, "Say it louder."

"Your Momma's Real Pretty!" Gilbey shouted.

When Del returned, Gilbey said, "If it would be OK, my family's just got home. If I could, I'd love to take a real quick shower, then I'll scoot home an' see everybody. If you could give me some time for family reunion before . . ."

"Of course, Gilbey, go ahead. Have your shower," Pascal said. He looked pretty done in. He gestured to the big white Chester. "Please," he said, "do sit down." Del said thank you. Pascal asked how she took her coffee. "Black," I said, "she takes it black." He brought Del a mug of coffee, put it on the little table in front of the Chester.

"Aren't you having any?" Del asked him. He said he planned to get some sleep as soon as possible, so he wasn't going to "risk caffeine."

Gilbey was swinging down the stairs. She'd French-braided her hair and looked fresh, clean and, as usual, beautiful. I could see Del noticing this for the first time. "Before you go, Miss Tarr, I have a lovely surprise for everyone." She got up, went out to the Morgan. She came back with a little white plastic shopping bag. "Rosie mine," she said, "it looks like you've gone into the family business."

It was, I'm sure, major kid-goof behavior. Pascal was probably completely grossed out by it. I don't know. For a change, I wasn't looking at Pascal. I was looking at a large photograph of a record album (what Del said was a "rough assembly")—*The Yobs—Live at the Cow Palace!* The album cover in the picture was MY CARTOON! When Del pulled it out of the plastic bag, and Gilbey and I realized what it meant, we started to scream. We jumped up and down, danced around, high-fived eachother. We kept on screaming. When I did check out Pascal, he was sort of pressed against a wall, smiling as much as a wasted 42-year-old guy who'd been driving all night, and who had just met the mother of the teenager he was fucking, could possibly smile. "Look, Pascal!" I cried, thrusting the photo at him. "Look, it's my cartoon!"

"So I see. That's wonderful, Prowlet."

"Wunnerful? It's fuckin' awesome! Oh, excuse me, Mrs. Chappell."

"It's all right, dear, I've heard the word."

Gilb giggled. "Oh, right. Roe does use it all the time, duddn't she? Hey, I gotta run home and check in or I'm gonna catch hell. See you guys later. Congratulations, Babygirl! It's dyno!" She hugged me really hard, laughed and was out the sliding doors, running up the beach.

"Very pretty girl," Del said.

There was also a contract for me to sign. (Del, as my grown-up, had already signed it, but she thought I'd like to also sign for my first album cover. She was right.) I did that, in the best penmanship I could put together. Then Del, smiling a little, handed me a cheque. From "Camden Lock Productions, Ltd." Signed by Derek Rubin. "Pay to the Order of Roanne Chappell." For $10,000 U.S.!

"Well, I am truly exhausted, ladies, and I'm sure you've much to catch up on. So, if you'll excuse me, I'm going to have a lie down before I have a fall down. Please, make yourselves at home. Help yourselves to whatever you need. Have a swim in the sea if you like."

"Thank you, Mr. Douglas-Hyde, is it? That's very generous of you."

"My pleasure. Ah plootahr, see you later," and he headed up the stairs to the *QE2*.

"'See you lay-tah.' Not if I see you first. Pompous po-faced public school twit! Douglas-fucking-hyphen-fucking-Hyde. Known that type all me life, I'ave, or 'raw-ther,' avoided knowing them."

"He's a good guy, Del. He's been really kind to me."

"Oh, I just bet he has. Douglas-fucking-Hyde."

"Come on, Del, give him a break. Actually, he just uses 'Douglas.' He's a photographer. Those are his on the wall. It was me using the hyphen and the Hyde, it was me showing off. Gilb and I just call him Pascal."

"'Pascal'? That's even more affected than 'Douglas-Hyde.' His mum named 'im fucking 'Pascal'? She must be even more of an upper-class snobbo than he is."

"She is, actually. She's also French."

"Oh."

People she doesn't like are Del's least favourite thing. Her second least favourite thing, at least in the time I've known her, is when you deke around and don't come to the point. "Fuck, Rosie, just spit it out!" was a big expression between us. So I just spit it out.

"I want to stay here."

"Yeah, I thought you might."

"Can I?"

"It's 'may I.'"

"May I?"

"No."

"*Why not?*"

"Don't whinge."

"Why not?"

"How old is Douglas-Douglas-Hyde-Hyde-Hyde?"

"I dunno. Forty-something."

"That's why not."

"But I don't live with him. I live with Gilbey. And her family."

"No, Rosie. You do not live with Gilbey. And her family. You may be visiting with Gilbey at the moment, but you actually live with me."

"O.K. But, if you said I could stay here, which I supermuch want to do, I would live with Gilbey and—"

"Her family, I know. And how old is Gilbey?"

"Sixteen."

"And where does she go to school?"

"She doesn't. She's an emancipated minor and doesn't have to."

"No, Rosie. It's not about bloody emancipation. It's about that Gilbey, and what in hell Yank insanity is it to name y'r daughter after a bottle of bloody gin, it's about that Gilbey is clearly so bloody beautiful and, more to the point, so bloody rich that she doesn't have to go to school! You, on the other hand, are a good-looking enough kid whose mum is a freelance artist, and who plans to support herself by doing bloody cartoons! Such a person needs to have some sort of fall-back plan!"

"You don't! You never did!"

"How the fuck do you think I know that *you have* to!"

We had started out really well. Jhontee. Gracious. A discussion. A heated debate, even. But it had gotten louder and louder, in the way it pretty much always does, and then Pascal was at the top of the stairs screaming louder than anybody.

"LA-A-A-DIES!! I WILL NOT HAVE THIS SORT OF BARROW-BETTY CATERWAULING IN MY HOME!"

"DON'T YOU 'BARROW-BETTY' ME, MATE. THIS IS ME BLOODY DAUGHTER!"

"AND THIS IS MY BLOODY HOME! YOU, MADAME, ARE IN MY HOME!"

"AND YOU, SIR, HAVE VERY LIKELY BEEN IN MY DAUGHTER!"

"JESUS, YOU TWO! STOP!!" The last bellow came from me. I was as surprised as anybody, and everybody was surprised. "I don't *believe* you guys. Is this how I get to be when I get to be a grownup? Well, I think it sucks!" And I ran out onto the beach and down to the water's edge. I wasn't going to drown myself or anything. Just wanted to get away from those two screaming jerks in the house. I sat down on the sand and, because I didn't know what else to do, tried to see China.

"Prowlet?" He was standing behind me. I didn't turn around. He squatted down next to me. "May I talk to you?"

"Yeah, I s'pose."

"Look at me."

"Right. Looking. What?"

He crouched on his knees, hugged me and, from outside the bigness I was inside of, he said, laughing a little, "Oh, I do love you."

It wasn't just lower holes. Every part of my whole self clenched. I pushed at him lightly with my hands so I could be where I could see his face. "You what?"

"Easy. I probably don't mean that the way you heard it. What I mean is that I find you an extraordinarily alive, bright, funny and lovable creature. Girl. Young woman."

"Yeah, right. Go ahead, back up from it. You're so chickenshit, Pascal."

I tried to get up, so I could walk away, to wherever, but he grabbed my wrists.

"Yes. Yes, I probably am, as you put it, 'chickenshit.' Not the word I would've chosen, but . . . the reality of it is right. I do not love in the way you want to be loved. And you have a right to be loved in that way. We're incomplete, my brother and I. We deal with it differently, but it's the same—"

"Oh, shut up, Pascal. If you're gonna fire me, just fire me and I'll fuck off."

He put one hand on each side of my face, almost slapping me. "No, Prowlet, dammit. I am *not* 'firing' you. Had your mother not shown up, completely committed to taking you home with her, I would do whatever I could to keep your . . . joy, your energy, your enviable sense of wonder, as near to me . . . as I could possibly bear. Let you leave when you were ready. And mark me, you would one day, perhaps even one day soon, be ready."

"No!"

"Yes! I think yes. In any event, your mother has come for you. And she will not leave without you. We both know this. We both also know that she loves you a lot. And that you love her. I think she's scattered, loud and vulgar. It is also clear that she will fight your corner in a way that is very rare these days. Go with her, Prowlet. Write me. Ring me. Find me when you can. I will always want to see you. One of the good things about fellas like me is that we'll never love anyone *other* than you either."

I didn't care if Del saw, which I was pretty sure she could. I cried my guts up and Pascal held on until I was ready to stop.

When we walked back from the beach to the house, I asked him to take my picture next to the original Prowlet. He went in to get a camera. Del came out, saw me standing next to the carving. "Ah. I see," she said. Pascal's camera made a whirring noise, taking lots of pictures very fast, from different angles. He asked Del to stand on one side of the prowlet. She didn't want to, but when I asked, she did. He took more pictures. Then we sort of stood there. "My stuff's at Gilb's. I need to get it. And to say 'bye. I want to go there on my own. I won't run away."

Gilb and her father were somewhere away, "'aving ze talk." Clarissa was somewhere upstairs, "'aving ze sleep." Donnie had an envelope for me, from Buffalo Bevilacqua. I opened it. There was an American passport. And a note.

Dear Roanne.

They was able to replace your lost document quicker than I thought. Couldn't find you for the go ahead so I went ahead. If you found the one you lost, give this one back, and I'll give G. back her donation. I hope your happy. I'm enclosing my card here. Call me if there's any questions. I could not, like I told you, find your exact name. Maybe it was different when you were born, know what I mean? It was a pleasure doing business with you.

your Sincerely,
B. Bevilacqua

Under the typing, he'd scrawled, like a little kid who'd just started writing, "Buffalo." His card had buffaloes on it. I realized I could actually pay Gilbey back with my own money, as soon as I got a chequing account. I opened the passport. The dead baby, my second in a week, was named Langley. She was from Spokane, Washington. Born Oct. 17, 1960. Her first name was Roseanne.

Dear Gilb,

I have to go back to Kits with my mum. Tried to find you, to say a proper "bye for now," but Donnie said you were somewhere with yr father. Sorry I didn't get to meet him. Next time. There WILL be a next time. I'm just going to have to work on Del for a while. All this must be pretty intense for her. F., it's pretty intense for me!

Can you please call Dart R. for me? Tell him thanks for the job, but that I had a "family emergency" and had to go back to Canada. Tell him I'll phone or write him, and that if the job's still open when I get back, I'd love to do it—even if I'm a rich cartoonist!!! And tell him thanx for Venice. I really want to see those buildings coming out of the sea, but it doesn't look like I'll make it back in time, and I don't want to hang him up. I know he wanted to take "bookends"—what about replacing me with that Faboo guy (ha ha).

Seriously, you are the best friend I've ever had and I love you a lot. We HAVE to stay in contact! You should also come to Vancouver and let me show you around. We have some cute guys and some good music/dance clubs. You could stay with us.

You split before Del gave me the album-cover cheque. $10,000! U.S.!!! And none of it would've happened if you hadn't brought Dickie to "our" birthday party. Just one of the things I owe to you. So, let me buy you an air ticket to Van. I know you can do it on your daddy's plastic, but I'd love to buy it for you. Write! Phone!

Love, love, love,
XOXO,
Roanne (Babygirl)

P.S. Buffalo did the thing. It's great. I have lots of $$$ now (from the Yobs record cover) so please, please, please tell me what you paid him, and I will give it back to you, OK?

I wrote out my address and phone number at the bottom and left the letter on Gilb's bed. Donnie gave me a little suitcase, with initials all over it, for my remaining stuff (everything else was still in Pascal's rent-a-car). She also wanted to give me food, but I knew I'd barf if I even looked at food. Didn't put it that way, just said thanks very much, but that my mum had brought food for the trip, and that it would hurt her feelings if I didn't eat it. I diddled and dawdled, hoping Gilb would come back, but it wasn't happening, and I didn't want Del to freak. So I hugged Donnie and went back to Evil Owl.

Pascal and Del were seated on opposite sides of the room, the way the Indian kids and white kids did at school dances in Burnaby. It looked just as stupid in Malibu.

"You ready, Rosie? We have a long drive."

"Quick shower? I'm really funky."

"Here?"

"Yes."

"Right."

The bleeding had completely stopped. I took off the taped pad. Wrapped it in lots of t.p. and stuffed it into a covered wastebasket.

The room-sized black-tile shower was the beginning of my first explosion night. The water was hot, and the room was full of steam. I held onto the wall and cried. Probably looked like a jerk, but nobody saw.

It was good to be in my jeans again. And in Pascal's big denim shirt. I put my jean jacket on over the shirt. The humungus cheque and my new passport went into the jacket's inside zippered pocket. Tied the catbaby tightly around my neck. I was borderline to being a major blubbering mess. Put on my big "Ventoo Boovar" shades, just in case. Didn't dare go into Pascal's bedroom, or I'd hide in the closet and have to be dragged out biting, kicking and screaming. Figured if I'd left anything in the house, he could send it to me. Or, dammit, I'd get it when I, for fucking sure, came back.

"Nice shirt, Prowlet."

"Thanks for it. It's my favourite."

"I'm glad." Even Del, who superhated this whole thing, knew better than to get in the middle of it. The middle of it, between Pascal and me, was a frying place, like with electric fly zappers.

"Take care of yourself. Keep in touch."

"You too. Both things. And tell Gilb I really tried to find her."

"Where is she?"

"Somewhere with her dad."

"Ah."

We didn't touch eachother. Not even to shake hands. I said I needed to get my stuff out of the rent-a-car. We did that, the three of us, and loaded it into the Morgan.

Del thanked Pascal for "your kindness to my daughter. I hope she wasn't too much trouble."

"No trouble at all. Drive safely."

"Always do. See you." She got behind the wheel. I knew how Pascal hated crises, hated scenes, hated blubbering.

I wanted to be cool, to say something really grownup, really sophisticated.

"Gosh, Pascal," I said. "It's all so . . . so ephemeral."

"Do you know what that word means?"

"No."

"Good guess, Prowlet."

We didn't say much on the drive. Del asked if I were hungry. I said no. I tried not to look at the sea too much, which, normally, I like to do. But this wasn't normally. This was a Lopez-Garcia on my half-born new life. Del asked if I had my Yobs cheque in a safe place. I said yes. I realized I'd spent a lot of the past couple of months going up and down the Pacific Coast Highway. At one point, when Del was gassing up the Morgan and had gone to have a piss in one of those cold, smelly, mouth-breathing gas station loos, I thought, "You have money, Roanne, make a run for it," but I knew she'd chase me down, in the Morgan, and it would be hairy and crazy and awful.

"We're just outside of this really sweet little Danish town, Rosie. It's called Solvang. Why don't we stop there. They make super butter biscuits."

"If you want."

• •

"You really have to go to school, Rosie. At least to finish grade 12."

"Why? You didn't."

"That's not the point."

"It is the point. Do you know what school is like for me? What those kids, those teachers are like?"

"Yes, yes, I do, but you just do your work and get through it. And then, before you know it, you've done it."

"Like you did?" The big blonde Danish lady brought our butter-biscuits and tea. I could tell by her face that we had been keeping our voices down, which was good.

"You're going to keep throwing that up to me, aren't you? 'You buggered up, so I've a right to bugger up too.'"

"But you didn't bugger up. You lead your own life. You've raised me. You've supported me. You make this super art. Guys like you. You've got a great car. If you're not proud of you, at least I am, and that should count for something."

I really truly meant what I was saying, but I could also see that it hit her hard. I had to stay with it, to make a fight for the amazing thing I'd found.

"Del, you're not a bad example. You're what they call a role model. At least for me. You say you know what it's like in school, but you don't. You couldn't and still want me to be there. The teachers think I'm an arty little tramp. I heard that term used, when the witch-faced math teacher didn't know I was there. 'An arty little tramp,' she said. And the other teacher, Mrs. Campbell, who I thought liked me, said, 'What do you expect? The apple doesn't fall far from the tree.' That's you, 'the tree.' I'm the apple. And every fucking day, Little Apple goes bopping into these fucking schools, where these dumb-ass guys wait and hide and try to feel my boobs, feel my ass, feel my crotch. And they shout stuff and pass notes and leave dogshit and cups of piss and cum in my locker. And the girls! They laugh and whisper and point, and one of them, Melanie Haig, beat the shit out of me. Twice. While her buds cheered her on and—"

"What? Why didn't you tell me? I'll cripple the slag!"

"That's why I didn't tell you. You couldn't just cripple her. You'd have to fucking kill her. Take her out entirely, and all her buds. Otherwise, every shot you took, I'd get paid back double. And that's where you want me to be. Where you want me to learn. Instead of in a world with amazing people, people who actually like me, people who know more stuff than any school I've ever been in!"

We were both crying and the noise level must've gone up. The Danish lady asked us to please keep it a bit quieter. We paid our bill.

I didn't want to risk the Morgan. Being inside the Morgan meant heading north. I asked if we could sit in this little parkette for a few minutes.

Del wiped the water under my eyes with her finger. "Oh, Christ, Rosie. I had no idea. I knew it was less than brilliant, but . . ."

"Please let me stay in California. I have friends. I have some money. I have an offer of an honest job, sorting out the books in a very sweet old gay man's library. And Yobs albums usually sell like mad. I might get other covers to do . . ."

"That man is older than I am."

"This isn't about him. It's about me. And Mad Jack was way older than you when you left home and lived with him. And he was a seriously major drunk."

"And a wonderful man. A lovely guy."

"Exactly. Who taught you stuff, and cared about you, and left you his house."

"That was different. I didn't sleep with Jack. You know that."

"And I didn't sleep with Pascal."

"Of course you did. You think I'm bloody stupid?"

"No. Do you think I am?"

"No."

"Well, in the way you can suddenly know stuff, I know you slept with Jack. And that it was cool. That it was a part of how you took care of eachother."

"Blokes. Guys. This is about guys, innit, Rosie? About what happened with Marcus."

"No. Not anymore. I mean, it was in the beginning. I split to figure out what we were gonna do about guys. I even wrote out a sort of agreement to show you, to ask you to sign, so we wouldn't get involved with eachother's guys."

Del laughed and looked sad at the same time.

"Crikey. I'm really sorry about Marcus, Rosie. I didn't know you were . . . he didn't mean . . . I'll sign it. I'll sign your agreement, I'll—"

"No. You don't have to. It's past that now. In a good way. What happened was I found a place where I seem to fit. With real friends. With teenagers and grown-ups who don't think I'm weird. I love this thing I've found, Del. I want, I need to keep it, to build on it. I've just started to do that. How can I stop when I've just started? I bet you couldn't. Bet you wouldn't. I *know* you wouldn't. I know you *didn't.*"

"Oh, God. I dunno, Rosie . . . you're so bloody young."

"Less than a year younger than you were. And it's a different time. My almost 15 now is the same as your almost 16 then, older even, maybe."

"Dammit, Rosie! People will say I let my—"

I stood up. "People will say? You said, you *always* said that what people said didn't matter as long as *we* were solid about something, as long as—"

"But I'm *not* solid about this."

"I am. I'm solid about it. It's way solider than what you had when you left home. You didn't have a mother who loved you, who'd be there for you, who'd let you come back home, whenever and if ever you needed to. I do."

"Yeah, you do."

In the middle of the parkette, there was this large statue of a Danish king. I was thumping really hard. Needed a break. Walked over to it. Larfed. "Hey Del, this guy's called Harald Bluetooth!" Del smiled. Came and stood next to me.

"Reckon they didn't have dentists . . . Rosie . . ."

"Look, they've got all sorts of home study courses now. From real schools. I'll take tests, send you the results, you'll always know where I am, I'll call once a week, you can call back, I can come visit, I can—"

"You're gonna bolt, aren't you? If I take you back to Kits."

"First clear shot I get. And as many times as I have to."

I knew she would never hit me, but, for a moment, Del looked really angry. She shook her head, like she was trying to get rid of major brainclutter, started walking away from Harald Bluetooth and out of the parkette. I followed.

There were people, very blond people, in Danish (I guess) costumes, singing in (I guess) Danish. There were lots of them, so we sort of had to wait there, or be very rude by going through them while they sang.

"Where would you stay? I'm not saying yes, just—"

"At Gilbey's. Like I told you, I'd stay with Gilb. It's cool with her folks. I'd stay there at least until I can sort myself out, get the job thing going. I could also stay in Pascal's little guesthouse. Del, Pascal does not want a girlfriend. Not at all. If I want to stay his friend, and I do, being underfoot all the time is a superbad idea. And if I'm going to work in town, living in the Colony is a major hassle. Maybe Dart has a small space for rent. He's the guy with the library job. D'Artagnan Roland."

"His name's D'Artagnan?"

"Uh-huh."

"Fuckin' 'ell!"

For the first time that day, we both laughed full-out. Together.

"You'll ring once a week? I'll always know where you are?"

"Promise."

"Until Christmas. I want you home for Christmas."

"Of course. For sure. I *want* to be with you at Christmas."

"Your word?"

"My absolute word."

"Oh, God . . . all right. We'll try it. I must be crazy."

Don't scream, I thought. Don't giggle. Stay cool. Speak. "'Course y'are. It's a family trait."

"Yeah, I s'pose. I love you, Rosie."

"I know. Me too you."

"I know."

We were hugging and crying. The Danish blond people looked embarrassed. We apologized, which made them look even more embarrassed. I suggested to Del that we walk.

"Good plan," she said.

I had this megacheque in my pocket but was really low for actual cash. We were standing in front of a bank. I asked if, maybe, I could cash my cheque there.

"No way," Del said, "on account of it would be deeply stupid to be wandering about with all that money on yer person. Besides, you need all sorts of ID to cash a cheque in this bloody country."

I wanted to try my new passport, but it seemed better if Del didn't know about that. Besides, if it didn't work, there I'd be, busted by Danish-Americans as a full-grown dead baby from a foreign country. Del did her English movie voice with the teller, showed everything she had with her name and/or picture on it, got me a hundred dollars ("A loan, Rosie." "Definitely"). She drove me to the nearest bus depot, where I bought a ticket for Malibu. We did a lot of hugblubbering and reviewing of the rules (including my promising to get some sort of birth control from Gilbey's Famous Gynie as soon as I was back in the Colony). I made sure she had all the phone numbers she could possibly need.

Since I was little, Del and I have had this sort of weird game. In this game, I'm not allowed to begin a question with "Who is . . . ?" but I am allowed to make a question with a specific name. That's how the game works.

We were waiting for the bus. "Trevor Doone. Is Trevor Doone my father?" (I'd asked about Dickie years ago.)

"Trev? No. Wish he were. He's a lovely guy."

Another rule of the game was sort of Rumpelstiltskin—if I ever said the right name, Del had to say yes. So Trevor wasn't my father, but "lovely guy" meant they'd had some sort of Sex Thing. For the first time, I was tired of playing the "Is So-and-so . . . ?" game. Felt too old for it. Also felt that, if I pressed it, Del would finally tell me. The thing I knew, absolutely knew, was that she'd try doing a deal on it. "Come home and I'll tell you." Too risky. Decided it could keep until Christmas.

The bus was taking forever to come, so Del hugged me some more, then took off north in the Morgan. I watched until I couldn't see even a racing green dot. And there I was. On the point. Standing in the middle of the road, somewhere between somewhere and everywhere else.

• •

When I got to the guardhouse, Grady was glad to see me, but Murph seemed strange. I asked him to ring Gilbey's.

"Gilbey's?"

"Oh, sorry, Murph. I meant 'the Tarr house.' Gilbey's my friend. The daughter."

He pressed a few numbers. Said, "Miss Chappell is here, sir, to see Miss Gilbey."

I played with Grady, thinking how buzzed the Gilb would be to see me, how buzzed I would be to see her. Then Pascal was standing there. He looked awful.

"Hey," I said, laughing, "you did say to see you as soon as I could. Bet you weren't expecting it to be this soon, eh? Actually, it was Gilbey I rang. I'm waiting for—"

"Prowlet, Gilbey's dead."

• •

When I was 10, Martin Drew, a boy in my class, hanged himself in his family's shed. Everyone said it didn't make sense, that little kids didn't kill themselves. Even without Martin as proof, I knew that wasn't true. Little kids think of killing themselves all the time. Pretty much every day. It's just that other stuff comes along and they forget about it. Until the next thing reminds them. If something reminds them, and nothing else comes along, sometimes they give it a shot. Sometimes it works.

It seems Johnny Tarr didn't want to move the family to Europe. Just Gilbey. Alone. To go to school. In Switzerland. Johnny and Clarissa would stay in Malibu Colony. It seems Johnny was going to take away all Gilbey's credit cards so that she'd be stuck there unless he got her out. It seems Clarissa made him choose and he chose Clarissa. Said it was about wanting Gilbey to have a proper education, but Pascal said the school in Switzerland was a "wank school" for rich Eurotrash fuckups and Saudi kids whose families got tired of watching them drive their Ferraris back and forth in the desert. "She'd learn bugger all in that place that she didn't already know," Pascal said.

"How'd she do it?"

"Cut her wrists in the bathtub."

"Jesus. She bleed all over Clarissa's house?"

"No. She didn't bleed anywhere but in the water. And she did it here."

"Here?!"

"In the guesthouse." He lit one of his gypsy cigs. I took one as well. Lit it, but only smoked a little.

"It's how I met her. Two years ago. She chose my guesthouse when Johnny married Clarissa. On their wedding day. Said she thought I was big enough and cool enough to deal with the body. She thought that was a compliment to me. It wasn't, you know. It was just Gilbey's animal knowing that a certain deadness of soul can be useful at such times."

I knelt in front of where he was sitting. "No, Pascal. Look, I don't really know fuck-all about your dead soul thing, but I do know, just like you told me when I first came here, that Gilbey was a good kid, she thought you were a good guy, a real friend. She told me that."

"'A real friend.' She said that about *you*. In her note." He handed me a folded paper.

Hey, 'Scal,

Unless I fuck up a second time, when you get this I should be outta here. It's way too hard, 'Scal. I'm flat out of "It's Cool," and I don't know how to get more. Not without Johnny. I know you don't like him. But we were a team. Johnny's playing for Clarissa's team now. Remember how you told me about how snakes sleep all tangled up in a ball because they're cold-blooded and can't get warm? I've felt like that since I was little. Even with Johnny. Except the night I slept in the big bed in your freezing-ass cold other house. With you and your little fuzzy brother and Roanne. I was warm then. Roanne left me a note. Said I was her best friend ever. She was mine too. If you tell her it was me who took her catbaby, make sure you point out that I also put it back in the car. First time I ever did that. First time for everything! This'll be the first time I really died. If you do get to come back, I'll see ya.

Yr Pal,
G.

The police came (they'd already been one time before). Asked Pascal some more questions. Asked me questions. I said my name was Roseanne Langley. Showed them my passport as ID. It worked. I said I'd been staying with Gilb. They asked where I'd be if they had any other questions. Pascal said "Miss Langley" would be here at his place. When they left, he said, "Buffalo?" I said, "Uh-huh," and asked about Donnie. Pascal said she'd already gone home, that she probably didn't know yet. He said a doctor gave Johnny Tarr some pills so he could stop screaming and get some sleep. I didn't ask about Clarissa because I didn't care.

We fell asleep on the Chester. When we woke up, Pascal put together some clear soup and bread for me. I ate it. Asked if Dart knew. He said no, that it would be in the morning papers, but, for now, it was known only in the Colony, and that Colony people close ranks around this sort of thing.

"'This sort of thing'? Does this happen a lot?"

"Enough."

I thought I should ring Dart, make sure the library-organizing job was still there. Figured I'd wait a day. Go see him, talk to him about Gilb. He was another person who seemed to honestly like her.

"Pascal, why did she take my catbaby? I mean, she could have any 'thing' she wanted."

"She could never get enough. It's that cold problem again. She did a fair bit of thieving in the Colony. Johnny'd just pay the tab on it. When we got back from Mexicali, while you were in the loo, I rang her, told her to give it back. She said she didn't know what I was talking about. But then she came scooting over here, in the middle of the night, and returned it. A first. She did it for you."

"She was just afraid of you."

"No. She wasn't afraid of anybody. Like my brother, she didn't care all that much about living and dying. Makes you fearless, that. . . . Oh, speaking of my brother, you have a letter."

I asked Pascal if I could sleep in his arms. He said he'd like that. I asked if I could use his study for a while, to write in my journal. He said, "Of course." I took Didi's letter upstairs with me. Read it. Wanted to, but couldn't, draw. Except eyes. Eyes, over and over. They were spooking me, all those eyes, so I stopped. Wanted to, but couldn't scream. Could feel the scream, just under. Frozen, locked. Wrote and wrote. This journal is now up to date.

22 novembre 1981
Inn Nainity

Ma chère Cendrillon (Cinderella),

It was very good to see you. And to meet your friend, Mlle Gilbey. She is very, very beautiful. Very sad also, I believe. Fait gaffe, Petite. Malibu is also very beautiful, but also not so happy. I know you are having Cinderella now. I can see this. It is good to see. But Cinderella also has the midnight, with the pumpkin and the six mouse.

As concerns Pascal, you will both do what you want. He is a very good brother.

Listen, Petite, if you have the time, it would please me much if you come to visit with me. I have an influenza, but it should not rest too long. In all cases, you cannot catch this. My doctor say it is an influenza only for pédé. True! It is called GRID, "Gay Related Immune Deficiency." Can you imagine, my very own influenza! Très chic, non?

Je t'embrasse, très fort,

Didi